Gothic Pursuit

Tim Simpson, in charge of the Art Investment fund of White's Bank, sets out to acquire a piece of furniture by Richard Norman Shaw, the late nineteenth century's most brilliant domestic architect. When his first informant is murdered, Tim realises the trail to his acquisition is fraught with danger and finds that he himself is under suspicion – and at risk...

Mortal Ruin

The last thing Tim Simpson expected when he arrived in Chicago on Bank business was to be attacked by three men – and caught in a web of high-finance intrigue involving Morton Frewin, well-connected money-maker with a deadly reputation.

Tim's quest to assess the real value of Frewin's gold shares leads him to Ireland, where only a dramatic confrontation will expose the truth.

JOHN MALCOLM

Gothic Pursuit

Mortal Ruin

Diamond Books
An Imprint of HarperCollins*Publishers*
77–85 Fulham Palace Road
Hammersmith, London W6 8JB

This Diamond Crime Two-In-One edition
published 1994

Gothic Pursuit © John Malcolm 1987
Mortal Ruin © John Malcolm 1988

The Author asserts the moral right to
be identified as the author of this work

Drawings for *Gothic Pursuit* by Robert Staermose

ISBN 0261 66256 2

Cover photography by Monique Le Luhandre

Printed in Great Britain

Gothic Pursuit

PROLOGUE

The *Cospatrick* caught fire at night on November 17, 1874, somewhere south of the Cape of Good Hope. She was a three-masted London emigrant ship of the Shaw Savill Line, with more than four hundred voyagers bound for Auckland, New Zealand. In those creaking clippers of an extinct era, fire at sea was a terror always in the thoughts of passengers and crew. This one started in the bosun's locker.

The standard procedure when such a disaster happened in the forward part of the ship was to get her head before the wind to prevent the natural draught from spreading the flames. At first this went well. The pumps were started and the crew began to douse the fire with water. Then, somehow, by mistake, the *Cospatrick*'s head got into the wind, fanning the blaze. The bosun's locker was full of oakum, rope, paint and varnish. Roaring flames burst out in terrifying gusts from below decks and ran up the tarred shrouds. Billowing clouds of choking acrid smoke enveloped the whole ship in confusing, blinding thickness. It became obvious that she was doomed.

The emigrants panicked. A starboard quarter-boat was lowered but, in their terror, a mob overfilled it and it capsized, spilling them into the ocean. The bow of the longboat caught fire as it was swung out over the rail, putting it out of action. Amid the shrieks and dreadful fear of 429 passengers and 44 crew, only the port and starboard lifeboats got away, with 42 and 39 people on board respectively. These lifeboats stayed near the unimaginable horror of the burning hulk for two days, until November 19, when the main and mizzen masts of the blackened, charred and smoking vessel fell on to the crowded after part of the ship.

Screams were heard from those crushed to the cindered decks. At the stern of the clipper the handsome Blackwall quarter-galleried glass panes were blown out by the dreadful pressure in a final explosion. The onlookers saw the captain, a luckless man called Elmslie, throw his wife overboard before jumping himself. The *Cospatrick* sank.

The survivors in the boats wore only their nightclothes and had no food or water, sails or equipment. One boat had only one oar. The other, with none, drifted away in roughening seas and was never seen again. Bad weather kept filling the boat that was left and, amid desperate baling, a sea-anchor was rigged. Men, women and children died in steady progression from thirst and exposure as the days passed. Those clinging desperately to life tore open the dead bodies around them, ate the livers and drank the blood. A foreign ship passed only 50 yards away in poor light and did not hear or ignored the feeble cries directed at it. Soon, there were only five men left: the second mate, called Henry Macdonald, two able seamen, an ordinary seaman and a passenger who had gone mad. This pathetic group were finally and miraculously picked up by another vessel, the *British Sceptre*, en route from Calcutta to Dundee, but the insane passenger and the ordinary seaman subsequently died, so there were, in the end, only three survivors.

We know what happened to the *Cospatrick* because Henry Macdonald gave evidence of the last of the old frigate-built ship at the inquiry. In other cases it is perhaps better that we remain ignorant for our peace of mind. The Shaw Savill Line was a bit unlucky with fires and disasters in its early days; it had fifteen sailings a year to New Zealand from London in the 1860s, with several fast little clippers that could still take four or five months to reach their destination. Many a tremulous emigrant, driven by courage or despair to seek a new life in the days before the Plimsoll Line, must have quaked as these little ships, mostly between four and five hundred, but none above one thousand tons, packed with people, beat round the Cape and then went eastwards into the Roaring Forties, where the passengers could clutch fearfully on to something fixed to steady themselves and listen to 'the whistle and scream of the westerlies on a dark and sobbing night'.

It was a hazardous business. The *Pleiades* and the *Halcione* were wrecked. The *Merope* burned off the River Plate on the homeward run. The *Caribou*'s cargo of coal caught fire in 1869, taking the wooden ship down in flames. The *Avalanche*, en route for Wellington with 60 passengers, collided with the *Forest of Windsor* in the Channel off Portland and only three crew members, who jumped on to the colliding ship, which also sank, were saved. The *Marlborough* just disappeared in 1889; no Henry Macdonald survived to tell the tale.

Eventually the passage became much safer and Shaw Savill, after merging with the Albion Line, became one of the well-established, highly-respected pillars of the British merchant fleet. Distinguished operations continued until comparatively recently, when the Furness Withy Group quietly absorbed the company. All in all, there was no particular reason why anything to do with the Shaw Savill Line should have disturbed the even tenor of anyone's ways until, quite suddenly this spring, an evil spirit from those fate-ridden 1870s came back to look for victims.

CHAPTER 1

She had the look of a woman who, the morning after, is not only confident of the role she has played the night before but feels that she has banked up an indefinable credit which can be called in at a carefully-timed moment. Her face, close to mine, was relaxed and beautiful in early morning repose, even if there were slight signs of that swollen languorousness one comes to recognize with experience. She gave me a meaning smile.

'I suppose you expect me to marry you, now,' she said.

I laughed. She's very fond of these role-reversal lines, culled from standing the conventional morality of a number of years ago upon its head. It made me chuckle but, in a way, I was both surprised and pleased. References to marriage are usually taboo with Sue; she has her reservations on that subject.

'Not at all,' I responded. 'Anyone who behaved herself quite so unreservedly as you did last night must be entirely unsuitable for matrimony. My mother warned me about girls like you.'

I won't say what she tried to do but I had to move quickly and I managed to grab her wrist in the nick of time. There was something of a struggle after that but it was interrupted, maddeningly, by the alarm clock bursting into a clamour far too late.

'Damn it,' I said, switching the ruddy thing off. 'I'd forgotten I was going to have a slight lie-in this morning. The place doesn't open until ten.'

'Serve you right,' she said, primly. 'I've still got to be at work on time, so you can get breakfast.'

I swung my legs over the side and put my socks on while

she disappeared into the bathroom. Normally I am well away before her because, despite what people think about merchant banks and the City of London, I do tend to get cracking before the Tate Gallery does. It's a bit further for me to get to the City from our flat in Onslow Gardens than it is for her to get to the Tate, where she's worked for some time now. I donned a large dressing-gown and set about getting breakfast with a degree of enthusiasm, for I was hungry and, although we don't go in for bacon and eggs with all the trimmings, we do rather like a bit more than a cup of tea—for me—and a beaker of coffee—for her.

In due course she arrived at the little table we have by a long window overlooking the gardens and sat down with an appreciative nod at the material I'd laid out. She was crisply dressed as usual, rather neat and buttoned-down, like one of those female executives with black briefcases you see in business hotels who cultivate the impersonal stare and the distant expression. Not that Sue ever carries a black briefcase: she has a sort of leather satchel-handbag into which she scoops everything, like a prep-school boy bundling homework and playthings together in an indiscriminate jumble.

'A boiled egg!' she crowed cheerfully. 'How nice! Where on earth did you find the eggcups?'

I gave her a reproachful expression. When you live with a girl like Sue there are great areas of domestic responsibility which are never defined, so that neither side can attribute blame for failure to perform. After nearly a year of happy cohabitation this situation had not changed but I was trying to exert some sort of control over her sway in the kitchen, where no sense of order seemed to prevail at all. I knew that it was almost useless, though I had my hopes, but I wasn't going to press the subject on one of the first warm mornings of April, when the sun actually shone into the gardens and

spring might be going to happen if you didn't w
closely.

'The Victoria and Albert Museum,' she said thought
ignoring my expression. 'You and Jeremy are just like little
boys really, aren't you? Any excuse for a trip out of school.
Is there any real need for you to meet there? Let alone to
drag Geoffrey Price in?'

I reacted with justifiable indignation.

'Of course there is! It's absolutely essential!'

'Why?'

'Why? Why? Well—er—we all have to be quite clear
what it is we're talking about. Question of fundamental
communications.'

Sue sank her white teeth into a crisp slice of toast. 'Nonsense. You could brief them at the office.'

I gaped at her, aghast. 'At the office? In the City? I most
certainly could not! This is a matter for the Art Fund, Sue,
not the Securities Department.'

She paused, holding a spoonful of marmalade above her
plate. 'What difference does that make? You've got all your
reference books, catalogues and photographs in your office
there, haven't you?'

Her blue eyes watched me steadily as I picked up my
teapot. Why do women always feel this need to challenge?
If I'd been sharing the flat with an old College friend or an
ex-rugger man he'd never dream of probing in this way.
Never. He'd simply have said oh, off a bit late, are you,
down to the V & A, well you lucky bugger it's the nine
o'clock grindstone for me as usual, see you in the Dog and
Duck for a pint around six, then? And I'd have said OK
fine, I'll have one set up for you, and he'd have pushed off
after taking an aspirin for his hangover. Simple as that. I
gave her a scowl.

'It has become our practice—' was that perhaps a shade
pompous, I wondered, but too late now—'it has become

our practice to view and discuss in detail, indeed in depth, the next type of article we are going to acquire for the Art Investment Fund so that we are all quite clear and absolutely agreed on the decision taken. On these occasions—' I held up a warning teaspoon to restrain her, because she'd opened her mouth—'on these occasions I always make a sort of presentation to Jeremy and to Geoffrey, explaining the logic and the background to the investment so that they are both quite happy about it. One does not commit the odd hundred thousand nicker, or even just the possibility of it, lightly. Not in our business, anyway. I can't answer for the Tate Gallery, of course.'

That impressed her. She had been about to swallow some coffee and now she put her cup down. 'A hundred thousand? Tim, are you—are you serious?'

'Absolutely.' I didn't explain any more. It seemed to me that I'd done enough already. I filled my teacup and drank some tea with relish. She was still looking at me when I put the cup down. Christ, I thought, she's a good-looking girl, is Sue, but I should have known that glint in her eye.

'I thought you were going to be completely tied up with this timber thing that Jeremy has sicked you on to.'

I sighed. Trust a woman to spoil the morning. 'Now why did you have to bring that up? Eh? You know very well that I'm not pleased with this timber job, even if it does have historic significance for White's.'

I should perhaps explain that White's Bank was founded by an original merchant adventurer White in the early nineteenth century, importing rosewood from Brazil. Over the years White's had expanded into many other things and had become a proper merchant bank, if a bit idiosyncratic and specialized, but they had retained their timber interests. They still imported a range of hardwoods from their Brazilian company and, indeed, more recently, some softwoods too. They had a substantial operation in the Far East and Australasia doing the same thing, all handled into London. It was a good solid business, if a bit unexciting, and Jeremy had been taken aback when the other members of the Board had pressed him hard on a possible acquisition into distribution throughout Britain, requiring a commitment of capital into what Jeremy had always looked upon as part of the Bank's semi-colonial, possibly even moribund past. Jeremy White, you see, is something of a high-flier and a financial wheeler-dealer. He doesn't like industry much—in common with many of his City friends—and he'd rather gamble away on commodities and shares and securities and foreign exchange when he isn't setting up insurance schemes that avoid tax one way or another. So he'd tried to resist, but the Board for once had stuck to their guns and Jeremy, cornered, did what he often did on such occasions. He turned to me.

'You'd better look into it,' he'd said. 'You and Geoffrey, that is. It's right up your street.'

I protested vigorously. 'Damn it, Jeremy! We've just reorganized the whole Bank structure into proper departments! Geoffrey's in corporate finance and I'm supposed to be looking after overseas operations.'

'This is to do with overseas operations,' he responded gamely. 'The timber all comes from abroad, doesn't it?'

There's not much you can answer to that, so I'd been landed with the job as principal, Geoffrey offering moral and professional support. It hadn't pleased me; looking into a possible deal with a UK timber operation, possibly even having to buy it outright, needed careful research, assessment and risk analysis which, on top of other things I was doing, were unwelcome. I'd been sulky about it.

Sue gave me a wicked grin over the breakfast table but her eyes now showed concern. 'I think you're trying to avoid getting on with the timber thing, so you've lured Jeremy out for a hooley.' She wagged a finger at me. 'I think it's a diversion from serious business.'

I shook my head. 'Nonsense. The Art Fund may not be more than an amusement for Jeremy and me in some ways but it is a serious commitment of the Bank's to customers wanting to invest in Art. When an opportunity comes up to acquire something original, in the broad stream of our policy, then we have to react to it. There's no playing hookey on hoolies about it.'

She didn't say anything immediately but she finished her coffee and she got up, tidied herself and got ready to depart, satchel-handbag slung over her shoulder. She was wearing one of the neat suits I always associated her with but her blouse was open at the neck and she looked a real heart-stopper, so important to me that I must have done something odd or shown it in my face because she turned back from her departure and came across to kiss me gently, putting her hand on my flannelled shoulder to squeeze it.

'You and Jeremy have met at the V & A to look at potential investments before,' she said. 'And you know the sort of things that have happened.'

'Oh Sue! Now really—'

Her fingers, scented and warm, stopped my lips. 'Stick to the timber business, Tim, please? Get the other over quickly.' She took the hand away and walked to the door before looking back. 'And come home early,' she said.

She didn't say why.

CHAPTER 2

Twin gables capped the edifice. Overlapping discs were painted on the surfaces under the peaked tops, giving way to stripes above the arched spaces under the gables, each bisected by a turned column. An odd gallery connected the gables across the rooftop, starting from the solid sides where, at the front, bulbous turrets projected from the edge, rather like those medieval turrets that bulge out from the four corners of Scotland Yard, the old striped New Scotland Yard that overlooks the Thames, not the new cement-coloured New Scotland Yard off Victoria Street. Under the gables were more massive, turned oak columns, fronting shelves of heavily-bound copies of *Punch* and leather volumes of indeterminate subject. Then there was a slope, yellow with marquetry. Under that there was an incredible blocked colonnade of Gothic arches, bound top and bottom by long iron straps that were hinges; the whole colonnade was, in fact, two great doors secured by a complicated iron lock. Here and there, in a careful row, were inlaid discs of symbolic patterns, like pies. Four small drawers, with iron ring-pulls, ranked under the bottom iron strap-hinge. Then there was a writing-surface, projecting out above more columns with turned collars and a drawer. Beneath this surface was a bottom cupboard, contained by two square-panelled doors, criss-crossed with numerous stiles. The whole effect was massive, mediæval, architectural, a celebration of jubilant ecclesiology and secular decoration. It towered above us. I got Sue to do one of her architectural sketches of it afterwards and even in that it came over as a formidable creation.

'Good God,' said Jeremy White, his rich Park Lane tones for once hushed with awe. 'It's more like a Town Hall than a piece of furniture.'

Geoffrey Price gave a nervous giggle and looked quickly round, like a schoolboy caught whispering in chapel. I gave him a reassuring grin, as though to confide that the respectably filtered light on the second floor back in the Victoria and Albert Museum was not ecclesiastical and that a distant, uniformed porter would not surge forward like a churchwarden to hush his nervous rupture of the sepulchral silence. Around us stood the grave furniture of a distant age, most of it rather sombre. Only an occasional shine of bird's eye maple or satinwood, only the odd bounding scroll, spiralling into a query, broke the grained surfaces.

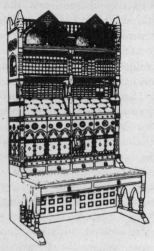

'It's supposed to be the most important piece of nineteenth-century furniture in the whole collection,' I said.

Jeremy shook his head in amazement. 'Furniture? Furniture? What on earth was it for?'

'It was his office bookcase. Cabinet. Call it what you will.'

'Office! Good grief! If I put that in my office at the Bank they'd send for the men in white coats.'

'It was an *architect*'s office,' I reproached him gently. 'And it was at the height of the Gothic Revival bit. Not that this is pure Gothic, of course. The circular motifs, pies and that, are of Japanese origin. He put his blue-and-white Oriental jars up in those spaces under the gables.'

'*Very* architectural.' Jeremy's sarcasm was heavy. '*Most*

necessary in an office.' His eye went up and down the aisle, taking in the various pieces, peering further inward to the gloom where William Morris's medieval cabinet, with its painting by Burne-Jones and others was ranged along the wall. I knew what he was thinking. Opposite the Morris, which had been exhibited with this very bookcase in 1861, were the Godwin pieces; the chairs, the tables and, more important, the sideboard. He gave me a scowl, telepathic as ever.

'Didn't have anything to do with Godwin, did he?' It was an aggressive question so I smiled back, blandly.

'Of course he did. They all knew about each other in those days. Not intimately; Norman Shaw wasn't a bohemian type at all. But there's Bedford Park; both worked on that.'

The scowl deepened. 'I'd hate to think that—'

'Of course not, Jeremy! This is quite different.'

Geoffrey Price cleared his throat, nervously. 'I think that what Jeremy is thinking, Tim, is that—'

'I know what Jeremy is thinking.' I didn't like to interrupt Geoffrey because he's a nice chap and an accountant, and you get your expenses paid by accountants, but this was between Jeremy and me. 'Jeremy is thinking that if I go off to locate this bureau-bookcase or cabinet or whatever it is, there may be trouble. Just because there have been one or two little incidents in the past.'

'Little incidents! Little incidents! Why—'

'The Art Investment Fund—' I raised my voice to over-come his indignation—'has made lots of purchases—correc-tion, *I* have made lots of purchases for the Art Investment Fund—without the slightest hint of any problem whatso-ever. There is no reason to suppose that this will be in any way different. None at all. If the cabinet exists, that is. If it is genuine. If—'

'All right! All right!' Jeremy was peremptory. 'There's no need to go on! Geoffrey is quite justified in his query. You

may recall, my dear Tim, that you and I agreed—once—
that no good ever seemed to come out of the Aesthetic
Movement.' He waved a hand towards the ebonized furniture, gleaming with silver hinges in the dusk nearby. 'Godwin and Wilde and Whistler, that whole Tite Street crew,
bankrupt and bumptious and—'

'Brilliant. I quite agree. What you have conveniently
forgotten, Jeremy, of our discussion in Brighton after that,
er, unpleasant imbroglio, is that we agreed that perhaps we
should have stuck to muscular, middle-class Christianity
instead of the atheistic Aesthetic Movement.'

His face wrinkled. 'I'm not having any of that Morrisian
nonsense in the Art Fund.'

'I'm not saying that we should. But we are not talking of
the Aesthetic Movement either. Richard Norman Shaw was
a sensible, professional, God-fearing Scot who became the
most brilliant domestic architect of the late nineteenth century. And this piece of furniture—' we all three swung
back to look up at its massive power—'is streets ahead of
Morris's.'

'It is incredible. Quite incredible. But do you seriously
think there is more of it about? Surely it would have come
to light by now?'

I shrugged. 'He got tired of this piece when he went off
Gothic. His daughter was in a convent so he gave it to them.
You wouldn't believe it—it turned up, completely forgotten,
in 1962.'

'Good grief. What must it be worth?'

'Ah. That's hard to say. My guess is into six figures. If it
ever came on the market, which it won't.'

'A hundred thousand pounds?' Geoffrey Price sounded
quite aghast. 'A hundred thousand? Jeremy, Tim is propos-
ing—'

'Not a lot, really.' Jeremy's murmur was quite ignorant
of Geoffrey's astonishment. 'Not for a major, unique work

like this. I mean, look at those Mackintosh pieces. Give me this any day. Scotsmen might think differently, of course.'

'Shaw was a Scot. And the man who made this—to Shaw's design—was called Forsyth. Another Scot, I suppose. But any idea of price for this is pure speculation. My guess is that although this is more important, much more money would be paid for a highly-painted Gothic job by Burges or one of those Morris pieces like that over there, painted by Madox Ford or Burne-Jones, or both.'

'Burne-Jones! Burne-Jones!' Jeremy's voice was suddenly full of contempt. He practically wheeled full round, sweeping the gallery with a commanding, imperious glare. 'Man painted as though he'd never seen a pair of buttocks in his life.'

That's the amazing thing about Jeremy. Most of the time he goes round behaving just like a typical City merchant banking yahoo, as though Eton and Oxford had done nothing but teach him how to sail, shoot and gamble. Most of the time now he appears to be a classic member of the Board of his family's Bank, White's Bank, addicted to finance, insurance and horse-trading, loftily indifferent to the world outside. Then suddenly you find he has a real eye for a painting and has read extensively, read things you've forgotten or locked away in your own memory-bank as esoteric or indulgent.

'*Point Counterpoint*,' I murmured, hearing my voice isolated in the hush of the museum.

Geoffrey Price stared at me, bewildered. Jeremy grinned with pleasure at my spotting the reference: a statement about Burne-Jones from the Bohemian artist-figure Bidlake, based perhaps on Augustus John, from Aldous Huxley's novel. It was just the sort of thing John might have said: Burne-Jones's androgynous figures would not have been to the liking of the old goat himself, whose perception of the sexes was all too sharp. Jeremy clapped me on the back.

'Bravo! Let us have no truck with Morris and his circle.
I hope Norman Shaw didn't?'

I shook my head. 'He knew them well, of course; he was
in Street's office learning his trade at the same time as Philip
Webb. And he used the William Morris firm, to begin with,
for some furniture. But not for long. He said he couldn't
afford to buy from a "socialist for well-to-do people". He
exhibited this piece—' I gestured at the great bookcase—
'with Morris in 1861, but he was just getting started them.
That was about it.'

'Good! Then tally-ho! After 'em, Tim! I like the idea of
the Art Fund taking on a piece, a really important piece, by
Norman Shaw.'

'If it exists.'

'If it exists, of course, if it exists. What a splendid find it
will be!' He pulled himself upright majestically, allowing
his tall blond figure to pose for a dramatic moment in the
aisle as he waved a cautionary finger at me. 'If there's any
hint of any trouble, though—any hint at all, the merest
suspicion d'you follow me—you're to drop it, Tim. Do you
hear?'

'I hear,' I said. 'I absolutely hear.'

Geoffrey Price pursed his lips as his eyes closed for a brief
second. Then he pulled himself together and cleared his
throat.

'I do hope there will be no complications,' he quavered.
'Really I do. But since you're both here and we are surrounded by the material, so to speak, do you think I could
have a word with both of you—now—about the timber
business?'

CHAPTER 3

The offices of that popular journal, *The Modern Façade*, are in Covent Garden. I reflected, as I strolled down William IV Street, cutting through from the Charing Cross Road, that this was very appropriate. The area north of the Strand has housed many publishers in its time, a lot of them involved with magazines of one sort or another. The area tends to attract advertising agents now, great phalanxes of the bullshit brigade, all dressed in trendy suits and quacking marketing platitudes as they scurry about with their folio cases full of artwork, but there are still some older, traditional outfits in residence. The Chatto & Windus building caught my eye on my way through to Chandos Place but that's a female preserve now, a case of the rib running Adam, so I suppose I didn't count it as I tracked on towards the office where, not too far from the operas he so dearly loved, Toby Prescott perched on the first floor above what had once been a vegetable wholesalers.

A girl stopped me at the reception desk, where back numbers of *The Modern Façade* were carelessly scattered with careful abandon, their brightly-coloured covers arranged in unconflicting chromatic order. As is so often the case with those involved with successful consumer goods and the media, there was a tinge of condescension in the way the girl received me, an impression that great patronage might somehow be conferred by your admission to the premises. I smiled at her unconcerned, since the boot was on the other foot.

'Toby's expecting me,' I said. 'Tim Simpson, of White's.'

He came barging through from his inner sanctum himself, mouth stretched in the familiarly broad frog-like grin I remembered so well, eyes bulging as ever, so that he looked as though he would be off, at any moment, to play the spoilt, aristocratic motorist in a local panto production of *Toad*.

'Tim! Dear boy! How are you? My goodness! You still look so—so muscular. Life at the Bank obviously suits you.'

I grinned at him in unashamed delight. You might not think that we had been contemporaries at College, but we had. Toby's few years more than mine entitled him to his avuncular style, not unlike Jeremy's; the reading of architecture at Cambridge is a much lengthier process than my modest degree had imposed, so that he seemed altogether to belong to a senior generation. In fact he wasn't quite forty. He wore a suit of a material that I would have thought of as definitely architectural in the modern sense: a grey, slightly knotty, slightly hopsack sort of cloth with a consciously woven texture to it cut in a style belonging to the cavalry, which clung tightly to his legs—my own itched at the thought of that rather tweedy contact—but had enormous fullness in the jacket flaps, as though to contain poacher's pockets. The effect was to enhance the Toad-image in a comically endearing way, to make a bulky grey ball of a body stand on narrow, strutting legs. A scarlet tie pouted from under his white collar, set on a red-striped shirt. His black brogues glistered with polish.

'You old *crapaud*,' I said, prodding him in the ribs. 'Who on earth d'you think you're fooling, hey?'

'Tim! Really! You can talk!' He shot a glance at the reception-girl, clearly entranced by our meeting, and I felt a pang of conscience at my lack of unction in front of one of his employees. 'You indeed! A merchant banker! I never knew such cheek!'

We both laughed loudly and he trotted me through a secretary's ante-room to his office, where two large windows overlooked the street. Despite what I've hinted there was a working atmosphere to the whole place, a profusion of coloured images, photographs, piles of copy, posters and bits of artwork stuck to hardboard. Along one side of his office, taking up a whole wall, was a huge set of bookshelves, full of very large architectural volumes; my eye caught works on Lutyens, Frank Lloyd Wright, the Adam brothers, Voysey, Hawksmoor, Casson, Corbusier and Siefert before I sat down, creaking, on a rather strange rush-seated Queen-Anne-repro corner armchair of racy style that Toby placed beneath me, beaming with bonhomie. He then trotted round to the other side of a large oak Gothic desk that separated us with pronounced serrated edge-moulding. I tapped it cautiously and cocked a querying eyebrow at him.

'Sedding,' he said, cheerfully. 'Almost certainly Sedding.'

'Not Seddon?'

'Aha!' He wagged a finger at me. 'Of course not! I'd have sold it to a museum and retired if it had been by Seddon. My goodness, Tim, you have changed!' His eyes, twinkling at me, were kindly as ever, but more respectful. 'It's true what they tell me, obviously.'

'What d'you mean? What's true?'

'Have some coffee?'

'Thanks. What's true?'

'Or would you—I say—what about a glass of, a glass of *white port*, now, with it?'

'Toby! We're not back at College, you know!'

He giggled. 'So what? Why are you so conventional, all of a sudden? You'd have said yes ten years ago.'

'Twelve,' I corrected him. 'I forgot that you were up for seven years, so these academic habits have persisted. Don't let me deter you, though.'

He pouted. 'You've spoilt it now. We'll just have coffee. It'll be better for us, I suppose.' He poured coffee from an elegant silver jug into bone china cups. 'You were such a *hearty* at College. All rugby and beer and pub-crawls. Now everyone says you're so knowledgeable about art and things. What happened? How did you do it?'

'Memory.' I took the bone china, refusing sugar. 'Just memory. I remember you told me once that memory and intelligence are not connected. Well, I got interested in antiques—my ex-wife did that—and then in art history so I read everything I could lay my hands on and memorized it. It passed a lot of time when I was travelling, staying in digs—I was a business consultant, remember—before I met Jeremy.'

'Ah yes, Jeremy. How is he? I only see him from time to time now. He's become such a tycoon. "Boom! the Banker of Bhong!" and all that.'

'He sent you his best. I hadn't realized you were well acquainted. What a small world.'

'Ah,' Toby's face went reminiscent. 'It's a while ago, Tim. After he left Eton. When he was at Oxford, actually.'

'Oxford? I didn't know you visited Oxford much.'

'Oh yes. My second year. Before you came up.'

Memory suddenly embarrassed me. I drank cautiously from my cup. 'Sorry, Toby, I remember now. The friend you had from—where was it—Sarawak? Wasn't he at Balliol or—'

His smile was kindly on my embarrassment. 'Indonesia. Java, to be precise. Taught me Dutch, Malayan and Tamil.'

'That's it. You introduced me once. Just after I'd come up. He was over from Oxford for the day. Christ, I was impressed. You were collecting languages like a schoolboy does postage stamps.'

His wide beam never faltered. 'I know. Which is why I cultivated you so assiduously, Tim, to start with. Your River Plate Spanish and your rather, er, individual Portuguese were so endearing. Of course—' he threw himself back in his chair and rolled his eyes at the ceiling—'once you'd become such a *famous* rugby player and got a *Blue* and become a sort of *God*, lesser mortals like me couldn't—'

'Toby! Pack it in!'

He giggled. The moment had passed; the painful memory had become a scar. It was hard, now, to remember his distress when the Indonesian friend had broken off with him, how he'd come round with me, cracking bad Spanish jokes as he drank himself senseless every night on appalling East Anglian beer until, in sheer compassion, I'd agreed to drink wine with him. The friends I'd played rugby with had looked at me a bit oddly at first, but once they'd realized it was just good friendship and superb conversation—Toby's experienced wit was on a level well above ours—quite apart from a crying need for company, they'd accepted him and liked him. Besides, no one was quite sure about Toby; sometimes he would bring the most magnificent girls up from London, Resting Actresses no less, and they obviously stayed with him at his digs and liked him and one or two were all over him, no mistake about that . . .

'You've gone all dark.' His voice startled me and I now saw his face again, the wide smile condensed, the eyes knowledgeable. 'You used to do that. You'd go off into a sort of trance and we couldn't get you back. Come on, Tim; have another coffee. I'm glad you haven't changed that much.'

'Thanks.' The mood had passed. I accepted more coffee and peered at his Gothic desk. 'Do you remember when you made me go with you to see the Handley-Read Collection? At the Royal Academy, years ago?'

'Indeed I do! Indeed I do! You hated it. The look on your face! It was a picture.'

'Well.' I smiled ruefully. 'I didn't know all about Burges and that lot then. Alfred Waterhouse—he was a pal of Shaw's, wasn't he? They all designed furniture. And they were all architects. Like Godwin.'

'Indeed they were.'

I looked at him. 'It was just before you started all this lot. Haven't seen you much since then. Tell me all about it.'

He shrugged modestly. 'Nothing much to tell.'

'Come off it, Toby! *The Modern Façade*! You're synonymous with success! Style, fashion, interiors—the whole Covent Garden bit. Nothing to tell!'

He laughed. 'It's true, Tim. Really. There's no money in it, you know. I looked round—mid-Seventies it was—and there were magazines on interior design, you know, women's things on *curtains* and that, and there were one or two very serious architectural journals and of course there was *Country Life*, but there was nothing in between. So I hd the idea of starting a magazine, more town-based than country but not didactically so, which combined an architectural approach with something of interiors, something really exposing people to what style was all about and how architectural history fits in. I had a little lump sum, as they say. Started very small, very modestly, but I did have some lucky connections, people who were looking for something new, foresaw the Art Deco bit—'

'And you're a great communicator and you have the advantage of being extremely witty when interviewed, so the TV boys like you—and the girls—and you know half the architects who matter and most of the designers, so Bob's your uncle. *The Modern Façade*. Very clever and not at all easy.'

'Flattery will get you nowhere.' He was pleased. 'I work very hard and I meant what I said. I love it but there's no money in it.'

'Is that why we are being given a chance?'

'Of course. If I had the money I'd buy it myself.'

'Fair enough. Tell me about it.'

He smiled knowingly. 'First you tell me what you knew about him.'

'Richard Norman Shaw?' I waved a hand at the book-shelves and pointed at one book, a large paperback with a blue-and-white spine. 'I've read that. That's all. Oh, and Mark Girouard, of course.'

'Andrew Saint.' He got up and took the book out almost reverently. 'A great biography. Marvellously done. The Paul Mellon Foundation. Saint's biography of Shaw will stand for ever.'

'There's not all that much about furniture in it. I read it up yesterday.'

He gave me a sharp glance. 'There's enough. Certainly enough balance in the context of his career. Shaw was a great domestic architect, remember, not a furniture hack. You obviously didn't use your memory on this book so well.'

'Why not?'

He gesticulated at me. 'Open your knees.'

'I beg your pardon?'

He grinned. 'Don't get the wrong idea, you old Rugby thug. Open your knees. Look between them.'

The green corner chair creaked as I rather cautiously opened my knees, revealing the forward sharp sweep of the seat-rail and the swerving cabriole leg built into the front corner; the other legs were just turned and straight.

'What can you see?'

I gaped at him, perplexed. 'The edge of the chair. The seat rail.' I pressed back a bit. 'Rushing. My flies. What else should I see?'

'Look, Tim, look!'

I peered again. 'There's a stamped mark on the front edge. Chair must have been in an institution or something. It's—'

'Can't you read it?'

'No, I can't.' I peered closer, testily. I hate exams. 'It's just a stamped mark, a maker's mark or something. It says, let me see—Christ! It says R.N.S.!'

'Richard Norman Shaw!' we both shouted, together.

His delight was infectious. 'What else?' I realized that he had a marker in the book and was waving a photograph of the chair, clear on the page, at me.

'There's a sort of—sort of sunburst impressed above the initials. Just a few lines, like a Japanese flag.'

He nodded sagely. 'Sunbursts and pies. Sunflowers and scrolls. Symbols of the Aesthetic Movement. Sweetness and light. Victorian Queen Anne. A whole philosophy, Tim, a whole philosophy, lost and gone.'

I put my hand on the chair, reverently. 'You old bugger, Toby. Where the hell did you get this?'

'I bought it for a few quid at an auction in Kent.' His pleasure was smug this time as he handed me the book with the photograph. 'They hadn't the faintest idea what it was. Thought it was nineteen-thirties repro. In fact it's from Willesley. A farmhouse near Cranbrook that Shaw extended for the Royal Academy painter, Horsley.' He giggled. 'They used to call him "Clothes" Horsley because he disapproved of nudes. It was Shaw's very first country-house commission and it made his career.'

'And no one knew? About this chair, I mean? At the auction?'

'Nope. No one. Shaw was fond of corner chairs. They're very masculine. I keep that one here for enjoyment. No one has recognized it, yet.'

'Not me neither. I suppose I've failed the test?'

He laughed. 'You're in good company, Tim. A lot of so-called experts haven't given it a second glance.'

I stared at the photograph of the odd, curving chair, made to a design based on a Queen Anne, or at least an early eighteenth-century type, but somehow different. 'What sort of date is it?'

'Willesley? Eighteen-sixty-four.'

'Christ! I'd have thought this chair was much later. You

mean that they started Queen Anne repro as far back as that?'

'Shaw did. Interesting, isn't it?'

'Bloody hell. Makes you realize how little you know.'

'Drink deep,' he murmured, 'drink deep.'

'"Or taste not the Pierian spring."'

'Exactly.'

'Pope. I quite agree. Shallow draughts may well intoxicate the brain. May I now be guided? I've finished my coffee and am all agog.'

'Of course, Tim, of course.' He picked up an umbrella. 'Shall we go?' His eyes were twinkling and he was obviously enjoying himself. I had to clarify one last point.

'It's quite agreed, then? We will pay you a suitable, er, emolument as the finder and introducer of this piece if it does turn out to be genuine and we buy it?'

He nodded briskly. 'It's agreed. As we discussed on the phone the day before yesterday and as gentlemen. I take your word for it.' He opened the door. 'I know you, Tim.'

Not recently you don't, I thought, but still: a responsibility like that is tighter than five monkey-lawyers' contracts.

'Where are we going?'

'Not far, as it happens. Hay Yard. Just off Long Acre.'

'Heaven's sake! Is the piece there? So close?'

'No, I don't think so. Alf will advise us, provided all is in order and we give him certain, er, guarantees. As I explained to you, Alf is a failed architect but a fine bookseller, a technical man, who deals in architectural books and does a bit of design work on the side. He didn't get beyond his intermediate exams. He isn't actually in Long Acre itself— that would be too expensive—but he's in a passage off it. Quite a snug little place with a high skylight. Books right up to the heavens. He came into my office a day or two ago and said he was handling a piece by Richard Norman Shaw that was available. A cabinet or a bureau-bookcase; he was very defensive about details. Alf is always like that—gruff and brusque until you can open him up. Anyway it's like my desk, apparently; he gestured at it with a sort of stiff, casual wave that was so off-hand and mysterious that you wouldn't believe it. "That sort of style," he said. "It'll be a big price, very big. Architect's pieces always are."'

'He was right. Especially those nineteenth-century ones. Eastlake and Burgess and Godwin and Talbert. Not to mention Mackintosh, although he's twentieth-century really. But like your desk? You mean it's Gothic? Like the thing in the V & A?' I looked dubiously at his desk, with its rather attenuated Gothic influence, weakened by its distance in time from the 1861 Exhibition. The further away you get from Pugin the less impressed you are; Sedding was an architect whose offices were next door to Morris and Company and I guessed that the piece was made in the eighteen-eighties, when Gimson was articled there, well after the powerful Gothic Revival of the Sedding cabinet we had looked at that morning in the V & A and about which Jeremy had been so peremptory. 'Are you sure you can vouch for this, er, Alf? Does he know his stuff?'

'Oh yes! Indeed he does. A lot of people—dealers and the like—consult him as well as buying his books. I think that he was just indicating the style, not necessarily the detail.' Toby's voice came down to a soothing note. 'He's very knowledgeable but a bit, well, resentful, if you know what I mean. Thinks he was cheated in his Finals. I'm not sure that he wasn't; I know quite a few qualified men who haven't got half his expertise. It makes him brusque. I've given him quite a few commissions for the magazine and I've bought God knows how many books from him' He gestured at the shelves. 'Most of those, anyway. I don't think he'd come up with a cock-and-bull story. Not to me. You can't tell Alf anything about architectural history, not where this country's concerned. He has a world-wide mailing list.'

'I can't wait. Lead on, Toby.'

We strode out of the office and down to the street, Toby expounding on the architectural degradation of the area now that it was turned over to tourism. He moved surprisingly quickly considering his appearance and I was amused to stride alongside his briskly strutting legs as we eventually entered Long Acre about half way up, from the south side. No sooner had we done so than Toby turned right, south again, down a wide side-passage between two large shops. A well-painted sign pointed the way to Brown's Books and a door set in the left-hand wall where the passage opened out into yet a wider court repeated the same title. Toby knocked sharply and went in with me following deferentially, anxious to convey a good impresion to the man with the passport to a Norman Shaw piece. I had a sudden twinge of disbelief, as though no really important work of furniture could be forthcoming through so incidental a set of circumstances, but then suppressed it; past experience had taught me lessons about the way valuable works of art get winkled out.

The first impression was of good daylight, surprisingly so for an inner court. Then my eyes went up vertically to the skylight Toby had mentioned, set high above me in a sloping roof about twenty feet up. The room was quite large, perhaps eighteen feet or so square, making the proportion pleasant. Books lined the walls and went on up to a gallery ten feet up, where more books could be seen lining the walls like an elegant library. There, however, the half-floor also contained a small drawing-office, below the skylight, with a draughtsman's drawing-board set up beside a folio chest.

On the ground floor, beside me, was a large table and, towards the back, a big office pedestal desk strewn with papers. However much Alf Brown might have resented his failure in his Final examinations, there was much about the whole set-up to envy; it was the workroom and bookshop of a neat, competent sort of man, a skilled technician of self-sufficient character, with an evident degree of professional discipline. I liked it. The only problem was that there was no Alf Brown in it.

'Does he know we're coming?' I inquired, perhaps not very tactfully, but I was keyed up. I always get tense before events like this, before big purchases or the possibility of them; it's part of the excitement, the sort of fear that suffuses the system with nervous anticipation.

'Of course he does.' Toby looked around and then up at the drawing-board work-platform above us. 'I told him yesterday. Alf?'

He wasn't irritable or snappy or anything, just slightly perplexed, and he wandered, without showing too much concern, over to the big desk with its papers strewn about. He clucked his tongue. 'That's not like Alf,' he said, 'leaving papers muddled like that. He's always so neat. He—'

I had been looking curiously at the rows of books, big volumes many of them, pretty valuable in some cases, that lined the wall near me up to the place where the stairs rose to the cat-walk above. It was the way Toby suddenly stopped that made me look up to see him, head turned to his left, frozen at the big desk with his slightly bulging eyes opened wider than usual. I couldn't see what he was looking at because it was under the stairs so I walked across to him, to his left side and looked, following the direction of his gaze to a point under the stairs that had been concealed from me.

There was a man lying down there, staring at us. He was slightly built and his legs were stuck outwards, twisted in a way that must have been uncomfortable. His face didn't move.

'Alf?' Toby's voice was full of surprise at first, incredulity, as though he'd found a maiden aunt in bed with the milkman. 'Alf? What are you doing? Are you all right?'

Alf didn't answer. I didn't expect him to. It's very difficult to answer when your head is over at that angle because to get that way your neck has to be broken, broken severely enough to ensure that you are dead. I know, you see; I've seen that angle a couple of times before.

'Alf?' Toby's voice had lost its incredulity. It was hoarse now, and full of fear.

I knelt down beside the late bookseller to check that he was dead. He was, and he hadn't fallen from the gallery above because to get where he lay he must have been propelled very violently across the room. What little learning Alf Brown had possessed about architecture had turned out to be a very dangerous thing indeed.

CHAPTER 4

Sue did a turn up and down the flat. She actually wrung her hands. It's a condition you often read about but never seem to see in real life; a person wringing their hands together in agitation, elbows stuck out, knuckles whitening, the odd joint cracking. Her eyes glared at me. Her breathing was rather short-winded.

'I did get home early, as you asked,' I pointed out. 'Look on the bright side, if you can. I've made tea for you.'

Her mouth opened and closed. No sound came out.

'There didn't seem much point in going on to the Bank,' I went on, gloomily. 'Jeremy would only have been upset.'

'My God! Jeremy! Is that—is that—all you can—'

'It took a long time, I must say.'

'What? What took a long time?'

'Oh, you know, for people to arrive and all that sort of thing. You remember Motcomb Street? A bit like that. Then we all had to go off to a police station—Holborn, it was—

and there was all this taking of statements and interminable explaining to do. It's no wonder they have to keep on recruiting more policemen. The bureaucracy is unbelievable. I can't understand how any of them actually get out on to the street. Well, they don't much, do they? They have everything set up for putting into computers now, you know, it's like being at an airport, telly screens everywhere and people typing at keyboards. That's where they dug up Nobby, I suppose.'

Sue stopped her pacing, bang centre in the middle of the carpet. 'Nobby? Nobby Roberts? You mean poor Nobby has had to be dragged into one of your scrapes? Again?'

I looked up at her indignantly. 'What do you mean, *poor* Nobby? There's nothing poor about Nobby, let me tell you. Chief Inspector, inflation-proof pension, lots of praise from Maggie Thatcher, plenty of tea to drink, minions cringing about kowtowing like blazes, and then usually someone else like me has to do it all for him.'

'Oh no! Oh no! No you're not!'

'Of course I'm not.' I tried to be soothing. 'Just a figure of speech. I mean I just had to, before. Not now. I can't really say that I'm delighted to be sort of *known to the police*, if you get me, but that's evidently what happens when they punch my details into the box. A flag goes up saying refer to Chief Inspector Roberts, Scotland Yard, and that's what they did. And before you could say Bob's your Uncle round came Nobby in a white Rover, old Plod in person, irritable as a singed porcupine, he was.' I chuckled. 'Didn't half take him aback to see Toby.'

'Toby.' A new look had come into her face, a sort of meaning look, if you know what I mean. 'I might have known that—tell me—Toby's never married, has he?'

Strange how women bring up these irrelevancies.

'No.' I kept it casual. 'No. He never has. Why?'

'Nothing.' Her voice carried a thousand shades of meaning. 'I just wondered. He's obviously a friend of yours, so you'd know.'

'Oh, I'm sure I must have told you before. Never has. Not the type.'

'The *type?*'

'You know Toby, very intellectual, cultivated, a bit donnish really, loves the opera, food, wine, mad on his magazine, married to it, not a family type at all. Detests children. No, not the marrying type.'

She pursed her lips. 'Well. I'm not the one to discuss old friends of yours.'

'Really? I thought we'd discussed old Nobby many times.'

'That's different.'

'Different? Because he's a rugger player too or because he's happily married to Gillian and loves his kids and all that—that—'

'What?'

'Domestic you-know-what. Have some tea?'

She scowled at me. I could tell that we were getting off the subject and into deep water. Sue's conviction that I constantly get into the sort of situation we had had in Long Acre really won't stand statistical analysis but it is unfortunate, I must say, that one or two odd occasions like it have happened before. She was involved in the first one, in Motcomb Street, and in another in Chelsea, which she took rather well. She's fond of Nobby and Gillian, very much so, despite the fact that Nobby can be extraordinarily prickly about himself and his job, a sort of moral vocation it is, no sense of humour about it at all. You wouldn't think we'd been at College together sometimes. He was a cracking good wing threequarter was Nobby, twelve years back, and went on playing for a lot longer than I did.

'I take it that Nobby and the other policemen involved warned you—very seriously—to let them handle everything, absolutely everything, connected with this man Brown's murder?'

'Oh yes. Absolutely If it is murder. To the point of tediousness. Repetitively. Toby became quite restive about it. I don't think he and Nobby would get on very well now, you know.'

'Did they ever?'

'Oh—well—they weren't exactly *close* but they were quite congenial at one time. When I was with them, anyway. Years ago.'

She sat down and picked up the cup of tea I'd poured for her. She drank a bit, put the cup down, bit her lip and tapped her foot on the carpet. Then she stared at me before she spoke. It was the sort of stare I don't like; it had the look of a schoolmistress about to address a mob of recalcitrant schoolchildren to whom she feels an ultimatum is due. I hate being treated that way: I'm very bad at learning lessons.

'Tim?'

'Yes.'

'I'm going to have to say something to you.'

There was a pause. I could have screamed. I'm not a child to be put through responses. I waited.

'Are you listening to me?'

Her voice betrayed tension. '*Mirame quando le hablo,*' I said.

Now she glared. 'What does that mean?'

'It means, "Look at me when I'm speaking to you." Latin schoolmarms are just the same as ours.'

'Tim! I'm serious! If you don't leave everything—*everything*—to the police and keep out of this dreadful business I will leave you. Do you hear? I will *never* come back. Is that clear? I've a mind to pack now.'

'I hear you,' I said. 'Don't pack. Please don't pack.'

'I mean it! You attract trouble!' Sue held up an imperious palm to check me because my mouth had opened. 'I know what you'll say! It's not your fault, you'll say, it just happens. Well, this time it's going no further. Nowhere.'

I spread my hands. 'How can it go further? I know nothing of Alf Brown. Never met him. Not involved. Feel no emotion about him.'

'The bookcase! I know you. You'll want the bookcase. It'll be a challenge to you. Please, Tim, *please*, I beg you, yes, I beg you, let the whole thing drop.'

I sighed. I bet the first person to think of saying the pledge was a woman. Public commitment and apology: they're mad on them.

'I don't see that I have any choice. The trail began and ended with Brown. Toby can't throw any more light on things so what else can I do? I have no forensic skills and I'm not interested in avenging Brown's death. It might have been quite unintentional; manslaughter, not murder. I have a pile on my plate with this timber business. There's no time.'

She wasn't convinced. I could see that she wasn't convinced, but there was no point in going on because she'd never believe me, would she, and I'm damned if I'm the sort of man to make public declarations, professions of faith and intent; I won't. She picked up her cup and saucer again and gave a long-drawn-out moan.

'If only I didn't know you so well,' she said, with rather more dejection than I liked.

CHAPTER 5

'Tell me,' I said to Nobby Roberts, putting a pint of bitter down on the pub table in front of him, 'why have you been lying to me for the last two or three years?'

His lean, sandy face checked as he peered at me. A stiff

look set into his gingery, freckled features and his muscular jaw closed tight for a moment before he spoke indignantly. 'Lying? Me? To you? Bloody cheek! When I think of how you've behaved and the trouble you've got into! How I've had to compromise myself over and over again while you've avoided telling the truth! What do you mean? Eh?'

He's quite ungrateful, is Nobby. To hear him talk you wouldn't believe what I've done to help him solve cases that have added to his swift promotion. Like all moralists, Nobby suffers from the delusion that it is his character, the strength of his purifying convictions, that have led to his elevation, quite apart from the sheer hard work and unremitting motivation that have moved him since we left college together. Because we were such close friends in those days we've never really drifted apart since, but Nobby looks on me rather like an early Christian with his beady eye on a sinner: if only he could dissuade me from my way of life he thinks that I might Join the Throng, if you follow me. To him, my defection from business consultancy, which had a degree of evangelical activity associated with it, and my move to stewardship with Jeremy and White's Bank constituted a Fall from Grace. Merchant banking, to Nobby, is a mercenary, unprincipled, low-down form of usurious swindling that is more appropriate to a lounge lizard than to a decent, hardworking, productive, stalwart, taxpaying citizen of the realm.

He's probably not far wrong.

'I mean,' I said, sitting beside him and taking a first cooling swig from the jug, 'that you've always given me the impression that you were in the Fraud Squad and you're not.'

'Eh?'

'Don't act innocent! You had to come over from Scotland Yard yesterday. I found out that the Fraud Squad—the real Fraud Squad, that is—are in High Holborn. You have never been stationed in High Holborn. Ergo, you are not in the Fraud Squad. You have deliberately misled me. And others. What are you in? Special Branch? Or daren't I ask for fear of salt mines?'

He looked quite defensive. Attack is the only way to deal with Nobby, otherwise he swamps you in moral fervour. He bridled a bit before he spoke. 'I did not say I was *in* the Fraud Squad. I may have conveyed that impression, but—'

'Oh yes you did! The Art Fraud Squad. I remember it, definitely.'

'I said I was *attached* to the Fraud Squad. On special duties. You are quite right; the Fraud Squad proper, the one that deals with financial and, er, City-related matters, is in High Holborn. I am not, structurally, a part of it.'

'Structurally? What amazing minds you coppers have. How is your structure today? Not too rigid, I hope, after your unpleasant surprise yesterday? Frightfully formal you were. I mean, I understand that you have to maintain your proper position, your rank and station, in front of all those mere constables but you were very stiff with Toby. I'm used to it, of course. I understand that you don't really mean it when you're so bloody rude, but he was quite put out. Old College friend, senior police officer, turns up loyally when old pals are being sniffed at by woodentop bloodhounds and instead of clapping all and sundry on the back, beaming bonhomie, the old "Don't worry, Sergeant, these gentlemen are friends of mine, can vouch for them, pot of tea and some fairy cakes on a tray'll do fine," you go all sniffy and cold and—oh splendid, she's brought our Ploughman's.'

There was a pause while the barmaid set down two plates in front of us, each loaded with the regulation doorstop of crusty bread, slab of Cheddar, scoop of butter and about half a pound of pickle and chutney, without any of those wisps of lettuce and watery slices of tomato that some pubs seem to have become infested with. For once Nobby looked quite approving: his face softened with interest and his mouth, which had become grimmer, curved outwards in the beginning of a smile.

'A proper Ploughman's,' he murmured. 'I must remember this place.'

We were in a pub south of Trafalgar Square that I had chosen, partly out of previous experience and partly because it was not too far for Nobby to walk but out of range of his colleagues in Broadway. There was silence for a moment or two while we both tucked into a preliminary mouthful and then he managed to speak, working the words round a hefty compendium of bread, butter, cheese and pickle.

'I don't know how you do it,' he mumbled. 'Actually, I've given up getting upset about it. You're a sort of magnet for corpses. Especially if they're involved in the fine art trade.'

'Well, you should be happy. It's your specialization, isn't it?'

He shook his head. 'It *was* my specialization. It's not now, not more than a watching brief and my past experience being available.'

'Oh I see. Well, I'm sorry if I've dragged you back to your murky past. What are you supposed to be doing now?'

He scowled. 'I do not have to reveal what duties I am undertaking now.'

'Ho! So that's the tone. Proper procedures and complete discretion, is it? Investigating one of our cabinet minister's relationship with a Bulgarian masseuse, are you?'

'I certainly am not!' He grinned suddenly. 'I wish I were. Might be more interesting than what I'm doing. Contrary to popular belief, a large amount of police work is very dull.'

'There you are. I try to make life interesting for you and all I get is dog's abuse.'

His eyes looked at me steadily as he munched further into the bread and cheese. 'Talking of relationships, I'd no idea that you'd kept up with Toby.'

'I hadn't.' I bit off a chunk myself. 'I hadn't seen him for years. Heard of his progress, of course. *The Modern Façade*, very *à la mode*. But then he contacted us a few days ago. About this piece by Richard Norman Shaw that the late Alf Brown had put up, like a gun-dog. You know the rest; it's all in the statements. It was great to see Toby again: he hasn't changed. None of us have. One never does.'

'Hm. You always liked Toby, didn't you?'

'Of course. Brilliant chap. Architecture, languages, culture. Learned a lot from Toby.' I picked up my beer-glass.

'We often wondered. You were such good chums for a while, at College.'

'We often—' I put my glass down. 'Now what do you mean by that?'

'Don't get excited! I'm not inferring anything, you know, untoward. Just that it was an odd mixture, you and he, that's all. Nothing else.'

'Now see here, Nobby—'

'No! No violence! You must know what I mean. We all knew you were absolutely straight, my God, it was obvious, but Toby, well, we were never quite sure what was what, were we?'

'You were pleased enough to know him, your first year. Short memory you've got. I can recall one Saturday night down Mill Lane when one of the lush girls he'd brought from London took a shine for you and you nipped outside with her and—'

'Tim! No!' Breadcrumbs sprayed the table.

'—found you in the meadow, skirt up round her ears and you going at it like a—'

'Tim! For Christ's sake! People will hear! Stop it!' His agitation was comic. 'That's the past! The past! Can't you ever forget anything?'

'No. To be honest. Biographical detail is something that sticks in my mind. All I'm saying is that we had some hilarious times together in our first year. After that, of course things changed. We were into rugger and we didn't see that much of him any more. Of course I know what you mean. Maybe Toby was—is—ambidextrous. It's not my business. I've always liked him for what he was to me; witty, generous, sophisticated. He's a mine of information and he's very well connected.'

'With more than one social world.'

I gave him a sharp glance. 'Ah. You've obviously started your inquiries. Very quick off the mark.'

He stroked his glass thoughtfully. 'That sort of outfit, Tim, a semi-fashion, semi-serious magazine; think of it. Connections in printing, advertising, design, journalism, architecture, art, bookshops, paper, distribution, photography. A concentration not only on buildings but on objects, things, materials, even landscape gardening. Almost anything, in fact, connected with a household. Brings in all sorts, doesn't it, and needs a man as—versatile?—as Toby Prescott to keep it all together. Quite a selection of talents, in fact. Used in several different worlds and rubbing shoulders with all sorts. Did Toby have money?'

The question was abrupt, short, taking me by surprise. 'No—I—no, I don't think so. He said he started *The Modern Façade* with a small nest-egg, but it doesn't make any money.'

Nobby's mouth gave a twist. 'That's all relative, Tim, as well you know, being a banker. We'll know what he means from the accounts, anyway.'

'Why? Why are you digging into Toby? He didn't do it, that's obvious.'

He raised his eyebrows. 'Is it? You said yourself it didn't take long to get from his office to Long Acre. The full report won't be available for a while but Brown had been dead for a few hours. Whoever it was visited him around opening time and no one else seems to have been into the shop until you arrived.'

So there it was, I thought dully. While Jeremy and Geoffrey and I were standing in the Victoria and Albert Museum gazing at the Gothic bookcase, talking about it, someone did in poor Alf Brown almost as though our voices, our decision, had sent out vibes that set off the deadly process.

'Not much sign of an argument,' Nobby mused. 'Papers on the desk ruffled and searched. My guess is that Brown knew his assailant. Perhaps a customer. Not afraid of him, anyway. He was struck a few blows and then got the one that did it. People don't realize how fragile we are sometimes. All that cinema-cowboy trash. If you hit a man the way John Wayne was supposed to in some of his films, especially if the recipient wasn't expecting it, you'd very likely kill him or maim him for life. Brain damage, anyway. Brown wasn't strongly built. Broke his neck on impact with the wall. Unlucky for the attacker, perhaps.'

I know, I thought, I know, and you know I know. Well, not all of it you don't and I'm never telling you: mine was in self-defence.

'Have another beer?'

'Just a half, thanks, Nobby.'

'Same here.' He shuffled off and I finished my plateful. A mental image of Toby rose to reproach me. He had kept his nerve remarkably well, but then Toby was no panicker. I'd left him in the bookshop while I summoned a policeman. Toby had been sitting alone, shaken and pale, when I came back but he was composed. We talked to each other briefly while more officials arrived. At Holborn they had taken our statements separately but we'd waited about together quite a bit. We were both comically apologetic to each other, feeling an individual responsibility for what had happened. The ebullient mood of our meeting earlier had seemed blasphemous; in a way I felt as I imagined a drunk driver does after a hilarious party which has ended in a smash and his presence in the cooler. What a mess, I thought, what a mess; if we had been about to renew an old friendship its rebirth had been most nastily blighted. Once Nobby had arrived it seemed worse; there had been Nobby's disapproval and uncertainty, his official position, his exasperation to contend with. He had been pretty cool with Toby. Nobby's very square nowadays, very moral; it must be something they do to them at Hendon, but I was willing to forgive him that because his heart is in the right place and you can depend on him. In a way he was now keeping very calm and friendly compared to the outbursts I've had from him before; perhaps, I thought, he's reached a philosophical accommodation with my tendency to get involved in these things.

He arrived back with the half-pints and gave me a rueful smile. 'I bet Sue gave you an earful when you got home?'

'She did. More in sorrow than in anger, though. "Nanny is not cross, she is just very, very disappointed" sort of approach. Much more effective in many ways.'

He laughed. 'You are a dreadful man, Tim. All I hope is that you'll be sensible this time and keep out of it.'

'Of course.'

He gave me a sharp glance. 'You've said that before.'

I spread my hands. 'Could I help it? Could I?'

'Yes.'

It was my turn to laugh and give him a silent toast as I lifted my glass to sip the first sip. 'Touché and cheers.'

'Cheers. And that goes for Sue, too.'

'What does?'

'Keeping out of it. You dragged her in last time.'

'Now that's unfair and you know it. She insisted.'

'Only because she wanted to keep tabs on you, what with your reputation and all. I'm telling you, Tim—'

'I'll come to a bad end? You've said that before, too, but here I still am.'

He sniffed as he put his glass down. 'Well, I wouldn't call White's unsurious Bank a good end but we'll not squabble on that subject again. You've made your bed, Jeremy White's bed as it happens, so you can lie on it. Just don't expect me to scrape up any gory remains, that's all.'

'God, you are becoming a dour old bugger, Nobby. There isn't any Scots Calvinist blood in you by any chance, is there? Or Wesleyan? You'd have made a good companion for Carlyle or Knox, you would. You could have sat moaning together about the misery of man's ways and really cheering each other up with a glass of fresh water. What are they doing to you at Scotland Yard?'

A grin came back to his face. 'Depressing me, it's true. I'm sorry if you think I was a bit strong with Toby Prescott. Actually, Tim, it was almost a relief to get called out to Holborn and know that you were misbehaving again.'

'Me? Damn it, Nobby, I'm not—'

He held up a hand. 'All right! All right! Don't get violent! What I was going to say was that I'm bogged down with paperwork and technical stuff, which stultifies any keen policeman because although someone has to do it the real job is out there. Out here.' He glanced round the pub. 'So I'll keep a distant eye on the Holborn crowd, won't offend them, and I'll let you know what happens.' He held up a finger. 'Please, Tim, please, I *beg* of you; keep your distance.'

'I will. I promise. I'm off to the Tyne for two or three days so you can't keep much further distance than that, can you?'

He stared at me gloomily. 'Alaska would have been better,' he said, 'but I suppose the Tyne will have to do for the moment.'

CHAPTER 6

I'm not going to bore you with the timber business. Britain was once covered in the stuff, just a vast forest, but what with random domestic heating, cooking, houses, wooden ships and charcoal for smelting iron there hasn't been much left for the last two or three hundred years so we import most of it. A lot of the softwood comes from Scandinavia and gets in through the east coast ports. From further afield softwood and hardwood come to places like Liverpool and Cardiff, but London still handles huge quantities of both, so it's not as though White's were out of the centre of things. When the other directors demanded action of Jeremy and he passed the ball on to me, Geoffrey Price went into a great gloom and started quavering on about the best use of our money and whether we shouldn't conserve management resources. I had to tell him, somewhat briefly, that I wasn't charmed with the subject myself but that a job was a job and I might as well do it thoroughly. He mumbled disgruntledly as he dug out a folder on Edwards & Coe, timber merchants and importers, giving it to me with a shake of his head.

'If only Jeremy had kept his mouth shut this would never have happened,' he grumbled. 'Bloody yachtsmen.'

I cocked an eye at him. 'Yachtsmen? What have they done? Sunk Jeremy's boat?'

He gesticulated at the folder. 'You'll see it in there. You know that Jeremy keeps a boat on the Hamble. Well, so does Sir John Coe. Head of Edwards & Coe. Lives in a big pile in West Sussex when he's not here in the City. Convenient for their operations at Shoreham; Shoreham's a big softwood port now. He and Jeremy met on the Hamble.

Next thing you know, Sir John Coe's putting up the idea of a merger of our timber interests, or even a takeover or something. Jeremy blabs about it in the Bank dining-room, never thinking anyone'd take it seriously, and here you are or rather here we are, pair of us, up to our ears in bloody woodwork. So the great wheels of industry grind on.'

'Ever smaller.'

'Ever smaller. To dust or, in this case, to sawdust.'

I shook my head at him. 'Mustn't be negative, Geoffrey, and especially not with humour. Places like the North-East are swimming in timber. From what I hear, Coe's crowd are very strong up there and not too dusty elsewhere outside London. We are pretty much concentrated here. He may have a point. Put us together and who knows?'

'Who knows indeed? We're not the only ones who can put two profitable operations together and lose a fortune. Just try us.'

There's no dealing with Geoffrey when he's in one of those moods so I left him, clutching my folder, and got to work. Edwards & Coe seemed to have extensive interests, depots everywhere, a transport company and no Edwards. Of the originators, only the Coes remained. I gave a cursory glance at the list of directors, sighed at the balance sheets, and decided to start as far away as possible and work my way back. I got hold of Sir John Coe's secretary, fixed appointments of a very discreet nature, told Sue I'd be away for a couple of nights, got out the Jaguar XJS and tooled off up the Great North Road determined to get it all done in the quickest and most efficient manner possible.

I got to Immingham first, took a look at the Humber, scouted the Edwards & Coe operation and then went back a bit to Scunthorpe. After that, Goole. I said I wouldn't bore you with the timber business and I won't. The next stop was Hartlepool. I spent a night in Newcastle, looked at South Shields and then, for no really pressing reason, went to Blyth, which is where the temptation happened. Up to then I had been behaving logically and dutifully. I worked hard, taking copious notes, and listened to those I interviewed respectfully. My head was stuffed with timber, its handling and its markets. It was at Blyth, after I'd looked at the docks, around lunch-time, that I realized I'd seen all I was going to and, instead of keeping my head down to the grindstone, I raised it, quite in disobedience to Sue, who I'd 'phoned the night before and assured of my good behaviour. She said she was going to bed early after tidying up the flat, which was so much more controllable in my absence and I said yes, men are trouble, and she agreed. I left the conversation at that and heard her laugh to herself as she put the phone down. Well, at least she's cheered up a bit, I thought, probably because I'm out of danger for a few days or at least out of mischief and she can make arrangements to fix me properly when I get back.

It all goes to show that there's just no telling. I sat in the car at Blyth, where it had turned damned cold by midday, with the freezing rain that April gives to the North-East bursting itself and its sleet on my windscreen and suddenly, from musing about tonnages and cubic metres, containers and veneers, my mind ran on to what the stuff is used for: furniture. From furniture it wasn't a far hop to bookcases and Norman Shaw, with something I'd read somewhere in Andrew Saint or Mark Girouard rustling the wet flat leaves rotting themselves to fibre under the dark trees of my brain. A tingle of apprehension went through me. I've never really wanted to seek for trouble, you must understand that, but there are things, unfinished things, necessary connections, nagging queries, that will not let the mind rest, over which I have no control. I hate unanswered questions. I was in Blyth, you see, where the road signs indicated the way back down to nearby Tynemouth via Seaton Delaval and to

Newcastle; that was one way. The other way was to Bedling-
ton, Morpeth, and further north.

Morpeth, that was what did it. I looked at my watch. Not
yet one o'clock. I had a mental image as I closed my eyes
of old black-and-white photographs of panelled rooms with
arched or panelled ceilings, heavy, containing furniture
that was either gravid sideboard oak or spindly, thin-railed
chairs, ebonized in dusty black like all Aesthetic Movement
furniture based on the Japanese. There were two or three
of these old black-and-white image-photographs: in them I
could see a rich patterned carpet on the floor and expensive
wood going up the walls or, in one case, plasterwork arching
to the great window-ceiling of a picture gallery. Below, on
the heavy carpet, was furniture; in one case furniture lined
the walls just like the paintings.

'Cragside,' I murmured out loud, to the noise of icy rain
drumming on the roof. 'Of course.'

The car seemed to know the way. Once round Morpeth
you take the road further north towards Rothbury, where
the National Trust now direct you carefully round the 1,700
acres that Sir William Armstrong planted with millions of
trees, until you are wound in among them as you enter the
country park. I drove carefully through the huge conifers
that block the light until, at the end of the tarmac, beyond
the intervening trunks, I could see the astounding house,
piled teetering above the Alpine-style gorge of the Debdon
Burn in a landscape that seemed to belong more to the
Black Forest than to Northumberland.

I use the word house, but the hunting lodge that Richard
Norman Shaw converted to a country residence for the
inventor and armaments manufacturer Sir William Armstrong is more like several houses to look at, welded together
into a huge and solid and well-kept mass, with an extraordinary medley of impassive stone walls, calm Gothic arches,
half-timbering of black-and-white brightness and sharp red

roof-tiles, capped by a tower with a strange, timbered hutch-roofed top to it, stuck like a miniature Swiss chalet above the rambling concourse of buildings that make up the total called Cragside. I sat in the Jaguar, pulled up in the gravelly earth of the car park carved from the sloping hillside and the trees, gaping at the sight around me until, by force of habit, I got·out to stretch my legs and ease a bad knee I inherited from a collapsed scrum in a long-distant rugger match. Still stooping to put the key into the door-lock, I glanced up over the car roof and caught sight of a big Ford Granada estate with a trade rack on it, about six cars away in the line. There was a movement which had caught my attention as the driver opened his door to get in. His back was turned to me but I could see he was a tallish, slender man bulked up by a blue plastic anorak. His check trousers went down to a pair of unmistakable brown suedes with rubber soles. I nipped round the back of the cars and, as he got in, I clapped a hand on his shoulder.

'Gotcher!' I exclaimed, cheerfully.

He gave a great start, dropped his keys, cursed mildly, leant on the horn, jumped at the blast and twisted round to gape at me.

'Christ! Tim Simpson! You bugger—I nearly had heart failure.'

'Guilty conscience,' I replied, grinning. 'All you Brighton Boys are the same. Antiques and women: you're all guilty.'

He gave me a reproachful glance, put his leg out of the door and emerged, blinking, to stand up and shake hands with me. Stan Reilly is not really one of your typical Brighton Boys. By that I mean he is not a chunky, cockney-accented, aggressive bloke who waves fivers in your face. It's unfair to quite a lot of the Brighton trade but I'm afraid a section of them have produced that image: tough, unrelenting, confident coal-heavers with a reputation for rapacious door-knocking. Stan is one of the other sort; rather thin, almost weedy-looking, and tall, but quite stringy and resilient, with a hatchet-shaped narrow face like an inquiring bird or a curious librarian, almost ascetic but slightly skew. When he speaks his voice is quiet with a faint Sussex accent emphasized by the use of local phrases like 'made up', to mean pleased. 'I heard you were made up with that,' he'll say, meaning he'd heard you were pleased with it. The gentle manner is deceptive; his shop in Hove is a pleasure to visit because he always has something unusual or attractive in it and you have to be sharp to keep that up. Stan has always been a bachelor as far as I know, so my remarks about women were of no relevance to him; antiques were his obsession and he never seemed to need close relationships of any sort. He shook his head at me.

'You are a terror, Tim, really you are. What on earth are you doing here? England isn't safe from you any more.'

I chuckled. 'I didn't think this was one of your stamping grounds either, Stan.'

'Everywhere has to be a stamping ground for a poor, hard-working dealer like me these days. Everywhere. Goods are so hard to find. Don't tell me you're buying up the National Trust now?'

'No. Not me. It is a long way from London, I agree, but it's even further from Brighton. Sorry, I mean Hove.'

It should be explained that Brighton and Hove, in the manner of south coast towns, have run into each other until, to the stranger, they are inseparable, rather like Hastings and St Leonards. In the same way, Hove rather fancies itself as a bit superior to its more famous neighbour and resents being lumped in together with it in any casual geographical reference. Stan's shop is just into Hove but a chance visitor, moving west through the tangle of streets, would never know wherethe borderline lay. He gave me a cautious smile.

'It is,' he admitted. 'But I've done a run up to the North-East many times before, Tim. I'll say no more.'

Etiquette dictates that a dealer keeps his sources of supply to himself unless he volunteers them. It is bad form to press him on the subject of where he buys; not only bad form but commercial ignorance. Older dealers often used to help new ones by telling them of the good 'calls' in a certain area but with increasing competition this is becoming less common and, in any case, auctions are steadily replacing other dealers as a source of supply. I nodded sagely and changed the subject, gesturing at the pile above us.

'Culture time then, Stan? Come to see how the great men used to live?'

He nodded quietly, following my glance up to the gables. 'Quite something, isn't it, Tim? Quite something. You can't imagine anyone having the money to build a place like that now, although I suppose it still happens in America and the Middle East. I've just stopped off to do a tour, for interest, like. Might learn something, I thought. Have you been round it? Before, I mean.'

I shook my head. 'My first visit, too. I've been up on business—not antiques business, Bank business—so I just thought I'd take a gander on spec. Playing hookey really.'

He laughed, looking over me carefully and keeping his eyes on mine watchfully. 'Lucky man. You're not thinking of buying the place for White's Art Fund or something?'

'Oh no. Once in the National Trust, forever in the National Trust. We can't buy Cragside. What's it like? Inside, I mean?'

He wagged his head up and down with affirmative pumps of the neck. 'Quite something. Really quite something. Well worth seeing. I had no idea what it was like. Armstrong must have been a remarkable man. He must really have liked contemporary art, too. But see for yourself.' He waved a hand at the great house. 'I've had my lunch-break: much too long a lunch-break. Won't say that it was wasted, though. You always learn something when you visit these places; you get a better feel for the furnishing and design of the period. You get to understand a bit better what they felt was the latest thing. It always helps.' He smiled gently. 'I suppose they'll say the same about a David Hicks room in a hundred years' time.'

'I suppose they will.'

He held out his hand. 'Nice seeing you, Tim. Take care, now. I must be off. There's a good call I can make before this afternoon's out.'

'All the best, Stan.'

He retrieved his keys from the car floor and I watched the big Granada lumber over the bumps to the surfaced road, where it straightened itself out and then slid off towards the house, disappearing under a wide, pointed stone arch in the side wall. I strolled after it thoughtfully; it was a long time since I'd seen Stan and I knew of his bookish interest in all old things but somehow it felt odd to meet him there, in the cold damp forest on the rocky hillside by the house. It seemed incongruous to mix the reality of Brighton's commercial trade with this carefully-preserved tourist attraction. A spatter of rain hit me and I shivered as I hurried to the entrance.

The interior is quite staggering but I'm not going to make life tedious with a guided-tour monologue on Cragside. The room that sticks in my mind the most is the library, which was finished in 1872. It is panelled in oak to a height of five feet and has a beamed and coffered ceiling. Between the two there is snuff-coloured wallpaper. On the wallpaper hang Pre-Raphaelite paintings, which are another story in themselves, but I was looking for furniture, of course, and, despite the distractions of Morris stained glass designed by Rossetti, and gilt panels with painted leaves, and blue-and-white porcelain, I saw plenty of furniture.

There was no Gothic bookcase, though.

There were ebonized black chairs with cane seats and

leather back-panels stamped with gilt and pomegranates.
There were red leather sofas. There was a Gillows writing-
table and there were even four corner chairs of 'Queen
Anne' style but not quite like Toby's green one. These were
pitch black in shiny ebonizing, more stolid, and they had
stronger back legs with turned stretchers between for added
strength. The front leg was a cabriole though, like Toby's
green one. The back slabs were painted and the seats had
leather coverings, not rush, gilded again, like the other
chairs in the room, so that they were very decorative as well
as being very masculine. It was a glorious room, the room
of someone who really liked art, and it made me begin to
understand what most of the Aesthetic Movement had
tried to do and failed, whereas Shaw had succeeded
magnificently.

I explored the rest of the rooms enthusiastically but there
were no more clues to the existence of other Gothic bookcases
or pieces like the one in the Victoria and Albert Museum.
Nothing like it came into sight. This house and its furnishings were a different exercise, something else, a movement onward in style and taste. I collected all the
information the bookshop had in print and got back into
the car. Serve you right, a little voice said, for doing your
terrier-act again; you've wasted your time. No, I haven't,
another voice replied; time spent viewing places like this is
never wasted. Tucked away in the memory-bank now are
impressions that will never fade, just as Stan Reilly said, or
something like it. The pleasure of that library was worth
every minute of the trip. And the corner chairs, they were
great, I thought, I must remember to tell Toby about those.
When things have died down a bit, of course.

CHAPTER 7

If you put your foot down it takes five hours or so to drive from Newcastle to London. I let myself into the flat in Onslow Gardens some time around ten. Sue was sitting in front of the fireplace, on the big sofa, with her legs curled up under her, reading. She put her book down hurriedly and scampered across to greet me with considerable enthusiasm. After a while I let go of her and we went into the kitchen to brew a pot of coffee while I foraged about for something to eat. Sue tends to be a health-diet faddist, so when I had found a beefburger, three sausages, eggs and a clod of cold mashed potato she gave me a reproving look.

'I'm not cooking that for you,' she said. 'There's some salad things and the remains of a fish stew you could have.'

'That'll do to start with. While I cook the sausages.'

She shook her head sadly but before I had been tending the grill for long the fish-stew-salad appeared in a bowl with some dressing and I wolfed it down, chatting lightly to her about the attractions of Scunthorpe and the treeless rawness of Newcastle. She quizzed me quite closely for a while and it wasn't until I'd finished my miniature grill and we had taken our coffee into the living-room, where she regained the sofa and I had a sprawl in one of the armchairs, that I realized she hadn't said much about herself, apart from asking me to note how tidy the flat looked.

'What about you?' I demanded. 'Surely not two whole days and nothing to report?'

'Oh no,' she said, 'it's been very quiet. Two full days at work and two early nights in bed like a good girl.'

'Some chance. Alone?'

She pulled a face at me and I grinned, reflecting that

there had been no need to mention my visit to Cragside, although I would very much have liked to have discussed its contents with her. Sue is not very keen on Victorian romantic painting or, come to that, on anything very much of the decorative side of the British scene before 1890 or so. French Impressionists, now, that's another matter: Sue is an expert on them. The big picture gallery at Cragside, like the vast drawing-room with its enormous marble double-storey chimneypiece, originally had Armstrong's Victorian paintings in it, with work by Millais and the superior Pre-Raphaelites, all sold off in 1910. Cooke was present with his marine painting, and Horsley, through whom Shaw got the contract to design Cragside for its famous owner. I sipped my coffee. Shaw must have enjoyed himself hugely with that house, just as Armstrong did. The library I had liked so much was the first room in the world to have permanent incandescent electric lighting, powered by a hydro-electric generator that Armstrong had connected to a turbine, driven at the dam he had erected to form Debdon Lake. The whole thing was an enormous play-castle for a man with unlimited private funds; the work that was done on the grounds, rearranging huge rocks and planting vast forests, was a major occupation, quite apart from the interiors that Norman Shaw had so carefully considered for his client. Thinking of him and of Cragside, I quickly decided that I'd have another glance at Andrew Saint's book, and Mark Girouard, some time when Sue wasn't about, just to check my facts. It wasn't that the temptation to persevere had dominated me—not yet—but intellectual curiosity needed to be satisfied that I hadn't missed something in my tour. So, while smiling at Sue over my coffee-cup I shot a quick glance at the big set of bookshelves on the wall opposite where we jointly kept a great range of books on fine art and related subjects.

The Andrew Saint wasn't there.

Still smiling, I looked quickly back at Sue to make sure she hadn't noticed the direction of my gaze and answered a banal question of hers about Jeremy and Geoffrey's attitude to the Coe's timber operations. As she half-turned to put her coffee-cup on the side table parked by the settee I took a much longer, steadier look at the place on the bookshelf where Saint's biography of Richard Norman Shaw, with its distinctive blue spine lettered in white, should have been. Then I let my eyes range right along the serried volumes before looking back, just in time, to intercept a glance from her.

It definitely wasn't there. Nowhere in the bookcase.

Finishing my coffee, I eased myself up to my feet and stretched luxuriously, as a man who has driven solidly for five hours and then eaten needs to do, flexing my bad knee before I put the cup and saucer down on the mantelpiece beside me. The April night was dark outside and it was pleasant to look at the room, with the paintings assembled separately by both of us hanging carefully on the free walls. Behind me, over the fireplace, was the big coastal marine by Clarkson Stanfield that Sue didn't like so much; in front, my Seago next to Sue's Stanley Spencer. To my left was a wall containing an etching of Dorelia by Augustus John and a Picasso print. Elsewhere my Wilson Steer had to contend with all Sue's ladies: Sylvia Gosse, Laura Knight, Elizabeth Stanhope Forbes, Dod Proctor and Ethel Walker. It was a nice room, calm, unperturbed and unruffled: I liked it. I smiled down at Sue, with her shoes kicked off and her feet tucked under her, propped against the arm at one corner-end of the sofa. She smiled back.

'You must be tired,' she said.

I eased myself off the mantelpiece, took a step across the hearthrug and sat in the middle of the sofa next to her knees and feet. 'Not that tired,' I said.

A look came into her face, the sort of look that said

ho-hum he's been away and now that he's back and he's
fed he thinks that the next logical step is a bit of you-know-
what but he's not just going to do that, oh no, I'm not
having that. Still smiling at her, I slid my hands along the
sofa, one on each side of her, so that I was leaning over her,
bringing my face close to hers.

'Tim! Now look here—'

Too late. Slumping down on her as though to impose a
kiss and pinning her body beneath my chest and shoulders,
I slid my hands right to the end of the sofa and then up and
under the cushion supporting her back. My right hand
hit something hard and I grabbed it, pulling it out and
straightening myself up with a triumphant shout as the
bright red-and-white photograph of Scotland Yard on the
cover of the large, chunky paperback came into view.

'Well, well, well,' I crowed. 'Fancy that! What have we
here?'

She straightened herself out, flustered, pulling her skirt
back over her knees and smoothing her woollen sweater
down.

'You bastard,' she said.

'How extraordinary. *Richard Norman Shaw*, by Andrew
Saint. Under the cushion at the back of you. Most odd.
Quite peculiar. I wonder how it got there. To bed early,
you said? With a good book, perhaps? What a funny thing
—especially after your little homily to me three days ago.'

She scowled blackly. Her mouth set in a line. Guilt
emanated from every bit of her expression. I wondered if I
might not have cause to regret this little victory but suppressed the idea: I was too pleased with myself just then.

She found her voice. 'All right, Clever Dick. I've been
reading it. So what?'

'Curiosity killed the cat, that's what. So what were you
looking for?'

She pouted. She's a very pretty girl and I love her, but I

managed to sit severely on the middle of the sofa, away from her feet.

'Get me some more coffee and I'll tell you,' she commanded.

I went through to the kitchen with our cups, replenished the coffee and came back into the living-room. She was sitting more upright and had tidied her dark-brown hair carefully. Her large blue eyes looked at me without blinking. She has a slenderish figure but with a good bosom and her lips are full. I handed her the cup of coffee and she sipped it before speaking so that I could admire her for a brief moment.

'I had to make a decision,' she said.

'Decision? What decision?'

She pointed at the door. 'Whether to walk out through that door, bag and baggage, traps packed, or whether to stay.'

'Walk out? What on earth are you talking about? Why?'

'You know very well why! Don't think I don't know you! I've either got to be a part of your hopeless love of snooping or pack up! It was the same with the Whistler business. Either I'm a part of your life, Tim, or I'm not. I'm not going to sit here like the meek little woman while you gad about chasing that Norman Shaw cabinet and get yourself killed. I'm not! So do you want me to stay?'

'My dear Sue, sweetheart, of course I—'

'Well then! I'm not that much into architectural history but I do know a bit about it. I decided to bone up on Norman Shaw. I was keeping it quiet for a bit. Until you asked for help.'

'Thank you for making that decision,' I murmured courteously, 'but I do feel that your getting involved is a bit— um—well, Nobby nearly killed me for endangering you over the Whistler. This is quite different, of course, but—'

'But nothing. Blow Nobby! I really think I must have a

word with Gillian. His attitude to women is so old-fashioned.'

'Perhaps she likes that.'

I got a withering glance. 'I had no doubt that you wouldn't leave the matter with Nobby and the police. So I'm going to be involved, Tim. That is, if you want me to stay?'

'Of course.'

'Good. What did you think of Morpeth?'

I gaped at her. 'Morpeth? I never said I'd been to Morpeth.'

'Of course not. But you did say you'd been to Blyth. So naturally you must have slipped up to Morpeth too; it's very near. On the way to Rothbury.'

'How did you know that?'

'Oh, Tim, really! I have an Oxford degree and a diploma from the Courtauld!'

'Not in geography. I didn't go to Morpeth. There's a bypass.'

'Now stop it!' A reminiscent look took over her face. 'If you really want to know, I once had a boyfriend up there.' The look went smug. 'A very good boyfriend too.'

'A Geordie? I didn't know you liked a bit of the rough in your younger days.'

'You are insufferable sometimes! He was not a Geordie. Not in the sense that you are inferring. His family had large estates in Northumberland.'

'Wild country. Full of strong silent men.'

'He asked me to marry him. I'd have had a large farm and my own hunter by now.'

'A horse? How very boring.'

'There is nothing wrong with horses!'

Horses bite at one end and kick at the other, but there's no telling Sue. A horse is the most bone-headedly violent animal you can think of, liable to take fright at a gesture intended for someone a quarter of a mile away and kick its owner to death as a result. In England they ride horses on hard thin saddles and hold the reins with both hands, which is ridiculous. Where I learnt to ride in South America they put a sheepskin on the horse first so that the saddle sits like a club armchair and you only hold the reins with one hand, as does everyone else in the world. It leaves the other hand free to wave your sombrero or fire your revolver. I decided to say nothing; Sue has that English girl's sentimentality about horses which defies all logic.

'You'd have been bored stiff. No art to speak of.'

'There was plenty of art at Cragside.'

'Huh?'

'Cragside. You did go there, didn't you? It was inevitable. Was there anything there that gave you a clue?'

I put my cup and saucer back on the mantelpiece, crossed the rug again, and sat down beside her on the sofa. 'No, there wasn't. And I'm glad I'm not married to you,' I said.

'Why?'

'Because if I were your husband I would feel considerably endangered by a wife with such prescience, or insight, or whatever it is. I wouldn't feel safe.'

She smiled. 'It didn't take much calculation,' she said. 'Once you'd mentioned Blyth I was practically home and dry.'

I leant across and kissed her gently. 'So we're quits?'

'Quits.'

'Sue, please don't do anything I don't know about, will you? Please?'

'Don't worry. I'll let my big strong bodyguard know everything. Providing he does the same.'

'Done. It's a deal.'

'Then I reckon it was for Nesfield.'

'Eh?'

'The cabinet, Tim.' She became brisk. 'That's what we're

after, isn't it? A Gothic cabinet or bookcase like the one at the V & A? Shaw designed that for himself in 1861. Well, what about Nesfield? They set up office together, Shaw and William Eden Nesfield, in 1863 or so. They were partners in architectural practice, two famous men together for about three years, later on. In 1869 they split up the partnership but continued to share offices. What could be more natural than that? Nesfield might have admired Shaw's bookcase and asked him to do another one, maybe the same, maybe different?'

I sat back from her. Once she gets the bit between her teeth, horses have nothing on Sue. 'There's only one thing wrong with that,' I objected.

'What?'

'Nesfield was as famous as Shaw, to start with. Perhaps even more so. He designed a lot of furniture, I seem to remember, which has all disappeared, but he was a well-known furniture designer. Surely he would have designed his own office bookcase?'

Her mouth turned down a bit. 'Oh dear. You've got a point, Tim. I just naturally thought, since they were so close in the eighteen-sixties, that the only other person Shaw would have produced a cabinet for would have been Nesfield. They were so influential together.'

'The Old English and Queen Anne styles, you mean? Possibly. But they worked quite separately. Nesfield was a bit of a *bon viveur* and mixed in different circles to Shaw. I have a feeling he died youngish.'

'Fifty-three.'

'Eh?'

'In the late eighties, eighteen-eighties. About eighty-eight I think. Cirrhosis of the liver. He was fifty-three.'

'How odd. What a coincidence. Godwin was fifty-three when he died. Also a *bon viveur*. Like Sir William Orpen. Also a *bon viveur*. Remind me to be careful in my fifty-third year. The ladies and the drink were prominent in all three cases.'

She gave me another of her looks, the sort that ignore what you've just said while registering it for future use. 'Anyway, I believe Nesfield's furniture was not unlike Shaw's. They even designed some together, I think.' She brightened. 'Suppose this is one of those pieces? Designed by Shaw and Nesfield together?'

'That would be a coup!'

'Wouldn't it? Oh Tim, how exciting!'

He face flushed. Her eyes sparkled. I couldn't help feeling her enthusiasm come through to me as well. 'I suppose it's possible, Sue. Alf Brown could easily have been mistaken. The only problem is that we don't know where it is. We have no idea. Presumably all of Shaw's estate was well-documented at his death even if the V & A cabinet had escaped to a convent. Nesfield would be much more difficult to trace. He more or less died in obscurity didn't he?'

.'Yes, poor man. He married a widow—quite late in life, around fifty—and retired to Brighton. Died three years later.'

The room went quite still and I suddenly heard, clearly, a bus going down the Old Brompton Road two hundred yards away. Sue stared at me. 'What's the matter? You've gone pale.'

'Brighton? Did you say Brighton?'

'Yes.'

'Nesfield died in Brighton? Was buried there?'

'Yes.' She rummaged about in the book, found the page and nodded emphatically. 'Nesfield died in Brighton in 1888, aged fifty-three, after marrying a divorcee, not a widow, called Mary Gwilt, who was an architect's daughter. "A pathetic end for an architect of genius." Why?'

'I forgot to tell you—I ran into Stan Reilly in the car park at Cragside today.'

'Stan Reilly? That rather studious dealer from Hove?'

'Yes.'

Sue closed the book slowly. 'Stan Reilly. He's virtually in Brighton.'

'It may just be a coincidence.'

She shook her head. 'I can see you don't believe that.'

'I have to go to Shoreham tomorrow. Shoreham, Sussex. It's a big timber port now. A couple of miles or so from Brighton and Hove. I think I'd better call on Stan. He virtually admitted he'd never been to Cragside before. Why the sudden interest?'

She jumped to her feet. 'I'm coming with you.'

'You can't! You've your work at the Tate!'

'I'll 'phone them. Tell them I'm ill.'

'You can't! I—I'll be tied up at the timber yards. Nearly all day.'

'I'll wait. In the car.'

'Oh Sue! No!'

'Tim Simpson, have we just agreed on something or haven't we? Either I'm in or I'm out. Permanently. Which is it to be?'

I sighed. I've said that there's no stopping her and I meant it. Even Nobby Roberts has been defeated by Sue's determination and heaven knows how much moral force he can bring to bear. I sometimes wonder, in those tremulous moments that one gets, whether Sue hasn't stayed with me the way she has simply out of a desire for the excitement that my involvement with art sometimes brings. She mostly disagrees with me about the commercial aspects of it all; her view from the Tate is very purist. But then the view from the Tate can be very dull, and Winston Churchill once said that people need change and excitement, otherwise they become bloody-minded. Winston Churchill understood people well and power even better; I had to keep my place with Sue, even at a cost. 'OK,' I said, as firmly as I

behind the office because Stan always maintained that the presence of sawdust or shavings on the premises, or the smell of hot glue, was bad for customer confidence. He always got his structural repairs done elsewhere by freelance restorers. What there was, however behind the shop area itself, was another large storeroom, its floor down three steps from the shop due to the slope on which the houses were built. This storeroom was quite big and, because of the slope, much loftier than the shop. Stan kept his unrestored and unpolished pieces there along with items he didn't want to bring out yet or which had been sold and removed from display. Access at the back of the building via double doors made it a convenient point for loading and Stan often used the storage area for cleaning, staining and polishing; the smell of polish was good for customer confidence, he said.

Sue and I moved into the centre of the shop and waited for Stan to emerge. I had a quick look at his display stock and felt a bit disappointed. It was rather run-of-the-mill, nothing exceptional except perhaps for a satin maple sofa table against one wall and a good marine painting of the Pool of London by Dixon above it. Usually, Stan would have something very decorative or exotic to make a splash; the shop was a bit subdued that day.

'Stan?' I opened the office-partition door and called up the stairs. No reply. Shrugging, I beckoned Sue and went to the door to the storage area, plumb centre in the back wall. Beyond the doorway it was darker, shrouded by the squares of furniture, so I felt round the door-jamb and switched on a light without thinking that if Stan had been there the light would have been on already.

'It's a bit empty here, too,' I said out loud, apropos of nothing except that it normally held much more than the stock I could see beyond the three steps down. Neon light-bars flickered and then clicked into a bright glare that revealed a bare space of whitewashed wall at one side, a blank gleam of spotty white brickwork that awaited the arrival of something solid to cover it up. I trod down the three stairs. 'Stan?' I called again, in case he turned out to be in the alley outside, loading up and ignoring the bell-jangle of the front door.

No one answered. Sue followed me down the steps into the storage room with its garish fluorescence of vivid artificial daylight. Polish and white spirit fumes pricked my nostrils with the happy aroma of antique finishers; Stan seemed to have been at work here recently. Stepping round the edge of an oak chest of drawers, I moved towards the large blank space of wall where the smell seemed stronger, and nearly trod on an overturned tin of paint, spreading a dark stain across the floor.

'Tut, tut,' I said, out loud again. 'Clumsy.'

It was blackboard paint. Not black blackboard paint, you understand, but green blackboard paint, the colour of the better class of blackboards, of ping-pong table tops, a satisfying matt sage green like old, old baize cloth. The tin, with its white label printed in red, lay on its side and the paint had ebbed from it across the cement floor.

'*Very* clumsy,' said Sue, her warm soft body pressing up behind me and her dark brown hair brushing the back of my shoulder. 'Look, someone's trodden in it.'

It was true. A dark green footprint, mostly a shoe-sole outline, printed itself across the floor in three fading, reducing marks to the back door out to the alley. I shook my head with a chuckle and walked carefully round the mess to reach the door, throwing it outwards to step across the lintel and out into the service road behind the shop.

There was no one there. No van, nobody loading. Behind me, Stan's big Granada estate stood against the wall, carefully parked with its nose facing the way out. Behind it straggled the backs of other houses and shops, with occasional dustbins against their gates. The sharp April wind blew straight down between the walls, making Sue shiver.

'It's cold,' she complained, 'and there's no one here. Let's go back in.'

We retraced our way back into the storeroom, up the steps, into the main shop display area.

'Stan?'

No answer.

'This is silly,' I said, more to myself than to Sue, and strode through his office partition-wall up the staircase and on to the landing of his flat at the top. Looking back down, I saw Sue halted at the foot of the stairs, her eyes wide as she looked inquiringly up at me. I turned left, towards the front of the building and went into his living-room over the shop, with a big multi-paned window facing south-east that made it very light. He wasn't there either, so that wasn't what made me stop. It was an untidy room, as befitted a solitary dealer-bachelor, littered a bit with papers, comfortably dug into the space in front of the fireplace and the television set, with a big sofa to lounge on. On the sofa there were some books, pulled most probably from the big bookcase on the wall where Stan kept all his reference books, for he was a studious bugger, was Stan, and he had a lot of the classic reference books like Edwards, MacQuoid and Cescinsky. It was the one open on the sofa that stopped me. There was a thick hardback, quarto size, open at the flysheet, across which I could see a familiar legend: *Studies in British Art*. I knew then. I knew, not because that is what is printed by the Paul Mellon Foundation across the flysheets of their books and what is, therefore, printed across the flysheet of Andrew Saint's book on Richard Norman Shaw. I knew because the bookseller, in the manner of old-fashioned booksellers, had stuck his own little monogram-label inside the front cover, facing the flysheet. And I knew I could bet, if I looked inside some of the other art reference books that Stan Reilly had on his shelves, that I would find the same

little monogram-label inside them too, and that like this one
it would say, quite simply:

> A. Brown. Bookseller.
> Hay Yard, Long Acre,
> London W.C.2

and that the sight of it would make me feel, as I felt now,
overcome by a dreadful fear, a paralysing dose of the willies
that locked me in position, staring at the little label until
Sue's voice from the bottom of the stairs where she had
stopped, perhaps in trepidation herself, sharply called
'Tim?' in a nervous tone and jerked me back to the capability
of movement.

I knew. I knew even though the bedroom was empty
and so was the kitchen. I knew even though, when I had
summoned the courage, I swung open the storeroom door
and found nothing in there but junk. I knew then that the
last room, the bathroom, would contain him and that the
reason the door wouldn't open properly, even though it
wasn't locked, was that the body was slumped against it
from the inside so that I had to steel myself to push it open
enough to peer round into the white-tiled space. Stan Reilly
was there, bundled awkwardly in a heap, limbs doubled
against the pedestal of the lavatory. My guess was that
whoever had strangled him had slipped the belt round
his neck while he was standing having a pee, completely
unawares, and had twisted it tighter and tighter while
Stan struggled and writhed, eyes popping, arms and legs
thrashing, until he was down on the floor and, after that,
until all life had gone.

I went back to the stairhead and leant against the corner

of the landing wall. Sue stared up at me. My legs started to shake.

'The Hove police first,' I said. 'Then I'm afraid we're going to have to upset Nobby Roberts all over again.'

CHAPTER 9

'This is appalling! Appalling!' Jeremy White did a sort of two-step up and down his carpet. 'It is absolutely disgraceful! Irresponsible! You—you—my God, we are due to meet Sir John Coe in minutes and here you are admitting, yes, openly admitting, that you have once again—quite *blandly* I may say—interfered disgracefully in a criminal matter and got yourself further, no, not just further, much *deeper* involved! Hm? Eh? Am I wrong? Geoffrey? Am I wrong?'

Geoffrey Price closed a notebook with a snap and scowled at me before speaking. He's not a bad chap, Geoffrey, quite human for an accountant and loyal to his friends, but he has his weak moments and the Art Fund always brings them out. 'I've always maintained,' he said, with a manner superficially pompous, like a politician asserting a matter of principle, 'that the Art Fund was quite risky enough, quite outside normal investment practices, without adding to it these dreadfully squalid cases that Tim always gets himself into. Without the Art Fund perhaps none of this would happen.'

Jeremy stopped in mid-two-step with a sort of hop and glared at him. Geoffrey had put his foot right in it. 'There's nothing wrong with the Art Fund! Nothing! It has done well!' He gave a glance around him. 'It's just that Tim *always* behaves like a—like a—Jack Russell after a rat on these occasions.'

'Now you're talking like your Uncle Richard.'

Jeremy dropped his fountain pen. I knew my remark would hurt. His office at the Bank is not bad as City offices go but it's not the Chairman's nor is it as grand as the one he'd had at Park Lane in the old days and it didn't have a portrait of the original White, posed in blue coat and white silk breeches in it. There was some panelling, some good carpeting under a respectable mahogany pedestal desk, a long table and chairs for meetings and a window with a view towards Bishopsgate. On one wall hung quite a large painting of Wapping by Whistler himself, depicting the tangle of barges and sailing ships on the curve of the river behind a man and a woman, modelled by Alphonse Legros and Jo Hiffernan, on a balcony in the foreground. Jeremy's glance around him had taken that in and had inferred silently to Geoffrey that the Art Fund had had its successes despite the somewhat murderous events that had brought the Whistler to us and the resistance of his uncle, Sir Richard White, once chairman of the Bank but now departed. On another wall was an earlier painting of a three-masted timber ship en route from Manaos to London which Jeremy had inherited with the office.

'I am *not* talking like Richard!' He picked the pen up with a petulant gesture. 'Although Richard may have had a point, you know, Tim, when he inveighed against your somewhat—somewhat—'

'Tenacious?'

'Precisely. Tenacious qualities. Stubborn qualities.' His face twisted for a moment, darkened, then broke, briefly, into a radiant smile. 'Damn it. Tim! You always do this to me on these occasions! I will not be equated with Uncle Richard. Even if you will continue to attract mayhem. You must accept that as a Director of the Bank, and a member of the main board, I have to warn you that your behaviour is consistently irresponsible in dogging about pursuing criminal leads when you should be getting on with the business!'

'Do you want me to resign?'

'Resign?' A look of absolute horror crossed his face. His voice rose in pitch. 'Resign? Have you gone raving mad? Of course not! Ridiculous! Whoever suggested such a thing? Eh? Geoffrey?' He wheeled towards his accountant.

'Good God no! Absolutely not! Never crossed my mind!'

'Well then!' Jeremy wheeled back to me. 'What on earth are you talking about?'

'Well,' I said, mildly, 'you can hardly expect me to ignore the possibility. I come in here, tell you fully and frankly what has transpired, how these unfortunate and unrelated events have happened, events for which I have had no responsibility, discovered while quite innocently pursuing information in my own time, and what do I get? Dog's abuse. You call me appalling, disgraceful, irresponsible and —what was it—a Jack Russell. Incidentally a Jack Russell terrier is incapable of being bland, which is the other adjective you used.'

'Tim! Don't be flippant, damn it! This is serious.'

'Yes. I'm sorry. But it's quite unfair. The bookseller Brown whom Toby and I discovered was found while on official Art Fund business. I met Stan Reilly while visiting Cragside in my lunch-time. I went to his shop after a missed lunch-hour simply to chat to him.'

'Pah! You admit that the Nesfield connection intrigued you! You always do this!' He gave a dismissive gesture. 'It's no good. I can see it's no good. You'll never learn. All I can hope is that the good name of the Bank will not be impugned in some way. That you'll at least consider your responsibility on that score?'

'Of course, Jeremy. As we always have.'

He flushed, but his eyes twinkled at me. In the old days,

when I started with Jeremy in Park Lane, where he ran a quite separate personal investment brokerage, he would inveigh continually about the Bank, its stuffy and moribund directors, its lack of initiative, its lack of profitability and its stultifying paternalism. As a junior nephew of a cadet branch of the White family his place at the bottom of a pyramidical hierarchy had pressed heavily upon him and his financial freebooting had earned him much pompous censure and patronal reproof. Jeremy's opinion of the Bank then had been expressed with extreme sarcasm and bitter humour. Now, however, he recognized that he would slowly turn into a typical White himself unless someone like me and his charming, shrewd and pretty wife, Mary, once Sir Richard's secretary, kept him from ossifying by stimulating his natural iconoclasm and entrepreneurial flair. He wagged a finger at me and picked up a bunch of papers from his desk.

'To work! To work! No more of Norman Shaw! Coe will be here any minute.'

Geoffrey Price's face was still pained. He gave me a long look of reproof and then got out his own papers so that we could prepare properly for the meeting with Sir John Coe. For some time Geoffrey and I had worked hard to get Jeremy to prepare for meetings properly instead of shooting from the hip, as was natural to him, and it was gradually working. This time he had actually studied the figures and read my reports on the various port facilities and depots, so that when Clara, his secretary, buzzed him that his visitors had arrived, we were all for once satisfied that the others knew their stuff.

There were three visitors. The first to enter was tallish, grey-quiffed, well polished and dressed in a dark grey three-piece pinstripe suit with a striped shirt capped by an old-fashioned stiff white collar. His tie was a red paisley job and his blue eyes were bright under thickish white eyebrows. I remembered his age—sixty-six—from my folder of facts and figures.

Jeremy surged forward. 'John—how are you—may I introduce you—Tim—Geoffrey—Sir John Coe—'

His grasp was very firm. It was immediately clear why he and Jeremy had hit it off. In about twenty years Jeremy would be like this: taller by an inch or two, and fairer, more commanding perhaps, but with the same quick movements, active, well-exercised, clear of speech. The two men behind him wouldn't.

He turned to introduce them. 'Jeremy—our financial director, my nephew, Robert Baker—'

The nephew was in his late forties, quietly dressed in plain dark blue, rather diffident, bespectacled. He and Geoffrey nodded to each other in understanding, chartered account- ant to chartered accountant, professional membership con- veying a mutual experience. He gave me a pleasant handshake and a slight smile.

'My son Peter—our distribution director—Jeremy—Tim Simpson—Geoffrey Price—'

Son Peter was around forty and nothing like his dad except in height. He also wore a pinstripe suit, without a waistcoat, but there the resemblance ended. He was slightly taller for one thing, and thicker, but his movements were nothing like as active and his grasp didn't really try. Brown hair, parted at the side, flowed slightly long over a forehead that had met with little weather to beat it. The complexion was pale and the blue eyes had much less penetration, sliding away a little as he shook hands. Whatever function the directorship of distribution conveyed it occurred to me that it couldn't involve much standing outside watching lorries being loaded with timber. Peter Coe was definitely an indoor man, probably one of your computer-package optimum-distribution calculators, bent over a flickering screen. Sir John was obviously the driving-force.

We settled down to a fairly hefty session which involved each side trying to get the other to come out first and commit itself to some sort of proposal which would give the other an idea of what the first was really thinking. On our side most of it was left to Jeremy, with Geoffrey and I chipping in the odd contribution as we did a sort of tour of the various possibilities we had agreed to explore. After a while it seemed to me that Coe wanted two things: a lump sum of money and the survival of Edwards & Coe in some form that, even if only part of White's timber operation, would ensure the jobs of most of the employees, including his fellow-directors, in service contracts for two or three years. A share swap would be involved and he, Sir John, would stay on the new board for some time but not excessively. I guessed that he wanted to retire and sail; that he had calculated that his fellow-directors were not up to running the business without him; that he wanted to make the best and most responsible deal he could for them before ducking out himself. Understandable and very worthy; the business was in good shape and he was following the admirable principle of quitting while he was ahead.

'Splendid.' At the end of the morning Jeremy was still alert and more enthusiastic than he had shown himself since the start of the affair. 'I'm sure I've got enough to go back to my Board with and we'll take it from there.'

'So have I.' Sir John Coe nodded briskly. 'I'll do the same. Can we fix another meeting now?'

'Certainly.' Jeremy consulted his diary. 'Fairly soon, if possible?'

'Indeed.'

'Oh dear.' Jeremy's face creased. 'It looks a bit difficult next week. Then I have to go to the States.'

Sir John leant back. 'A suggestion: are you going down to the Hamble at all in the next two weekends?'

'Well—let me see—I suppose I could—I—'

'Because for obvious reasons I'd like to keep our meetings as confidential as possible. You'd be very welcome to drop in at Candwell on your way, no, I've got it—why don't you and Mary stay overnight? That's it! At the weekend?' He sat forward again with a slightly apologetic look, as though he'd gone too far, and gesticulated slightly. 'If that's not too —er—pressing for you?'

'No, not at all! In fact it's a very good idea. I'd a plan to go down this month and this'll make Mary concede. Say on Saturday after I've visited the yard? There's some work they're doing that I need to look at.'

'Good! That will suit admirably!' Sir John sat back again. 'Your colleagues are most welcome too, of course. Come for dinner and stay over.'

Three pairs of eyes watched us. Geoffrey shook his head slightly. 'That's kind but I'm sorry: I'm away that weekend.' His eyes met Jeremy's squarely. 'The business you and I have discussed.'

'Oh yes.' Jeremy suddenly nodded at the recollection of whatever it was Geoffrey had been directed to do. His eyes turned to mine. 'Tim. I think that would be a good idea.' It wasn't a request, it was an order; Jeremy needed a henchman. 'Would you bring Sue? Mary hasn't seen her for a while.'

'Your wife is most welcome too, of course.' Sir John's voice was hospitable and he grinned suddenly. 'I can assure you of plenty of room.'

Damn it, I thought, this bloody timber business, I wanted that weekend, but I smiled back. 'Thank you. I'd be delighted. So would Sue, I'm sure.'

'Splendid.' Jeremy and Sir John stood up, chorusing together. There was another, final, round of handshakes before Jeremy did the honours in showing them out, leaving Geoffrey Price and myself together. Geoffrey gave me a steady, grey, bespectacled stare.

'Timber talk in a Gothic retreat,' he ground out. 'Please don't take any kindling of any sort along with you, Tim, there's a good fellow?'

CHAPTER 10

'It was Leyswood that did it, really.' Toby Prescott smiled his broad, corner-crooked smile across the table as he forked some more leaf spinach up from the place where it nestled against the veal on his plate.

'Did what?' Nobby Roberts's voice did not actually snap or growl but it wasn't exactly soothing. I gave him a warning glance, which he ignored. So far, my attempt to reconcile him with Toby and to smooth him over about the events in Long Acre and Hove had not been a total failure—he was surprisingly unaggressive—but I hadn't counted it a success yet.

We were in a small Italian restaurant in Covent Garden, not far from Toby's office. It was the sort of place which depends on businessmen because although no individual dish seems to be very expensive, the sum total of your meal always is. So the bill would be mine, not that I objected, because I was the one with the expense account and I was the one, in addition, most wanting to gain from further discussion. Toby had agreed with enthusiasm to meet me for lunch, clearly wanting to overcome the disastrous start at Brown's bookshop, although his voice had hesitated when I had told him that Nobby would be there. Toby obviously still felt great reserve about Nobby, whose attitude was similar, but I knew I had to deal with both until this affair was resolved and I wanted to save time, quite apart from reconciling them to each other.

'Made his name.' Toby spoke round a mouthful of spinach. 'Caused an absolute sensation. It was the turning-point of his career.'

'I thought you said that Willesley did that,' I objected.

Toby waved a fork in negative vehemence. 'No, no! Willesley was his *first* country house commission. For "Clothes" Horsley. He got a lot of commissions from artists—RAs—after that. Lots of them. E. W. Cooke was one, with Glen Andred at Groombridge. But Leyswood—only half a mile away—was the decider.'

'Why?' Nobby, for once, showed genuine interest. 'What was so different about it? It was just another big country house, wasn't it?'

Toby smiled, another frog-beam of delight at getting himself an audience, a live audience this time, not just a printed-page one, and popped another wodge of spinach, supported by a piece of veal, into his wide mouth.

'Leyswood was built in eighteen-sixty-eight to sixty-nine,' he said. 'The drawings for it were shown at the Royal Academy in eighteen-seventy. Every newly successful Englishman, from Royal Academy painters to Manchester cotton manufacturers, decided that this was just what he wanted. It was old, it was quaint, it fitted superbly into the countryside and it looked as though it had grown there over a period of time. So the fact that it contained a number of different styles, all old and rustic rather than, say, "modern" or "new", was no problem. Indeed, it was an advantage. Think of it; think of our bloody British society. What was the one thing that a newly-rich Victorian manufacturer wanted to appear more than anything?'

'Not newly-rich.'

'Precisely, Tim! He wanted to be like the landed gentry. Even though land was ceasing to be a major source of wealth and power, to be a country house owner, to have some sort of ancestry, or to appear to have, was the only way to social acceptability in this bloody stupid society of ours. You can trace the whole source of this country's failure to maintain its industrial power, its technological base, to this ridiculous cultural fact. To your English upper class, industry and trade are symbols of gross Philistinism, boring crassness, unmannerly usury, unacceptable. The horse and the country house reign supreme. The country cottage, damp and insanitary, has a much better image than the well-designed, warm, efficient bungalow. The irony of it is that intense Socialists like William Morris fell head-first into it as well. Country was better than town, hand-made better than manufactured, and so on. Unbelievable. Take a look at any fashion magazine now, take a look at the Sloanes, the *Tatler*, *Country Life*. Horsey women with protruding teeth but without a penny to their name are socially far superior to a computer software manufacturer's pretty daughter.'

I chuckled. 'You've left Leyswood behind somewhere, Toby.'

'No, I haven't! It was built for a shipping magnate. Norman Shaw and Eden Nesfield had hit on a real winner when they brought out the Old English style for country houses. Businessmen flocked to it. Nesfield faded, but Norman Shaw kept right on with it. The list is enormous. The formula was nearly always the same: within commuting distance of their work by the new railways that were springing up all over, but not too near the station to be noisy or vulgar. There were three houses at Groombridge; several at Cranbrook, which is five miles from the Staplehurst station, and so on. You can take it that Norman Shaw virtually invented Stockbroker's Tudor single-handed.'

'That's a bit unfair to him. He was much better than that.'

'Of course he was. Take a look at anything he did. He was brilliant. What I mean is that a whole horde of imitators crowded on to the bandwagon. The country suddenly became stuffed with half-timbered, tile-hung, multi-gabled houses in a sort of mock-vernacular tradition derived from Sussex and Kent. Nesfield and Shaw did that, Shaw more spectacularly perhaps, but the two of them to start with. It was an amazing achievement.'

'Which makes an important piece of furniture by Shaw, or by both of them, so desirable.'

'Indeed.' Toby's smile suddenly faded. 'Even if it does belong to his earlier, Gothic period. Well, perhaps even because of that. How awful this has all become, Tim. I realize that you—well, I hope you won't take this the wrong way—you've had prior experience, so to speak, but I was quite fond of Alf Brown, resentful though he sometimes was. You could always get round that aspect of him and he was a mine of information, really he was, on anything architectural. Now he's gone.'

'I wonder,' I said casually, without any forethought, 'who'll take his place. Someone must be interested in a specialist book business like that.'

'My dear Tim—' Toby's smile returned—'you *have* become the banker and businessman, haven't you? As a matter of fact I rather think that I shall take it over myself. Buy it from his estate.'

I put my knife and fork down in surprise. Nobby gave him a curious, open look of inquiry without speaking.

'You will?'

'Yes.' Toby's face went serious again. 'I've been thinking about it. *The Modern Façade* is a leading architectural magazine. It makes entirely good sense for us to have a specialist bookshop arm which stocks all the great textbooks on architecture and the collectors' items. We get inquiries for them all the time.' His voice gained enthusiasm. 'We could do reprints of out-of-print books that people obviously want. Who better? It would be a fitting memorial to Alf. Brown's Books will live on.'

'Interesting.' Nobby's face was still absolutely open. 'I'm

sure you're right. From what I understand, Brown's clientele was very extensive and he had a lot of overseas customers, particularly Americans. His mailing list must be worth having.'

'Of course. I mean, the business isn't worth a fortune, you could tell from the way Alf lived, but it's a good specialist business and, tacked on to my efforts here in Covent Garden, it would be even better.' Toby's face suddenly gave a spasm of remorse. 'Look here, this all sounds horribly mercenary so soon after poor Alf's death, really it does. You must think that I'm the most frightful vulture.'

'Oh no. It's only natural. You'll have to wait a bit until matters are cleared up, of course.'

'Ah.' I saw my chance at last; Nobby would have to be drawn out with care. 'How are—er—matters—going? Any progress?'

He gave me one of his pursed, recalcitrant looks. 'I long ago decided that to try and keep you out of things is a waste of time and effort. You only go poking about and making matters worse. You and Toby can, I suppose, be trusted to keep confidences?'

'Really, Nobby! That you need to ask!'

He ignored my indignation. 'As far as Brown's concerned, the Holborn boys are not having a lot of luck. They've pieced together his movements for the last few days before his death and his other contacts. Going through his list of customers and his mailing list is a massive job. There are several thousand on it. What we are looking for is a connection with anyone who contacted him about furniture of any sort. Now that a connection with this Hove dealer has been established, *one* of the lines we are working on is your bloody Norman Shaw bookcase, or whatever it is. The two things might not be connected, remember. Brown might have been killed for some other reason and so might Reilly. Or, one might be the bookcase and the other not. Knowing your past form, however—' he gave me another very sharp glance—'it is likely. We've got photographs of the V & A one and we're circulating the trade. Auctioneers, runners, everyone.'

'Nothing so far?'

'Nothing so far. I must say it's a very distinctive piece but it's likely, now, that whoever approached Brown and/ or Reilly will have gone to ground with it.'

'But it must have come from somewhere.'

'Yes. And let us hope that whoever or wherever that was, someone will come forward. At present, Brown's connection is very difficult to establish. Reilly is a much better prospect. The Hove CID are running through all the information connected with him—his movements, his purchases, contacts and habits. It's a much more straightforward policing job because we have all his petrol receipts and auction catalogues, his invoices, all that sort of thing. There's nothing in the shop that resembles what we're looking for but the local trade are, for once, being very cooperative. I believe that we stand a very good chance of detecting the murderer there. Which I hope will lead us to Brown's killer too.'

'Good,' I said carefully. 'Don't forget that anyone with green paint on their shoe must be a suspect.'

He gave me a withering glance. 'Thank you. Most helpful. All I hope is that you will take no further interest in this business until we resolve it. I am grateful to you for the lunch and I do hope that, by keeping you informed, I can keep you *out* of any further involvement?'

'Yes, Nobby.'

'You'll not try to pursue any further leads of your own?'

'No, Nobby.'

'If anything *does* occur to you, you'll simply inform us and take no action yourself?'

'Yes, Nobby.'

'That goes for Sue as well?'

'Yes, Nobby.'

'Pah!'

'No, Nobby.'

'God! Give me strength!' He turned to Toby, who had been grinning and giggling throughout, for support. 'I know I can rely on you to keep your distance, but this man is impossible. Impossible. Put up the scent of a work of art for his bloody Fund, thwart him from getting it by some crime or another, and he's off like an Irish foxhound into the bog. Short of arresting him and keeping him locked up, there's nothing to do.'

The conversation degenerated after than so there's not much point in recording it. We finished our lunch pleasantly enough, however, and Nobby shoved off back to Scotland Yard leaving us with a last cup of coffee together as I paid the bill. Toby Prescott was obviously quite well known in this particular hostelry—he had suggested it—which didn't surprise me because he's always been fond of food and the waiter deferred to him in a way that indicated pleasure at dealing with someone knowledgeable. One or two people at other tables had nodded or waved in his direction and it occurred to me that Toby, in his way, must be quite a local celebrity because, apart from being the editor and producer of his magazine, he carried quite a lot of influence. I thought his idea of buying up the late Alf Brown's business was a good one and it pleased me to find someone like Toby thinking in expansionary terms instead of the usual doleful recital you get about how bad things are and how investment will be too difficult. The only thing that interested me idly, in the back of my banker's mind, was how he was going to finance it. After all, he had said very strongly, on the day that we'd first met again, that *The Modern Façade* was great fun but that there was absolutely no money in it.

CHAPTER 11

The drive down to Sussex on a late Saturday afternoon in April was pleasant enough, so by the time we had skirted Horsham I was in a reasonably tolerant frame of mind despite the loss of a valued weekend evening. Sue hummed vaguely to herself in the seat beside me and seemed to be enjoying the ride. Eventually I turned off the main road and we plunged into a wooded section of the countryside, threading our way through the narrow lanes until we turned into the gates of Candwell Park, passing a rather quaint lodge with a steeply-pitched roof and thick white-painted mullions to the windows.

At first, the view of the house was obscured by trees but, quite suddenly, the curve in the drive came out of the thick tangle and Sue gave an exclamation as we got a clear sight of the house. It was large but compact, clustered round a tall tower that ended in a pitched and pointed roof whose eaves beetled out like eyebrows over the windows set in the walls at the top of the tower. The design was derived from the almost-obligatory Gothic of Northern France that so many architects of the 1860s and 1870s felt the need to use but it was lighter, less threatening, and the roofs leading up to it, which piled in a bank around it and sheltered the complex house beneath, were steeply-pitched in a charming, child's-cottage set of angles rather than the massive or ecclesiastical slant of the severe mid-Victorian mansion. Late afternoon sun gave a cheerful light to the building and I felt my heart lift as we came to a halt with a crunch of gravel next to Jeremy's Jaguar saloon near the front door.

Sir John Coe came down the front steps to greet us as befitted the captain of industry playing host in his country seat. He shook my hand firmly, took Sue's with considerable charm and crinkled his active face with pleasure at my appreciative stare upwards, head craned, to look over his roofs.

'Not bad, eh? I understand you and Jeremy actually run your own Art Fund and fancy yourselves as connoisseurs. What do you think? Whose work is it? I can tell you that Jeremy failed the test.' He grinned at us in an amiable challenge.

I gave him a rueful smile. 'Very difficult. If I didn't know better I'd say it might have been Godwin. It's not unlike Beauvale Lodge but it's a bit bigger and it doesn't have that rather French or Belgian half-timbering. Just brick and tile-hanging. The roofs are super. What do you think, Sue?'

'School of Godwin,' she said, firmly. 'Influenced a bit by "Queen Anne" but still hanging on to a touch of Gothic.'

'Bravo! Both of you!' Sir John Coe's pleasure was genuine. 'School of Godwin is right. One of his admirers. Man called Bateman. Didn't do anything much else to speak of. Died youngish.' He put a finger to his nose. 'Fond of the bottle, so the rumour went. But he was a great follower of Godwin's, knew him quite well and consulted him while Godwin was writing all those articles for the *Building News* magazine. In fact, the legend has it that Godwin helped him more than a bit here. Visited the site and advised a few modifications. All those little gables in the roof on the east side?' He put his finger to his nose again. 'Legend also has it that the reason why Godwin was happy to visit the site was that he had a lady friend nearby. Wife of a London man. Building Candwell was good cover for Godwin to be down here.' He gave Sue an open, disarming smile. 'Shocking, I'm afraid. But then Godwin was a bit fond of the ladies generally. It's a weakness one can sympathize with, I think?'

Sue smiled back at him. 'Indeed. I suppose one can. Tell me: have you lived here long?'

'My grandfather bought it shocking cheap just after the First War. The demand had collapsed. Death duties an' all that. It was a bit dilapidated but not too bad in condition. Running it would have been the problem but Grandfather was a bit ahead of his time there. Got the company to buy it, put big timber storage sheds over beyond those far woods to the east and called this the offices. Regional branch, distribution centre; didn't own it personally. Actually, to be fair, the servants wing is in offices but only for local matters. There's an enormous stables and coach-house, quite separate, behind the house; Bateman's client was mad keen on broughams and four-in-hands, that sort of thing, but we don't use it. The clock's been stopped for years. Mostly we're in the house as a weekend place, a sort of flat. And a management training centre or lecture hall.' He smiled a vulpine smile. 'The management being mainly ourselves, of course, although we do have some senior people here from time to time. Seem to get away with it. But come in, come in.'

We followed him up the steps into a large hall with a floor tiled in encaustic patterns and a large marble fireplace. A member of Sir John's staff in a white coat showed us up the wide staircase and we plunged along an upper corridor until he led us into a rather pleasant, dormered room and disappeared, after announcing that the others were having drinks downstairs. Sue looked at the twin beds, smiled a mysterious smile and started hanging up things from her small case in a mahogany wardrobe.

'How's Mrs Simpson?' I demanded, walking to the dormer window.

She put her tongue out at me. 'I've spoken to Mary. She's told the others our real condition.'

'Ahh. How disappointing. I was hoping to get a thrill by posing as a married man.'

'Bad luck. You should call yourself Smith.'

The light was fading and the view from the window was across complex roofs to a dim block with a clock over it. The hands had stopped at quarter to twelve. Evidently Sir John's management training facilities had neglected that particular building and any sense of time's importance for it, but I was pleased to find that he had used the investment allowances connected with business education to install a decent bathroom off our bedroom. I had had uneasy thoughts of Victorian excursions down draughty passages to far-distant ablutions.

We descended to a large high-ceilinged room off the hall where the murmur of voices could be heard over the occasional clink of glass. The same white-coated retainer was acting as barman. He provided Sue with a gin-and-tonic and me with a Glenmorangie while we were hailed by Jeremy with what I thought was evident relief.

The room had a great bay window of full height, dispro-portionate to the rest of the space, that overlooked a large terraced lawn and distant trees that rose above rhododen-dron bushes. Facing it was a large fireplace with a complex overmantel and grouped round a fairly dismal fire were Jeremy and Mary, with Sir John Coe and his wife, who was introduced as Ann. Two other couples stood slightly apart, talking together, and I recognized them as Peter Coe and Robert Baker, with their own wives, to whom we were soon introduced. It seemed to me that there was an implied hierarchical grouping in the way they had placed themselves and that I would be needed to engage at the lower level, so I left Sue chatting animatedly to Mary—they've always got on well—and Lady Ann while I grappled with Peter Coe and Robert Baker.

Baker was dry, but pleasant. I found out that he lived outside London at Kingswood, which is in the better Surrey fringes, and doubtless his house was a shrewd investment.

His wife was pleasant too, but noncommittal. Both of them played golf.

Peter Coe was harder to assess: his conversation came and went in bursts of sudden confidences and equally disconcerting reserves of silence or lack of response. His wife had moved off to talk to Sir John's group when I found that they lived in London.

'Well, not London really,' Peter Coe confided. 'Acton Green.' His teeth showed in an apologetic grin. 'Older suburbia.'

'But very convenient now,' I said amiably. 'For the M4 and Heathrow.'

'Under the flightpath, you mean?'

'Why, er, no. It isn't quite, is it?'

'A good deal of the time.' He shrugged. 'Chiswick High Road, Kew, Richmond. They are quite high up—the planes, I mean—but not high enough for me. Or Patricia.'

'But still, for the convenience—'

'My wife hates it.' His voice was suddenly abrupt. 'She's an interior designer. Would prefer something more trendy. She says once you get beyond Earl's Court you're finished.'

'Oh.' I didn't know quite what to say.

'You live in town?'

'Er, yes. Onslow Gardens.'

'Oh well! Patricia will approve of you!'

'But I'm sure you'll have much more space.'

His face lit up. 'That's right. As a matter of fact that's why I like it. We couldn't possibly afford the same house nearer in.'

I was just congratulating myself silently on having said something at last acceptable to this tall, moody man when I felt my elbow being taken. With great aplomb and not the slightest hint of deliberate separation, Jeremy joined our conversation, drew my attention to the darkening garden, pointed out the 'pies' encrusted into the moulded ceiling, moved me closer to a painting by Herkomer on the wall and succeeded in isolating me from everyone else in such a way that we were quite apart together in a far corner of the room. His voice lowered itself to a murmur.

'How thankful I am to see you, dear boy. Sir John is most pressing. Claims he has another Interested Party.'

'What a normal negotiating ploy,' I murmured back, inspecting my nearly-empty glass.

'Yes. He may be telling the truth. But that is not the point. There are complications.'

'Complications?'

'Yes. It appears that the clever grandfather—the one who bought this place, apparently—set the ownership of the company up in such a way as to avoid the dreadful death duties that Lloyd George, or someone like him, set up after the First War.'

'Very wise.'

'At the time, Tim, at the time, maybe. The share owner-ship is, however, complex. Our own Board are going to make a dog's breakfast out of it if we aren't careful.'

'Why?'

'Because acquisition will require a treeful of careful law-yers. The thing is not simply in the hands of the Coe family.'

'Oh.'

'He hasn't gone into this in detail before because he wasn't sure of our real interest.'

'Whereas now he is?'

Jeremy smiled, transferring the smile to the room in general and then back to me again. 'It seems like a good business to me. What about you?'

'So far so good. There are bits we will have to, er, divest ourselves of.'

'As always. Anyway, I thought a word to the wise would be in order. Not too enthusiastic—well, I know you wouldn't show that—but much sucking of teeth, please, when we get to the difficulties of the transfer of ownership.' He gave me a sad look. 'Sir John will be the last of the Coes in this business. I hope it never happens to White's. The others here will be like me when it goes—or at least as I would be now if we sold.' His eyes produced one of his steeliest stares. 'Give it a little more effort and I'll own a *real* share of White's by the time I've finished.' The look vanished. 'With your help, of course, Tim. And Geoffrey's. Shall we rejoin the ladies?'

Quite often Jeremy allows you to forget his real ambition in life but it surfaces frequently enough, like the periscope of a lethal submarine, at moments like these. There are many men who, born into the fringes of a family like White's, are prepared to bask in the name, study the family tree, take pride in their peripheral association. Not so Jeremy: his need for a place in the centre of family affairs is no mere aspiration; it is an intention, a calculation, a purpose, a resolve. The achievement of that objective is an obsession compared to the wild folly of my occasionally obstinate pursuit of an interesting piece of art. It is, I sometimes think, the reason why Jeremy and I understand each other so well. He comprehends very fully that there are certain things in life that you need to finish, even at considerable cost.

We drank another glass before going in to dinner in another high-ceilinged room which I guessed was the original dining-room. This did not have a bay window, which helped to give the walls a better proportional balance. I found, however, that for my taste the ceiling was too high for the floor area, like so many Victorian rooms. Evidently the architect Bateman did not quite have the touch of his admired Godwin and I saw a faint look cross Sue's face as she sat at the other end of the table, where Sir John Coe had carefully placed her within his own ambit. She evidently felt the same disappointment as I did but was too polite to show it; I wondered with amusement whether Sir John had placed her near him after meeting her or whether she had been put there after Mary's doubtless quiet advice on our unmarried status. Sir John might be just old-fashioned enough to be interested in Sue as, conceptually, a mistress.

I found myself between Baker's wife, on my right, and Peter Coe's on my left. Peter Coe was across the table at an angle. It was a good dinner, certainly good enough to invite a man to, on Johnson's dictum, so the conversation flowed easily enough on more or less unprovocative matters. When the table had been cleared Sir John Coe apologized to the ladies, escorted them to the door, explained that none of us was so old-fashioned as to want to remain behind without them in the old style, but that we needed a little time for discussion. They forgave him with considerable charm and left.

I have promised to deal with the timber business briefly. Actually the part we discussed took us about an hour. Some of the points were quite detailed. We even touched briefly on Candwell Park. Earlier, Peter Coe had mentioned that the distribution side was very short of space so I jokingly suggested we open up the coach-house for lorry parking. He replied very shortly that there was no planning permission for use of the house and outbuildings for anything other than office, educational or residential purposes, so I decided that humour was not appreciated or that perhaps he was touchy about the thought of the family losing its erstwhile country seat. That set me off thinking about Toby and his peroration on the English country culture and that in turn led me to thinking how recent most so-called English traditions are; the majority can be traced back no further than Norman Shaw's time. I half-heard, half-missed a monologue by Robert Baker during this train of thought, in which he dealt with some aspects of the family trust's share ownership. I hoped I managed to look sufficiently worried and uneasy to convey the impression that this might be a considerable obstacle. There seemed little point in trying to understand it; lawyers would have to deal with it in conjunction with accountants. I wondered what we would do with Candwell Park if we got it and how, almost certainly, if we wanted to alter it or knock it down, some idiot would make a song and dance about preserving Bateman's work for posterity. Otherwise everything went reasonably well and we rose to join the ladies with Sir John and Jeremy in such good fettle that they told yachting stories for what seemed like hours while we drank brandy.

Eventually we all retired and Sue set herself very primly into one of the twin beds in our dormered room.

'One person, one bed,' she said, smugly. 'Very democratic.'

'Democracy has triumphed over civilization yet again. I think it's been done deliberately.'

'Nonsense! All the rooms are twins. Mary told me.'

'How depressing. Do you realize that at the turn of the century there would have been much coming and going in the passages at night? Now that we all have individual bathrooms there's no excuse. Hygiene has much to answer for.'

'Whose attractions would lure you out into the passages? Into which room would you want to go?'

'This one.'

She smiled with saccharine sweetness as she turned away to sleep. 'In that case you have got your wish. The only difference is that instead of getting one combined arrangement you have got two separate ones. I'm afraid life's often like that, Tim.'

'Only if you want it to be,' I retorted, pulling off a sock. 'Remember what Mark Twain said about a verb: it has a hard time enough in this world when it's all together. It's downright inhuman to split it up.'

'What have verbs got to do with it?' Her voice was muffled as she sank further under the sheet.

'I'm not sure. It just seemed like a good quote to me.'

Sue didn't answer. She didn't need to; as it came about, she was the one who'd been prophetic, not me.

CHAPTER 12

Sunday morning was fine, with a brisk breeze clearing the sky of the few clouds inclined to linger. Our room was cottagey rather than Gothic and the daylight view from the dormer over the back of the big house, across the roofs of the office-servants wing, gave a country-farm impression.

Beyond the steep slated surfaces beneath our window you could see across the weed-strewn courtyard, perhaps sixty yards wide, to the neglected block with its clock-tower poised above another steep roof over a series of high, solid double doors made with diagonal planking. That, obviously, was the unused stable building that Sir John had mentioned, with smaller windows in a pointed row over the big doors. These doubtless gave light to the rooms where the grooms had slept over their charges and the coaches they had assiduously maintained. We take our transport for granted now; all I had to do was to walk out to my XJS and turn a key to give me instant, powerful freedom of movement at colossal speed. The men who built this house and those who had lived in it would have envied me the ability to dispense with the servants, preparation, equipment, bulky fodder and hypochondriacal horses needed to achieve a stately movement through the countryside to the nearest railway station.

The stained glass of the landing windows over the big oak

staircase took the atmosphere quickly back to a guilt-ridden Victorianism as we came down to breakfast. This was served in a high morning-room, also partly glazed with stained glass, so that the morning sun was shot through with blue and red patterns that reminded me that today was Sunday, a day for church and considerations of sin and mortality. The breakfast was cheerful enough, however, with Jeremy hot in discussion on roll-furls and capstans with Sir John, Mary and Sue agreeing with Lady Ann that sailing was a dreadful bore for womenfolk, unless sailors themselves, and myself exchanging minor pleasantries with Robert Baker. Peter Coe came in late, wearing rather muddy brogues which had evidently borne him through wooded walks of an energetic, pre-breakfast kind. He nodded to me affably enough as he helped himself to orange juice, bacon, eggs and coffee. 'I've been pigeon shooting,' he explained. 'Bagged a couple before they all flew off. Are you off too—back up to London this morning?' He drained his juice with a gulp as he asked and set to his plate with a vigour that made his wife, across the table from Lady Ann, raise her eyebrows with amusement.

'I expect so,' I said, glancing across at Jeremy, who was still deep into consideration of genoas with Sir John. 'You too?'

'Oh,' he said carelessly. 'I'm in no hurry to get back. We'll probably enjoy the country for a bit longer. Sussex is a great place for countryside.'

'Yes.' I stared at him for a moment as his words touched a chord. 'Yes. How right you are. Pity to waste it, really.'

'Mmm.' He munched on some toast. 'Stay for lunch if you like.'

'No, that's very kind.' An idea was forming in my mind. 'I'm afraid we have to get on.'

He smiled, a slightly barbed smile that carried a hint of the condescension of the wealthy towards the striving. 'You go-getters. I expect you have to keep up the pressure. Even on Sundays.'

That, I thought, was slightly unnecessary. It revealed just a disturbing existence of aggression. I smiled back blandly: I suppose if your father is selling the family business you can't be expected to like the new owner's bailiffs but I would have preferred to keep matters polite. Looking across at him, however, that Sunday morning, with the particularly Sunday feeling that an old Victorian house can convey, an atmosphere ridden, as I have already indicated, with overtones of guilt and thoughts of duty, I had a sudden desire to leave which was much more powerful than concerns with Peter Coe. Despite the enthusiastic yachting jargon and the bright interest of the ladies in each other, the room brought a profound gloom to me. Work had been finished the night before; I wanted to get out. A sense of claustrophobia had started, perhaps emanating from an old spirit left from the days when this house conformed to its original, rigid, stifling routine, very heavily, without levity or tolerance. I gave Coe an impersonal stare, thinking of his remark about Sussex countryside and imagining Toby's cheerful, bulge-eyed face over the Covent Garden lunch-table. Wiping my mouth on a linen napkin, I turned to the ladies near me.

'Sue.' I interrupted their chatter across the table. 'Sorry to have to break it up but you do remember, don't you, that we have to get on? I'll bring our things down and see you in the hall?'

The look of surprise that had come to her face disappeared almost as soon as I'd detected it. She reacted with intelligence and loyalty as she caught my eye. 'Oh dear,' she pouted, 'I suppose we must. Just as Mary and Ann and I were really getting started. All right; I'll see you in the hall.'

I left the table with a nod to my host and a smile to my hostess and was back downstairs again, carrying our things, five minutes later. There were formal goodbyes, thanks, a quick word with a slightly consternated—if that is the word —Jeremy that I'd see him tomorrow in the office and then we were in the car, heading for the lodge gates.

'What was all that about?' demanded Sue, smoothing a tweed skirt over her knees. 'I didn't want to go straight back to London. I rather fancied a day in the country.'

'You're going to get one. In Sussex, too.'

'What? Wha—what do you mean? Your face was so set to go I didn't dare inquire. You told Peter Coe you were going back. To London.'

'Yes, well, Peter Coe was getting just a little bit tetchy for some reason best known to himself. He did remind me, though, that Sussex has its attractions and we're going to look at one or two of them. It'll be far better than hanging about at the Coes listening to yacht-talk and being polite to the rest. Business was over last night.'

I drove out of the gates, past the quaint keeper's lodge and turned eastwards. She shook her head sadly. 'Tim Simpson, you are a caution. Where are we going? It's bound to be connected with Gothic bookcases.'

'It's a surprise.'

'Not Hastings? That's your usual haunt when in Sussex?'

'No.'

'Brighton?'

'No.'

'Hove? To Stan Reilly's?'

'*No*. Now look here, Sue, I said it was a surprise, not a guessing-game.'

She ignored me. 'Let me think, now, we're going east. Ha! I know!' She clapped her hands. 'Cranbrook?'

'That's in Kent.'

She pouted. 'We could have lunch at the Willesley Hotel. That's Norman Shaw.'

'No. Sussex I said and Sussex I meant.'

'Tim!'

'Sue! Cranbrook, I mean Willesley, was emptied of all its furniture years ago. It's an hotel.'

'It was his first country house commission. I know it was only really a sort of re-build, an extension job, but it was very comprehensive. It might tell us a lot.'

'I don't think so.'

'Meanie.'

'All right, all right! If we finish what I want I promise we'll try to go to Cranbrook.'

'Give me a clue, then. Where are we going?'

'To the border.'

'The border? Of Kent and Sussex, you mean?'

'Yes.'

She paused, a long pause. I could practically hear her thought-processes grinding.

'Hawkhurst?'

'Hawkhurst? Why?'

She scowled. 'Because it's on the border of Kent and Sussex. Divided right through. And Norman Shaw did quite a lot of work there. Or around there.'

'Wrong. Not a bad guess, but wrong.'

She pouted hard this time. The scowl remained. As I accelerated across yet another back-country crossroads she leant across and pinched, painfully, inside my thigh.

'Ow! Don't do that!'

'Tell me! No wait a minute; I've got it!' Her face cleared. 'Isn't Groombridge on the border?'

'Well done! Yes, it is.'

'Of course. You're behaving to perfect pattern, Tim. As I said at Shoreham. It just took time to guess.'

'No doubt. But see how much better you feel when you find out for yourself. The sense of accomplishment, the—ow! I'll kill you if you do that again!'

She grinned and settled herself back with a contented

smile. Cats are no different; we had one at home that purred as it stuck its claws into your trouser leg.

The cross-country journey took longer than I'd anticipated. It was nearly an hour or so later when we came into Groombridge and, after getting directions from a perambulating churchgoer, we turned by the Victoria Hotel up Corseley Road and went back out into the country again. After a dip into a flat valley containing a pumping station the road rose up from the green meadows back into woods on a rugged hillside and, suddenly, on our left, beyond yet another quaint gatekeeper's lodge, rose the gables of a very large house set back among the trees. Sue let out a low whistle.

'Glen Andred,' she said, having read the sign on the gate. 'My God. Unmistakably Norman Shaw. To think that a painter could afford that.'

I pulled into the side of the road where there was a good view so that we could both have a goggle. There are times when I let myself forget that Sue works at the Tate Gallery and has strong emotions on the subject of art and of painters. She doesn't really like romantic nineteenth-century painting —my Clarkson Stanfield doesn't enthuse her—and I recalled vaguely that Glen Andred was built for E.W. Cooke, who was in the same line of business as Clarkson Stanfield.

'It's enormous,' she said. 'Absolutely enormous. It seems to be divided into two now.'

I stared across at the red-and-white building, lined almost parallel to the road. 'It was after he did Willesley for Horsley, wasn't it? Horsley put him on to E.W. Cooke and from then on Norman Shaw was *the* architect for all the successful RAs. Town and country. Queene Anne style for London and Old English for the country. Cooke had both.'

'But my God, Tim! How many successful RAs in England *now* could afford to have a house like that built for them?'

I nodded soberly. 'Not many. If any at all. Well, there must be some.'

'But Cooke wasn't by any means the biggest name! He was a marine painter, good enough, but not really *great*. Norman Shaw built houses for dozens of them. Luke Fildes, Marcus Stone, Sidney Cooper, Goodall, Webster, Benjamin Williams Leader, Frank Hall and God knows who else. Even Kate Greenaway. Could that many artists afford Shaw houses now?'

I chuckled. 'That was Whistler's fault,' I said.

'Whistler's fault? Why?'

I grinned at her. 'You're the art historian, not me. It's a theory of William Gaunt's. He reckons that Whistler buggered up the art market. At the time we're talking about, RAs were successful members of bourgeois society. They painted, and what they painted was recognizable. Everyone knew what a good painting was and rich men paid big money for it. Then along came Whistler and said absolute crap, you English have no idea about painting, the French are the boys; only the painter himself, or his fellow-painters, know what a good painting is. That did it: if only a painter knows what a good painting is then how can a rich man know what to pay for? Gaunt says you can trace the decline in money paid for contemporary paintings in England from the time of Whistler's Ten o'Clock lectures. Men like those—' I gesticulated at Glen Andred—'could earn thirty or forty thousand a year until Whistler came along. That's the equivalent of a million today. Who earns that now?'

She scowled. 'Whistler! That—that showman. It was Norman Shaw who had to pick up the pieces of the Peacock Room fiasco. And you've reminded me: Nesfield and Whistler.'

'What about them?'

'I read my books over again.' Her eyes met mine. 'There's

an account of Whistler going round to box with Nesfield at Argyll Street in London. At the offices he shared with Norman Shaw. The famous bookcase must have still been there then.'

'So?'

'So maybe Nesfield's was still there too.'

'If he had one. Sue, that still doesn't help us find it.' I put the car back into drive. 'Toby said that Leyswood was the key. Come on, let's go and look at it. It's only half a mile up the road.'

'What's left of it.'

'Mmm?' I gave her a look as the car moved forward.

'There's not much left of it. Just the stable block with its Gothic tower.'

I felt a pang of disappointment. 'Oh well. You never know.'

Indeed you don't. We came to the gates of Leyswood further up the road and I turned in, perhaps impudently, but I was determined to see what I could see; I have this peculiarity about visiting the sites of things, as Sue says.

We were caught completely unprepared. The drive swept through trees carpeted with fresh grass, curved round a bend, emerged from trees below a spectacular rockface and went up a gorge between boulders.

'Stop!' called Sue sharply. 'Look! Oh look, Tim, look!'

I pulled up short and we both stared in delight up to our right where, above a jumbled face of boulders, the remains of the house looked down at us. The top of the Gothic stable-tower was clearly visible back from the edge, peaking high above the superb setting that Shaw and his client had adapted. I realized that, with arrogant confidence, the rocks must have been blasted to make a mini-gorge for the drive to ascend, giving the visitor this spectacular and humbling approach to the house. It was a sensational thing to find in so soft a landscape as Sussex normally provides: Cragside,

Scotland or Wales were the normal associations with this kind of terrain.

I eased the car up the drive, between the rocks, and came to a circular carriage-sweep facing the entrance under the Gothic tower. To our left, a large white-painted gate with decorative canopy was set in a thick bank of evergreen bushes above a flight of brick stairs. To our right was the Gothic tower, with its arched entranceway and the stable block attached to it on the left. Through the arch was a tantalizing view of a courtyard that ended in space. The house, half-timbered and gabled in comfortable Old English prosperity, was missing; our gaze went straight out over the edge of those spectacular mini-cliffs to the wooded rolling beauty of Sussex instead of stopping at the far side of the courtyard which had enchanted the potential customers of 1870. There is, however, something about the work of an architect of genius which always arrests the attention no matter how little remains; even the way the dormer windows were cut into the steep roof above the stables was distinctive, carefully thought out, painstakingly proportioned. It was a brilliant work.

'There's someone living in it,' whispered Sue. 'We ought just to say something or apologize perhaps. We are intruding really, you know, Tim.'

'OK.' I got out of the car, went through the door in a castellated brick wall that enclosed the stable-yard and rang a bell. There was no answer. Whoever inhabited the remains of Shaw's house was out, perhaps fortunately; I beckoned Sue and, feeling like a pair of burglars, we trod carefully under the arch to peep into the draughty remains of a courtyard törn open to the winds by the removal of the welcoming house on the other side.

'It must have been *fabulous*.' Sue spoke very quietly, as though inhabitants or ghosts might overhear us. 'What a shame they had to pull the house down. Even what's left is still absolutely terrific.'

'The billiard-room's there,' I said, looking back to my right. 'Plus the stable-block, the servants' wing on this other side of the courtyard, and the tower. The tower is great.' I walked back up the drive towards the car to take another look at it. 'It's very sort of French-Gothic, isn't it?'

'Yes.' She came back up the drive to join me. 'Very. Actually I think he got it from Nesfield, who'd done it elsewhere. Cloverly Hall.' Her voice became absent. 'They'd both toured Northern France when studying and had drawn all that early French Gothic from building there. This was about his last gesture to mediævalism of that sort. The rest of the houses were Old English, without the Gothic. This was superb, though; a spectacular approach, almost forbidding, a mediæval tower-arch to enter, and then, there across the courtyard, your homely English rustic house with big fireplaces and inglenooks. Very clever. It reminds me a lot of Sissinghurst in its way. The tower is a relic of grim days when big houses had to be fortified against invaders and enemies; the other buildings are timbered or mellow brick, domestic, unchallenging, built in peacetime. The impression is that the place must have grown up over the ages, not that it was, in fact, brand new.'

'Ideal for your rich successful artist or businessman. Amazing. This wasn't for an artist though, was it? Toby mentioned a shipping magnate.'

'James Temple. Shaw's cousin. He was very rich.'

'Really? I thought that Shaw came from a fairly impecunious Scots family.'

'He did. Although his father was from Dublin originally; before setting in Scotland. Died when Shaw was young. The old story: strong Scots Protestant mother, successful sons.'

I smiled. 'The old story. I didn't register Temple somehow; just that he was the client.'

'Dear Tim, how unlike you. You normally store all these biographical details avidly.' She smiled, putting her hand on my arm to reassure me that she was only teasing. 'Didn't you know who Temple was?'

'No.'

Her smile broadened a little and then faded slightly as she turned back to look at the tower. Like that at Cragside, the battlemented parapet was surmounted by a gable-roofed hutch, but this Leyswood version, the original, instead of being romantically half-timbered, was brick-and-tile, very sober, with an almost helmeted side-tower like a sentinel at the corner. Turning back to the car, she took out her handbag, opened it, removed a white pad and got out a pencil.

'What are you doing?' I demanded.

'We haven't got a camera with us. I'm making a sketch of this. Somehow I want to remember it clearly.

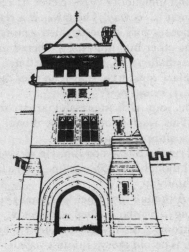

'Well you're the trained artist. Couldn't be better.' I watched her as she started to make quick brisk strokes on the pad. 'You still haven't said who Temple was.'

'Toby was right. Temple was a shipping magnate. As it happened, he became the managing director of the firm Shaw's brother founded.' She frowned up into the light as she turned the pad and put another line into the sketch. 'I don't need to tell you the name of that. Do I?'

I grinned at her, because it was all too easy to answer. These fateful phrases slip from our lips with a facility that astonishes later.

'The Shaw Savill Line,' I said confidently, right there in the spring sunshine with the tower looking down on me like an armoured warrior from a mediæval saga.

CHAPTER 13

'Ships.' I spooned some more marmalade on to my toast, took another swig of tea and pointed across the tangled table-top at Sue with the spoon. 'Ships. This thing has something to do with ships. I feel it in my bones.'

'Look at this mess. The flat is an absolute tip. There's hardly a book in place. The kitchen's full of dirty dinner things. You got up three times last night to check something. I feel absolutely *drained*.'

It was Monday morning and drizzle had started outside, making the whole atmosphere turn grey. The bright spring sunshine of the day before seemed remote. True to my promise, I had taken Sue all the way across to Cranbrook, lunched at Willesley, admired the Japanese pargetting with bottle-ends stuck in it, the peacock and the sheer rashness of a young, unknown architect who could build such a jumble of 'Old English' idiosyncrasy on to what had been a severe, rectangular Georgian farmhouse. There was no original furniture in it or near it. Despite enjoying the trip, the lunch and the view of the house I had felt frustrated.

Long discussion with Sue had followed our return to Onslow
Gardens, gone on through our dinner and long into the
night. Sleep had been impossible. Ideas kept occurring to
me, and dates had to be cross-checked. I felt irritable. Sue
had dressed herself neatly for work again and was looking
suitably subfusc but smart. I was in a City pinstripe that
felt crumpled. Damn it, *I* felt crumpled.

I sighed. 'There's something not right.'

'You've said that rather often.' She helped herself to more
coffee. I drink tea for breakfast, she drinks coffee. Oh,
I've told you that before. Well, that's how I felt; repetitive,
short of ideas, hacking over the same information, needing a breakthrough. Sue looked quite composed for all
her complaint. 'Actually,' she said, 'I think Andrew
Saint says somewhere that Glen Andred and Leyswood
are like ships. Ships on land, a bit rakish, riding above
the landscape like ships over the waves. Cooke was a
marine artist and Temple a shipping magnate. It's a nice
thought.'

'Indeed? It's a nice *fancy* I would rather say.'

'Grumpy! Just because the Robert Shaw theory doesn't
seem to fit.'

'Thanks. I agree. I am. I thought I'd got it with Robert
Shaw. There he was, industrious brother, clever salesman,
winning the business for Willis Gann and they got jealous
of his success. Cut his salary. Typical City bastards. So he
takes his assistant Walter Savill, who is a demon organizer,
with him and founds the Shaw Savill Line. Who better as
a candidate for a magnificent piece of Shaw furniture in his
office? A far better bet than Nesfield, who would have done
his own. I'm sure that the Nesfield theory was a wild goose
chase.'

'Thank you! Very much! It led straight to poor Stan
Reilly!'

'Yes. Well. Sorry. There was that to it, I must admit.

Anyway you were quite keen on the Robert Shaw theory for a while too, weren't you?'

Sue shuffled her cup. 'Yes, I was. Until we found that he'd died of a heart attack. Aged only forty-two.'

'Business risk, poor chap. Anyway he died well before Norman Shaw built the Shaw Savill offices in Leadenhall Street and if he had had a Gothic bookcase or anything like it I think it would have been detected long ago. It must have been a tremendous choice for Norman Shaw. When his brother died in 1864 he was offered the chance of taking his place in the Shaw Savill Line. I mean, Norman Shaw was only just getting started as an architect and he had to take over responsibility for his brother's widow and children. Yet he never hesitated with his refusal. The cousin, James Temple, was already in the business so he took over from Robert and became Savill's partner. Four years later Shaw built him Leyswood.'

'So maybe the bookcase was for Temple. At Leyswood. After all, there's a Gothic tower. Why not a Gothic bookcase?'

I rubbed my chin. 'I don't know. Maybe there was. The house was pulled down quite recently: 1955. The V & A bookcase came to light in 1962. We're not getting anywhere. There are too many missing pieces. I must talk to Nobby.'

Sue gave me a look. 'On that note I have to go to work.'

'So do I.'

I put my raincoat on and we departed our different ways, Sue down to the Tate Gallery and me to South Kensington Tube Station and the City. The morning at the Bank was quite uneventfully hard work until, at about eleven, Jeremy burst in.

'Tim! There you are!'

'Been here all morning, Jeremy.'

'Now, now! None of that.' He paced across my bit of carpet-space and plonked himself down in the spare chair.

Like me, Jeremy was back to his City pinstripe but he looked a great deal better groomed than I felt. His blond hair gleamed under the electric light. 'Dreadful weather. Had the best of it yesterday. Talking of which, you pushed off rather smartly after breakfast, didn't you?'

'Did I? Well, Sue and I wanted to get on. You and Sir John were obviously into sailormen's natter so I didn't want to spoil it for you. There wasn't anything more on the business side, was there?'

He eyed me suspiciously. 'You never said you'd be in a hurry to get away when we met on Saturday.'

'Ah no. Just wanted to play it by ear. If we finished, we finished. Question of timing. Would have stayed if the business had demanded it, of course.'

'Ye-es. Pity to rush back to town, though. Lovely day like that.'

'Mmm.'

His gaze became more searching. 'Something special, was it?'

'What?'

'That you had to rush back for?'

'Oh, that. No, not really. Just promised Sue we'd nip back smartly if we could.'

The gaze became accusatory. 'Sue didn't want to come back at all! Mary was certain of that! You're hiding something.'

I struck a dignified pose. 'Really, Jeremy. My Sundays are my own, you know. When business finishes. I really do not have to account for my movements in this Inquisitorial fashion. I—'

'Rubbish! Guilty conscience! You're up to something! What is it?'

'Jeremy, I—I—really—I—'

He slapped his hand flat on my desktop. 'I knew it! I could tell from your face as you left! I know that look. Read

you like a book sometimes. You're ferreting again. That
cabinet business. Bookcase. Whatever.' He held up a finger.
'Please, Tim. I beg of you. Stay-out-of-trouble-this-time.
Got it?'

'Yes, Jeremy.'

'Hopeless. You're hopeless.'

'Yes, Jeremy.'

'To work. It's useless to talk to you. Listen: I've sounded
some of the board this morning. The Edwards & Coe thing
looks to be on. Subject to certain provisos, conditions and
reservations.'

'Naturally.'

'Naturally. Don't look so unenthusiastic. I know I didn't
want to get involved at first but it's a good business and it'll
fit in with us very well.'

'I have to admit that.'

'Good. Now, the Shoreham operation is important. I want
you to go back down there, avoiding Brighton and Hove
please, and look into—'

You may stifle a yawn at this point but for those engaged
in it, the timber business can be complex, original and
challenging. To outsiders it is just a question of moving
wood about. Most businesses are the same; talk about
business to women and ninety per cent of them glaze over
at the eyeball. Talk about businesses to men and ninety per
cent of them wait for a gap in your peroration and proceed
to tell you all about their own businesses, which induces a
mutual glazing of eyeballs. Nevertheless, to those involved
there are tremendously stimulatory aspects and Jeremy and
I managed to get through an hour before, suddenly realizing
he had things to do before attending a luxurious lunch with
a firm of brokers, he shot off, leaving me in peace again. I
made a telephone call, got my coat and went out, turning
through the dull streets with my hands in my pockets.
When I got to Leadenhall Street I strolled up and down

thoughtfully before calling a taxi. It's no good looking for the bright plastered building that Shaw built for the Shaw Savill Line now; an incendiary bomb did for it in 1941. When it was put up and its drawings were shown at the Royal Academy in 1873, it was controversial, like much of Shaw's London work. It cocked a snook at the dull, respectable business façade of City architecture, for it was a deliberately light-hearted medley of 'Queen Anne' white ornamental plasterwork, oriel bay windows, square brick columns, overhanging cornice and other cheerful features of the late seventeenth and early eighteenth century not unassociated with mercantile life. From Shaw, Nesfield, Stevenson and the Morrisian architect Philip Webb we have inherited a London of cheerful houses in red brick and white woodwork multiplied by a throng of imitations of 'Queen Anne' and Pont Street Dutch, but to the conservative City of the 1870, the offices of the Shaw Savill Line must have been quite a shock.

My taxi dropped me off opposite Charles the First's equestrian statue at the south side of Trafalgar Square and I strolled down Whitehall until turning off into the relieving cheerfulness of the pub. Nobby was already at a table with two pints in front of him and, as I approached, a barmaid sidled up with two large plates of ploughman's lunch.

'Just in time to pay,' he said cheerfully, pushing his sandy locks back from his eyes. 'Your timing is excellent for once, Tim.'

'How kind.'

'Thought you'd love to.'

'Such a privilege.'

'Temper, temper. No need to turn nasty. Out of bed the wrong side this morning?'

'Something like that.'

He gave me a shrewd glance. 'Not losing sleep over amateur detective work, I hope?'

'No.'

'Thought you were. Sticks out a mile.'

'Bastard.'

He grinned. 'Now you know why policemen seldom laugh. Want to tell your Uncle Nobby everything, do you?'

I drank a lot of my beer and bit into a hefty slab of bread, cheese and pickle. When I had got it down I started talking, telling him about Cragside, Leyswood, Willesley and all the things Sue and I had gone over. He shook his head sadly at the end of my account.

'This is rubbish. Mere vapourings. Not like the old Tim Simpson at all. Idle speculation based on quasi-pseudo-art-historical conjecture. Roaming about Sussex in an æsthetic daze. You say you've even paced up and down Leadenhall Street in a sort of gormless, unfocused sleepwalk? Eh? Good grief, Tim, God knows I don't want you getting involved in a *real* investigation but if you're going to visit Norman Shaw sites for inspiration you'll get arrested for vagrancy by the time you've finished. I mean, look at London alone. You'll be on the corner of Pall Mall and St James, goggling from one corner to the other at the insurance buildings, and then Regent Street quadrant; then you'll be in Chelsea on the Embankment near Tite Street, back to Sloane Street and Queensgate and Kensington and Melbury Road and Hampstead and Albert Mansions, Jesus Christ, before you even *start* on Bedford Park. As for the provinces, the mind boggles. It'll take you to the end of the century.'

I looked at him curiously. 'You've become very knowledgeable all of a sudden.'

'Well.' He took a draught of beer. 'As it happens, there are one or two lads at the Yard who are quite keen fans. One of the older men worked at Scotland Yard, the old one. Another man was at Kentish Town Police Station. They're both Norman Shaw.'

'I know.'

'Yes, well, there you are. We're not just thick Philistines, you know, despite what you think. And we certainly don't let wild imaginings get in the way of real police work.'

'So you've made an arrest.'

He scowled, pausing with his glass halfway to his mouth. 'Now that's enough of that! If you're going to be like that today, I'm off.'

'Sorry. Let me get you another beer.'

'I should think so.' He handed me his glass. 'It's a touchy subject. We haven't made an arrest. I think we should have. So I've been roped in to being official co-ordinator for the two cases.' He glared at me. 'See what a fine mess you've got me into now, Stanley?'

'Oh dear. Caught between Hove and Holborn, are you? I'll get refills right away.'

When I got back he fiddled about a bit, finished his cheese, crooked his glass in my direction, drank and wiped his mouth with a paper napkin. 'The Reilly murder is straight policework,' he stated. 'I can't think why they haven't sewn it up. We have all Reilly's receipts, auction records, petrol vouchers, cheque stubs, stock books, the lot. We've pieced together where he went and more or less who he saw for the last three weeks of his life. Everyone accounts for their movements.'

'No Gothic bookcase?'

He shook his head. 'Nope. Nothing. He didn't half get about a bit. But there's nothing, no receipt or goods described anything like that. And think of it, Tim; that piece at the Victoria and Albert is enormous, *bloody* enormous. It'd be like shifting a building. No one would miss it.'

I cocked my head on one side. 'Nobby Roberts, I do believe you've actually been to look at it!'

He blushed. 'Of course I have. I do like to know what I'm talking about, you know. We circulated a photograph. Most of the trade fell about laughing. Said if they'd seen anything like that in the last month or two they'd hardly have missed it. You know what I'm beginning to wonder, Tim?'

'What?'

'I'm beginning to wonder if there really was a significant connection between Reilly and Brown. Over this, anyway. Whether the connection isn't just coincidental. And I'm also beginning to wonder whether Brown really had found a Shaw bookcase. If he did, I'll swear it wasn't in the trade anywhere. Not in auctions or shops anyway.'

I bit my lip. 'It might be in a shipper's warehouse somewhere. Hidden from view.'

'That's possible. Just. It would have to have come from a private source, though. A thing like that would never have escaped trade comment.' He stared at his glass. 'Another thing struck me: we've assumed, just assumed, that it's in this country. You realize that that bookseller Brown had an international mailing list? Supposing someone abroad had the bookcase and sent him a photograph? He could have been acting as agent for a foreigner, couldn't he?'

'Yes, he could. Well, I suppose he could. What about the Holborn boys, then? Did they turn up anything like that?'

'No.' His voice was gloomy. 'They didn't. Spent hours combing his office and his papers. Nothing. Not a sausage.'

'Then there's something wrong. Something obvious has been missed. I can't believe that those two murders are unconnected, purely coincidental, and nothing to do with the Gothic piece Brown was trying to sell. It just doesn't make sense.'

'Well, I can't see it. We've done fingerprints, the lot. Some time or another the piece has to come out of the woodwork. I've gone through Toby Prescott's statement about Brown very carefully. Brown said that the piece was a "cabinet or a bookcase, that sort of style". Like Toby's desk. I've been to look at that, too. It's nothing like as

fanciful as the V & A Norman Shaw but you can't mistake
that sort of grim oak semi-religious stuff. Revealed joints
and all that—that—'

'Moral fervour?'

'If that's what you want. Not my description.'

'It doesn't make sense. You've missed something somewhere.'

'Well, all right, Clever Dick, tell me where.' He looked
at me expectantly for once, without the usual guarded
keep-off-the-grass expression that he uses on these rare
occasions, so I felt a twinge of conscience and a real desire
to help.

'Listen, Nobby, it's a long shot but look: Brown's connection is too vague, it could be anyone, but Stan Reilly was a
dealer. Just concentrating on him for a moment, have you
got a full account of his movements for the two or three weeks
before he died? Auctions he attended, shops he visited?'

He nodded hesitantly. 'We've pieced it together, mostly
from receipts. Things he bought. Petrol receipts. It's not
absolutely hour by hour but it's quite good.'

'Was he at auctions much?'

'Seven in that period. He bought quite a few things. Left
bids on some, went personally to some. We've been round
all seven. With a photograph. No luck.'

'Did he pick up all his purchases himself?'

'No. I don't think so. He used carriers for some. Obviously, being a one-man band, he couldn't do it all himself.'

'He'd have needed help for a piece like that.'

'There wasn't one.'

'Damn it, Nobby! This is all wrong! That piece has to
be somewhere and someone has committed murder for it.
Twice.'

'Well, it wasn't in any of those auction rooms. We checked
very thoroughly. They're nearly all provincial; two are South
London but not fine art trade, you know, run-of-the-mill

furnishings. An occasional bit of Victoriana. They'd have wet their knickers over a Gothic bookcase like that.'

'Then the thing has to be somewhere else.'

He gave me a sarcastic smile. 'Brilliant. Where?'

'What will you give me if I tell you?'

'A severe sentence for withholding information from the police.'

I got up, brushing crumbs from my trousers. 'The trouble with you, Nobby, is that you're an ungrateful bugger.'

He did the same, punching me lightly on the arm after he'd swept himself down. 'And the trouble with you, Tim, is that you won't leave matters to the experts.' He gave me a meaning glance. 'Anything that occurs to you—anything —you 'phone me. Right?'

I sighed. 'Right. But I'm thoroughly out of ideas now. Don't expect anything soon.'

CHAPTER 14

I arranged my trip to Shoreham at short notice with Peter Coe's secretary. I couldn't get hold of him personally because she said he was out with one of their vehicles checking on a distribution pattern, which he often did, so I revised my opinion of him as a computer-screen man. Obviously he did real work sometimes. I left a message saying that I'd contact him because I needed some facts on the distribution side. Edwards & Coe were quite large in transport, as you might expect, having bought up one or two haulage companies in their time. To get them, they had had to swallow a couple of removal operations and I didn't really fancy White's going into that, nor did the board of directors, so there were matters to be resolved.

It took quite a time to get through the things Jeremy had

asked me to cover at Shoreham and it was early afternoon when Peter Coe came on the telephone, having got the message from his secretary, and asked rather briefly what I wanted. I explained to him in some detail and he said he didn't have the figures with him because he was in the City, not at his desk, but he could dig them out.

'That's all right,' I said, rather casually. 'I could 'phone you at home later if you don't mind. I've got your address in all the company details—Acton Green somewhere, you said, didn't you? If it's not too much trouble I'll ring you there. If you'll be at home? I have to go back to the Bank now but I meant to check on these removal company operations you own; I'm afraid I've got to get some detail.'

There was a moment's silence, a hesitation, and I thought he was going to be difficult. Then he spoke, his voice a bit muffled. 'That's all right. I tell you what—what time will you be at the Bank?'

'Oh, not before four. I'm staying there a bit late before going on to see a friend in Covent Garden. I won't leave before six.'

'Good. No problem, then. I'll have the figures sent round to you at the Bank in an hour or two's time. You'll have them before you leave.'

'That's very kind. Many thanks.'

'No sweat. Anything else?'

'No, thanks.'

Efficient fellow. Doubtless he guessed that White's were anxious not to buy themselves too deeply into ramifications of his father's empire which spread beyond timber and the hauling of it. What quite we aimed to do with the businesses, if acquired, was another matter.

I finished at Shoreham and dutifully skirted round the north of Brighton and Hove, avoiding them as Jeremy had instructed. In no time I was on the A23 and then the motorway, the M23, heading for London. You know how it is on motorways: you blaze along for a while and then you get bored, so you start to notice the commercial traffic in front of you, the lorries and the vans, with their company names, companies you've dealt with or been associated with or whose products you eat, wear or drink. I'd passed Gatwick and was racing northward when a big removal van came up ahead, washing along in the light April drizzle. Pavilion Removals it said, right across the back of the pantechnicon doors, London and Brighton, Weekly Service. Telephone numbers in London and Brighton were marked underneath, visible above the spray from its back wheels.

Well, well, I thought, small world, that's one of the removers that is a subsidiary of one of Edwards & Coe's haulage companies, I remember from the files. Not a bad outfit by the accounts. I was overhauling it fast. A standard weekly run and a bookable special service for moving house or other needs. The huge side of the vehicle came into view, repeating the great Pavilion Removals' legend and the telephone numbers with a bit more detail on the street address in Brighton and a depot in London's Turnham Green.

Turnham Green. For a moment I nearly threw a wobbly on the wet road surface. Nobby had said I was wasting my time in capering or vapouring about at Norman Shaw sites. But I'm superstitious, and if ever there was a pointed reminder this must have been it. Only a strong sense of duty persuaded me to fulfil my obligation to return to the Bank and go on to visit the offices of *The Modern Façade* afterwards; when you get a pointer like that you feel you must follow it up immediately, in case it vanishes or your mind slips it, out into a bit of the memory-bank that doesn't have a recall system. I trembled on the verge of turning off to the west when I came into the outer tangle of south London but then duty called, and it was raining, so I steered my way obediently to the City.

As it happened, I worked very hard once I got to my office because there were corners I couldn't cut and the figures Peter Coe had sent needed more than a glance, so I was a bit late leaving. I got to Toby's office just as the staff were abandoning the place in that casual way that magazine and media staff in London have of drifting out towards pubs and boyfriends and home. There was a cheerful litter of the same paste-ups, art posters, heaps of paper and smart weeklies or monthlies that I had seen before. Toby came out and greeted me himself because the snooty receptionist had gone, leaving her rubber plant and the coffee table fanned with the coloured copies of *The Modern Façade* in such careful arrangement behind her. I traipsed after him into his office, refused a drink and accepted coffee before sitting down on the rush-seated corner chair with the sweeping cabriole leg at the front.

'My goodness!' His face looked concerned behind the bantering front he always puts up. 'You do look glum! What on earth's the matter?'

I sighed. 'There's something wrong about this whole Norman Shaw business. Something doesn't fit.'

'What?'

I couldn't put my finger on it. I tried to explain to Toby, peering at him across the panelled back of his desk in an unfocused way that took in the careful Gothic edge moulding without caring to register it closely. I explained to him how far things had got, or rather had not got, and he beamed and said I was incorrigible but if it would help we could talk it through because, apart from Alf, whom he'd liked and known well, the whole question of the missing Shaw piece was making him lose a lot of sleep, too. It was after some time that I suddenly couldn't hold back any more and said that I had this funny feeling that the thing was somehow connected with ships or shipowners.

'Ships? Of course!' His face bulged at me across the desk-top. 'You should have asked me: I'd have told you straight away.' He waved a hand at the shelf-covered wall, lined with books. 'It's all in there, Tim. Yes, dear, yes, I'll lock up.'

The offices of *The Modern Façade* had been steadily emptying and, from time to time, a different female face would appear round the door and say good night, she'd put her lights out and would Toby please lock up and he'd say yes, yes, like that, impatiently, and we'd go on talking and drinking coffee from a big red percolator-jug he had plugged in to a socket at the side of the Gothic desk. He had a shirt with broad blue-and-white stripes under a white collar this time, and a startlingly electric-blue tie with white polka dots. The suit looked like the same one as before: a grainy, slightly coarsely-woven grey, almost hopsack cloth that gave a deliberately textural effect such as only an architect would insist upon, as though to make sure that you knew that his suit was made of cloth and not something else, something artificial and smooth and perhaps plastic.

'An association with the sea and ships can never be separated from Richard Norman Shaw,' he repeated. 'Look at his major private clients, the really big ones. Three out of four of the great newly-rich ones were shipping men.'

'Really? Who are you talking about?'

He smiled happily and began ticking them off on his fingers. Like so many editors, journalists and publishers, Toby was something of an evangelist, a compulsive lecturer and preacher. Direct opportunity made him happy. 'One —your Leyswood man, James Temple. From him came not only Leyswood but warehouses and the Shaw Savill Line offices. I know he was a cousin but he kept up the shipping connection. In fact it was no accident that number two,

Ismay of the White Star Line, provided ships and crew for the Shaw Savill Line when they got into financial difficulties in the 'eighties. Shaw built Dawpool for him; he died long before the *Titanic* disaster. Then there was Leyland of the Bibby Line; another Liverpudleian, like Ismay. He was one of the grandest. Shaw could deal with him better than most —he was difficult—and picked up the pieces at Princes Gate when Leyland and Whistler parted brass rags over the famous Peacock Room. Shaw was amazing that way; quiet and unostentatious and Scots, but a magnetic personality. He had no trouble with rich clients and could handle them all with confidence.'

He stopped and topped up my coffee. 'Shipping tycoons seem to have been able to make money quickly. Those three men were all in their forties when they became rich.'

'You said three out of four. Who was the odd man out?'

'Your own Armstrong of Cragside. He was in armaments, as you know. And older. Shaw got him through a contract with Horsley at Cranbrook. Armstrong's wife saw the work there.'

I shook my head. 'Somehow I keep ruling Cragside out. I've got this thing about ships.'

'Really, Tim, you are a funny fellow! You're not psychic or clairvoyant are you? You? One of the most practical, the most—er—most prudent sorts of men?'

'I think that the Shaw Savill connection—which was his earliest really maritime client—was important to him. I think he might have designed a splendid piece of furniture for Temple.'

Toby's face puckered. 'I doubt if it was at Leyswood. You think it was at the offices? New Zealand Chambers in Leadenhall Street? Impossible to find out, I'd say. The partners—Savill and Temple—shared an office there, a big semi-circular office specially designed for them. All bombed out in the war. Dead end. More coffee?'

I got up. 'God, no. I'm bursting already. Where are your loos?'

'Loo. The loo. My loo is just across the hall. I *hate* sharing loos with my staff. *You* are welcome to use it.'

'How discriminatory. And how kind.'

The hall light was not particularly strong and the rest of the offices were in darkness. The desk behind which the condescending receptionist normally sat was empty. Toby's own personal toilet facilities were beyond a door to the left of the entrance and comprised a cubicle with the usual pedestal and a tiny washbasin with a blue-and-white hand towel which would have matched his current shirt perfectly. Not that I was terribly interested at that moment; I simply stepped inside quickly, only half-closing the door because we were alone, and got on with the business I needed to do so urgently.

It was a hell of a relief. Such a relief that, when I had finished, I was quite oblivious of anything except zipping myself up again. So that when the swing of the door fanned a movement of air on to the back of my neck I didn't really bother and, in any case, it had been a long day what with driving down to Shoreham and back, getting to the Bank, looking at figures and now trampling all over the same ground again with Toby, trying to speculate—

The band constricted my neck so suddenly that my head jerked up in an astonished rigor of stiffened reflex. The material bit deep into my flesh, throttling my windpipe. It was like being hanged, but more slowly. In immediate reaction I made the classic mistake of whipping both hands up to grab the noose, too late. I couldn't get my fingers between it and my flesh to obtain a relieving purchase. There was a great thrust into my behind and I realized that the assassin had driven a knee into it so as to brace me backwards, taking the purchase off my feet. My lungs expanded without achieving any inhalation at all: a tightness squeezed my chest. My eyes began to bulge as darkness fringed the edge of my vision. Silver spots started to coalesce into big patches as the throttle tightened from excruciating to terminal. I let out a great half-croak, bitten off by lack of air.

Now the noose was being twisted at the back of my neck to bite in deeper. I tried a backwards head-butt in stupid desperation, only making things worse by giving a better purchase to the binding, squeezing, contracting strangle-band. A blinding intelligence came to me that this was *it*, finish, all over unless I did something really drastic in the next few seconds before, taken completely by surprise, I lost consciousness. How stupid, I thought, I haven't used my arms yet or my legs, I've been a classic victim, pulled backwards off balance and next thing down I'll go to the floor and that will be it.

There was obviously only one way to go: backwards. I put one foot up on to the lavatory basin-edge and found, with my left hand, Toby's dinky little washbasin. Then I drove backwards with those purchases and all the muscle I could muster.

Partial success. There was a great slam and grunt as I rammed backwards into my attacker and, locked together, we hit the door-post. Even better, as the solid upright stopped us I jerked my head back in a last desperate back-butt and connected hard, very hard, with a skull behind me that was already stopped short against the jamb. I heard a great crack and a gasping grunt, the noise of someone badly hurt, as bright stars flashed among the silver patches and blackness that had now taken over my vision. Over-balancing, I went down backwards on to the lavatory floor, hearing vague noises of distress as I collapsed into semi-consciousness, grasping now at the murderous binder round my throat.

I got a purchase on it and pulled, my head jammed

against the wall under the washbasin. Just when the last black-pressured agonized moment seemed about to arrive there was a tight rush of air as the noose slipped out an inch. The pressure dropped. With a painful whistling I got a merciful gust down into the system. Then, as I pulled, the band round my neck, twisted at the back, slackened and gave way completely, leaving me heaving, gasping, choking and coughing on the tiled floor of Toby's personal blue-and-white loo.

I don't know how long I was there. It might have been several minutes or it might have been tens of seconds. All I know is that it took much longer to get back my vision than I would have liked and I went on gasping and heaving and croaking until, intelligence returning, I managed to pull myself up via the wash-basin and sit, bent double, on the lavatory basin I had so recently used with gratitude. Then I managed a lot of deep breaths, which got my oxygen back towards normal and my whole, racked physique back to a more acceptable level of discomfort. Boiling with rage, I lurched out of the cubicle and into the hall, looking for someone to murder. I found I was holding a paisley-pattern tie in my hand, clutching its twisted material from where I had freed it from my neck.

Toby's black-polished shoes came into my vision first. They were right outside the door, pointing upwards. The rest of Toby was stretched out beyond them, flat on its back. As I moved quickly forward to kneel beside him I saw the blood on his forehead where a great gashed contusion marked the blow that had laid him out. I didn't try to move him; I went straight to a telephone. I didn't see the other contusion on the back of his head where, apparently, he must have hit the receptionist's neatly magazine-stacked coffee table as he went down. They told me about that much later.

CHAPTER 15

The police arrived before the ambulance. The two uniformed coppers took a careful look at Toby, asked me a few
questions where I sat, still half-throttled, and made notes
until the ambulance men arrived and carried him carefully
off on a stretcher. I gave the policemen more information,
told them to contact Holborn and Nobby Roberts if they
could, and repeated what had happened for the fourth time.
They seemed to have difficulty believing me but, as I got
fairly emotional and demanded that a doctor look at me too,
they relented and took me with them in the car they'd left
outside. It all seemed to take ages.

One of the policemen sat with me as I waited in casualty
and then, as more people came and went, I began to get
news of Toby's condition. Apparently he did not have the
same thick skull structure that I have and the head-bashing
he'd received had cracked his, rendering him deeply uncon-
scious even if not actually in a coma. As time went by Nobby
arrived with a Holborn CID man, all irritation and lack of
sympathy for my painful neck. They pushed me to one side
and went off into the inner depths of the hospital but they
couldn't get anything out of Toby at all, just very vague
responses and murmurs, not even a recollection of my visit,
let alone the attack. The doctor got angry with Nobby for
pressing the point and shooed him out. Nobby got very
stroppy and said that not only was he a senior police officer
but he was a personal friend of a senior physician at the
hospital with whom he'd played rugger, and the young
doctor then grinned and said he played rugger too, so what?
Then Nobby and the CID man left, taking me with them,
after making arrangements for a policeman to wait at the

hospital until Toby improved. We went back to Covent Garden, to the offices of *The Modern Façade*, and I described the whole thing as best I could and they looked at each other significantly before calling a forensic specialist who started to take scrapings and samples off the door-jamb and everywhere else that mattered and didn't matter, it seemed to me.

I sat down in a chair in reception and watched them. The back of my head was bruised and tender but it was my neck that was the real trouble. It was bloody painful; very stiff and extremely sore. My breathing still seemed to be impaired. They had taken a look at me in the hospital and murmured a few condolences before announcing that there was nothing wrong, nothing that a few days wouldn't improve, that is, and made light-heartedly impudent remarks about the thickness of my neck, which annoyed me. Nobby wasn't much better: he kept looking at the paisley-pattern tie, now in a polythene bag, and asking me whether I'd ever seen it before and I answered for the umpteenth time that I hadn't, it was just an ordinary mass-produced tie of the sort you see everywhere. No one I'd been in contact with recently had one like it. I even thought of Sir John Coe, but his was a different colour. Toby, of course, had been wearing his blue polka-dot job which was just as well for him because Nobby and the CID man were fairly clearly marking him down as suspect number one in their minds, despite unbelieving protests from me.

'You were alone in the office with Prescott just before it happened?' the CID man demanded.

'Yes, but—'

'You didn't see or hear anyone else in the office?'

'No. No I didn't, but—'

'You've said you have no idea who came up behind you? Didn't see him at all?'

'No.'

'He didn't say anything or make any sound that you recognized?'

'No.'

'Just walked in behind you and slipped the tie round your neck?'

'Yes.'

'Must have been about the same height as you, or taller, and pretty strong.'

'I suppose so.'

'Funny that he knew exactly where you were. In this manager-only toilet.'

'Well, he might have seen me go in. If he was hiding in the office somewhere.'

'Mm. Prescott's about your height.'

'Yes, yes, I know, but—'

'You banged your head backwards into your attacker *after* you'd driven him up against the door-jamb. He can be expected to have a contusion of some sort somewhere on the front of his head and on the back.'

'I suppose so.'

'Prescott has both.'

'But that's from the table in here. The back one, I mean.'

'Possibly, sir. Forensic will have to establish that. With any luck there'll be hairs on the door-jamb although it's not a certainty.'

'And on the coffee table here.'

'If that has been involved too, then yes, there may be. Again, it's not a certainty.'

'No.' I felt very glum. It was inconceivable to me that Toby could have been my attacker. If he really was involved in this whole affair criminally, why wait until I was on his premises before trying such a thing? And though Toby was not weak physically, he knew from college days that an ex-rugger Blue, a front-row scrummager, is not a man you attack lightly, even if you do have the advantages of surprise and rear purchase. He would have to have been desperate. I racked my brains in going over our conversation that evening, what I'd said and what he'd said. All of it came back to my conviction about the shipping connection and the Shaw Savill possibility: was there something I'd said about that or the possibility of the Gothic bookcase being made for Temple that had sparked something off?

Nobby drove me home and abandoned me on the doorstep, very late. He wouldn't answer questions and he just grunted at most of the half-speculations I threw at him. It made me very cross. I couldn't argue with the line he was taking: that this attack would have to be treated on its own merits and its evidence sifted for conclusions quite independently of the other attacks, on Brown and Reilly. Each new attack opened up its own line of evidence, adding to the total in a way that would help to solve all three perhaps, but only perhaps. I began to realize that Nobby was holding back a bit in sympathy for me because he knew that I liked Toby enormously and his own suspicions would upset me. That irritated me, too. The only consolation was that Nobby seemed to have taken over his co-ordination role with great seriousness. He let slip that he had the complete file on the Reilly murder with him at his office, so he was evidently trying to do better than the Hove crowd had managed to do so far. I said good night to him feeling a bit happier in the knowledge that Nobby was getting deeper into things himself.

Sue was waiting up for me. I'd phoned her from the hospital and told her, very approximately, what had happened, emphasizing the danger to Toby rather than myself, but she was still extremely edgy.

'Oh Tim! Look at your neck!'

She grabbed me very tightly and, gratified, I put my arms round her and made soothing noises. I was immensely grateful to see her in a way I couldn't properly express, so

I just held her and kissed her while she demanded to know everything that had happened, everything in every detail. After a while I steered her to the sofa and told her the whole story, which seemed simple enough in the re-telling. Her eyes were wide.

'Do you think it was Toby?' she demanded.

'I can't believe it.'

'Why not?'

'It doesn't make sense. Think about it. If Toby wanted the piece, why approach me in the first place? Why not tell Alf Brown he would have it himself? Or Stan Reilly. Or whoever. Unless he changed his mind after contacting me. But why attack me right there at *The Modern Façade*? What would he have done with my body?'

'Dumped it,' she said, promptly, and with a conviction I didn't like.

'Alone? Without help?'

'It's possible.'

'Possible, but not probable.'

'Nobby and his lot seem to think so, from what you've said.'

'Yes, I think they do. I simply can't accept it. I can't believe that my conversation with Toby could have suddenly made him so desperate.'

'Tell me again. Come on: everything you discussed.'

With a sigh, I went over it all again, sitting on the sofa holding her hand with the big Clarkson Stanfield marine painting looking down at us. When I got to my remarks about the shipping connection a troubled look came into her eyes.

'What's up?'

'It—it's a strange coincidence, in a way.'

'What is?'

'The shipping connection. I've a confession to make. I had to go to the Westminster Library today. To look up a reference in the art section. Nothing to do with Norman Shaw.'

'So?'

'So on my way back down I passed the general section and I couldn't resist going in to look up anything they had on Shaw—the brother, I mean—just in case, you know, just in case there was anything, anything at all. It was visiting Leyswood that did it.'

I chuckled, which was painful, but still. 'Sue, you are incorrigible. You're getting worse than me.'

'No, I'm not—it's just your influence. Anyway I couldn't find anything on him or on Temple but I did find a book on those emigrant ships to New Zealand that covered all the trade in the early days. There was quite a bit about the Shaw Savill ships in it.'

'Really? Anything relevant?'

Sue shook her head and then, still holding my hand, she told me about the bad luck the Line had had in those early, perilous days, about the dreadful fate of the *Cospatrick* and then the *Merope*, the *Caribou* and the others that were wrecked or in collision or simply disappeared. She had noted down the names and she told me the story simply and factually, which somehow made it seem all the more stark and horrifying and so remote from the grand houses, the celebrated furnishings and the art collections of the men who had remained on land to finance and organize the dangerous reality of life at sea in the nineteenth century. There was a long silence when she'd finished because somehow I felt even more strongly, now, the inexplicable pull of the shipping connection with what had been going on.

'Keep your notes,' I said, getting to my feet. 'With any luck Toby will return to consciousness tomorrow and this whole thing will be cleared up, especially if he recognized the attacker. So we may not need them. Whatever happens, though, there's one last place I have to go to, one last location to check. I know that Nobby says I've been wandering about vapidly but I do get more information clear in my head, a better picture, when I visit these places.'

She looked up at me from the sofa with a smile. 'Dear Tim, where on earth do you want to chase to now? Still in hot pursuit, just like a terrier? I'm coming with you, you know, so you'd better tell me. Where is it?'

I reached down and lifted her up off the sofa to stand in front of me so that I could put my arm around her waist. 'It's very intellectual,' I said. 'We're going to Turnham Green.'

CHAPTER 16

'William de Morgan tiles,' I pointed out, raising a pint glass in their direction. 'Never thought I'd be so glad to see such things again. Not that I don't admire William de Morgan's ceramics, I do, but somehow I never thought I'd view them with gratitude, if you follow my drift.'

'I suppose I do,' she said, looking first at me and then down at her hands, quickly.

We were in the Tabard Inn, Bedford Park. Just round the corner from Turnham Green station, West London, that is. You can see it from the Underground train going out to Heathrow if you want to, because the Underground goes Overground at that point, in fact it's elevated well above ground level and I'm rambling, aren't I, but I was feeling somewhat light-headed that morning. Waking up with a much less painful neck had helped, and having Sue beside me, and the spring sunshine. It made me feel decisive and dynamic. I had checked with the hospital: no change in Toby yet, but hopeful signs. I left a message at the Bank, avoiding Jeremy and Geoffrey, recovered my car and took Sue, late morning, over to see what was probably the first Garden City suburb in the world. Bedford Park was laid out by a man called Jonathan Carr and mostly architected by Richard Norman Shaw, although E.W. Godwin managed to get a couple of houses in at the beginning. There's still a good deal of it left because a plan the local borough had, after the 1939–45 war, to raze it to the ground and build council houses over it was shelved. Bedford Park survived; its leafy roads still contain most of the original brick-and-tile houses, with their white-painted balcony balustrades, their little Dutch gables, oriel window-bays and other cheerful 'Queen Anne' features.

I had driven Sue carefully down the principal roads: The Avenue, Woodstock Road and, finally, Bath Road, where we came across the celebrated pub called the Tabard Inn, which Shaw placed across the road from the church, facing it and even rivalling it, because the Inn building included a stores and club all under one long roof, with seven gables aimed at the street. The pub is at the end and the sight of it had made me thirsty, so I parked nearby and took Sue in. Although the William de Morgan tiles are still present, there have been changes; for one thing the walls have been re-papered in a William Morris print, which would have made Shaw writhe, particularly since it is a design that you see on so many settees nowadays. Alcoves contain cubicled bench seats with tapering oak Voyseyesque uprights in an Arts-and-Crafts manner and a 'Morrisian' patterned carpet. The front ceilings are still heavily moulded, however, in their original Renaissance design and, despite the bloody jukebox and the wretched fruit machine, the multi-paned windows in the doors, with their ovals and heavy, painted glazing bars of 'Queen Anne' style remind you of what the original must have been like. That, the sunshine and the relief of feeling that my neck actually worked again counterbalanced any loss of expectation that the interior of the Tabard Inn might have caused.

Sue gave me one of her looks, the ones that convey the sense of my incorrigible nature, over her glass of white wine. 'Well? Now that we are on site, so to speak, what conclusion have you come to? That the bookcase went for six when they pulled Tower House down? Or that it's standing in the church vestry opposite and all we have to do is hire a gang of removal men, pretend we've been sent by the Commissioners to take it for restoration and off we go?' Her smile mocked me.

'Church vestry,' I said. 'That's a thought. I doubt if it's there but we could look. As for removal men—it was seeing the Pavilion Removals van that reminded me of this place. Their depot is here somewhere.'

She shook her head in mock sadness. 'I think that Jeremy and Nobby are right. You're hopeless; you can't resist prowling about like this, sniffing for inspiration. You really should leave professional police work to professional police-men and forensic science.'

'They take too long. Besides,' I said, indignantly, 'what about you? Raking through out-of-print books on sailing clippers in the Westminster Reference Library? Hey? All that esoteric stuff about the *Cospatrick* and the dreadful *Yarn of the Nancy Bell* type of story? What is that but hopeless sniffing for inspiration?'

Her chin lifted. 'Well, it's been as much use as your researches go as far as finding this enormous piece of furni-ture is concerned. I may have nothing to show but nor have you, either.'

'Ouch.'

'I try to help you with your intuition about shipping and all you do is to deride my efforts. *Yarn of the Nancy Bell* indeed. The only Gilbertian aspect of this affair is the sight of you, going round in circles.'

I gave her a significant stare. 'Don't be too sure of that. Quite apart from writing *"I am a cook and a captain bold, and the mate of the Nancy brig, and a bo'sun tight and a midshipmite and the crew of the captain's gig—"'*

'Stop it!' She shivered. 'That's a horrible rhyme for me, now. Horrible. Gilbert had a macabre sense of humour. He—'

'He did indeed. He re-named his big house in Harrow Weald. He called it Grim's Dyke. Its original name was Graeme's Dyke. Guess who built it?'

She stared at me. 'Of course. Richard Norman Shaw.' Another shiver made her tremble.

'Right first time. Smack on. For Frederick Goodall, actually. The Royal Academician. I seem to recall that Hesketh Pearson called it a "sham Tudor" house. Shaw might have had a few words to say on that. Anyway Gilbert bought it later on, in the 'nineties. So who knows—Gilbert may come into things yet.'

'Tim, you don't think that—that Gilbert got *The Yarn of the Nancy Bell* from reading about the *Cospatrick*? Do you?'

I shook my head. 'Don't think so. I think the Nancy Bell was written in the 'sixties, well before the *Cospatrick*. But it was rather strong meat: *Punch* turned it down.' I gave her hand a reassuring pat before lifting my glass for a soothing draught, and, carelessly looking up, got a view through the Inn window of the Gothic-arched stone mullions of the church opposite. I put the glass down thoughtfully. 'In the meantime, before we decide that *HMS Pinafore* or *The Pirates of Penzance* are the key to all this, let us follow up that suggestion of yours about the vestry and look over the church. I have a thing about looking around churches, as you know. Not for ecclesiastical reasons, of course; just the odd biographical curiosity at work. What was it? "If only because so many dead people lie around"?'

She frowned. I put my arm around her for a comforting

squeeze and we came out of the pub to face the church, opposite. St Michael and All Angels, Bedford Park, is an odd building, combing Gothic features with the 'Queen Anne' bits and pieces of the surrounding development in a low-key manner. That these features are derived from the Renaissance is merely a matter for purists. There is a long roof above the old red-brick body of the church and this roof has been re-tiled fairly recently in hard, livid-red shiny tiles which set the teeth on edge; they have no relation to the old tiles or to the mellow brick beneath. Cut into this roof are the three dormer windows of the clerestory, deep set in their stone arching and shaped in that 'Dutch' manner of the English Renaissance. Above the roof is a four-columned white bell-cupola that looks like one of the small belvederes that Shaw liked; the effect is somehow slightly Chapel rather than Church. Certainly it is not a Victorian church in the way that I have come to think of Victorian churches, all tension, high-notes and encrusted stone. It is much more like the Lutheran churches of Scandinavia or the cool simplicity of Wren, where the rational human being can worship without the attitudinizing that Victorian Gothic seemed to demand.

There was a green-painted notice-board outside, with white lettering, giving the usual information about services and the vicar. We strolled past it, into the slightly ponderous porch and then into the church via a door on the left. The first thing that hit my eyes was the font, with a 'Dutch' roof over it supported by four pillars, rather like the white bell-tower above the roof. Nothing could have prepared me for the second thing, absolutely nothing; it hit me so hard that I wandered deeper in with my mouth open and my mind in a daze.

The whole church was a sea of green. Not dark green or light green: a sort of mid-range sage green. Green panelling went half way up the walls, with green broken pediments above the entrance doors further down. The huge roof timbers were green. The screen and the near altar rail were green. Above the turned balustraded green screen were three words, Holy Holy Holy, set in gold lettering into the green. I noticed, irrelevantly, that the clerestory windows had narrow inaccessible balconies inside and that the turned balustrades to these were painted green. The side-aisles had boarded barrelled ceilings on which the tongued-and-grooved boards were white or cream but the cross-supports at regular intervals were picked out in green. Everywhere I looked my eye met green. Even the pews, with their turned supports, marching down the nave in rows and set at an angle in the aisles, were green, that mid-green, that sage-green . . .

Suddenly, I had to sit down on one of them.

'What's the matter?' Sue's voice was curious but concerned. She spoke in a low pitch influenced by the cool green calm of the nave and, when I didn't answer, she sat down quickly beside me and looked into my face. 'Is it your neck? Are you all right?'

'These pews,' I said to her in a hoarse whisper. 'They're green. Like everything else. Look at it. Green. Sue, it's a sort of—a sort of a *blackboard* green.'

Her eyes, peering at me, widened so that the large whites showed in the quiet gloom.

'Are you thinking what I'm thinking?' I demanded. 'Eh? The tin of paint at Stan Reilly's? That blackboard paint? Middling green paint. It was just like this.'

'But, but, Tim—'

I grabbed her arm feverishly.

'We've been looking for the wrong thing! I knew it! I knew it! You couldn't miss a thing like the V & A bookcase! You couldn't. The police haven't found anything. Anywhere. Nor has the trade!'

'Tim—'

'Think, Sue, think! Dark green was a favourite colour of the Gothic Reformers! Morris and Company used it on their Sussex range of chairs! God damn it, Sue—'

'Tim!'

'Sorry. Sorry. But Shaw used it too! That chair! The Willesley chair in Toby's office! It's green. Rush seats and green stain: I meant to talk to Toby about corner chairs— Shaw's favourite chairs—and the ones I saw at Cragside. I forgot. Hell! I completely forgot!'

'Tim!'

'That's what Alf Brown meant. He waved offhand, Toby said, he waved or gestured at what Toby thought was the desk. The oak Gothic desk by Sedding. It wasn't that at all. He was waving at the chair, the "Queen Anne" style green chair in front of the desk! "That sort of style," he said. Toby thought he meant the desk, but the chair stands in front of it. The green chair! The—'

'Tim! Calm down! You're shaking. And repeating yourself.'

I stared at her. Then I looked around me. My neck started throbbing again and my head felt hot, even in that cool, calm, quiet green church with its three bounding Gothic arches going down each side of the aisle on their turned stone pillars.

'It was the chair. We should be looking for a darkish-green piece of furniture, Sue. Think about it: Stan Reilly's tin of paint. He must have been touching something up. He always did that in his back storeroom. We've been looking for the wrong thing. Believe me, we—'

'Tim.' Her voice was quiet but the tone made me stop, despite a desire to babble feverishly on, alone with her there in the quiet church.

'What?' I checked myself. 'What is it? Eh? Sorry—sorry. I'll speak quietly.'

'The Shaw Savill Line.' Her voice, low-toned, still conveyed a significant urgency. I scowled at her.

'What about it? What on earth has it to do with—'

'Green?'

'Sue, please!'

She grabbed my hand. 'Until it merged with the Albion Line, sometime in the early eighteen-eighties, guess what colour the ships were painted?'

I couldn't move. I couldn't believe it. 'No. It's not possible.'

'They were green. I don't know what tone but they were green. I bet it wasn't light green.'

Her hands were squeezing mine so hard my knuckles cracked and she let go. I stood up.

'Come on—quick!'

'Wait! Wait! The collection box! Please, Tim.'

I found a set of slots in the wall near the door and pressed money through the one marked 'Building Fabric'. Then I rushed through with Sue in hot pursuit.

'Where are we going? Tim!'

'To the telephone. We need Nobby. Now, quickly. Before that bloody piece of furniture vanishes forever.'

CHAPTER 17

It took ten maddening minutes to get him to the phone and then he was resentful, irascible, obstructive and downright negative. He started off badly. 'I told you,' he rasped into his end of the line, 'that I would contact you if there was any news. Toby Prescott is still semi-conscious. It isn't expected that he'll be available for at least another four hours. At least four hours. Have you got that? Four hours.'

'I don't want Toby Prescott. Or news of him. I want you.'

'Eh? What for?'

'Have you got all the files on Stan Reilly there?'

'Now look here, Tim, I've told you—'

'God damn it! Have you or haven't you? For Christ's sake, Nobby, we've been barking up the wrong tree! There is no oak Gothic piece of furniture! We should have been looking for something green!'

'What? Green? Are you drunk?'

'Dark green. Or medium green. Like the tin of blackboard paint kicked over at Stan Reilly's.'

There was a silence. Quite a long silence. Then his voice came through again, the voice of an experienced interviewer and interrogator, sober, but tinged, however, with suspicion because he was talking to me.

'What have you found out?'

'Nobby, I'm in Bedford Park. I've just been in the church. The original pews are in it, still painted green. Everything is green. All the woodwork. Everything. Norman Shaw green. The chair in Toby's office, by the desk, in the same colour. It was a favourite colour in the eighteen-sixties and 'seventies. Morris used it on rush-seated chairs. Ford Madox Ford is supposed to have made up the stain. Oh God, I'm rambling again. But that's what Alf Brown meant: he pointed at the chair and said, "That sort of style." Toby thought he meant the desk, the oak Gothic desk. It wasn't; it was the Queen Anne chair. The green one.'

There was another long silence. 'That's just guesswork,' he said eventually. 'You're guessing. Besides, I think Toby—'

'Oh God! The tin of paint at Hove was guessing, was it?' Outside the telephone-box I could see Sue, between it and the car, staring tensely at me from the pavement. The Shaw Savill colour was green; it seemed too much to be true; what a girl!

'Well, I suppose we could check.' Nobby's voice on the line was less certain, grudging.

'Now, Nobby, now! In that file you've got! Is there anything—anything at all—that has a description that would fit? A desk, a bookcase, a cabinet, anything? That Stan Reilly bought in the last three months before his death? Anything? You must have his invoices and things there. You said he went to about six auctions. Anything in those?'

'It'll take time. I'll have to think about it.'

'Nobby Roberts, if you don't well bloody well check *now* I'll come round there and kill you, by God I will! There's no time to lose! Somewhere that piece exists and is the clue to three murderous attacks! Get off your bloody arse and *look*, damn it! It won't take a minute! You've already been through everything he bought, looking for a Gothic bookcase. Well, there isn't one; there's something else. Ninety-nine chances out of a hundred that it's wrongly described. You and your crowd won't know. You've *got* to tell me, damn it! It may not give the colour! Please!'

There was a silence, another long one. Then the telephone crackled and banged as I heard him put the receiver down on his desk and I could hear the rustle of papers shifting. His voice muttered resentfully in the distance. Sue still stared at me from outside, the sun making her brown hair shine. A great red bus thundered by, shaking the cubicle. More paper-ruffling noises came down the line. The phone banged again as he picked it up. His voice was almost triumphant; he loves to prove me wrong.

'There's nothing. Nothing like that. Certainly nothing green, anyway.'

'There has to be! What did he buy! Read all the purchase invoices out to me!'

'Damn it, Tim, I'm supposed to be in an important meeting!'

'Read them! There can't be that many!'

Put a man on the spot and he'll take short cuts, even if

only to save work or to get rid of someone. Nobby's voice was defensive.

'The only purchase anywhere near at all is nothing like.'

'God help me! Have you any Irish in your family? What was it?'

'A lot at Baines and Baines auction. Chipstead.'

'Chipstead? South of Croydon? Brighton direction?'

'Yes.'

'What?'

'A pair of desks. Lot 103. March sale. £375. That's all the invoice says.'

I clutched the phone. 'A pair of desks? Have you got the catalogue among his papers? He may have marked it.'

'For God's sake, Tim! What in hell?'

'Nobby! Are those two desks in his stock still? Or did he sell them? Either there's an outgoing invoice or they're still marked as in stock.'

Another silence, broken by ruffling and shifting. Another bus thundered past, followed, appropriately enough, by a Pavilion Removals van. I could have screamed.

'Odd.' Nobby's voice came back on the line. 'There's nothing in the stock. The Hove boys checked it thoroughly. But there's no sale either.'

My nerves were shaking now. I managed to get a hold of myself and sound calm. 'Nobby? See if the Baines and Baines catalogue is there? Check Lot 103. Read the description out to me.'

Another silence. Then the familiar voice. 'Well, the catalogue is here. Reilly had marked it at Lot 103 all right.'

'What does it say?'

'No luck, Tim, not on this one. Listen. Lot 103: a pair of Art Deco desks with turned supports and shelves and cupboards under and over, inscribed *ca* 1930. You see? Way out. Don't tell me that—Tim? Are you there? *Tim?*"

But I was gone by then, sprinting for the car so fast that Sue, who was nearer, only just had time to leap in and slam her door as I burnt the tyres accelerating away from the pavement.

CHAPTER 18

Chipstead is an area south of Croydon cut through by the main A23 London to Brighton road. I'd never been to it before or noticed it particularly but the location was ideal for a man like Stan Reilly who would have made regular trips through it. As we rushed towards it, weaving across from Kew Bridge and then tangling our way round Kingston and Ewell, I tried to put my thoughts in order enough to justify myself to Sue, who kept protesting about my excitement when she wasn't emitting cries of alarm at the supposed recklessness of my driving.

'Art Deco!' she kept repeating. 'What on earth are you thinking of, Tim? A pair of Art Deco desks of the nineteen-thirties! The earliest they'll be is around nineteen-twenty-five! Why the panic?'

'Look,' I said, patiently, squeezing past a bus by forcing a van up the pavement, 'you can ignore the description. They are the only things that fit. And they're missing. I must admit a pair worries me. 'Cupboards and shelves under and over.' So you know what that means? It means that they must each be a form of bureau bookcase.'

'An *Art Deco* form of bureau bookcase. Mind that old woman! Tim, that was a zebra crossing!'

'Forget the description. Out-of-town auctioneers are hopeless. Look at that duff Godwin sideboard that came up in the London Rooms a few months back. It was a copy or a fake of some sort but it was punted first in an auction in

Scotland. Do you know what it was described as in the catalogue there?'

'I remember,' she said. 'I remember well. Mind that Mini! Christ! It was listed as a wall unit.'

'There you are then. A wall unit! A Godwin sideboard, and it was a close approximation of one, catalogued as a *wall unit*. Provincial auctioneers have no expertise when.it comes to strangely-disguised furniture on the road to the Modern Movement.'

'This is hardly provincial.'

'Fringes of London. Fringes of Surrey. Call it what you like.'

'It's not Scotland. Mind that bike! The light was *red*, Tim, you were supposed to stop! The trade probably called regularly. I don't see it; I think you're grasping at straws. These people will know their stuff.'

She was wrong. Baines and Baines Auction Rooms were well off the main road through Chipstead. I had to ask twice to find them. At the end of the line of nineteen-thirties shops with metal windows there was a larger, double frontage of glass that might once have been a sizeable furnishing store. Outside, on the pavement, a wooden poster-stand proclaimed in large print that auctions were held monthly on Wednesdays and that all categories of goods, furniture, china, glass, objects of virtue, carpets and so forth were sold. Pressed to the glass frontage I could see, as I drew to a halt, the depressing accumulation of second-hand residue that comprised the Baines' catchment. There were armchairs, a sofa, ten-year-old dining chairs, a refrigerator, two oak wardrobes and a 'fifties coffee table with a broken leg. My heart sank. I got out, followed by Sue, and passed the immediate barricade of bedsitting-room rejects to enter the premises properly through the shop-door in the centre.

It was a miserable spectacle. Whatever sources Baines and Baines could tap for their sales could hardly ever have been prosperous. Boxes of cheap glassware stood on tables cluttered with dusty modern china. Spindly chairs were stacked beside electrical appliances on the dirty floor. An old porter in a long brown linen coat was pushing a broom across the far corner without enthusiasm and stared across at me without the slightest concession to hospitality.

'Too early, mate. Sale's not till next week. Viewing starts Monday. We're closed, see?'

I suppose that dealers have to cover every eventuality, every possibility, no matter how unlikely, how tedious, how demoralizing the effort can be. In all that clutter of rubbish there might be something on which a turn was possible, a Clarice Cliff pot, a Susie Cooper jug, sporting prints, a reproduction clock. Somehow this enterprise survived, vying with the local junk dealers for house clearances, probate goods, any source. Stan Reilly had come here, had bought here, not three weeks ago.

'Is the manager in?' Behind the far wall was an office-window through which I could see shelves of box-files, an electric fan.

'Nah. He's out.' The sweeping stopped and the old porter looked at me steadily without sympathy. Sue picked up a glass vase and a look of irritation crossed his face. 'Not on view yet, miss. Monday. Next Monday.'

There was only one way to deal with him. I got out my wallet and walked across to him, taking a blue five-pound note out of it clearly in full view, so that his eyes narrowed and then softened as he watched me.

'I'm looking into something on Stan Reilly's behalf. You knew Stan? From Hove.'

If Stan Reilly had bought here he must have dropped in regularly. The chances were he'd tipped this porter from time to time, asked him to leave bids. The face was lined and stubbly, pale with lack of exposure to the light, but the old man's body was lean and stringy, a body used to lifting with economy of effort, efficient leverage, careful movement. I guessed that he'd been a porter for many years.

'Stan Reilly? Yes, 'course I knew Stan. You're not police.' The statement came factually, watching the blue banknote. His eyes flicked to Sue, to make sure she wasn't pinching the lots.

'No. I'm an old friend. In the trade. London.'

He nodded, leaning on broom. 'Someone done him in. Last week.'

'I know. He bought two desks here last month. Your last sale.'

The old head nodded again.

'The catalogue says they were Art Deco. What were they like?'

A broad grin parted the grey-stubbled face, revealing yellow teeth that were surprisingly even but not false. He jerked a thumb at the vacant manager's office behind him and a look of scorn replaced the grin.

'He's a bloody fool, he is. Got no idea. Never been in the trade. Thinks anyone can set up and run an auction. Bloody fool.'

'Were they not Art Deco?'

'Haven't you seen them?' The eyes went sharp, resting full on my face.

'No. They've gone missing. That's why I'm here.' I put my wallet away and passed him the note. 'I just need a proper description. That's why I'm here.'

He took the note and palmed it down into his coat pocket with a single movement. His head jerked back towards the office of the absent manager. 'I *told* him they wasn't Art Deco. Bloody fool. He wouldn't know. I was thirty years in this trade, porter in the West End rooms, see? I knows antique furniture when I sees it. Retired here, I did. Took this job to help out, keep me in beer money. Fool. Just 'cos they was a bit different, bit odd, he calls them Art Deco.

Art Deco my arse, I says, but it was too late then. He'd sent the catalogue off to print. Too proud, anyway. Wouldn't change because of me.'

'What were they?'

He grinned. 'Stan Reilly knew. Knew as soon as he saw them. Art Deco he says to me, Christ, some Art Deco. I know, I says, they were never twentieth-century, those. That's that Art furniture, I says, ain't it, and he grins and says keep it to yourself as usual, and I did. He was good that way, Stan, there was always a bit in it for you if you looked after him, see?'

'Art furniture? You mean like that late nineteenth-century Victorian stuff?'

'Yeah. What do they call it now. Ess something. Essthetic, is it?'

I felt a dreadful block of disappointment raise itself in me. 'Not Aesthetic Movement?'

'Yeah. That's it. Aesthetic Movement. You know, they 'ad shelves and doors and panels and things. They had a funny top, tall they were, with a sort of balcony. Fussy, I call them. Never liked that stuff meself.'

I sighed, feeling my shoulder slump. Another dead end. 'Aesthetic Movement. You mean they were ebonized? Black lacquered?'

His jaw muscles clamped angrily. 'I know what ebonized means! 'Course they wasn't ebonized! Black? Who buys black? Eh? Trade don't like black, do they? Stan Reilly wouldn't have bought black, now would he? What would he do with that black stuff?'

'I—I'm sorry. Didn't mean to upset you. It's just that most of the Aesthetic Movement furniture is black, so naturally I —what were they then? Oak?'

'Nah! Oak! 'Course not! Would *he* have catalogued them as Art Deco if they'd been oak? It was the colour that fooled him, see? Green, they were. Darkish green, well, a sort of mid-green I suppose, like that bloody awful carpet over there. Funny furniture, I says, painted green like that, but Stan liked them and he got them even though the two local boys bid him up to nearly four hundred. Art Deco! *He* thinks that anything green like that has got to be nineteen-thirties, he does.'

Sue's face was a picture. Come to think of it, mine must have been quite a sight. I could practically hear my heart thumping. 'Green? Good God. Where did they come from?'

The answer was prompt. 'Depository. Croydon way. We got a load of old stuff they'd had since the war. No claimants. Turned it out to get rid of it. Some good armchairs there were, and some office furniture, way out of date. Wooden filing cabinets. Didn't fetch much. Only the desks.'

'Green.' Sue's voice was full of wonder. 'Green bureau bookcases.'

The old head shook vigorously. 'Nah. Not bureaus. No bureau, see? Desk, it was. Desktop, sticking out. Didn't have a fall, like a bureau. Didn't have to open it, see, miss, it was fixed. Made special for someone, I reckon. Heavy, they were. Gone missing, have they? Rare lot to go missing, I reckon. How'd they do that? Lose 'em? Someone scarper with the whole load, I suppose? Happens quite a bit now-adays. Or did they just ship 'em by mistake?'

My mouth was dry. 'No,' I said. 'I don't think they were lost or shipped. At least I hope not. Not yet.'

He shook his head. 'Bloody amazing. It'd have to be a big bush to lose those under. Mind you,' he chuckled, 'they did have their initials on 'em. Maybe someone'd lost them before.'

'Initials? What initials?'

'Up top. Inscribed, wasn't they. With initials.'

'They weren't—they weren't R.N.S., were they? The initials, I mean?'

'Nah.' He shook his head again. 'Nothing like that. There

was a 'W' in them. Don't remember the others; I didn't really bother. Don't like that stuff. But they were different. Not the same.' His face took on a disgruntled look. 'Don't get much worth anything here. Load of bloody rubbish. Look at it.'

'Er—yes. Thanks. Thanks a lot. We must go.'

I took Sue's arm carefully and steered her to the door. 'Thanks,' I called back to the old porter again, but he'd already started his sweeping and made no response as he created more dust particles to settle on the glass, the china and the used, unlovely furnishings stacked in that unlikely birthplace of a violent resurrection. A thought struck me and I put my head back through the door.

'Was it you who helped Stan on with them?'

The brushing stopped. He stared at me with almost the contempt he'd had for his manager. 'On with them? What d'you mean, on with them?'

'Load them up. On to his estate car.'

The yellow, even teeth appeared again in a broad grin. 'Them two bits wouldn't even go on Stan's brake. Never. You should've seen 'em, mate. Nah. He got a carrier to pick 'em up next day.'

'A carrier? Stan usually took things himself, on his Granada.'

'Well, he didn't take these, I'm telling you, mate, 'cos I helped with 'em on myself.'

'On what? Whose?'

'Eh?'

'You helped who? Who were the carriers?'

'The London-Brighton boys. The regular run. He used 'em before. Trade all use them. They didn't lose them, did they? Big pieces like those?'

'Who? For Christ's sake, who?'

He glared at me angrily and gripped his brush in self-defence.

'The one they all use, of course! Who the bloody hell else? The trade boys: Pavilion Removals, mate.'

CHAPTER 19

'Instead of one combined operation,' I spoke out loud, 'we have two separate ones. Life's often like that, you said.'

She didn't answer. I had made the mistake of sitting in the Jaguar at the kerb for a few minutes to try and get my thoughts straight. Sue had gone completely silent and waited for me without expression, staring ahead into a far distance that obviously didn't contain our surroundings in Chipstead within it. Occasionally her brow furrowed. I got out my briefcase, opened a file, read carefully, closed it and looked across at her as I replaced the briefcase.

'We're parked on a double yellow line,' she said. 'And I'm completely lost. I don't know how those two desk-bookcases fit but I take back what I said. It's incredible. Green. All the time: all the time we were looking, we'd missed the obvious thing from the start.'

'Stan's tin of paint.'

'Yes.' She put her hand on mine. 'What are you going to do now?'

'I think I know where those things are. Might be. Possibly.'

'Where?'

I started the engine. 'I think we'll go and look. Right now.'

Wrong now. I said that I made the mistake of sitting at the kerb to think and a mistake it was. A minute earlier and I'd have been clear, but the dark Rover cut across my path so quickly and stopped so close that it was almost touching. Sue let out a strangled cry of shock but I was out of the car by then and my feet must have hit the ground at the same moment as the two men who sprang from the Rover. I found myself, fists bunched, face to face with Nobby Roberts. Behind him stood a dark-suited bloke with a hard-packed physique that I didn't like the look of at all. Not at all. I let my fists slacken.

'Caught you,' said Nobby, his face right in mine. 'Almost got away, didn't you? Mind you, I'd have been here five minutes ago if there hadn't been a march through Parliament Square.'

'Good driver, is he?'

'One of the best. Grabbed him as soon as you rang off on me. You bugger.' His voice carried no resentment: it was just flat and uncommitted, official. 'I ought to arrest you.'

'What for?'

'Obstruction. Or something like it.'

'Solving your cases for you, you mean? Saving you from making a fool of yourself?'

He grinned. 'Jumping the gun again, Tim? The case isn't solved yet. And I'm not pleased. I'm not pleased because you've tried to rush off on your own to muddy the waters and I'm not pleased because you've got Sue with you and we are dealing with a very dangerous criminal. So tell me all.'

'Otherwise?'

'Otherwise I shall tell my driver here, who happens to be a very good detective-constable, to arrest you and lock you away in the nearest nick. I mean it. Then I shall go into those auction rooms—if they can really be called that—and find out what you've found out and why it's made you keen to go careering off again so urgently and where to.'

'You won't, because you won't be able to put two and two together the way I can from my angle.'

'But I'll have you in chokey and I'll demand that you tell me.'

There's nothing you can do with Nobby when he's in one of his high-handed, official moods so I sighed, nodded acceptance, and made him a proposal. 'Why don't you follow me and I'll explain when we get to the bookcases, or where I think they are?'

He shook his head. 'I don't trust you. It isn't that you are good enough to shake off my driver but you might play a trick of some sort. So I'll offer you a deal: you and Sue get in the back of *my* car and you can be telling me all about it while we drive to wherever you tell my driver to go.'

I sighed. 'OK. But I'll have to move my car. It's on a double yellow line.'

He held out his hand. 'Just give me the keys. My driver will park it for you while you get in the Rover. Both of you.' He held Sue's door open and ignored her expression. 'Hello, Sue. This way, please. If you don't mind.'

So that was it. We piled into Nobby's police car, a police car without signs or flashing lights, and his driver parked mine and came back with a satisfied look on his face as he returned the keys. Then I gave him instructions and, as we drove back to the A23 and the motorway, I told Nobby that we had found out, where we had got to and why I thought what I did. He sat listening attentively and asked very few questions; even the driver asked one or two and they were pretty intelligent so I hoped that I'd given them a reasonable view by the time we turned in past the gates by the picturesque lodge with its white-painted windows.

'Not the house,' I said to the back of the driver's head as the tower came into sight. 'Keep on round the house till you come to the stable block. That's where we stop.'

We pulled up in the weed-scattered yard and clambered out in front of the big diagonal-planked doors under the clock. There were lights on in the office-block but no windows from that side gave on to the stableyard and it was curiously quiet and shadowed, out of the sun; a cold yard, I thought.

'They don't look as though they've been opened for years,' said Nobby, prowling along the line of high doors. 'No: wait a moment. These have been moved.'

There was a padlock and hasp securing the double set from the outside and Nobby hesitated for a moment. He gave me a very keen stare. 'You reckon this is it?'

I hesitated for just a moment. 'I—I think so.'

He nodded at his driver, who walked across, looked at the padlock, smiled a faint smile, took out a bunch of spidery keys, fiddled about for a minute and then clicked the padlock open. We all grasped the doors and swung them wide apart.

'A pantechnicon,' said Sue, her voice surprised. 'What on earth is it doing here? It's enormous.'

'Pavilion Removals.' Nobby's voice was soft as he looked at me. 'That fits.'

The back of the huge van was locked too, with a padlock, but the policeman made even less work of that. We let down the back flap and pushed the big roller blind up out of the way so that we could clamber in unobstructed. It was quite light enough to see what we wanted to see but Nobby's man, efficient as ever, went back to the car and fetched a torch.

They were about eight feet high; high enough to look impressive but not too high for most ceilings; certainly not for Victorian ones. They stood facing each other across the van floor, strapped by canvas webbing to the side battens so that they wouldn't fall over. As your eye went naturally from the projecting writing surface that each had—for they were identical—it followed the lines of the vertical divisions set in the left-hand side of the upper half, rested on the green fielded door to the right, rose to an arched gallery under the top balustrade and then saw the dark, tiled roof set back from the balustrade, like a seventeenth-century house which has had a Georgian façade added to it. Then your eye went back to the writing surface, which was fixed and permanent, supported by green, turned pillars, and you remembered that the fall-front bureau was right out of fashion in the eighteen-sixties and eighteen-seventies, so that even though the designer was emulating the great bureau-bookcases of the 'Queen Anne' period he still could not bring himself to include a fall front and had instead made this a gentle, fixed slope with tooled leather set in the green surround.

Each piece was about three feet six inches wide and, beneath the writing surface, set back under the slope, were more shelves and cupboards with arched, fielded panels to the doors that emulated the curves above. The green stain was scuffed here and there but it was the same tone as the pews in St Michael's church and I had the impression of looking at a similar combination of Gothic sentiment, conveyed by the slatted-tile roof, stained nearly black, and 'Queen Anne' styling that I had noticed in Bedford Park. Incised lines in various surfaces showed remnants of subtle gilding deep in their recesses where some part of the design, some emphasis of decoration, had been carefully strengthened to the eye. But it was above the upper gallery of four arches, just below the roof balustrade, that my gaze went to the faded gold initials: J.W.T. on one and there, opposite, W.S. on the other. Sue did one of her sketches later and it was the initials that she, too, remembered so vividly; the Leyswood ones, as it happened.

I found that the other three were staring at me, waiting expectantly for an explanation, so I pointed at the initials in turn.

'James William Temple,' I said, my voice sounding unexpectedly loud inside the van, 'and Walter Savill. J.W.T. and W.S. The partners in the Shaw Savill line when Norman Shaw built the new "Queen Anne" offices in Leadenhall Street. And designed these bureau-bookcases, partners' desks, whatever you want to call them, for their big semi-circular office on the first floor back. One each, with their initials. I bet his own stamp is somewhere on them.'

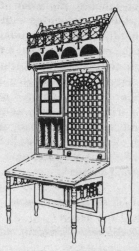

I looked closely at the writing-slope on the nearest desk, tracing the green-painted wooden surround with my fingers. At the top, in the centre, just where each partner would have looked every time he used the surface, I saw the faint impression stamped into the green surface: R.N.S. It was the same stamp that had been so prominently placed on Toby's chair, between my legs, with its five 'rays' fanned out in a tiny sunburst above the initials set in an arched rectangle. I stared up at the balustrade around the sloping 'roof' which replaced the double domes or the parapeted mouldings of real Queen Anne furniture. A 'roof' on a piece like this had more to it than an architectural effect, more than a genuflection in the direction of Gothic. It had a vaguely sinister, very grave, almost threatening air about it that reminded me of the ominous roofs over the tower at Leyswood. It hinted at protection, fortification, in an armed way that conveyed grim strength to the approaching way-farer. Had they been sitting at these desks, bookcases, whatever description should fit, when the news came through? Sailing ships were not for men with weak stomachs. Somehow the work of Shaw, the artistic interest of the chase, had made me forget the real courage that created the wealth for those great houses, those happy artistic indulgences. The *Cospatrick* had foundered only a year after they had moved into Shaw's light-hearted building in Leadenhall Street; they bought the old frigate-built ship at the time of their move. Had the partners come back then, after the dreadful details had emerged, to sit at these desks in horrified silence, with the rhythm of Gilbert's gruesome, mock-macabre humour beating in their minds?

> *The next lot fell to the Nancy's mate*
> *And a delicate dish he made:*
> *Then our appetite with the midshipmite*
> *We seven survivors stayed.*

Nineteenth century shipowners needed strong consti-tutions and hard fists; there is a thesis to be written some-time, not by me, on the relationship between art and commerce, a relationship which Temple and Savill were unlikely to dwell upon. They would not have had much time for the Arthurian fantasies of the well-heeled Morris and his circle; it was no wonder that the practical but cheerful Shaw, with his easy understanding of armaments manufacturers and other big shipowners, was their man. At these pieces of furniture they had probably run their company for many years after the building of New Zealand Chambers, facing other disasters, human and financial, until the 'nineties, by which time both men were gone. I wondered how much they had used the desks, whether they had liked them, whether the cousin and the dead brother's partner had appreciated them and found them practical. Shaw himself, fit, devout, sensible, had lived on until 1912, so he would have known if the desks had been relinquished. By then perhaps he would not have cared, for he had become a Classical reviver and said that the Gothic was dead. I did know, whatever their history, that I was looking at two very important pieces of furniture, things worth murder to a dedicated man, or a greedy one, and that poor Alf Brown and Stan Reilly might have guessed what they had found.

'What the hell is going on? What are you doing here?' The voice, angry and hoarse, broke my reverie and the silent examination the others were making. Peter Coe, tall and angular, stood in the double doorway holding a shotgun whose bright double-barrels pointed at me as the nearest person. There were no country tweeds on him this time, no mud-stained clothes: he was in a working suit. 'Who gave you permission to break in here?'

There was a moment's silence as I sensed Sue moving guiltily behind me. Nobby and his man didn't move.

'Pigeon-shooting?' I don't know why I get flippant on these occasions, I think it's probably nerves; I just can't help it. It could have been elation, though: elation at seeing a great dark bruise on his cheek.

'You.' The word contained great hatred. 'Simpson. You haven't bought us yet, you know!' The voice rose to a shout. 'You're trespassing! I could—I—' The gun moved as his arm tensed and I heard Nobby step quietly out beside me.

'Mr Peter Coe?'

He got a livid glare. 'Who the hell are you? Another of White's vultures?'

'I am a police officer. I am making inquiries into the deaths of Alfred Brown in Long Acre, London, and Stan Reilly, antique dealer of Hove, within the last three weeks.'

The voice had become official, flat, a monotone carefully devoid of emphasis or emotion. Coe stared at him in disbelief for a moment, flicked his eyes sideways to the plain-coloured unbadged Rover and then back to me, Sue, the other two men. He jerked the shotgun in a spasmodic movement.

'Rubbish! I know what you are! Traders! Working with White's Art Fund. You're trespassers!' He glared at me again, swinging the double-barrels back with the line of his eyes.

'Were you on the van when it picked them up? At Baines and Baines?'

He didn't answer or blink.

'Doing one of your checks? On distribution patterns and timing?'

No sound.

'I think you must have been. You knew immediately what these were, or you guessed pretty closely.'

His eyes narrowed at me. For a moment I thought he was going to fire. 'I haven't the faintest idea what you mean.'

'The Orchard is in Bedford Park,' I said, not flippantly.

The eyes widened, losing focus. 'Eh? What?'

'You said you lived in Acton Green. I wondered why you didn't want me to look up your address. Technically, you are on the edge of Acton Green. But when I looked it up, The Orchard struck a bell. It's on the western side of Bedford Park. The place you don't want to leave, despite your wife. Beautiful houses, aren't they?'

He licked his lips. I could practically hear the numbed mind's mechanism whirring for answers.

'I suppose you've always been keen on Norman Shaw? Living in Bedford Park? When you saw them being carried into the van you must have had a very good idea what they were? Green, like the woodwork in St Michael's? Wouldn't Stan Reilly sell them to you? Or did he sell them but want too much? He must have helped you, the second time. The time you took them out of his store and put them in this van. Pavilion called on Stan regularly; no one remarked on that particular visit. Rather like the milkman in a Father Brown story. You murdered Stan Reilly for them. And you tried to murder me; you thought I was much nearer to them than I really was. I suppose Alf Brown was an accident? Wouldn't he go back on his agreement with Stan?'

He cleared his throat. 'I don't know what you're talking about.'

'Then how did these get here? Only twenty miles from Hove? To a building you knew had been unused for years and wasn't likely to be? And how did you get that bruise on your cheek?'

He licked his lips. 'This is fantastic. You've no evidence.'

'Tons of it. The forensic evidence, that is. Your hair on Toby Prescott's door-jamb, for instance.'

There was silence. Uncertainty etched into his face. Nobby suddenly couldn't stand it any more. He stepped forward and Coe waved the shotgun.

'Don't move!'

'Peter Coe, I must ask you to accompany me to answer inquiries connected with the murder of Stan Reilly at Hove. I must warn you that you are not obliged to say anything but that anything you do say may be taken down in evidence.'

'Stay where you are!'

Nobby paid no attention. 'Put that down,' he snapped. 'If you put that down now, I shall simply accept that we met while you were intending to go pigeon-shooting and say no more.'

'No!'

'There are four of us here. And God knows how many people in the offices behind you.'

'Stay where you are! God! Simpson!' Suddenly the shotgun swung back to me. 'I'm warning you, I—I'll kill you!' Tears began to run from his eyes. 'I'll kill you! I will!'

I shook my head. I don't know why, but I'd never felt more exuberant. 'Not a hope. You'd have done it by now, if you could. You only get one chance at a pigeon. You should know that.'

'Put it down! I am warning you!' Nobby's voice rasped nervously. 'We are police officers! We are armed! Put it down!'

Armed. Turning fractionally to my left I knew, now, why I hadn't felt comfortable about the look of Nobby's driver. Trust Nobby: he'd brought his hard man with him and his hard man was standing at the edge of the van, apart, with a clear vision to Coe. A black police revolver was in his hand now; no expression altered his unemotional face. He stared straight at Peter Coe without moving or even bothering to bring his handgun up into both hands in the normal firing position. The double-barrels moved, swung, wavered and then dipped, despondently. The head behind them drooped. Nobby tramped down the sloping back-flap to the ground and took the shotgun from Coe without resistance.

'Very sensible,' he said, taking an arm and turning back to beckon the silent driver. 'You wouldn't have got half way to squeezing the trigger before he shot you, Mr Coe. Assuming that this is loaded. Is it?'

CHAPTER 20

Jeremy White's drawing-room on the first floor of his house in Kensington is an elegant room overlooking the square-cum-crescent filled with trees outside. There were four couples there that evening: Jeremy and Mary, of course; myself and Sue; Nobby and Gillian, lending, as Jeremy facetiously put it, an air of respectability to what would otherwise have been a raffish gathering, and Toby Prescott, together with a very voluptuous Resting Actress who had put her hand on my arm three times that evening in dramatically affectionate gestures which caused Sue to produce glacial glares and to stiffen as though someone had stuck an easel down her back. Not that there was anything for her to worry about; the Resting Actress was, quite clearly, totally taken with Toby and was merely showing me friendship in that tangibly insincere way that theatre people have. Toby and I were examining Jeremy's paintings together while the rest of the group lingered over port or 'stickies', as Jeremy described his liqueurs.

'Thomas Whitcombe,' murmured Toby, hospital plaster still adorning his forehead. 'A frigate off the Cape. Very nice. Very expensive.'

'Quite appropriate, too, if about a hundred years premature. The *Cospatrick* was a frigate-built ship.'

'Really, Tim. If every time one looks at a fine eighteenth-century marine painting of a frigate one is going to be reminded of that ghastly disaster, life will be impossible.'

'Sorry. It just happened to be off the Cape and a frigate. That's what reminded me. Nothing else. Whitcombe is a fine painter.'

'Indeed. And so formal. Think what a dramatic fiasco an artist of the eighteen-seventies would have made of the subject.'

I laughed. 'You mean Clarkson Stanfield or Cooke or one of those?'

'Well—I wasn't going to—knowing your—'

I laughed again. 'You won't upset me by saying that eighteenth-century marine painting is superior to nineteenth. I might agree with you.'

'What an easy fellow you are to get on with. Not like the old Tim at all.'

'Thanks.'

He giggled. 'I suppose you won't lend me any money now?'

'Not a penny. But I fancy Jeremy will.'

'Dear Jeremy. He's obviously as pleased as punch about buying this timber firm of Coe's. And about the bookcases. I've never seen him look so successful.'

'Indeed. Now is the time to touch him for a loan for your bookshop if ever there was one. I'm very sorry about Alf Brown, Toby; it seems that Peter Coe, having seen Stan Reilly about the bookcases and been told that Alf was trawling for a buyer, tried to dissuade Alf from bringing you and me in to counter-bid. Alf knew, though, that he was likely to get a much better offer if we were given a chance. They had a row and Coe lost his temper. Nobby tells me that he would have got off with a manslaughter plea for that one; he didn't mean to kill Brown. But then he was in a fix; he went back to see Stan, persuaded him to let him buy the pieces and they loaded them up in the Pavilion Removals van that Coe had brought. Coe was in overalls, like an employee; he knew that Stan would soon put two and two together so he strangled Stan and drove off in the van like any delivery man, and put it in the stables. He was the distribution director, after all; when anyone queried where the vehicle was he told them he had it out on special loan. Nothing unusual about that in transport firms. All he needed to do when things died down was get a man from his firm, drive to wherever he intended to keep the pieces and get the man to help unload. Bob's your uncle. No one was looking for two green desk-cabinets, were they?'

Toby shook his head. 'It's quite horrifying. It could easily have worked.'

'It certainly could. We were all barking up a Gothic gum-tree.'

'Ah no!' He patted my arm. 'You would have got to it, Tim, in the end. No one escapes the Simpson curiosity.' He giggled again.

'Toby! Cut it out! Actually, it was extraordinary. Those pieces must have been taken out of Leadenhall Street at the beginning of the war and put in a depository for safe keeping. Bang down come the incendiary bombs in 1941 and records get lost. Hence the disappearance. Hence the eventual clearance and sale as Art Deco desks. Amazing.'

'And the Art Fund is certain of title?'

'Oh yes. The lawyers are quite clear. Stan Reilly bought them fair and square at auction and the depository owners, who are now as sick as parrots, were perfectly entitled to dispose of them after storage for so long. We have them from Stan's estate and, I may say, you will get your introductory fee. Some small compensation for the bang on the head.'

He touched the plaster automatically. 'I suppose I was lucky. It was you Coe was after. He must hate you on two counts: the family business and the cabinets. You were influential in depriving him of both as he seems to see it.'

I looked down at the carpet. 'He's wrong about the business, of course. That was between Sir John and Jeremy. I was just the runner in that one. But he obviously saw me as a threat to the Shaw cabinets and the timber thing simply added to my undesirability overall. He must have followed me to your offices that evening in absolutely reckless despair. When I went to the loo, he pounced.'

'Indeed. Just after you'd gone in I remembered there was no soap. I went out to the reception area to get a bar and there was this tall man I'd never seen before. I still don't remember anything after that.'

'He hit you with all the force of a seething maniac and then tried to strangle me. We're both lucky, Toby, not just you.'

'Tim! Toby!' Jeremy's voice sang across the room. 'Stop murmuring together.' He put down his glass and came across to us. 'And stop looking at my Whitcombe so covetously. You look as though you're plotting something.'

'Oh no.' I grinned at him. 'We were just discussing Toby's plans to expand the business.'

'Ah! Ah!' Jeremy was suddenly all attention. He beamed in a proprietorial fashion at Toby and put an arm around his shoulders. 'Of course, Toby, my dear fellow, of course. We must get together at the Bank and discuss it. We will be glad—of course we will, won't we, Tim?—to help you finance your expansion. Just the thing for White's. Publishing and book-dealing: I have some rather special ideas I'd like to put to you. Profitable ideas. One or two contacts of mine that might help *The Modern Façade* considerably. Eh, Tim?'

'Oh, er, yes,' I responded obediently, noting a slight expression of alarm cross Toby's face and then quickly disappear as he nodded at Jeremy.

'Super. Great. I'd love that. There's only likely to be one condition I'll insist upon if White's come in with finance— at the right price, of course.'

Jeremy stared at him. 'What's that?'

'That I can have Tim on the board as a non-executive director. I think I can trust him to look after things.'

I was so taken aback that my jaw must have dropped. Jeremy burst out into one of his high-pitched arpeggios of laughter as he wagged a finger at us. 'I knew it! I knew you were plotting! But of course! How very appropriate! I entirely agree; we would like someone to look after our interests if we finance a major expansion and I know Tim needs a change from timber. He finds it boring, you know, Toby, unless it's built into bookcases.' He leant forward confidentially. 'As a matter of fact so do I, but don't tell anyone at White's. They think I'm dreadful enough already.' He gave us an unrepentant grin. 'But enough of business; it's time we looked after the ladies.'

And so that was it, until the party broke up and we all made our different ways home. I let Sue into the flat and we sat and sipped coffee under the big marine painting that had acquired, like all nineteenth-century marine paintings, a different significance for me now. She gave me one of her looks.

'You are a dreadfully acquisitive bunch,' she said. 'You've acquired a timber business, a removal business, a Gothic house in Sussex, two desk-cabinets by Norman Shaw and now probably a stake in a magazine and an antiquarian bookshop. What will you want to possess next?'

I put down my coffee. 'I can't answer for White's,' I said, moving across to her. 'But for myself I have absolutely no doubt whatsoever.'

Mortal Ruin

CHAPTER 1

The immigration officer at O'Hare was very affable. He took my passport, after I had politely waited in line, and grinned at me as he thumbed the document open. His eyes took in my face, my dark suit, white shirt and sober tie. They flicked back to my broken nose before he saw the briefcase in my hand.

'You're here on business,' he said factually, checking my visa and my immigration forms before picking up one of those curious, metal, spring-loaded stamps they use, the sort that have only survived in Government departments and airports the world over.

'That's right.'

'What kind of business?' He moistened the stamp casually, on a pad.

'I'm a banker. An investment banker.'

To my left, the thick lines of arriving passengers rustled in half-impatient expectation. Chicago is a busy airport, the busiest in the world. Everyone seems to be in a hurry. I looked at the immigration man in his white short-sleeved shirt, noting the American vest beneath, with its rounded neck, an undershirt of a type you never see anywhere else, and wondered how long he would be.

'You investing in Chicago, Mr Simpson?'

I smiled at him. 'Possibly. We already have to some extent. We work together with Owens, McLeod and Casey.'

His eyebrows raised themselves a little and his head bobbed in a nod. Others may not have heard of Owens, McLeod and Casey, but locally they are a well-known firm of investment bankers, established in the nineteenth century, part of Chicago's business tradition. His face registered approval. 'Uh-huh.' The stamp banged down and my passport, with its papers, came back over the counter. 'Well, in that case, if you're here on business, you won't want to hang around. Welcome to Chicago, Mr Simpson. Hope you have a successful stay here.'

That's what I like about America. In half the airports of the world, if you make the mistake of saying that you're there on business they peer at you suspiciously, eyes narrowed. What business? they demand to know. Why? Who with? How much are you going to make? Have you got a business visa? What tax will you pay, which one, that is, of several they've got; you can't leave until we tax you; and so on. Not in America. In America business is business, refreshing thought, and you can get on with it. They really do believe that what is good for business is good for America and there you go; don't muck about, get on with it, you should be busy if you're here on business.

It was the same in the Customs hall. My suitcase came up on the conveyor. I took it and my briefcase to a Customs official, planked them down in front of him and handed over the declaration form. He looked at me. He was large, his grey shirt straining into the waistband of his dark trousers. He looked as though he lived on beef and ice-cream, happy days, none of your modern dietary fads. Our eyes met in friendly fashion.

'Here on business?' He held the declaration form at arm's length in order to read it better.

'I am.'

'In that case—' he leant forward and scribed squiggles with a piece of yellow chalk—'you won't want to hang around here, will you? Carry on through, right over there. Door on the right. Have a nice stay in Chicago.'

'Thank you.'

'You're welcome.'

So there I was. Just like that. I strode through the exit door and out into the arrival hall milling with people. I was feeling extremely cheerful. It had been a good flight, on time, quite comfortable. I hadn't drunk much. I was a bit stiff, one knee particularly, and slightly dazed, as one always is after eight hours or so on a plane, but I like America and I'm usually exhilarated by going there. Since Andy Casey had promised to meet me at the airport, I was entirely relaxed about getting to my hotel and down to business after a wash and brush-up. Everything was going to plan. I scanned the crowd, looking for his lean figure, his freckled face among the mob.

He wasn't there.

An impatient traveller half-collided with me from behind and I moved forward, apologizing. Something must have delayed Andy, or perhaps he'd sent a driver if an urgent bit of business had come up. I pushed gently through the people between me and the glass doors at the exit which gives to the roadway outside, where taxis and limos and private cars jostle with buses and courtesy vans. A dark-suited chauffeur with a peaked cap stood near the taxi desk inside the doors. I moved across to him and put my suitcase down for a moment as I spoke to him, holding on to my briefcase.

'Excuse me—are you from Owens, McLeod and Casey?'

He shook his head. 'Nope. Not me.'

I held up a placatory hand. 'Sorry.'

A man bustled in through the swing doors and I turned quickly in case it should be Andy because the shape was like him, over six feet, fairly lean and active, but it wasn't. I wondered if we had given the wrong flight details to each other somehow and turned back to pick up my case, a standard large green Antler fibreglass job with a band I put round it for identification because so many modern suitcases look alike.

It wasn't there.

My stomach went hollow. The suitcase wasn't there. I blinked at the empty spot, now crossed by striding people in a kaleidoscope of clothes, hurrying by. My case, I thought, slowly at first, then with rapidly-cranking speed as the adrenalin began to flow, my case, this is happening to me, not to someone else, my case has gone, just like that, everything had been going so well, I put it down there and someone has picked it up—

Luckily, I caught sight of it out of the corner of my eye. There was a grey-suited man carrying it, quite conventionally in his right hand, arm straight down, walking normally, not too fast, not too briskly, away among the crowd, no, he was turning now, going towards the exit doors further down to my right.

'Hey!' I called out, not too loudly, not wanting to make a fuss, you know how we English are, don't want to draw attention to ourselves or make a scene, but a case is a case when you're abroad and this one had all my gear in it. 'You've got the wrong case! That's—'

He went straight through the doors and outside without altering the rhythm of his walk at all, deaf to the world. I plunged out of the nearest door on to a pavement dotted with people carrying their own luggage, moving towards bus stops, cab ranks, God knew what. Fresh air pricked my nose.

'Hey! My case!'

He was slender, of medium height, not remarkable in any way, not striking, in fact very unremarkable, almost camouflaged by his conventionality. He went away from me at what seemed to be an increasing pace, weaving skilfully through the people and the pillars of the building, the signposts and odd kiosks, crossing towards a multi-storey car park opposite, beyond some roadworks that scattered earth and barriers between the park and the airport terminal.

'*Oy!*' I roared after him, as he nipped between barriers towards a pair of doors.

No one paid the slightest attention. I gripped my briefcase tightly in my right hand and sprinted after him, cursing at a twinge from my stiff knee, skidding past people and half-apologizing as I brushed them. I had a mental image of myself galloping up to this mistaken bag-carrier as he put the Antler into the boot of his car, parked inside the multi-storey somewhere; I didn't want to be too aggressive but if I didn't move fast I was going to lose my clothes and some papers, not important papers because those were all in my briefcase, but useful papers none the less. A sense of unreality, of unpreparedness, persisted in me.

The roadworks had striped barriers round them. Beyond the clutter of equipment and planking, the car park's concrete walls had various openings and doors in them. I pelted after the grey man down a short length of asphalt that led to a pair of swing doors made of rubber or plastic, the sort that fork-lift trucks can butt through en route to pallet racks or similar destinations. Without thinking, I hurled myself through them, only to stop short.

There were three men just beyond the doors. Behind them stretched a cavernous area of empty garage, devoid of cars. The grey-suited man was bending over my suitcase. Beside him stood a big fellow in a lumberjacket and jeans. To his left was another man, nearer to me, a slender black man with a grizzled non-shave to his face and a greasy peaked cap on his head. He grinned as I drew up, panting, in front of them.

'I'm afraid you've made a mistake,' I gasped at the grey-suited man. 'That's my case. You picked it up in the hall. By mistake.'

He straightened up and the three of them faced me. None of them spoke. Suddenly, I felt uneasy. Behind me were the big rubber doors, cutting off the outside world. In front of me was this oddly-assorted threesome, the cavernous garage area, a gritty concrete floor. I cleared my throat, getting my breath back.

'That's my case,' I said again, less firmly, but it was: the coloured band round it is unmistakable because the colours are those of my old college and a rugger club I once played for combined with a light blue streak. That's why I bought it.

The black man's grin grew wider. 'That your briefcase too?' He gestured at my right hand.

'Of course it is,' I snapped. It seemed to me that the time had come for firmness. I didn't like the way they confronted me, their attitude.

'Good.' He drew the word out, like a croon. The lumber-jacketed man now managed a smile too, not a smile I liked at all. He gave the black man a quick look of what seemed to me like satisfaction and the black man spoke again. 'It was real kind of you to bring it along. Just as we hoped.'

'Eh?' Spines started to rise down the back of my neck. Cold sweat suddenly chilled my back.

The black man's face went menacing, savage. His half-beard now gave him a vicious look. 'Hand it over! And your wallet! Quick, man, quick! We got no time!'

Great hackles pricked up on my back, somewhere between my shoulder-blades. Blood started pumping at high pressure from a source within, suffusing my face and neck in high colour. Automatically I tightened my grip on the briefcase. 'Like hell I will! Give me my case! At once!'

His hand came out of his jacket, sweeping the six-inch blade of a polished steel knife into view. The smile snapped off, his teeth bared in rage. 'You hand it over right now, man, or you get hurt real bad. Real bad! Hand it over! Now! Now!'

I suppose that's how all muggers do it. The immediate intention of the shout is to terrify, with their all-too-real willingness to maim and kill. The victim freezes to the spot, obeys, paralysed out of the ability to run away like mad, hoping to extract something from the disaster, praying not to get hurt. The big lumberjacketed man stepped forward at me, bringing his right hand out to beckon for my briefcase. To do so, his arm had to move across his body from right to left. It was a bad mistake because it made the arm inoperable from a fighting point of view and put his left completely out of the arena. Not that arms matter that much in a mêlée, human ones I mean. Any sportsman, and certainly any ex-rugby player, like me, knows that legs are much more powerful than arms and much more damaging, particularly when capped with good stout leather brogues with a thick, solid leather sole and welt rather than the soft, tennis-type shoes he and the black man were wearing. I shifted my weight backwards and, still holding the briefcase, kicked him as hard as I could on the bone to the inside of the knee, beside the kneecap. I didn't dare go higher, much as I would have liked to, because a real stopper into the place where it hurts most, higher up, might have missed; I was out of practice and could have overbalanced, leaving the field clear for them to do me in on the ground.

He gave a yell of pain and stopped to grab the knee, giving me time to block a horrific knife-thrust from the black man with my briefcase, which fortunately is hard black fibreglass. Then I had to drop it and use both hands to deal with the next thrust. As the knife-wielder came back at me, I stepped away from him and turned, gathering his forearm in my left hand to deflect the knife. For a moment we were locked side by side in a grapple, so I took the precaution of standing on his canvas sports-shoe with the heel of my brogue, transferring my weight to it. He gasped and tried to break away, leaving enough space open for me to wallop him with my right in the best short hook I could muster. His foot was still pinned to the ground; it's an old booth-fighter's trick a Cambridge friend, who got his blue for boxing, taught me, and it's very effective. With any luck you tear the tendons in the arch of his foot as you smack him backwards, unable to break from you or to ride the punch.

I scored a bullseye, a beauty, right to the side of his jaw while he couldn't shift away. His eyes rolled and his knees buckled like rubber. The knife dropped and he went down on hands and knees, jerking his head so that the greasy cap fell off. At that point the lumberjacketed one stopped hopping and hit me on the side of the head somewhere.

I went backwards in the direction of the rubber doors, my vision whirling the scene about me like a Catherine wheel. The momentum took me through them helplessly, flailing my arms wildly out of balance, but I got one sight, one momentary flash-image that, together with the keen Great Lakes air outside, served to freeze my focus on to important events. The mediocre grey-suited man had now picked up both my suitcase and my briefcase and had come out through the doors, heading towards the roadworks and a narrow lane between them that led to the airport concourse with its taxis, limos and buses. He still used the same determined walk, not a run, just like someone preoccupied with getting to a flight on time would do, quite natural, quite unremarkable. I almost had a second to admire the professionalism of it as I regained my balance by whirling my arms like a windmill. Then I leapt after him with the maddened zeal of a man seeing his precious possessions disappearing, shaking my head to clear the numbness from the blow.

I used to be known, in my day as a front-row forward, for a rather accurate up-and-under punt kick of the type normally associated with stand-off halves and similar ilk, disconcerting from a forward expected to do nothing much more than shove, run and blunder. I used it now, with unrepentant fury, on the back of his right leg above the knee but below the buttock, where there are lots of important tendons and muscles and stringy bits that doctors advise you to look after. The toe of my shoe was travelling with maximum velocity and muscular propulsion as it sank into the back of his leg and kicked it forward, up and high into the air, like a can-can dancer. He went over backwards with gratifying promptness and a shriek, dropping the cases and half-falling on them as his back and head smacked the ground. That gave me a chance to jump on him and tread about a bit with both feet as I turned to meet the certain arrival of the big lumberjacketed bloke, ignoring the squeals underfoot as I tried to refocus in the hard daylight.

It wasn't a promising situation. The suitcase-carrier was out of action and the black man was still evidently picking himself up, but my head was singing and I had a sudden onrush of reaction, of weakness, as you do after a clout. At that moment the lumberjacket got to me. He had paused for long enough to pick up the black man's knife and, although he couldn't move as fast as he might, due to a painful knee, he came on at me in a ferocious bull-rush, swinging the horrid knife in a terrifying arc. The only encouraging prospect was that there were now, from behind me down the roadway, cries and shouts where it met the main concourse, even a screech of brakes. I jumped off the grey-suited professional and the knife missed, but I had to abandon my position near the cases. Mind you, the grey-suited one couldn't do much with them; he now had both hands clasped to the upper part of his right leg and was making tragically damaged noises. I dodged the knife again and managed to hit out, connecting without much force or impact to my assailant's body. It was a feeble blow and made no difference to the lumberjacket; he crouched to leap once more.

Just then, the black man came out of the swing doors from the car park to rejoin the party, his eyes rolling as he lurched towards us. The lumberjacket grinned, knowing that they now had me properly outnumbered. He dodged to the left of me, stuck out the knife and gestured to the black man to come in on the right as he aimed the point at my ribs. The black man caught his gesture, nodded, stepped forward, paused, and then collapsed in a heap on the tarmac.

The lumberjacket was so surprised that he froze for an instant, gaping at the crumpled body on the floor. I didn't bother to explain to him that the effects of concussion can

be very unpredictable, as any rugger man knows, because
the sight had given me a great, joyous, resurgent spurt of
energy. I went in past the outstretched knife with one terrific
right to his face and then I was all over him, it was no time
to hesitate or let up, he'd kill me, so I let him have it, left,
right, left, face, stomach, face again, neck, jaw, nose—
   'Freeze! Police! Freeze!'
   I hardly heard the shout. I had the lumberjacketed man
against the nearest wall now, I was battle-crazy, mad, head
down, pistoning in punches like a maniac, I was going to kill
the bastard, murder him, hack the knife-wielding assassin to
the ground, stamp on him like a—
   'I said freeze! Freeze or I fire! Police! Police!'
   At this point I heard it. The shout had become a bellow
and made me turn my head. More strident voices penetrated
my hearing. Near me, pistol held in both hands, was a
policeman, youngish-looking, legs astride and braced, like
a well-trained man. The barrel of the gun was pointed
straight at my eye. Behind him, flashing lights whirled on
a police patrol car skewed across the construction site.
Behind that, another car was screeching to a halt, siren
wailing, lights rotating. His finger whitened on the trigger.
I stepped back.
   'Don't move! Don't move!'
   'I—um—I—er, this, these men—'
   'I said don't move! Stay where you are!' The pistol jerked.
Staring straight at it, straight down the barrel, it seemed to
me, I had the sudden impression that he was going to fire
right into my eye. It was a horrible moment, a split fraction
of a second when, if I had been drowning, my life with all
its sins might have passed before me. Guiltily I watched the
lumberjacket slide down the wall with a moan. The knife
clattered on the ground somewhere. Two more policemen,
burly in black uniforms, ran up alongside the young one
and I sensed, rather than saw, his muscles relax as the
shakes started to come over me. Ignoring his instruction, I

took a step or two away so as to be able to lean against a barrier for support. Behind the eyes I closed for a moment, in the darkness of my mind, the reproachful face of Jeremy White began to float before me. That the events of the last two weeks should lead to this, I could imagine him groaning; is there nothing that can be done to keep Tim Simpson out of trouble?

CHAPTER 2

If I had not been out of my office for a few days, doing the Bank's business elsewhere, Jeremy might not have got so steamed up about things. As it was, the report had been with him for that time without any explanation from me and, always the case with Jeremy White, he let his natural instincts run amok for a bit until he heard that I was back. He sent for me right away—it was about a week or two before my trip to Chicago—and was braying at me the minute I sat down, that sunny September afternoon, there in his office at the Bank. It's not a bad office as the Bank's offices go, oak-panelled but light, reasonably light anyway, decorated with one of Whistler's paintings of Wapping, all ships and spars and tangle above the models' heads, and another painting I admire, one of a three-masted White timber ship en route from Manaos in the mid-nineteenth century. The Whites founded their business by importing rosewood from Brazil but White's Bank is into many other things now, like stocks and bonds and corporate finance, quite apart from its overseas operations.

'Tim! This is horrific! Christerby's are going to make a complete cock of things!'

'I take it,' I said calmly, accepting a cup of coffee from his secretary, who winked at me knowingly before leaving the room, 'that you have received my interim management report on the state of the art—to coin a phrase—at the rooms?'

He glared at me. 'I have indeed! This is no time for flippancy, damn it! What on earth is that man Howarth thinking of? The business is still losing a fortune on its New York auctions and he's talking of an acquisition or even a green-fields branch in Chicago!' He waved a sheaf of papers at me. 'This report of yours should be pepped up and circulated to the entire board! What does Charles Massenaux think? Hey?'

It should perhaps be explained that White's Bank own a thirty-per-cent stake in the shares of Christerby's, International Fine Art Auctioneers, an investment made possible a while back through the happy intervention of my old friend Charles Massenaux, the head of the Impressionist department and now a director of the firm. To keep a watching brief on behalf of White's, I was on the Christerby's board as a non-executive director. This fitted in well with the responsibility I had for looking after White's Art Investment Fund, an invention of Jeremy's and mine intended as a service to those clients of ours who wished to invest in art without actually buying a Rembrandt themselves.

The man Howarth Jeremy was referring to was the presiding managing director of Christerby's International, a man not originally an auctioneer, but a supposedly proven international businessman and marketer, very acceptable to the financial institutions who had invested in Christerby's and, apparently, to its public shareholders. Like its competitors, Christerby's was heavily committed to developing its US business and started with a great fanfare in New York, where some record prices had been achieved. Alas, like one or two of its competitors, Christerby's had found the costs to be astronomic and was not yet showing a profit on its substantial investment over there.

'Charles,' I said, sipping my coffee, 'is an expert on

Impressionist paintings, sculpture and various other subjects. He is an extremely competent director of the British company. But he is no expert on marketing in the USA, even if he does have a sound knowledge of the relevant collections our American friends have amassed.'

Jeremy gave an impatient wave. 'Really, Tim! Stop flannelling! What does he think?'

'He doesn't like it.'

'There you are! Neither do I!'

I put my coffee down. 'Jeremy, whatever you may think about Howarth's intentions, the USA holds the key to much of the future for fine art auctioneers. The overall business, right now, is comfortably profitable—'

'Only because of London and Europe!'

I ignored his interruption. 'The overall business is profitable despite losses in New York, which can be regarded as an investment for the future. In due time New York will be organized on a profitable basis, but Howarth's contention is that if he waits until then before expanding and establishing the business in other American centres such as Chicago and Los Angeles, his competitors may have got in ahead and pre-empted his expansion. Ergo, he is looking to do it now.'

'Madness! Throwing good money after bad!'

'Jeremy,' I said patiently, but with an effort because I'd had a busy week with quite enough to endure already, 'Jeremy, it is perfectly reasonable for the chief executive of the company to look at such expansionary options before deciding on where next to allocate his resources.'

'Now you're waffling. Like a management consultant or something.'

I gritted my teeth. 'I am a management consultant. Was a management consultant. When you met me. You found such things useful once.'

He shot me an amused look. Jeremy is a peremptory devil but he and I get on well most of the time. When I had first met him, Jeremy was still very much the junior member of a cadet branch of the White family, running his own little outfit in personal finance in Park Lane. With his natural flair for money-making, tax avoidance and publicity, plus a certain amount of assistance from me and others, he was now a full board member of White's Bank in the City of London. At the beginning, things had been very different; he was then struggling to establish himself and needed more expertise behind him than his own entrepreneurial qualities could muster. I had been sold into his office to organize his chaotic administration and to recruit an accountant or finance director for him. When I finished this task, he suddenly offered me a job. Jeremy and I had much in common on art and antiques, had mooted the idea of an Art Fund together, and he was obviously a high-flier. I had not been long divorced from Carol, my ex, and was not very inspired by the worthy firm of consultants I worked for. I joined Jeremy with cheerful abandon, thinking that I might as well have a bit of fun for a couple of years. Now here we were, nearly four years later, becoming gravid and respectable and serious; it seemed extraordinary. Jeremy still retained his energy, his blond imperious looks, his sudden Etonian arpeggios of hilarious laughter, but he had responsibilities now, much bigger responsibilities. Conservatism was setting in.

The telephone rang. Jeremy picked it up with a quick grab of his yachtsman's hand. 'Yes, Clara? Oh, splendid, Andy Casey. By all means put him through.'

I looked at him in surprise. On the whole it was I who tended to deal with Andy Casey since I had charge of overseas matters, but there was no reason why he and Jeremy shouldn't be in direct contact. Jeremy clamped his hand over the mouthpiece.

'I asked him to phone,' he said. 'So that you and he can arrange your visit.'

I gaped at him. 'My visit? What visit?'

'My dear Tim! To Chicago, of course. We can't have this man Howarth splashing our money out on wildcat projects without checking the facts ourselves. You must go there. And to New York. Find out what on earth they're intending to do.'

My jaw dropped. 'For Christ's sake, Jeremy! I'm not an executive director of Christerby's! Even if I were, this would be an unwarranted intrusion. Howarth might be furious.'

'Of course not! If he wants to expand into Chicago he'll want finance. Our arrangement with Owens, McLeod and Casey exists to handle that sort of thing. It's quite in order for us to see them locally.'

My jaw dropped even further. 'Howarth can arrange finance from where he likes. He doesn't have to use us or our contacts just because we're shareholders.'

I got a full view of the whites of Jeremy's eyes as they flared open. 'Oh yes he does! We exist for the purpose of financing such things. Let him try for finance elsewhere at his peril.'

There's no dealing with Jeremy when he's in one of these moods, so I waved at the telephone. 'You'd better say hello to Andy. He is in Chicago, waiting patiently, I suppose?'

He scowled, but unclasped his hand from the receiver. 'Andy? Jeremy here. Hello there! How are you? Splendid, splendid. Tim is bursting to speak to you, so I'll hand him over. Mine to your lot too, thanks. Fine, fine. Here's Tim.'

The look I gave him as I took the instrument was entirely lost on him. He picked up his sheaf of papers and avoided my stare. It meant that my trip to Chicago could not be avoided. Jeremy's decisions on such matters amounted to commands; argument would be useless. To Chicago I would have to go, willy-nilly. Andy's pleasant tones sounded in my ear, turning my irritated mind from the maddening prospect of Jeremy. 'Tim? Hi! How's Sue? Great. Are you going to bring her over with you? Or has she done the wise thing and left you at last?'

'No,' I said firmly, in answer to both questions. 'No, I'm not. Bringing her with me. I'm afraid that this will have to be a short business trip. I gather that Jeremy has talked to you about Christerby's business plans?'

'Nope. Just that you wanted to fix a visit to see me about something they want to finance. I'm all ears, Tim. What's it about?'

How bloody typical, I thought, how absolutely in character, Jeremy as usual, firing from the hip, leaving the 'detail' to someone else, poking his nose into everything but leaving the slog to me. 'It's quite an interesting one, Andy. Christerby's look like setting up a Chicago branch, either from grass roots or by acquisition. I will have to look at the idea pretty thoroughly.'

There was a momentary silence before the voice at the other end spoke. 'Set up a branch? Here in Chicago? You mean a full-blown auction house?'

'Yes. That's what they're looking at.'

'Wow! I thought they were still taking a tough ride over in New York?'

'They are. But Howarth doesn't want to wait for that to come right before getting his network established.'

Another brief silence. 'Well, I'll be glad to give any help I can. It'll certainly cost money. I guess we'll be involved in the action, if it goes?'

'That's the idea. I need to see you and then maybe we'd go to New York to talk to them there. I know that there are already one or two good auction houses in Chicago and we can talk about them. Maybe even talk to them as well.'

'OK. When are you coming over?'

We exchanged dates and I promised to telex him my exact plans. I knew Andy Casey well enough to understand his somewhat noncommittal mid-West conversation. Emotional backchat is not the style of your Chicagoan banker; the English are positively garrulous compared with them.

We were just about finished and I was moving the receiver back towards its cradle when I heard Andy call out and put the instrument back to my ear.

'Hey, Tim! I almost forgot! You're just the guy!'

'Yes, Andy?'

'Have you ever heard of an Englishman called Frewen?'

'Frewen?'

'Yes. Frewen.' He spelt it out.

I frowned in thought. 'No, can't say I have. In connection with what? When? To do with banking, or art, is this?'

There was a chuckle from the other end. 'Neither. This is to do with old gold-mine shares, Tim. He was once a rancher, I'm told, Wyoming area. About a hundred years ago.'

I chuckled back. 'Can't say it rings a bell, Andy. Before my time. I'm not much up on gold-mining, or cowboys. They're a strictly American zone. We never had a Deadwood stage.'

'Sussex family,' said Jeremy suddenly, still scowling at his sheaf of papers. 'Very old. Hunting.'

'Jeremy?'

'Frewen,' he muttered, turning the papers with another scowl. 'Sussex.'

I gave him a look, which he didn't see, and spoke back to the telephone. 'Andy? Jeremy says it's an old Sussex family. If that's any use?'

'Mortal ruin.' Jeremy's voice was thick and his head shook. His face was congested over the papers attached to my report. I clapped my hand over the receiver. I'd had enough of this.

'Now see here, Jeremy, it's quite bloody unnecessary to exaggerate like this! Mortal ruin indeed! Damn that! Christerby's are in good shape overall. New York will probably come right soon and you're taking a ridiculously pessimistic attitude, to my mind. Nothing venture, nothing gain. Where's the merchant adventurer spirit, eh? That sort of hyperbole is quite offensive, especially when my report points out—'

My voice trailed off. He was staring at me in a way that, together with an imperious gathering of his pose, stopped me. His face set in disbelief. 'My dear Tim! This really won't do. You're becoming obsessive. It's not like you to become so defensive about a thing like this.' He waved the sheaf of papers. 'I was talking about Moreton Frewen, my dear chap, not these. Mortal ruin.' He grinned wolfishly. 'It's a pun, my dear boy. Mortal Frewen. Moreton Ruin. Get it?'

I held the telephone still. Valuable seconds passed. 'Jeremy,' I said feebly, at last, my voice croaking a bit, 'what on earth are you talking about?'

'Moreton Frewen of course! Who else? Andy was asking about him, wasn't he? Frewen was known in the City as Mortal Ruin. All his backers always lost their money. On every scheme he ever had. Ask my cousin Donald. His father lost his shirt on a couple of Frewen's crazy investments. Some time ago, mind, but bankers have long memories, you know. My dear Tim, I do sometimes worry about you nowadays. You don't really seem to have quite the same *grasp* that you used to have.'

I managed to get my hand off the telephone receiver. One of the amazing things about Jeremy is that you never can tell what his mind is going to come up with next. It's stocked with the sort of esoteric knowledge that people claim mine is cluttered with. 'Andy? Are you still there? Was this man called Moreton Frewen?'

His voice came back sharply, interested and keen. 'That's it! Moreton Frewen. Does Jeremy know something?'

'Jeremy says he was known as Mortal Ruin in the City of London because everyone lost money on his schemes. Does that help?'

There was a laugh from the other end. 'Mortal Ruin, eh? That figures. It's no great shakes, Tim, but we handle a certain amount of our older clients' trustee business. One of them came into a pile of old stock certificates, shares you'd call them, some in a gold-mining company that had mines in Utah and Colorado. It was some kind of share swap deal originally, I guess, because this guy says that Frewen must have taken them in exchange. He probably left them with a security company of some sort at one time for safekeeping, because they've got writing on the envelope they're in. Something about keeping them with the sergeant for safety. Our client isn't too excited though, fortunately. Most of those mines were worked out years ago, if they ever had much gold in them to start with. There are other shares relating to South Dakota, too, I'll tell you, since you brought up the Deadwood stage.'

'Oh really? You said that Frewen was a rancher in Wyoming. Didn't leave any cattle ranges to your client, did he? They might still be worth something.'

Another laugh came down the line. 'Heck, no. Frewen pulled out of Wyoming way before this gold-mine thing. A lot of Britishers invested in cattle in the 1870s and 1880s, Tim, that's history from Chicago down to Texas. Most of them lost their pants as well as their shirts. The ranges got overstocked and a few bad winters wrecked the grazing. That and the rustlers and the settlers coming in; led to the Johnson County War, I seem to recall, but I never did listen to my history lessons much.'

'You've lost me. And this call is costing you a fortune. Is that all you needed? It sounds as though the certificates might have more value as collector's items.'

There was a pause. 'Oh—well—I guess—look, if it's no trouble, just to please the client. He is one of our best investors. Anything else that you can find. Find easily, I mean. Don't take a lot of trouble.'

'OK, Andy. 'Bye now.'

''Bye, Tim.'

I put the phone down. Jeremy was still frowning. 'You

seem in no hurry to leave,' he said peevishly. 'Can't you go to Chicago before next week?'

'No I can't! There's the Christerby's board meeting. I must attend.'

'Oh yes, of course. It'll be as well for Howarth to know that we're doing some reconnoitring for him.'

'Jeremy, really. I shall have to tell him that I'm going to be in the States on other business anyway and will simply take soundings at OMC.'

'OMC?'

I sighed. 'Owens, McLeod and Casey.'

'Ah. I do detest these cryptic initials. What business will you ostensibly be visiting for?'

'Oh God, I'll think of something. The Brazilian railway project. Gold-mining in Utah. Cattle in Wyoming. Something.'

Jeremy laughed. 'You sound much like Frewen yourself when you talk of schemes like that. No one'll believe you. You really must come to Donald's garden party on Sunday if this weather holds. It'll be the last of the season. He gives a good binge.'

'I really don't think' I said cautiously, 'that Donald altogether appreciates our presence, Jeremy, even if he is an expert on this Frewen bloke. We came in here, after all, when Donald got the push—early retirement, I mean— from your Uncle Richard, two years ago. I rather think that Donald will regard us as the Troops of Midian or something. I know that he's sixty-six but he wouldn't have retired for years yet if there hadn't been a Night of the Long Knives here at the Bank. We'd still be in Park Lane.'

'Nonsense! Enjoys his retirement. On the Hamble nearly every day of the week. Sails in fair weather and foul. Says it's the best thing that ever happened to him. He'll tell you about Frewen all right; his father used to rant on for hours about him. Besides, it's a good party and Mary is counting on your bringing Sue; she wants to see her.'

'I had no idea that White's were involved with this Frewen man.'

'Oh, they weren't really. Just Donald's father. An investment thing. More like greed, actually. Served 'em right. Frewen was very well connected, of course.'

'Was he? How?'

He scowled at the papers again impatiently. 'Frightfully. Knew all the best people. They were once big landowners. Sussex and Leicester and Ireland. Good county stock; Moreton Frewen was a great horseman. Superb hunter.'

'Oh. County stock. Horses.'

He gave me another of his looks. 'There's no need to curl your lip. He was Winston Churchill's uncle, after all.'

'You—you—you mean Sir Winston Churchill? *The* Winston Churchill?'

'Well, who else do you think I meant? I realize you were only a little lad at the time, or whatever, out on the pampas or at your prep school perhaps, but we did have a prime minister here, in the 'fifties, who, during the war, was—'

I left the room. There's simply no dealing with Jeremy when he's in one of those moods.

CHAPTER 3

The drive down to Haslemere was glorious. In case you had forgotten, summer last year was not exactly the greatest, but they tried to make up for it a bit in the early autumn, when the weather went into that sunny, misty, hop-gathering mood that makes England worth living in for its brief duration. London, especially our Brompton area, had a nostalgic glow over it. The countryside, on the way to Donald White's, down the Portsmouth Road and on over the Devil's Punchbowl, spread green and golden swoops of rolling mature fields and woods around us to emphasize, after an absence, that the Home Counties were still here and safe, beautiful and welcoming.

Sue hummed quietly as I drove the Jaguar moderately through this amiable landscape. She likes a trip out on a Sunday from time to time, even though Sue, like me, is a city dweller, preoccupied by city pursuits and art galleries. She works at the Tate, where she is what is known as a Curator, recently promoted to category D, whatever that may mean in the Civil Service apart from more money, which she was rather pleased to get. She was at Oxford, I regret to say, although I don't hold it against her, and then at the Courtauld. She is highly qualified in art history and various other aspects of the subject which I frequently find very useful, and she spends a lot of time immured in a sort of basement below the Tate, where they do research and cataloguing and muttering about special displays and so forth. They claim that you have to have considerable managerial, organizational and planning abilities to be a Curator, of any letter in the alphabet, and I rather incline to agree with them, because Sue certainly has all those. She's not exactly bossy, you understand, but she's rather crisp and headgirlish from time to time, exuding a sort of teacher-type quality of feminist confidence which can be disconcerting. Women will say that it is only disconcerting to a chap like me, whatever that may mean, but all I can say is that with a girl like Sue you can never take anything for granted, including her attitude to us, me and she I mean, which is modern to say the least.

I have actually been married once, fairly disastrously, and after the divorce Carol, my ex, went to live in New Zealand, which is about as far away as you can get and still only need to speak English. Sue and I have been together off and on for about three years, interspersed with a long year that she spent in Australia on an exchange with another gallery. You may well ask why the ladies of my close companionship evince a desire to rush off to the Antipodes and I'm not answering that; all I can say is that I missed her horribly, so I suppose that I'm more than a bit keen on Sue. She, however, takes the view that either I'm not yet to be trusted, or considered serious and responsible enough for marriage, or she herself is not yet ready for it, despite having reached her late twenties. I'm not sure which is the prevailing theory; it rather depends on what sort of mood she's in. All I know is that despite this she is a terrific girl, as passionate as could be asked for under the professional, businesslike exterior, and that the last fairly settled year or so while we have been living together has been great. I'm afraid that Sue has been a bit close to danger once or twice because of various unpleasantnesses that have happened in pursuit of works of art for White's Fund, but she's been very good about it and, no question of it, has contributed a good deal of intelligence to the proceedings.

That morning she was wearing a rather smart outfit consisting of a suit of light tweed that looked very simple but that I therefore suspect was rather expensive, and a blouse and some matching shoes and handbag. The handbag replaced Sue's usual daily satchel-like bag which she normally carries slung over one shoulder and which contains all her indispensable accessories, so I wondered how she would get through the day on her current smart but minimal equipment.

'Isn't Donald very old?' she asked, breaking a long silence that had taken in a sweep of hills around Hindhead.

'Not really. Well, he's sixty-six, if you want to be accurate. Retired.'

'Ah. I thought you and Jeremy weren't exactly his favourite people. Didn't he have to retire when Sir Richard agreed to having Jeremy on the board?'

'Yes, he did. But, to be fair, that happened before we joined.'

'The events were connected though, weren't they?'

'Er, yes. Sort of. The Bank was starting to lose a lot of money and some of the big shareholders wanted a change. Jeremy was acceptable to them. Should think so too. But he says that Donald doesn't bear a grudge. Spends all his time sailing from the Hamble. Sees quite a lot of Jeremy now for that reason.'

'I thought he had a tin leg or something.'

'He has. Lost a leg in the war. It doesn't stop him from sailing. He's quite nimble, I believe. Remarkable man that way.'

She shot me a glance. 'But not the business way?'

'No. Donald was part of the old guard who didn't understand what has happened to merchant banking and didn't like what they could understand. They hated our Park Lane operation. It's all history now, though. Thanks to Jeremy and a lot of work, we are at least decently profitable again. I shan't be drawing the dole just yet.'

'I'm glad to hear it. Hadn't fancied keeping you, Tim. Oh, what a nice house.'

We had turned off a side road into the entrance to Donald White'e establishment. The drive led down the side of an open field with a three-bar fence beyond which a bay hunter grazed peacefully near a copse. The house itself was not large, but it was of mellow brick with white Georgian window frames and looked settled, cheerful and well-kept. I put it down mentally as eighteenth-century, a farmhouse, and the outbuildings beside it, which included a stable block, looked as though they belonged to the same period. It wasn't large, any of it, but it was very useful, well-planned, the sort of place a country man would be able to run without too much assistance or outside help. As we drew up I saw people clustered on a terrace behind the house, talking animatedly. Jeremy waved as we got out of the car and came bounding towards us.

'Sue! Tim! Splendid! Donald's asked me to bring you over. Mary'll be tickled pink that you're here, says she needs

Sue to talk to. Haven't seen you for ages, Sue. You look absolutely gorgeous.'

She smiled and gave him a friendly kiss before we walked over to join the others. Jeremy married Mary Waller, as she then was, just after the big shake-up at the Bank. Mary was once Sir Richard White's secretary and knew the inner workings of the Bank like nobody else, so that in a way Jeremy stole a march on everyone when he joined the board. They'd been hoping to defeat him by his ignorance, but, with Mary's inside track, Jeremy had out-matched them all. Let me hasten to say that the move was not just a political expedient; Jeremy was madly keen on Mary well before that and she's devoted to him. It has been a very successful marriage, and Mary retired from the Bank to produce two children in fairly short order, so she's now *hors de combat*, as you might say. I have a sneaking feeling that she might return to the Bank one day, and it occurred to me that she would be glad to have Sue there that morning because Donald was part of her old days, when she sat outside Sir Richard's office, and was one of the Bank's secretaries, rather than a full-blown member of the family. She waved to us cheerfully, embraced Sue happily, kissed me with considerable warmth and then we went across to pay our dues to Donald.

I remembered his face quite clearly. I never had any direct dealings with him because by the time Jeremy had brought me in to the Bank from Park Lane the bloodbath was over and Donald had gone. Once or twice later, while we were wrestling with Sir Richard, trying to make sense of what he, the Chairman was doing, I had seen Donald around the Bank clearing up his papers, attending a pension fund meeting, that sort of thing. Then I lost sight of him. There was no reason for me to deal with him, he wasn't involved in the Art Fund at all; in fact, like Sir Richard, he disapproved of it, so I didn't see him again. The battle with Sir Richard had gone our way and now he had left as well, so that I had no contact with the older generation of White's and, frankly, hadn't had much desire to have it.

Donald White was a tall man, weatherbeaten and crinkly-brown of face, with sharp blue eyes and bright white hair, still fairly thick. He wore a navy-blue blazer of nautical cut, grey flannels and brown suede brogues. A dark marine-looking cravat filled the open neck of his spotless white shirt. He looked fit and active, as a yachtsman might. The first image that came to my mind was of someone impersonating the late David Niven. It was only when Donald stepped forward to shake hands with Sue that I noticed the slight drag of the leg, the stiffness of movement.

'How d'you do?' His smile at Sue was gallant and the eyes crinkled and twinkled with great charm. 'Sue, is it? What a pleasure. Ah, and this is the legendary Tim Simpson, I know. We have met before, I think? At the Bank? But alas, only briefly, eh?'

'I'm afraid so. This is very pleasant.' I tried to hide my embarrassment at the glancing reference to his departure. 'It's very kind of you to invite us down here. What a delightful place.'

'Glad you like it. It does rather suit me.' His smile was open and friendly. Sue was being led away by Mary to a table with a sherry on it. 'Gin and tonic?'

'Thank you.' A man in a white coat appeared with a tray of sizeable glasses, sizeably filled. I took one.

'Jeremy says you'd like to talk to me about one of my father's little *bête-noires*, old Moreton Frewen?' He grinned inquisitively. 'Thought we'd heard the last of him many years ago.'

I smiled back. 'Well, it was just an odd coincidence. Came up from Owens, McLeod and Casey. Some gold shares, gold-mine shares, that had once belonged to him. In Chicago. Jeremy seemed to think that you'd know something about him. Said he was called Mortal Ruin in the City.'

Donald laughed then, a full-blooded laugh that brought one or two more people to our side. He introduced them briefly and chuckled at me again, beckoning Jeremy to him as he spoke. 'You're absolutely right! Absolutely! He was a menace. My father always called him that. I should explain to you—I was born in 1920. Frewen was still alive then, of course, but only just. My father, as it happened, married twice, d'you see; first wife died. My mother was his second. Father was over fifty when I was born. He got involved in a few of Frewen's schemes around the turn of the century, when he first went into the thick of business. My God, there were some frightful projects! A Hoffman engine, vitrified bricks, incessant silver-mines. Frewen was a fanatical bi-metallist, of course. Gold came into it from time to time. There was a fluid called Electrozones. Disgusting stuff. Oddly enough—it was a sort of disinfectant—my dear old pa did quite well out of that later, when someone else took it over and called it Milton or something like that.'

'Milton? I thought that was a baby-bottle disinfectant.'

'It is. Moreton Frewen didn't always stick to gold, silver and ranching. But he lost out on Electrozones, and so did Horatio Bottomley, who collaborated in promoting it. My father had a lot to say about that. He became a dedicated disliker of Moreton Frewen. Ha! My goodness! I haven't heard that name for ages.'

'Oh dear. I hope I haven't raised old skeletons?'

'Oh no. Well, not really. How on earth did he come up after all these years?'

I took a refreshing draught of gin and tonic. 'From Chicago, as I said. Andy Casey asked about him.'

'Chicago? Chicago? Not very appropriate, surely? Frewen was anathema to Chicago. Tried to cut 'em out. What connection is that? If it's not confidential, of course.'

'Oh no, it's no secret. The old gold-mine shares are for mines in Utah and South Dakota. Colorado as well. A client of Andy's has come by them somehow.'

'Really?' Donald's delight was evident, conveying itself to the small group who had clustered around us. 'I love that sort of thing. Deadwood and the Homestake and all that. Wonderful. Were they Frewen's?'

'It seems so. They have his writing across them. Apparently he lodged them with a protection outfit, a security company of some kind. It says to keep them with the sergeant, written in what they think is Frewen's writing. Andy was looking for clues to their history, to help his client.'

Donald White laughed. 'Wild West stuff, young Tim! The Deadwood stage! Do you know that Frewen took his bride, Clara Jerome, out to his ranch in Wyoming on the Deadwood stage? Eh? And brought her back pregnant in it. Lost the child, I'm afraid. But there was an extraordinary sequel: Buffalo Bill Cody brought that stage to London when my father was in his thirties and used it in his show at Earls Court. My father went to see it. The cowboys recognized Frewen in the audience and got him to drive the stage round the arena. Extraordinary. Cody admired Frewen enormously, thought him a hell of a chap. They'd hunted together in Wyoming. Great excitement, there was. I've often thought that my father threw money into Frewen's schemes on the thrill of that Wild West Show. That and Frewen's tongue, of course. He could charm the snake out of a tree, Frewen could.'

'Oh dear. Did your father lose everything he put into them?'

'No, not everything. That was always the queer thing about Frewen. He wasn't a crook. Some of his backers made money. Most of them lost. Nowadays he'd have been a promoter, a PR man—even a merchant banker—no, not that; he couldn't be trusted with money. He didn't steal or anything but he had no business cool. It was bad luck on him in Wyoming; he was a great country man, that he understood perfectly, but no financier.'

There was silence. Donald looked reflectively into his glass. I cleared my throat. 'Well, thanks for all that fascinating background. I don't suppose it'll make the shares valuable. But I love that sort of history; it brings things to life. The dry documents, I mean. Gives them life.'

He grinned. 'I feel the same. Kept with a sergeant, you say?'

'Yes.'

'Hm. Frewen wasn't military. His younger brother was. But the Frewens were landed gentry in those days. Great horsemen. Hunting. Foxes, of course.'

My eye turned automatically at this towards the railed paddock where the bay paraded himself proudly on the green turf. Mary and Sue were headed irrevocably in that direction, talking animatedly. My stare after them drew an amused look from Donald, who nudged my arm confidentially.

'Don't let an old buffer's reminiscences detain you, my boy. Splendid girl. Wish I were your age. Go on, do your duty and join them. We can talk later. I've got to circulate over there with some locals. We'll catch up with each other, I've no doubt. Keep your glass filled by the way; I'll leave you to look after yourself.'

He turned off towards another group, leaving me decided that I liked Donald and that he was of the right material. I watched him greet a man in a tweed plaid suit and turned away myself, noting how Mary and Sue were changing their toncs as they approached the horse.

'Oh! Isn't he beautiful? Come on boy! Over here—have you got a lump of sugar?'

I shook my head sadly and ambled after them. Most of Donald's guests seemed to be prosperously-retired locals with a distinctly country flavour, rapt in conversations about winter barley and four-wheel-drive vehicles. There were a couple of yachtsmen and a stockbroker I knew vaguely, all clustered with Jeremy, who was holding forth about marine insurance. I decided that I could do a lot worse than join the ladies.

We stood at the pasture fence in the splendid sunshine, Mary and Sue making a fuss of the big hunter, who lapped it up, nuzzling them this way and that over the rough top rail. He was a stallion, which excited them; it's funny how girls, particularly English girls, have this thing about great powerful bone-headed brutes like horses. In my youth in South America I used to ride a bit, in comfort on a big saddle with a sheepskin under it, holding the reins in one hand, not two, but I never liked it that much. Here in England they have these mad girls perched on arse-cracking saddles and they hold the reins in two hands, so that you can't do anything useful once you're on the horse but ride it. It's a strange business. I gave the brute a leer and he grinned at me knowingly, pulling his big soft upper lip back to show his huge yellow choppers in a parodic reply, as though to say, 'If you don't pull one or both of these prize women, I'll have them for myself.' Disgusting. A man's horse, I realized, definitely a man's horse, no question.

After a while Jeremy excused himself from a group and came across to us. He grimaced at the horse. Jeremy is a yachtsman first and foremost; horses are not his style.

'Donald's always been keen on the gee-gees,' he said, relegating the fine animal to an amorphous category of hack. 'Before the war when his lot lived up in the East Midlands he used to ride a heck of a lot, apparently. To hounds and all that. Point-to-points. You name it.'

'He must have been pretty young.'

Jeremy glanced at me. 'Nineteen when the war broke out. Joined up right away. Cavalryman. Dashing stuff.'

'Not the Navy?' I swung in surprise to look at the blue-blazered figure, so neat and nautical, well away from us in a group towards the house.

'No, no. Donald's no naval man. Took up sailing much later. Armoured cars for him. He was in the 16th Lancers.'

I glanced back from the house, feeling rather than think-ing the line that without much reason or relevance came into my head. '*I 'listed at home for a lancer,*' I murmured, half to myself, half to the horse, who was still leering at me a bit in that aggressive way that horses have, rolling an eye without having the faintest idea what he was at.

'*Oh who would not sleep with the brave?*'

She's quick, is Sue. She shot the next line of the verse at me with an impish grin from close by, on my left, yet with a reflective smile replacing the first, meaningful flick of her eyelashes, as though she was sharing a long-held secret with me, partly suggestive and provocative, but also private, knowing that the sleep referred to was death, not what you might think. Her eyes shone and she squeezed my arm gently from her place close by, in a movement that I was sure Mary White noticed and which still, after all this time, turned my heart over in a way that no other girl but Sue has ever done. I winked back at her in complicity, and was about to continue the verse, when Jeremy's voice spoke behind me, making me jump.

'A. E. Housman,' he boomed, with a satisfied smile. 'Sort of poet you can't resist when you're in your late teens.'

The disconcerting thing about Jeremy, although why it should be I can't really justify, is this sort of occasional burst into literate utterance. He is, after all, highly educated. I mean, even Eton and Oxford have to have a civilizing effect of some kind on a man, but I suppose that because his exterior persona nowadays is so City, so banker, radiat-ing High City folklore and deals, financial jargon and Stock Exchange gossip, I tend to forget that underneath that aggressively business-besotted surface there is a well-rounded individual with a common cultural experience. I gave him a congratulatory bow for the accuracy of his identification but he was staring into his empty glass for a moment.

'Get you all another?' he queried, looking up. 'Mary? Sue? Tim? Another g-and-t?'

The girls refused and turned back to lavish their affections on the horse, so I offered to keep Jeremy company and strolled towards the white-coated waiter with him, feeling Mary's oddly disconcerted glance on my back for a fleeting moment as I turned to go.

'He lost his leg in North Africa,' Jeremy's voice was quiet. 'Chasing Rommel. He was twenty-two. It was a bad wound. Long time before they found him and his armoured car. All the others were dead. It took a lot of healing. He couldn't ever ride properly to hounds again. He tried for years and nearly killed himself with falls. The doctors got him to stop in the end and he just canters for pleasure now. Anyway, that's why he took up sailing and moved down here. It's only thirty miles to the Solent and he's got the pick of the places—the Hamble, Chichester, wherever. While he was laid up recovering from the wound, back in England during the war, he had a lot of time at home. He and his father got very close, then. He heard all the old man's stories—he was born in 1870. Probably did both of them a lot of good to have so much time together, with a big age difference like that, I mean. Anyway, that's how he knows all this Frewen stuff. His father was a bit obsessive about it.'

'Did he ever marry? Donald, I mean.'

'Oh yes. French, she was. Agnes, of all names. Nurse here during the war. They sailed everywhere together. No children, though. She was charming and adored him, but she died of cancer four years ago. He's had some bad luck, I'm afraid, has Donald. But he's made of the right stuff; doesn't show it. I'm glad I've come to know him much better. Through sailing, I mean.'

'Does he miss the Bank?'

'He did. Badly. Doesn't now, though. Like many retired men, I find, Tim, even the dedicated ones. Once you break the habit, somehow work doesn't seem that important.'

'I'm looking forward to that.'

He grinned. 'I don't believe you and don't try to convince me. You have a low boredom threshold, like me. Come on; we'd better join the throng again.'

We replenished our glasses and moved into the gathering, which was composed of couples, most of them older than me. I was promptly buttonholed by a stoutish matron in a woollen outfit which clung to her with rather more affection than she might have liked, but who turned out to be a sporting old girl whose son played full-back for his college. She displayed a remarkable degree of technical knowledge about rugger and claimed to have seen me at Twickenham in my halcyon years.

'You've weathered jolly well,' she bellowed flatteringly. 'I always thought that front row men went frightfully to pot once they stopped playing. D'you take exercise of some sort?'

'Er, not really. Try to keep off the beer as much as possible.'

'Don't jog, or anything?'

'Good God, no!'

'Wise man. They drop like cocks from heart failure round here once they try that. My husband—that's him over there, going gently purple—played for the Army for a long time but, thank God, never tried anything except golf once he stopped rugby.'

I decided not to point out that a reasonably youthful cove like me could hardly be compared to the splendid old johnny with flowing curves that she had indicated, but decided it wasn't worth it. It probably wouldn't have shocked her if I'd said that Sue kept me pretty fit too, but the old dear was off on the subject of the Stock Exchange by then, and had got the bit thoroughly between her teeth on that topic. She was remarkably shrewd, and obviously loved playing the market, so we got into animated conversation on the latest scandals—financial ones, I mean—until, all of a sudden, I realized that we were practically the only people left at the party and that Sue, Mary and Jeremy were regarding me with great good humour, waiting to go. I made my excuses and separated from the old dear.

'Didn't know you went in for generals' wives,' murmured Jeremy, as I joined the three of them.

'Now Jeremy, really—general's? Her husband? The puce old josser in the ginger suit?'

'Major-General McIntyre. Medical Corps. Has kept an eye on Donald for many years, when not in the Far East. Looks as though he's fuelled entirely on Singapore Slings, doesn't he?'

I chuckled. 'He certainly does. I don't know how good he is at mending broken bones, but I can tell you that his wife's hot stuff on the stock market, Jeremy. We should offer her a job in our broking department.'

An expression of pain crossed his face. Jeremy has always wanted White's to pep up their act in the broking world, long before the Big Bang, but older directors got in his way. He waved the subject aside with a rueful smile. 'We'd better say our cheerios to Donald. I'll be seeing him again soon—how did you find him?'

'I like him. Like him a lot. He's obviously got a sense of humour.'

'Oh yes, he has. Mind you, he has his off days, too. Calls it the Black Dog, like Churchill. Can hardly blame him. Anyway, we must be going.'

We moved across to Donald, who was bidding farewell to the medical general and his lady. They exchanged pleasantries with us and then Donald, who was in high spirits, walked slowly with us to our cars, talking animatedly. He gave Mary and Sue a fond pat of a decorous sort, saw them installed in their respective seats and then turned back to me. His eyes rested on me appraisingly.

'I wish you a successful trip to the States. Always liked the place myself. I'm sorry we didn't get a chance for another chat about our friend Frewen. Too busy nattering, I'm afraid. Old man's problem.'

'Never mind,' I said. 'Another time, perhaps? If I can come back to you?'

'Of course. Delighted. Bore the pants off you on that subject. Any time; just give me a ring. As a matter of fact something did occur to me during the mêlée back there, while I was talking to someone else. It was your mention of his nickname: Mortal Ruin.' He grinned at the epithet.

'Oh really?'

'Yes. Jeremy may have told you I was a cavalryman once. It hit me after we'd spoken. Frewen had a younger brother called Stephen. Another hothead, he was. Got into a row with General French during the Boer War. Stephen Frewen was Colonel of the 16th Lancers by then; got mentioned in despatches for leading the charge at Klipdrift during the relief of Kimberley. Anyway, that's not my story. It was your gold shares that reminded me. During the late eighteen-eighties Frewen—Moreton, I mean—started playing the gold market madly on the London Stock Exchange. All the younger Frewen brothers had been left an inheritance, about sixteen grand each, which was a lot then. Anyway, Moreton persuaded Stephen to come in with him to give more power in the speculation. He tried to take on De Beers and the gold market single-handed. To cut a long story short, he lost the lot. The whole lot. Stephen's inheritance as well.'

A whicker from the stallion beyond the rails took his eyes away from me for a moment and, following his gaze, I saw the meadow again, with the fine September sunlight on it, the warm-tiled stables, the old house and the beautiful countryside. When I looked back, Donald's eyes were on me once more, less reflective, more intent as he spoke. 'It wasn't the City that gave Moreton that nickname, you know, Tim. It was the officers of the 16th Lancers, Stephen's friends. They called him Mortal Ruin.' His eyes went back to the stallion and I saw the affection in them as he spoke to me again, almost over his shoulder as he started going across to Jeremy's car. His voice was still humorous and animated, but there was an element of caution that wasn't entirely banter in the tone as he spoke. 'My advice to you, young man, if you're going to look at anything to do with Moreton Frewen and gold shares, is to keep a sharp eye out. A very sharp eye out. My father used to say that Frewen and gold were financial nitroglycerine. Pure high explosive. And my father, bless him, was never wrong about things like that.'

CHAPTER 4

The cheering thing about board meetings at Christerby's is that we normally retire to a private room at the Café Royal afterwards for lunch. This particular Friday's meeting was no exception. After a rather boring business session, with various motions and counter-motions which made the real world of hammer-banging numerous works of art seem remote, we had consumed a very tolerable meal and were sitting back with our coffees in a relaxed, mid-afternoon frame of mind. It was true that there were clouds on the business horizon; turnover had gone a bit static, margins were very pressed, American expansion was still tough going, but a nice easy profitable business with no aggravation doesn't exist nowadays, does it, what with international competition and governments shoving their oars in at every turn. We had given Howarth, the chief executive of the international company, a sympathetic hearing and I, for once, had not asked more than a handful of awkward questions.

Harry Howarth seemed to be going out of his way to be friendly to me. He was a solid, chunky man of about fifty,

bald but not too fat, clad in a grey pinstripe suit, white shirt
and neutral tie. He looked more like a successful industrialist
than the head of a firm of fine art auctioneers, the sort of man
you might see in Coventry or Birmingham or Manchester,
dressed up for a day in London because his bank needed a
bit of a talking-to. What remained of his hair was neat and
short, only slightly speckled with grey around the ears, and
his skin was a healthy tan, a light brown colour, as though
he had been engaged in an energetic outdoor pastime rather
than lying on a beach or under a sun lamp. I knew that he
was well approved of by the banks and other institutions,
had run successful international property investment businesses and had once been an advertising and PR consultant.
He was a curious blend of smooth talker and brass-tacks
realist, a man who owed his appointment to good contacts
in both the City and the USA. I was placed to his left at
the top of the lunch table, rather to my surprise, because he
had seemed a bit suspicious at previous meetings. On his
right was a man I hadn't met before: the new director of
the American company, based in New York. This was
Alexander Carlton, a classy name if you like, a man who
had progressed to the board by working his way from the
unusual background of being an art expert. I say unusual
because a lot of art experts, as apart from art dealers, despite
suspicious and inquiring minds, are not very businesslike
or managerial. Carlton, however, seemed to possess these
qualities, too. Sue had heard of him and told me his history,
since he specialized, like her, in the Impressionists as well
as American painting and Cubism. Well, I suppose Impressionism is *de rigueur* for anyone connected with auction
art expertise these days, it being very much the top dog in
the money stakes, so Carlton was well placed to understand
the art market. He had studied in the States, London,
Florence and Paris before doing a stint at the Metropolitan
in New York, until someone—I think it may have been
Howarth himself—lured him from the marble halls of Cen-

tral Park to grubby commerce in the form of auctioneering.
He was eminently suitable for Christerby's because he was
Anglo-American, that splendid mix of blood, and sufficiently
'European' to be all things to all men in the art world of
New York. His father was American, his mother English.

Next to him sat Charles Massenaux, Christerby's London
expert on Impressionists and bronzes, now a director of the
UK board. Charles is an old friend of mine despite being
something of a smoothie; his dark brown hair flows in
unobtrusive waves over his aristocratic head and his coun-
tenance is slightly saturnine, worldly, and immobile in that
unimpressed cast that senior London auctioneers get. I
really shouldn't make fun of Charles because I like him, and
it was due to his intervention that White's picked up their
substantial stake in the firm. Charles and I thus formed an
axis, a relationship within the board that Howarth was
doubtless aware of and which could not always have been
too comfortable for him. Through Charles I had an inside
line to the London end of operations and much house gossip
on events in New York. Charles regarded my Art Fund
with humorous disbelief and occasional admiration; like his
competitors in the auctioneering world, he tended to speak
condescendingly of it while rather wishing that he had got
in on an art fund himself. Not that Charles isn't doing pretty
well; from being head of department to getting a seat on the
board when we helped to restructure it had done Charles a
lot of good and had brought us a bit closer than our previous
relationship, part-professional, part-friendly, had allowed.

'I thought you were very fair,' Howarth said at last,
lighting a cigar and sitting back. 'I'm obliged to you for the
copy, Tim.'

I made a self-deprecatory gesture. 'Thank you. It seemed
only right that you should have a copy of my report.'

He gave me a half-grin and a knowing look. 'I can guess
that there's a bit of resistance to my plans for the States?
That's why you've put things on record, so to speak?'

'Something like that. Well, not resistance exactly. Just, should we say, a need for clarification? A strategic rationale?'

His grin became broader. 'You're a tactful man, Tim. I can bet that Jeremy White is giving you problems. And if Jeremy's giving you problems, then White's board will be in a blind panic.'

I smiled. 'Jeremy has always been the most expansionist of the Whites. He's starting to pick up a few City traits these days, but his heart's still in the right place. He'll back you if he thinks there's half a chance of success.'

Howarth nodded slowly, but the new Alexander Carlton gave me a stare. 'You mean that the idea of the Chicago venture upsets the finance men that much?'

I nodded. 'They'd be happier about the idea if New York had turned the corner. A lot of money has gone into New York.'

'Surely it has turned the corner already? This year is going to be much better than last.'

'Oh yes, I know. But New York hasn't actually registered a profit yet, you see. Bankers always like to look at a black set of figures coming up, however temporarily, before you ask them for more money.'

Carlton pulled a face. 'Taking that philosophy to its logical conclusion, there'd be a hell of a lot of famous ventures in history that would never have attracted venture capital.'

'That's true. The problem is that history usually high-lights the famous successes, the great achievements, rather than the hundreds more failures, the losses.' I thought for a moment of Moreton Frewen. 'Drake's treasure ship coming home loaded to the gunwales with Spanish silver is an image we all retain from school; we gloss over the sunk galleons, drowned seamen and ruined speculators because we prefer not to think about them. Bankers have a rather unflinching way of looking at balance sheets. We think of them as miserable pessimists, play-it-safe, non-risk-takers. They say that if you want to gamble you can go to a casino.'

Carlton blinked. He was a thin man with gold spectacles, not much older than me, just a bit nearer forty, looking as though he had always lived his life indoors peering at impasto and X-ray photographs, but he was pleasant enough and shrewd in the way that art experts are; men used to tricks and deception and professional risk. He gave me a cautious smile. 'I thought you were a banker?' he queried. 'Are you saying that you don't associate yourself with your profession?'

Charles Massenaux permitted himself a broad smile as he leant in to the conversation. 'Now he's got you, Tim. You'll have to come off the fence and tell Alex just what you are.' He turned to Carlton, beside him. 'Tim's been running with the hares and chasing with the hounds for four years now.'

'I'm a *merchant* banker,' I said. 'That's a very broad-based calling, like the Church of England. It allows for a wide range of belief—and disbelief—to be accommodated within it.'

'Chicken! You're evading the question! You're not a merchant banker, either. I think you're still a management consultant *manqué*. You just like prying into other people's affairs and then telling them what to do.'

'How undignified. Quite wrong. I am a most respectable fellow these days. Prying into other people's businesses indeed. Me?'

Howarth laughed as he came back into the conversation. 'Yes, you. I have no doubt that you'll be prowling round this Chicago idea any day now, off on Concorde—'

'Concorde! We're not that extravagant, I'm afraid.'

'Well, off to the States anyway, just to snouse around.'

I gave him a disconcerted glance. 'As it happens, I am going to the States next week, but—'

'There you are!' Howarth blew an expensive and triumphant cloud of smoke upwards. 'I knew it! You'll be galloping over to see the Caseys, right there on the spot. Don't deny it!'

I shook my head. 'I will deny it. As it happens I am going to see Andy, but—'

'But! But! Come on, Tim, we've caught you out! Jeremy always works to pattern; I know him.'

I felt considerably defensive but Howarth was genial about this banter and I couldn't detect any malicious edge to it. He was still smiling broadly behind his cigar. From time to time he had winked at Charles and at Alex Carlton, who regarded me sceptically from behind his gold-rims.

'OK, we're bound to discuss it, but it's not the prime purpose of my visit. I have several things to catch up on with Andy Casey.'

'Oh really?' Carlton's voice had a tinge of irony in it. 'How convenient. Just at this time?'

'Yes. Just at this time.'

'What kind of things? Oh no—I'm *sure* they must be confidential?' He gave me a mocking look.

'Not all of them. Some are, some aren't. There are several joint ventures we have on at present.' I struggled to justify myself. 'There's even a thing concerning old gold-mine shares that a client needs advice on. That's not confidential; it should interest you lot, as auctioneers.'

'Old gold shares? Stocks, you mean? Stocks in old gold-mines? Or stocks in gold itself?' Carlton's interest perked up; his eyes had lost their mocking look.

'Mines. Gold-mines. An old client of Andy's has come by some old gold-mine shares. Utah and South Dakota. They belonged to an Englishman once, a man called Moreton Frewen, and—'

'Frewen?' Howarth put down his cigar. '*The* Moreton Frewen? The bi-metallist? The one who lectured everyone?'

'Er, I'm not too sure about that, but yes, he was a bi-metallist apparently. He had a bee in his bonnet about gold and silver.'

'How extraordinary. It must be the same man.'

I looked at Howarth curiously, seeing his broad, stocky figure stiffen from its relaxed pose as he leant forward to pick up his cigar again, tipping some ash off into a tray. 'Moreton Frewen,' he murmured. 'Gold shares? Him?'

'Well, they were his. Once. They or the envelope containing them have got his writing on them. He left them in the safekeeping of a sergeant for safety. At least that's what's written across them; keep with the sergeant for safety.'

'Extraordinary. They must go back a long way.'

'They do, I'm sure.' I looked across at Charles Massenaux. 'They may not be worth anything from the gold-mine point of view, but they might have value as documents. Like those old bonds people collect. What's it called? Something -ology?'

'Scrip-something-ology,' he said. 'Not quite our field, Tim. You need a specialist for that. Stanley Gibbons or someone.'

'Well, whatever. Andy asked me to find out anything I could about Frewen.' I looked at Howarth. 'Anything at all. Do I take it from your reaction that his name rings a bell?'

Howarth smiled. 'I do have a story about him.' He glanced at his watch and then at Carlton before turning to me. 'Alex is coming down to stay with us this weekend and I've promised my wife we'll be early. We have a cottage in the Cotswolds, you know, near Broadway. Gives me a chance for a bit of air after the week cooped up in London. I'll have to make it brief because we've just got time before the next train. Not that my story will help your gold-miner very much.'

'No?'

'I don't think so.' He pulled at the cigar. 'Part of my mother's family came from Canada. BC, actually. Vancouver and further north. Place called Prince Rupert. Ever heard of it?'

'Well, I've heard of it, of course, but not much else.'

'Ever been there?'

'No. No, I haven't.'

'You haven't missed much. Prince Rupert is a port at the end of the railway line. The old Grand Trunk route. Getting up towards Alaska. It was intended to be a new San Francisco. When it was decided that the line would end there a business entrepreneur called Hays, who was President of the Grand Trunk Railway, decided to promote the place. He needed to attract investment to develop the town. He needed someone with good contacts, someone persuasive, someone who could tap the speculators among the wealthy upper crust of British and Canadian society. By pure chance he invited just the man he needed on a trip across Canada on his railroad, in his private coach.'

'Moreton Frewen?'

'Moreton Frewen. Hays persuaded Frewen to promote investment in Prince Rupert among his friends. The reward was an option on some of the best land for Frewen himself. He could take up the option if his efforts were successful and the price of land rose. Frewen was good at that sort of thing. He said it was a deal.'

'When was this?'

'Around 1906, I think. Frewen was down on his luck, back from Kenya, which he also helped to promote. Anyway, he did his job only too well. They got all the investment they needed, Prince Rupert developed, and the price of land went up ten times.'

'Good old Frewen. So he made money that time?'

Howarth shook his head sadly. 'I'm afraid not. Hays and the Grand Trunk reneged on the deal. Frewen made the mistake of believing that Hays was a gentleman, like him, whose word was his bond. There was no written agreement even though the offer was made in front of witnesses. Hays got greedy. He wouldn't let Frewen have the option and he denied that the agreement existed. Frewen sued him and lost. Even the judge said that Frewen had been diddled, but they couldn't do anything about it legally.'

'What a bastard. Was there nothing Frewen could do?'

'Oh yes. That's where we come to the ironic bit. When Frewen's friends heard what had happened, they collared Hays. They were powerful men, who could make or break the Hays of this world. People like Lord Grey, who was Viceroy of Canada. They told Hays that if he didn't honour his agreement he was finished. Absolutely finished. They'd make sure he never did business in Britain or Canada again.' Howarth pulled on the cigar, which was burning down now, close to his lips. 'Hays knew that he was beaten. He capitulated. He agreed to let Frewen have his option, which was worth a fortune by then. This was agreed with Frewen's lawyer at the Savoy Hotel in London, just before Hays left to go back to Canada. They agreed to draw up the contract documents and send them on to him to be signed in Montreal. People like Hays and Frewen practically lived on the cross-Atlantic liners, you know; they were always buzzing to and fro.'

I restrained my impatience. 'So Frewen got his money?'

Howarth stood up, stubbing his cigar butt out. Fragrant smoke drifted away. He shook his head. 'Hays left for Canada immediately. He'd decided to cross on the very latest, the fastest, the best new steamship there was. Guess which one?'

'Oh no. Oh no!'

'Oh yes. It was 1912 by then. Hays sailed on the *Titanic*. No one ever saw him again.' He gestured to Carlton, who stood up to leave, and then looked down at me. 'That was the way with everything of Frewen's, Tim. Hays never signed the papers and Frewen never got the prime land, even though the case went on. My advice to you, if you're going to get involved with anything to do with Moreton Frewen—anything at all—is to look out for yourself. Look out for yourself very carefully indeed.'

CHAPTER 5

'Jesus Christ.' A very large, white-haired police sergeant stood near me, looking about him with disbelief. 'You're trying to tell me that these men were mugging you?'

'Yes, they were.' I pushed myself off the barrier I was leaning on and stood upright. 'They grabbed my case and then went for me. Attacked me.'

A flicker went over his face. 'Are you British?'

'Yes, I am. I've just arrived.'

He stared at me impassively. Close to him, the young policeman had put his revolver away and was looking dubiously down at the dapper, grey-suited man, now no longer dapper, rocking to and fro and moaning as he held his leg. The lumberjacketed one hadn't moved since collapsing but the concussed black man's eyelids were flickering in classic style. I didn't feel well; the side of my head ached horribly as feeling returned to it. I put my hand there.

'They hit you?' asked the sergeant curiously, as I made the movement.

'Yes.'

His eyes narrowed. 'What are you? What do you do?'

'I work for a bank. An investment bank.'

'A banker? You don't look like a banker to me.' He gestured at my cases, still flat on the ground beside the grey-suited man. 'What's in those cases that they were so anxious to get?'

'Nothing. Nothing special. Just my personal clothes. Business papers. Nothing valuable.'

'No? Well, we'll have to search them. Round here at O'Hare there's too many things come inside suitcases that people get excited about.' His eyes probed mine, making me start to get irritable.

'You can help yourself.' I took my hand off my head and looked right back at him. 'They're not locked. There's no gold bars or heroin or anything like that. Nothing. And the papers are just business papers, not the plans to the latest moon rocket. Or the President's love-letters.'

His expression didn't soften but I felt that I'd said something to reassure him somehow. He turned abruptly towards two of his men, still standing close by and staring at me. 'You call the medics?'

They nodded, without moving. 'On their way,' one of them said unemotionally, holding his truncheon down the seam of his trouser leg, as though pointing at a bug on the ground. The sound of aircraft, whistling jet engines and thunderous departures began to filter into my hearing. Nearby, I now saw people, ordinary civilians, grouped behind a policeman, staring at me. One pointed to the lumberjacketed man, who lifted a forearm from his sprawling, recumbent position and let it drop back again. Blood ran stickily from his nose and mouth. Unreality had taken over. This wasn't me, it wasn't happening to me, it was a dream, I was going to wake up, any minute from now, and Sue would nudge me and say .hey, you were having a nightmare or something, you—

'Tim! For God's sake! Tim Simpson! What happened? What on earth is going on here?'

The big sergeant stiffened, swivelling his head. The voice of Andy Casey bounced through the fogginess in my brain and I saw him striding towards me, a tall, lean, freckled man of my own age, as welcome a sight as I had ever seen anywhere. Andy Casey is about six foot three, and stringy in build, but he looks fit and alert, grey-suited and sober, like a model for any respectable citizen. His face was incredulous.

'Tim? I'm sorry, I got delayed and—what the heck? What on earth has been going on here? Who are these guys all over the ground?'

'I'm afraid there's been a spot of bother, Andy. I'm very, very glad to see you.'

He gaped at me. The big sergeant gave a jerk of his head in my direction. 'You know this man? You here to meet him?'

'Yes, of course, I—' Andy gave a sudden infectious grin. 'You mean there's been a fight here? Already? Heck, I was only ten minutes late, we had a break-in, I got delayed. I expected to find you over in the main arrival hall. What—what happened? Will someone tell me?'

'They tried to pinch my case. My cases. When I ran after them and argued they attacked me.'

'Three of them? Three of them attacked you? And you laid 'em all out cold like this?'

'No, no. Not three of them. Two of them—those two—they attacked me and that third one ran off with my cases. At least, he tried to. I kicked his leg.'

'He looks like he's crippled for life.'

'I wish he were.' I began to feel sour. 'But he'll get better. In rather a long time.'

Andy gave a snort of emotion of some kind and turned to the sergeant. 'I can vouch for Mr Simpson here. My name is Casey. I'm with Owens, McLeod and Casey, downtown. Here, I have a card. And plenty of ID.' He handed over a card to the big, black-uniformed man so that the policeman could read the legend I knew well. 'Andrew O'Brien Casey,' it would say, 'Vice-President, Owens, McLeod and Casey. Investment Bankers.' The sergeant stared down at it, a tiny white rectangle in his huge red hand. It struck me then, looking at his features and his white hair, that this sergeant was Irish, well, not really Irish, but American Irish, like Andy. His build was huge, like some of the Hibernian rugby players I've been up against, and played with, and his name was probably Daley or Houlihan or Mulvagh or Donahue or something like that.

'Maguire,' he said, interrupting my thoughts and looking

up from the little white card. 'I'm Maguire. Say, haven't I met you somewhere? Aren't you the Casey that's on the funding committee at St Peter's? Andy Casey? The banker?'

'Why—why, yes.' Andy looked at the sergeant with an affirmative but puzzled expression. That was a surprise; Andy is, I know, a practising Catholic, but he'd never mentioned any charitable activities to me.

The sergeant stuck out his fist. 'Tom Maguire. We met at the reception for the chapel restoration—the opening last April?'

Andy grabbed his hand. 'Of course! Tom Maguire! I'm sorry—I didn't recognize you with the, er, the—'

'Uniform?' The big sergeant chuckled. 'I guess not. It does disguise a man, now, doesn't it? And this, um, this British gentleman has come here to do business with you? You know him?'

'Yes. Absolutely. As I said, I can vouch for him. Tim Simpson is a friend and a banker too. Those muggers jumped the wrong man.'

'They certainly did. Wait here a moment, please.' With a wry smile, Maguire wheeled on the two policemen standing nearby and altered his tone. 'Well, come on! Let's move it here! Get that ambulance through. And keep those people moving! It's all over, folks. All over.' He beckoned to the young policeman whose revolver had given me such a fright. 'Go with those three and make sure they're booked. Don't let them out. OK?'

'OK, Sergeant.' The young one gave a brisk nod and then, hesitating, gestured at the grey-suited bag-snatcher, still writhing on the ground. 'We've pulled him in before, haven't we? Isn't he called Kamrowski, or something like that?'

'I know who he is,' Maguire growled. 'I've seen him before, too. And he's Kamrowski. Book him and keep him for me.' He began to issue more instructions and moved away from us as the tableau of watching people was stirred

into movement and my damaged attackers were shepherded
or loaded into suitable vehicles. Suddenly it seemed as
though the whole episode was over; the airport was returning
to normal again. I saw an aircraft lift away into the distance,
smelt aviation fuel, felt cold air on my face.

Andy touched my arm. 'Are you OK, Tim? You look very
pale.'

'I'll be all right in a minute. The air's clearing my head.'

'I'm really sorry I was late. We had a break-in this
morning. Or rather last night. They called me from a
meeting on the other side of town to check my office to see
if anything was missing. That held me up.'

'Oh dear. Was it serious?'

'Nope. Nothing. Well, a bit of petty cash. All the real
securities are kept safe. These small-time crooks see the
plate saying "bankers" on the door and think the place is
full of money. There was nothing much for them to take.
Made a hell of a mess, though.'

'What—in your office?'

'You bet. And some of the others. Turned everything
over. Papers everywhere. Ah, here comes the sergeant—
Tom Maguire. I knew he was a policeman, but I've never
seen him in uniform before. I only met him once. St Peter's
is on West Madison, right around the corner from the office.
It's kind of our local church, not for home and Sundays,
you understand, but right near us downtown.'

The large white-haired sergeant stood in front of me and
peered carefully into my face, searching my eyes with his
own. 'Are you OK? Do you want to go for medical treatment? Maybe you should.'

'No, thanks. I'm all right, really I am. I took just the one
big thump.'

'Sure? Sorry if I was a bit suspicious back there. We'll
still have to check your cases, like I said, just for the record.'

'No problem.'

'Good. Thank you.' He smiled at me for the first time. 'I

hope you'll excuse my asking, but were you perhaps a boxer or something, once?'

Andy grinned. 'No, Tom, he's not a boxer, despite his appearance. Tim here was once a rugby football player, a very distinguished one, over in England. He played for Cambridge University.'

Maguire nodded his black-hatted head sagely. 'Now I understand. Those three guys certainly did pick the wrong man.' He held out his huge fist. 'Pleased to make your acquaintance. Sorry if there was a misunderstanding.'

I shook with him. 'Not at all. No offence taken.'

'Fine. Good. Well, I'll have to ask you to come with me to clear up all the formalities. If Mr Casey here doesn't mind following us, he can take you on afterwards. We'll try to make it as quick as possible.' He walked over to a patrol car and held the door open. 'After all, if you've come over to see Mr Casey on business, you won't want to hang around here, will you?'

CHAPTER 6

The offices of Owens, McLeod and Casey are in the La Salle Bank Building, spang in the centre of Chicago's Loop business district. It's an older sort of skyscraper but still pretty tall, entered on the ground floor via a long, pinkish-marbled arcade of shops with lifts in the middle. If you could lean out of the correct back window, you might look out over the square in front of the main Post Office nearby on Dearborn and Adams, which has a modern red iron sculpture by Calder in it, resembling a sagging anchor but actually entitled Flamingo. Up in the company's conference room, however, tens of floors above ground, one is not tempted into doing much leaning out, even though, from time to time, I speculated on whether, if I did so and for far enough, I would be able to see right to the top of Michigan Avenue where it meets the Chicago River, and squint at the site of Fort Dearborn, marked in brass plates across the street to show where Captain John Whistler the Anglo-Ulsterman put up the palisades one hundred and eighty-odd years ago.

Over the prime fireplace position in the panelled conference room, the painting by his grandson James of that celebrated artist's English mistress, Maud Franklin, looked down at me with a pinched but knowing expression. It was a full-length portrait of her, hand on hip, carrying a muff. During our meetings, Andy Casey had seen me glance at it and had smiled an understanding smile as he silently re-called, like me, the way in which it had got there.* Neither of us mentioned it, but he knew it gave me pleasure to see it and, like our own painting of Wapping, I admired it as a work of art. Even those purists down at the Tate Gallery will admit that Whistler painted some smashing pictures.

I was feeling a lot better. My head didn't ache any more. I had had two very good nights' sleep at the Palmer House Hotel, not far away. My brain felt clear; and assurance from the police sergeant, Tom Maguire, that the attack at the airport was nothing personal or premeditated helped to release my thoughts for business and prevent any morbid worry about any deeper implications. Maguire was very reassuring on the point.

'A bunch of small-time pros,' he told us on the telephone during the second day. 'They work the stations and the airports. I guess they took you for a sucker when you put down your case in the foyer. The only real craftsman is Kamrowski—the grey guy who actually lifted the case. He's been around a while and has a record; usually he's too clever to catch. The other two strike me as being pretty dumb. No

* *Whistler in the Dark.*

ulterior motive as far as we can tell or that they will admit.
Just a random hit on a new arrival.'

With this unemotional, calming report, I felt free to work
unencumbered by larger suspicions. In a life which has had
its fair share of sinister, carefully-timed aggression, there is
a tendency to think of every such happening as being the
work of some Master Planner, intent on mangling Simpson
as part of a grand strategy too complex to comprehend. This
time I was cheerfully able to ascribe the attack to part of
Chicago's impersonal crime statistics, like those of any major
city anywhere. Soon, Andy and I were enmeshed in the
doings of our competitors in the Chicago area, the implications of opening up a new auction house in a major city,
and a welter of statistics and crystal-ball gazing. We could
leave my attackers safely to Maguire; it was useful to have
Andy Casey's solid reputation and church contacts to establish my well-being in Chicago. Charity may begin at home,
I thought, but in Andy's case it certainly has spread itself
out to finish elsewhere. Without Andy, Maguire might have
been much more difficult.

Andy, however, had his mind on other things. He was
quite excited, for a Chicagoan. 'That guy Frewen I asked
you about was amazing! Quite amazing! I mean, Tim, I'm
grateful to you for those stories you told me, but this is a
city built on cattle, originally, and Frewen was a cattle man,
back in Wyoming. Do you know what that crazy Englishman
tried to do?'

'No.'

'He tried to take on the Chicago Beef Trust!'

'The what?'

'The Chicago Beef Trust. Back in the 1880s. Can you
imagine? The big boys. Armour, Swift, Morris and McNeil.
I mean, we here at OMC started life as hide shippers, so it
wasn't difficult to get the story from some of the old records
here in the city. Those guys—the Beef Trust—dominated
the stockyards. Frewen understood distribution only too

well. His herds were on the Powder River in Wyoming. He had to drive them five hundred miles to the Missouri at Omaha, then load 'em on rail to Chicago. The stockyards bought the herds, fattened them up and sold them for meat. They made the big money. A lot of the meat went to England, either already killed or on the hoof for slaughter when it got to Liverpool or somewhere like that. What Frewen did was to try and cut out the middleman. He even tried to get the law changed in England so that he could import cattle and fatten them on farms over there, instead of having them slaughtered at the port of entry.' Andy shook his head in wonder at the thought of the scale of such a thing; the idea of changing the whole basis of the cattle industry. 'When they wouldn't change the law in England —lucky for Chicago that they didn't—he decided to cut out Chicago anyway. He bought land near Duluth, right at the western point of Lake Superior. A thousand acres. He built cattle sheds and fattened the cattle on free grain, rejected from the screenings at the wheat silos. The Beef Trust cut the price of dressed beef by half to try and ruin him. He fought back and he might even have won. Apparently, Frewen was the leader of the Wyoming Stock Growers Association in Cheyenne; he had the ear of the President of the USA and the Viceroy of Canada. The trouble was that the ranges were getting overstocked. There were too many cattle and too many settlers and rustlers moving in to steal steers and mavericks. Then they had two dreadful winters: 'eighty-four and 'eighty-five. Frewen knew by 1884 that the end was in sight. He cabled his directors in England to sell out before the collapse.'

'Don't tell me,' I interrupted him. 'I can guess what happened, so you don't have to be polite. They behaved like classic British boards of directors back in England and did nothing.'

'I'm afraid you've got it. They didn't follow his advice. Frewen's own contract didn't allow him to sell out his share.

They all lost their shirts. And pants. Frewen landed up heavily in debt. The land near Duluth became West Superior City and there are streets with his name there, but Frewen had to sell all that. Six years later, the land was worth ten times what he sold it for.'

'Good grief.'

'It was a hell of a crash. A lot of English and Scottish investors lost on cattle at that time. About ten million sterling, they reckon. Frewen was just another casualty statistic. He closed down the Powder River Ranch—it had a huge log cabin called Castle Frewen—and went back to England.'

'Disastrous. I'd no idea he was such a baron.'

'Oh, sure he was. He was quite a legend, Tim. I mean, when he and his brother Richard first went to Wyoming it was real frontier country. The Sioux were still dangerous— the Big Horn battle was still fresh in everyone's minds. Frewen knew Bill Cody well, and all the local bigwigs. When he led the Stock Growers he had a house in Cheyenne with leather on the walls. It's still called Sir Moreton Frewen's house. He entertained visiting British aristocracy at the Powder River with champagne and all the trimmings. Everything was in great style. Brought his wife out from New York in the Deadwood stage. He was a cattle baron, damn it. They lynched rustlers in those days and he knew it. Ever read Owen Wister's book called *The Virginian?*'

'No, I haven't.'

'Well, one of the local rustler-hangings figures in that. I've never seen that film rubbish called *Heaven's Gate*, but in 1892 Frewen was in Washington during the Johnson County War. He was busted from ranching by then, but he got Senator Blaine to send troops from Fort McKinney to relieve the besieged cattle owners, some of whom were his friends. Otherwise the rustlers would have hanged them. That was his account, anyway. He was a hell of a high talker, Tim. No one knew quite whether to believe him or not. He could ride and he could hunt and he was tough, that's for sure. A tall guy with a moustache and sharp blue eyes. In those days a cattle boss always carried a gun and Frewen was no exception.'

Andy paused, slightly out of breath. I hadn't seen him that excited for months. History is not usually your average American's favourite subject but this bit of it had grabbed Andy, all right. It was as though the smell of the stockyards, dust, leather, the far high ranges of Wyoming and the great revolver-toting story of the Wild West had suddenly come to life for him. I tried to steer the conversation back to the original point.

'What about the gold?'

'Gold? Gold? Hell, you can't separate Frewen from gold! He was always after gold! Mines, processes—he financed a patent crusher made by a Scotsman called Crawford— everything. When he came out to Wyoming, in 1878, the rush was on in the Black Hills.' He grinned happily. 'It was like a stampede, Tim. South Dakota borders on Wyoming. Wild, lawless things happened. Deadwood is right there in the Black Hills, and the famous stagecoach got held up regularly. They killed all the passengers a couple of times and left the bodies right there for the varmints to find. Just like the Indians did here at Fort Dearborn.'

'This was the same stagecoach? The one Frewen brought his wife out in?'

'The same damn one. She was Clara Jerome, Tim. Her sister was your Winston Churchill's mother. The Jeromes were big time in New York. Hell, Leonard Jerome, he—'

'Wait! Andy, wait! You're going too fast for me. I have to go on to New York after this. Am I going to get a chance to see these famous shares, stocks, whatever?'

'Oh, gee, Tim, I'm sorry. Of course you are.' He chuckled and shook his head at himself. 'I wouldn't be telling you all this otherwise. The guy who has them is an old client of ours called Victor Perkins. Been in real estate and other business all his life. He came by these stocks as part of a complex swap I won't bore you with. We haven't got them here because he doesn't think they're that valuable and he has a safe in his house out near Sunset Valley golf course. I haven't seen them yet but I'm going out there tomorrow to look at the documents. D'you want to come? I figured you would.'

'I'd love to.'

'Great. Victor'll be pleased to meet someone from England. His family was from Wales, way back. It seems that these stocks were kept by someone who moved to Chicago in the 'twenties. Mines in Utah and Colorado and South Dakota. The only mine still going in South Dakota, as far as I know, is the Homestake, and none of these stocks are in that. But they're in a big old envelope addressed to Mr Moreton Frewen of Brede Place, Sussex—you were right about that, or at least Jeremy was. Bang on, what he said about the Frewens being an old Sussex family. This Moreton must have been quite an adventurer. I had no idea until we did our researches that he was Winston Churchill's uncle. Victor Perkins will be delighted. He'll love it. It's a bit of history for him. They might have some value as documents, even if the gold-mines turn out to be a busted flush.'

'Can you check that?'

'Oh, sure we can. If he wants us to. It would take time, mind, so it would cost money. Perkins might want to do that himself, since he's retired and got plenty of time. But of course I figured to include you on my next visit to him, before you head over to New York.' He grinned. 'Knowing your propensity for history, I—'

The phone rang, interrupting him, and he scowled at it as he made an irritated noise.

'I told them not to disturb us.'

The phone rang again, insistently. Andy got up from the table, strode across to the side of the room and picked up the instrument.

'This is Casey. I left a message I didn't want—hey? Who? Oh. Oh, OK, put him on.'

He clasped a hand over the receiver. 'It's Perkins's son, Frank. Sorry. I guess I have to take this one. Seems like it's important.' He took his hand off the mouthpiece. 'Hello? This is Andy Casey here. Hi. Hi, Frank. How are you? I—'

Silence overtook him. He stood awkwardly, the phone to his ear, half turning to me, half to the wall at the side of the room. All the time the phone was pressed to his ear, the unheard voice talking on and on, his eyes were on mine. Not so much to start with, but more and more as the call continued, so that his stare intensified, narrowed, focused. It was a stare I'd seen in other people before, an unbelieving yet comprehending stare, accusatory almost, as though everything he was hearing, the shock, the disbelief yet the swiftly-following belief, the horror, the numb awareness of loss, could be engendered by my presence or attributed in some way to my involvement. When he put the phone down his face was white.

'Victor Perkins has been murdered,' he said.

'What?'

'Murdered. There was a break-in last night. Burglars. They made him open the safe. They took everything and they killed him. Shot him.' His voice was not normal, not in key or in steadiness. 'They shot Victor. There was hardly anything worth killing anyone for in that safe.' His eyes came back to mine. 'But they took everything. Including those gold-mine stocks. All of them. There's absolutely nothing left. The envelope I told you about, Moreton Frewen's envelope, went with everything else.' His stare was burning into me now, his eyes white, his face drained. 'What the hell could anyone have wanted that envelope for?'

CHAPTER 7

I stayed at the St Regis in New York. It's on Fifth Avenue, fairly high up to the right if you're looking at a map of mid-Manhattan, and therefore quite accessible to the big auctioneers, but not too far from what I still think of as the centre of events. The big auctioneers, in case you didn't know, are further up and well over to the right, over to the east in places like York Avenue, where their overheads are not as high as their first, mistaken addresses. It makes them still convenient for the high-spending elite of upper Madison Avenue and all that crowd. Christerby's New York premises are up that way and, after I had checked in to the hotel, I headed in that direction. Life has to go on, despite its calamities, and I had left Andy Casey in Chicago after what I hoped was a suitably decent interval. He was very, very upset. I knew what was on his mind; my violent arrival, his break-in, and then Perkins's death. It was as though the fact of my involvement had dictated such events, but he didn't want to say that. Andy is a decent, responsible citizen, and if he thought that Perkins's murder could be traced back to our inquiries, in no matter how remote a way, he would take it very badly. I tried to reassure him with Maguire's comforting report. I also suggested that his break-in was quite unconnected. I could tell that he wanted to believe me, but that doubts nagged him. I left him making preparations to go to Perkins's funeral and tried to drop the whole thing from my mind. It doesn't do to dwell on these things at length; the mind constructs all sorts of horrid scenarios when prompted to wander its way down the avenues of imagination in circumstances like those.

Big auctioneers are addicted to impressive foyers in their buildings so that clients can throng there. Ours was no exception. I say ours because, despite my principal allegiance to the Bank, I am a director of Christerby's and have a certain feeling of belonging, which made the deference I was greeted with by the foyer receptionist all the more enjoyable.

'Mr Simpson, sir? Welcome back to New York. It's nice to see you again. How are you?'

'Well, thank you.' That marked me as a foreigner, for a start. An American would have said good, thank you, with that strange love of ungrammatical usage that they have.

'Fine. Mr Carlton is expecting you. Please go right up.'

Alexander Carlton's office is above the foyer, on the first floor. You can take the lift or, like me, stride up a fairly wide staircase, with beige marble treads, to a carpeted landing. His secretary, in an ante-room, was already standing up and moving to greet me by shaking hands in a way that few English secretaries ever would. She was very attractive, so that an excuse to clasp her hand was all the more welcome. She smiled at me quite fondly, I thought.

'Hi! Mr Simpson. How are you?'

'I'm well, thank you. How are you?'

'Good, thank you, good. Alexander is expecting you. Would you like some coffee?'

'Love some.'

'Fine. I'll bring it right in after you.'

There's something about a warm welcome from an attractive woman that puts the Simpson constitution into a eupeptic state, so I tripped lightly through the next office door on lilting feet only to get a mild shock.

''Morning, Tim.' Harry Howarth's matter-of-fact, brass-tacks voice had an amused ring to it as he stood up from a chair in front of Alexander Carlton's desk. He swung round to greet me and grinned, a sturdy, grey-blocked figure which contrasted with the thinner, ascetic look of Carlton, who had also risen to come round his desk and greet me. 'Didn't expect to see me here, did you? I told Alex we'd give you a start when you got here. Now you see me, now you don't, hey?'

I recovered my poise and shook hands with his firm grasp. 'What a surprise. A pleasant surprise, I must say. Hello, Harry. Hello, Alex. How are you both? This is an unexpected pleasure.'

Howarth chuckled. 'I came over two days ago. Not by Concorde, if you're thinking what you bankers normally think. I don't believe in lashing out too much money on air fares. Business class is quite good enough for me. But things are moving here and we need to get on, so I came over. Ah, here comes coffee. You're looking well, Tim, and—good grief! What on earth have you done to your face? You've not been back on the rugger field, have you?'

I put a hand to the right side of my jaw, which, as I had turned to shake hands, must have come into stronger light. It wasn't really painful any more, nor was it swollen now, but I knew that there was still a fading, bluish-yellow mark, quite large, on the lower side, against the bone. Carlton, Howarth and the secretary all clustered round me and stared at it in embarrassing concern.

'What happened to you?'

'Do you need any treatment? Can I get you something?'

The secretary was proving to be more and more attractive. 'We have medication in the furniture hall where the porters sometimes—'

'No, no.' I waved my hands about. 'You're very kind. Thank you, it's perfectly OK. It's all over now. I had a brush with some muggers.'

'Muggers?' they chorused in horror, as though the States almost never, indeed very rarely, experienced such dreadful things. 'Were you badly hurt? Did they steal everything?'

'No.' I gestured at my briefcase. 'They tried to take my luggage. At Chicago airport. But they didn't get anything. It's all intact.'

'But you had to let them take something? Wallet? Watch?'

'Er, no. No, I didn't.'

'You mean—' the secretary's voice went into a thrilled, awestruck tone—'you resisted them? You fought them?'

'Um, yes. I'm afraid I'm a bit possessive about my kit. Unwise, perhaps. But I did.'

'But what happened? How many were there?' She was wide-eyed now; very flattering it was.

'Three. I had a bit of luck, actually. A chance right hook hit the bullseye and laid one out. Only one of the other two was up to much and I managed to do for him. Touch and go, but I was lucky.'

'But weren't they armed?' Her mouth was open.

'No. Not really. Well, a knife. Managed to avoid that.'

'And you—you *dealt with* all three of them.'

'Er, yes. More or less. The police arrived eventually.'

Howarth suddenly burst into a roar of laughter and clapped me on the back, gripping my shoulder in what seemed like affection. 'Fantastic! Tim, you mad dog! I might have guessed! Of all the men a mugger should leave alone, Simpson must be number one. What a useful citizen! Not a document lost! Eh, Alex? What did I tell you? He was one of the most aggressive forwards the game ever saw. That's our boy! Eh?'

Carlton smiled rather thinly and took off his gold-rimmed spectacles. 'Extraordinary. I must say it is unusual. To be honest, Tim, it was very foolhardy to do that. Resist, I mean. It is very dangerous. Most of these muggers are very, very violent. They'll kill you. Without a thought. The standard advice to everyone is to give them just what they want. If you hold things up, delay them I mean, they get psychotic. Really awful. Please don't do anything like that if it happens here in New York, please. They have guns. They'll shoot you dead, for sure.'

'Ah. Er, yes. I'm sure you're right. But still, it won't happen here, will it? I mean, I'll stick to a safe tack here.'

'Good. I'd feel terrible if I hadn't warned you.' Carlton

replaced his glasses and smiled with more warmth. 'We need you on our side, Tim. Hate to have anything happen to you while you're here. Let's have that coffee.'

The secretary was still looking at me with pure adulation. I'd forgotten that America, a violent place, still tends to over-admire the man who can defend himself with aggression. She was a brunette, about thirty, with a mature ripeness that made me suddenly conscious that I'd been away from Sue for several days and had been working hard, concentrating on facts and figures, quite apart from the other incidents in Chicago. I pulled myself together and managed not to leer at her too lustfully as she took the coffee from Howarth and insisted on serving me herself. We sat down round a low table in one corner of the office and the secretary left, swaying out to give a rear view that brought an even stronger pang of desire before the door closed.

'So how's it going?' Howarth was nothing if not straight to the point. 'Is it thumbs up or down for Chicago?'

I smiled carefully. 'I haven't got all the facts yet. Andy Casey and I have gone through a great deal of material and considerable analysis. I need information from you, now.'

'Really?' Howarth glanced at Carlton. 'What sort of information?'

I explained to them carefully how the assessment we were doing was calculated, and what sort of information had to be built into our model before we could run final analyses. What I particularly wanted was the source of current business by geographical area, if that was possible, and an assessment from each of their specialists on how much business in each category was volatile in the geographical sense. Would the business move or not if offered a Chicago facility, how much was prestige, New York-only business; things like that. Howarth rubbed his hands together vigorously when I finished.

'This is excellent! Excellent! Alex, can you dig out the info that Tim needs?'

'I should think so.' Carlton was cautious, reserved, keeping to his precise persona, the one that seemed more like a cost-and-works accountant than an auctioneer and art expert. 'It may take a little time to dig out, of course, but we'll do our best. And you're welcome to talk to our specialists. How long will you need?'

I put my coffee down carefully. 'Er, hang on a moment. This idea of opening in Chicago is your idea, Christerby's idea, I mean. You must surely have done some assessments yourselves? You must have some facts and estimates prepared already? I mean, my work is for White's, really. As a sort of back-up.'

Carlton gave one of his thin, wry smiles and looked deliberately at Howarth, who had started to grin like a Cheshire cat. 'I can't say that we have, Tim.' He let his voice go humorous. 'It's our idea of course, and we're serious about it. But there's no point in keeping a dog and barking yourself, is there? Sorry for the analogy, but I said to Alex that as soon as we moot the idea and Tim reports it to Jeremy White, we'll have White's best man clambering all over the place to check the idea. So why use up our own valuable resources? There's no one in Christerby's who'll do a better objective assessment than one of their experts, never mind what our gut feeling is. We'll get a professional analysis to check it out. And so it was; we got White's best man: Tim Simpson.' He grinned at me wolfishly. 'More coffee?'

'You—you fiend. You cunning, devious, good-for-nothing, property-dealing, advertising, PR-flannelling so-and-so!'

'Ha, ha!' He was laughing genuinely, with pure pleasure. 'You flatter me! I'm glad I've got your admiration. Words like that from Tim Simpson are gold, Alex, pure gold—which reminds me: how did the Frewen thing go? Another Klondike?' He poured out coffee with zestful enjoyment.

I shook my head sadly. 'I'm afraid not. Things didn't turn out so well.'

'Why not?'

I told them what had happened, not bothering with a long account of Frewen's cattle dealings, but giving a short version of old Victor Perkins's fate. It seemed to affect them almost as much as it did me. Telling someone else about it for the first time like that made me realize just how the murder had upset my visit to Chicago. I hadn't known Perkins, but I felt a dreadful sense of loss; I'd been looking forward to seeing him, quite apart from the thrill of holding those shares and their envelope, the historical link.

'How bloody awful,' Howarth said. 'Ghastly. Jesus! You have had a bad time, Tim. My dear chap. You must be upset. How did Andy Casey take it?'

'Very badly, I'm afraid. He somehow felt responsible.'

'Oh no. It can't have been any fault of his. But how dreadful. Appalling. That sort of thing makes you feel sick.'

'It does.' Carlton showed, if anything, even more concern. 'I'm afraid that life in big cities is becoming increasingly dangerous. The violence is horrifying. I hate it.' He shook his head sadly. 'And the documents are completely lost?'

'Yes. All gone. There's no sign of them.'

'How futile. Were they valuable?'

'We're not sure. Andy's trying to find out. He's going to phone me.'

'What a pity. I was quite looking forward to hearing all about them. Harry got me quite interested in this man Frewen. After all, we are in what was once his father-in-law's city. But that interest of mine pales before a tragedy of this sort.'

'I don't understand, sorry. His father-in-law?'

'Leonard Jerome. Didn't you know? He was King of Wall Street for a long spell. A fantastic man. Had a huge house on Madison Square with a private opera house attached to it. He was one of those larger-than-life characters.' Carlton smiled meaningfully. 'Jerome was keen on opera and its singers. Jenny Lind—he named his daughter after her—Patti, Fanny Ronalds, all those. He was a great yachtsman, too. Up at Newport, Rhode Island. Backed those cross-Atlantic races between British and American yachts before the America's Cup existed. That's how the family came to be at Cowes in the Isle of Wight. If Jerome hadn't been keen on yachting, Lord Randolph wouldn't have met Jennie. And then there would have been no Winston. Americans love that kind of story, Tim.'

'We're not unattracted to that kind of story ourselves. So Moreton Frewen must have been here a lot?'

'You bet. He knew all Jerome's contacts—Lorillard, Belmont, the Roosveldts—not that he didn't meet them in England, too. Frewen must have been well in with the top four hundred. Jerome lost a lot of money in his later years, but he was devoted to his daughters. He died in England, you know. Brighton.'

I spilled coffee into my saucer and on to the table as I gave an involuntary jerk. They sprang to mop up.

'What's the matter? Are you all right?'

'Sorry. Stupid of me. Just a bad reflex. It's nothing.' I tried to hide my fluster. 'Caught my arm the wrong way.'

To those of you who don't know, Brighton has figured only too prominently in a number of unpleasant episodes in my past.* Mention of the place is enough to cause the Simpson reflexes to jerk spasmodically. If any investigation, project, or art purchase features Brighton on its itinerary, I bridle like a horse confronted by a whistling loco. The very remote fact that Leonard Jerome died in Brighton was enough to give me severe palpitations about the whole Frewen–Jerome involvement. It was with relief that I found that the interruption had turned their minds back to the Chicago auction venture again and we started to work out

---

* *The Godwin Sideboard.*

a programme with names, timing and soothing professional routine. At the end of our meeting Howarth took me out for a very respectable lunch; Carlton excused himself on the grounds of work but, in fact, New Yorkers these days don't go in for business lunches much, nor for mid-day drinking, so I guessed that his rather spare frame eschewed such luxuries as a matter of principle. Howarth, however, was in robust form and did his food full justice.

'I hope you don't feel too aggrieved about my little subterfuge,' he said almost apologetically over coffee. 'Quite honestly, Tim, Christerby's haven't got the resources to do a proper assessment and I'd have had to call in consultants. Doing it this way we got something much better.'

'Flatterer.'

He smiled. 'Alex is a good man for our purposes but he's a bit light on that sort of business experience. What do you think of him?'

'He seems OK.' Caution lights flashed in my brain; I wasn't sure what Howarth was fishing for. 'He's an art expert, which helps, and he's very international. He can attract business and he understands the working of the markets. The accountants can support him from an internal, cost-catching point of view. He's a bit cold, perhaps. Why?'

'Oh, nothing. Just value your judgement. I agree with you on the whole. I think he can run New York for us, providing we back him up well. Which means provided I back him up well. Fortunately, thanks to Charles, London is looking after itself pretty well. What I'm not sure of is whether Alex can look after a country-wide organization here in the States. That might need a different animal.'

'Ah, I see. I'm not sure about that. I'd have to know him a bit more. People very often grow into jobs like that, Harry.'

'That's a consultant's answer.' He grinned. 'A merchant banker would shoot from the shoulder and say yes or no.'

I scowled at him. 'Merchant banking isn't about the

pheasant-shooting landed gentry any more. It's a modern business.'

He banged the table. 'Well answered! Actually, I agree. I'll talk to you about it again sometime, if I may. We have to get on, right now.'

He stood up and I got a full view of him, stocky, stalwart, all-of-a-piece, with his Lancashire name and his Lancashire manner that seemed odd in an ex-property and advertising man running a fine art auctioneers, but which fitted the role very well. It occurred to me that he and Jeremy would probably get on together splendidly if they didn't clash too much in these early days. They were both forthright, uncomplicated in their strange ways, so that you knew where you were with them. We parted genially.

It was a warm autumn in New York. The buildings there seem to stoke up heat during the summer and retain it, which makes the later part of the year much warmer than you get in London. I spent the next two days in and out of Christerby's New York rooms, working fairly hard. A couple of phone calls had me checking that Sue was all right; she was. It was one evening that the call I had rather been dreading came through, while I was working in my room at the hotel, with papers strewn all around me.

'Tim? Hi. Andy Casey.' His voice wasn't taut but it wasn't really relaxed either.

'Hello, Andy. What news?

'We've got nothing on the burglary. Not yet. I've asked Tom Maguire if he'll keep an eye out for me.' There was a silence. 'One of the advantages of having connections is that you can sometimes get an inside line on things.'

'Of course. What about the Frewen gold connection?'

There was a sigh. 'Jesus, Tim. You wouldn't believe the difficulties. Frewen was all over. I've had one of our researchers working full time. I feel I owe it to Perkins. My people have even been to the Frewen papers at the Library of Congress.'

'The what?'

'The Moreton Frewen papers in the Library of Congress. Didn't you know? That guy got into everything. He knew every President personally from Hayes to Wilson. But never mind that; I've traced his involvement in the Eureka—that's the Centennial Eureka at Cane Springs, Utah—then the Lewiston at Colorado Springs, and then there was Cripple Creek and, later, the Oroville Dredging—'

'Hey! Hang on! Hang on, Andy. Slow down. Were these the ones that Perkins had?'

'No—well, I'm not sure—but we may have some luck there. Frank Perkins, the son, says that his father sent the list of shares to a specialist to see whether any of the mines is still in production or worth anything. We're going to trace them that way. But I've been getting all this research done because I want to satisfy myself on all this. I need to check out all this Frewen gold involvement. I want to know about it. Really know.'

'Andy,' I said, as gently as I could, 'isn't this going a bit far? Shouldn't you wait until the police do their work? What does Tom Maguire say?'

'Oh, he says that all these different events are pure coincidence.' Andy's voice was impatient. 'That's hogwash, Tim. I know it is. Damn it, I know there's more to this than just coincidence. I know it! Someone rifled my office, tried to get your papers, killed old Perkins. It can't all just be coincidence. There's a connecting link.' His voice rose. 'My belief is that Frewen has something to do with it.'

'Hey, Andy! Take it easy. This is me, Tim, remember? You're starting to sound obsessive. Aren't you reading a bit too much into it all?'

There was a moment's hesitation. 'I—I don't think so. I know Tom Maguire doesn't agree with me. But what about you? You must have had the same thought, Tim, with your experience? Haven't you thought about it? What do you think?'

His voice was sharp. He was coming out with it at last, it was taking an emotional effort, but he was putting into words the things I knew he had avoided saying to my face in Chicago. Of course I'd thought through the same things. I shook my head as I thought of Leonard Jerome and Brighton, such an ominous pointer, and shivered a superstitious shiver.

'I've thought about it, Andy, but I can't possibly explain it. Life can't be like that. How did anyone know I was coming, for instance?'

'They broke into my office the night before you arrived. I had notes of your flight. I had Perkins's address. They could take it all from there.'

'It's fantastic. I don't see what there was to gain. I mean I had nothing in my documents to help anyone. I just don't believe that there can be a connection.'

'I do.' His voice was flat, hard. 'Someone wanted those gold shares, Tim. For some reason we don't know about.'

'Then why attack me? If they'd broken into your office, they knew I hadn't got them.'

His voice went down to a mutter. 'That's what Maguire says. Exactly the same. I'll test that theory somehow. I'll test it.'

'Andy! For heaven's sake! Leave it to the cops.'

'You're a fine one to talk. You never would. Not if it was your client. Not if you felt responsible.'

That silenced me. I held the phone without speaking until he came back to me again, his voice more conciliatory in tone. 'Look, Tim, I guess I'm kind of wound up over this. I'll call you again soon. Keep me posted on your movements. All right?'

'All right, Andy. Try no to dwell on it. And for heaven's sake let the police deal with it.'

He rang off. I sat in my hotel room and smiled a wry smile at my advice to him, advice I'd never taken myself. I hoped he wouldn't upset Maguire in the way that I have upset Nobby Roberts, my old Scotland Yard friend, in the past. Maguire might not be so tolerant; he and Andy might be involved with the same Catholic church, but that was hardly the same as having played rugger together, like Nobby and me, now was it? Work that one out, if you can.

Carlton was very cooperative for the next two days. I got all the facts I needed. From time to time he or Howarth would appear beside me, nod hopefully, and push off without interfering. I took taxis to and from my hotel and worked in my room at night. I didn't really have time to reflect that I was wasting the entire facilities for entertainment of the greatest city in the world for diversions; I had too much to do. Sue began to make noises on the telephone that indicated that now she had caught up with all her old girlfriends during my absence, and done the things that she claims my presence prevents her from doing, she was getting bored and it was time I was back. She did give instructions that I was to go to a couple of exhibitions in New York on her behalf and get catalogues; art catalogues, of course. I decided on the morning of the third day that I'd got all I needed for the moment; I could do the number-crunching back home. I told Carlton and Howarth that I would catch an evening flight back to London.

'Finished already? What's the verdict?'

'The jury is still out. I'll tell you the result after I've got back.'

'Infuriating fellow. After you've seen Jeremy, I suppose?'

'Of course.'

'Well, do your best for us.' Howarth looked serious. 'I'm more and more convinced that we must expand, and expand quickly.'

'I'll work as fast as I can.'

'What are you doing this afternoon?'

'Some shopping. Then I'm going to the Metropolitan.'

'Really? What to see?'

'I'm getting a catalogue for Sue. Then I'll look in on the

Rodin section. The Art Fund owns a terra-cotta by him of
Gwen John. The Met has some studies in plaster for the
Whistler memorial. One of them is unmistakably her. I
want to look at it. See how it compares.'

Carlton, standing next to Howarth, nodded. 'I remember
them. I'm sure you're right. Is that your full programme,
then?'

'That and the Whitney. I'm under orders to see that.'

'Ah, the Whitney.' He gave me a long, owlish stare. 'An
excellent exhibition. Is that a particular interest?'

'Well, yes, but mainly to Sue. She wants the catalogue.'

He nodded again. 'It's a good one. Lots of detail. Well,
I'm sure we'll be in touch.'

'When will you be in England again?'

He gave me a rather surprised look and glanced quickly
at Howarth. 'For the next board meeting, without doubt.
Assuming, that is, that we'll have your report and be taking
a decision to go ahead on Chicago?'

CHAPTER 8

I was up and dressed before she was, rooting myself out a
reasonable breakfast and setting it, together with her coffee,
on the table next to the long window that overlooks Onslow
Gardens. The autumn sun had the gardens all lit up with
amber and rust above the green grass across the road,
making me feel glad to be back for the time of year that is
London's very best. I had spent the day before at the Bank,
because modern flights get into Heathrow in the morning
and Sue had already gone to the Tate when I got clear of
the airport. Jeremy was away at a conference of brokers for
the day, so I'd worked undisturbed until evening, when I
returned to take Sue out to a trattoria round the corner
before an early night. She came out of the bedroom wearing

my thick white towelling robe wrapped round her, freshly showered she was, slightly tousled and healthy and delicious to look at above her bare feet and slender ankles. It gave me a pang of regret that I'd bothered to get up and get dressed.

'I think I can safely say,' she said, throwing her head back in a grandly masculine gesture as she sat down to her coffee with a nod of approval, so that I knew she was letting me have a quote, not a statement of her own, 'that without a single exception, the partners of my pleasure have either been charmed by my evident superiority or completely paralysed by the vigour of my performance.'

I had a mouthful of tea in place at the time she said it, and it went down so skew that it nearly came back all over the table. When I had finished coughing and spluttering I looked up to see her shrewd blue eyes resting on me sardonically and meaningfully with that mockery that women nowadays show for a man's conceit.

'Sue, really!' I heaved another painful cough and wiped my mouth. 'Really! I don't think that I have ever—I mean —I'm sure, not even when thoroughly plastered, have I ever uttered such a—a—'

'Chauvinistic?' She smiled sweetly.

'Well, yes, but not so much chauvinistic perhaps, but such a—a—self-satisfied—I—well—paralysed is hardly the word I would have—'

'You didn't.'

'Eh?'

'You didn't. Say it. I wasn't quoting you.' She smiled at my discomfiture. Women can be like that, especially after a night of—of—no, I won't risk saying it.

'You weren't?'

'No. I wasn't.'

Relief flooded through me. Tim Simpson may have his faults but, despite an attraction to the ladies, he doesn't say things it wouldn't be gallant to . . . Well, there may have

been times when I've felt a bit, what, *pleased* with events
perhaps, but I wouldn't, I mean, I really wouldn't . . . I
gaped at her.

'Then who the hell did? Where on earth did you get a
statement like that from? Eh?'

'Moreton Frewen.'

'What?'

She lifted her coffee cup, utterly composed. 'You mean
who. Moreton Frewen. He wrote it in his diary in later life.
He was a real Victorian hunting man of the old school. I
rather think he felt that the ladies were in luck when he was
about.'

'Men should never keep diaries. They—Hey! Wait a
minute! What do you mean? How the hell—how have you
been reading Moreton Frewen's diary?'

She shook her head as she buttered a piece of toast. 'I
haven't. Been reading his diary. Or diaries. I have been
reading Anita Leslie. Boning up on Moreton Frewen. I have
read—'

'Oh no! Now look here, Sue—'

'I have read—' she put down the toast and began ticking
them off on her fingers—'Anita Leslie's book, *Mr Frewen of
England*, which is straight biography. I have read *The Fabulous Leonard Jerome*, he was the father-in-law, then *Jennie*,
then *My Cousin Clare*—she was Moreton Frewen's daughter,
Clare Sheridan, quite a life that was, Charlie Chaplin and
Trotsky and F. E. Smith, you name them, the quote came
from that one—then I read *Edwardians in Love* and then—'

'Sue! Stop it! Stop it at once!'

'Then I read Ralph Martin's *Lady Randolph Churchill*—
my goodness, those Society beauties didn't half have a life,
Tim, she was Jennie Jerome, you know, Winston's mother,
she had a succession of—'

'I know! I know! For Christ's sake! I know who Jennie
Jerome was! I—'

'What on earth is the matter with you?' She bit a piece

of toast off very crisply and cocked her head on one side. 'You look quite congested. Not at all as relaxed as you were when you got up. What's wrong?'

I ground my napkin up into a ball on the table. 'You know very well what's wrong! You're—you're getting involved, damn it!'

'Why? Shouldn't I? Don't you want me to help?'

There was a look of casual unconcern about her, a gentle interest only, as though the question was totally unimportant. I recognized it. Pure gelignite. Absolutely lethal peril. I knew that look too well. This was thin ice, rapid quicksand, hot coals, the Niagaran tightrope, walking across the greenhouse roof in hob-nailed boots. Very light treading was called for.

'Um, no, of course, I mean, any assistance is always gratefully received. Most appreciated. It's just that I—well —I wouldn't like you to, er, to waste your time, that's all. Knowing how busy you are, and all that.'

She smiled. Prickles went down the back of my neck. 'Dear Tim. So considerate. Surely you should know that a woman's greatest pleasure is to help the man of her dreams?'

'Oh my God.' I put my head in my hands. This was going to be much worse than expected.

'I mean, it surely must be helpful to get to know one's subject in detail? Like Moreton Frewen and his contacts? The fact that he was one of Lillie Langtry's earliest beaux? The question of those gold shares? I know they're only of marginal importance to you and Andy Casey, but he is an old friend, isn't he?'

'Yes, Sue.'

'And you'd like to help him?'

'Yes, Sue.'

'And the story of Frewen's gold-crusher, for instance; that might be relevant?'

'Yes, Sue.'

'You knew about the gold-crusher?'

'Yes, Sue.'

'And the other mining ventures?'

'I—er—well, some of them.'

'They could be relevant?'

'Yes, Sue.'

'And I mean there's no harm, is there, in my reading up a lot of harmless old books while you're away, just in case something useful might turn up, just to help you? To pass the long hours of your absence?'

'No, Sue.'

'And I mean it's not as though there's any danger, is there, like there was with the Whistler or the Norman Shaw thing this year, nothing criminal or violent or anything?'

'No, Sue.' I shot a hopeless glance out of the window. The punch was coming from a mile back, I knew it, there was nothing to stop it, nothing.

'In that case—' her teeth flashed now, as she slapped her cup back into the saucer and leant across the table with her beautiful blue eyes narrowed into scowling slits—'why are you so upset about my interest? Why? More important, why is there the trace of a substantial bruise on the right side of your face, across most of the lower jaw? Why?'

'Oh.' I involuntarily put a hand to the place where the lumberjacket had belted me one. Morning sunlight is so much more revealing than evening lamplight. 'Oh, that. Oh, nothing. Just an accident.'

'Really? An accident? Don't tell me: you ran into a bus?'

'No.'

'You took on Marvin Hagler?'

'No. Now look—'

'Witherspoon?'

'Sue. This is quite—'

'Someone's husband caught you?'

'Sue, really! That's in poor taste!'

Her mouth drew into a humorous line. 'All right. I'll

withdraw that. I won't withdraw the suspicion of criminal violence.' She held up a finger. 'Don't speak! I know you, Tim Simpson. I know you. I knew when you left Donald White's. I knew it. I could feel it in my bones. There's going to be trouble over this, I thought, big trouble. There you were with that look on your face, all innocent and eager and wide-eyed, while Donald warned you. Just like a little boy. It sent a chill right through me. There's another one coming, I thought, another nasty violent chase after something long dead, something that should stay dead and buried, but he won't leave it, not Tim, that's not my Tim, assuming he is my Tim. He couldn't. And you know what I've told you before; either I'm part of it and I join in and help you and keep you out of more trouble than you'll get into on your own, let alone with other women, or I'm leaving. Right now. So make up your mind. There has been trouble, hasn't there?'

'Jesus Christ. I got mugged at the airport. Just an attempted mugging. So stop behaving like something from an Italian opera.'

'Pah!'

'I have to go to work. To the office. I'm going now.'

'You certainly are not! Not until you've told me!'

'There is nothing to tell.'

'Pah! Come on: cough it up.'

There's nothing you can do with Sue when she's in one of these moods. Absolutely nothing. She has that teacher-type quality that makes you feel like a recalcitrant prep-schoolboy caught with a large sticky toffee in the side of his mouth during a lesson on Religious Practice. You're never quite sure whether you've got a chance of surreptitiously swallowing the evidence or whether you'll have to bring it out on to the table top, all gooey and slimy and utterly disgusting. Either way, you know you're not going to get away with it. I stared gloomily at the charming cleavage where my bath robe had fallen open at the neck as she leant at me over the breakfast table. She sat quickly back and pulled the lapels tight up to her throat.

'That's enough of that! Come on—speak up! What happened?'

I sighed, replenished my tea and gave her a steady synopsis of everything that had taken place in Chicago, keeping it fairly brief. At the end of it I realized she was sitting absolutely still, with her eyes closed.

'Dear God,' she said.

'I'll get you some more coffee if you like.'

'No.' She held up her hand. 'Not yet. This is terrible. Much worse than I'd imagined.'

'Oh, come on, Sue.'

'Is there nothing—absolutely nothing—that you can do to avoid this sort of thing?'

'Sue, really.'

'I mean, could you not have let them have your case? No —no, I'm sorry. Of course you couldn't. They'd have—it wouldn't have made any difference. And that poor man. Thank God I wasn't there this time.'

'Yes.'

'Tim, you can't really believe that the mugging at the airport and the break-in at Andy's and the murder of that poor man weren't all connected?'

'Oh, come on, Sue, for heaven's sake! They might be, but they might not.'

'Pah! Of course they were. And the gold-mine shares have all gone?'

'It seems like it.'

'Who did you tell that you were going to see Andy about those shares before you left?'

'What, here? In England?'

Her mouth puckered. 'Yes, here. In England.'

'Look, Sue, everything that has happened has happened in America. It has nothing to do with people here. Nothing. There's no reason.'

'Then why did they go for you? You specifically. As soon as you got off the plane? Why?'

She was voicing suspicions I'd already had, suspicions I'd pushed to the back of my mind as unwelcome and disturbing. There was no future in that line of thought.

'If they knew Andy had asked me for information then they'd naturally be in wait for me. I'm sure the source of it all is in the States, Sue. Not here in England.'

She tapped the side of her cup impatiently with a tea-spoon. 'Who?'

I sighed. 'Jeremy, of course. One or two people at the Bank. The board of Christerby's. Donald. More than a few people at his party, who were listening.'

'That's hopeless! You might just as well have put a megaphone at the top of Bishopsgate and let the entire City of London know. Really, Tim!'

I felt my hackles rising. I'd had enough of this. There are limits to what I'll take. I leant forward over the table. 'There was no reason to be furtive about it, you know. It was all quite open and above board. I've had enough of this guilt-transference bit. A man owned some old shares, had good title to them, and wanted a bit of information about a previous owner, long dead. There was no breach of confiden-tiality. None. There's no need to act as though I'd broken the Offical Secrets Act, damn it.' I got up suddenly. I needed air. 'I did nothing to attract violence that could possibly have been foreseen! You sit there all bloody smug and I-told-you-so as though you or anyone else could have made the slightest difference! Or behaved differently.'

'All right, all right! Don't shout at me.'

'I will shout at you! I'm fed up with this! It'll be bad enough having Jeremy put on his Scottish-Elder-of-the Kirk expression of woe when I get to the Bank today without having you take me through a set of preliminary accusations. I thought you were on my side.'

'Tim! I am! Oh, I am! Can't you see that?' She flung

herself upwards out of the chair and grabbed me as I turned angrily away. 'I'm trying to help. Please, Tim; you came home last night and you didn't tell me anything. You weren't going to, either, were you? How can I help and be close to you if you won't tell me? I've had to wring it out of you.' Her mouth trembled slightly. 'You're not fair!'

'I don't want you in danger. I know—I've said I don't believe there's any part of it over here, it's an American thing, but I don't want any risk, any sort of risk at all. I don't want you involved, like before. It's been too dangerous, and I'm superstitious because of the mention of Brighton.'

She shook her head sadly and held me, a little less tightly, but not letting me go, putting her face close to mine so that I had to look at her right there, her breath smelling of coffee and her body of soap and damp towelling.

'You'll never learn, will you? I want to be with you and to look after you.'

'You? Look after me?'

'Yes. Me. Look after you. I have terrible fears about what might happen to you if I'm not there. You need a guardian angel, Tim. Try and think of me as that. Oh, of course I can't cope with violence or anything, but we work so well together and I—well—I can stop you rushing in where you shouldn't. No, don't look at me like that. You've had a lot of luck, Tim, a lot of luck. When I was away in Australia there was that woman and you got shot. One day, your luck'll run out. You're quick and strong and you never seem to be afraid; you've got such a temper when you're threatened, you don't seem to think of what could happen. I suppose that's what stops other people; they think of the danger and hesitate. If someone doesn't do that for you, one day it'll be too—Something dreadful will happen.'

How strange, I thought, her eyes have filled with tears and she's worried about me, as though I can't look after myself, when all the world knows it would be she who would be in danger. My friends would never forgive me if anything happened to her, never mind what I would feel. No one worries about me, I can handle myself, but my actions bring danger to her. How strange.

'I'm sorry, Sue.' I kissed her gently. 'Of course I know. I'm sorry. I'll tell you everything about this one, really I will. There won't be anything more to bother about over here, though. It'll be Andy Casey and the Chicago PD who'll bear the brunt this time. Really.'

She smiled uncertainly. 'I wish I could believe you.'

'It's true. Really it is. I must get to the Bank, Sue. I'm late already.'

She let go of me. 'Go carefully, Tim. Please go carefully.'

'Of course I will. Cheer up; we'll go out somewhere nice this evening, perhaps the theatre? What d'you say?'

'That would be great. But please, Tim, leave off chasing after any gold shares, will you?'

'Of course I will. And you can leave all those books on Moreton Frewen alone. We won't need any more information about Moreton Frewen. You can bet on that.'

CHAPTER 9

Jeremy White clasped his hands to his blond head in a dramatic gesture. It irritated me. I don't know if you've noticed, but people always behave with mock drama when you least want them to. Perhaps age is making me irascible, but I wasn't in the mood for another session on a cross-Atlantic view of events in Chicago, not after the one I'd had with Sue already that morning.

'My dear Tim! For the Good Lord's sake! Can *nothing* be done to—to—'

'Keep me out of trouble?'

'Precisely! Perfectly put. You go dashing about the world, barging into these situations with such predictable vigour.

Couldn't you possibly have managed, just for once, to avoid this sort of thing?'

'They tried to pinch my bags.'

'Why you? Eh? Why your bags? Why not someone else's bags? Can you answer me that?'

'No.'

'I mean, you can't treat a place like Chicago as though Al Capone was still running around, you know. Tim, this is nineteen eighty-six.'

'Jeremy—'

'It isn't as though you couldn't make an effort of some kind to be normal, respectable. Do you have to fly into airports with fists bunched, bashing out left, right and centre—'

'Jeremy,' I roared, standing up and shoving my face right into his, 'who was it that made me go to Chicago? Eh? I didn't bloody well want to go, but you insisted—yes, you—you made me go post-haste because of your typical desire to shove your nose into Christerby's business. Everything that happened happened because of you, not me!'

He sat back in his desk chair, startled, my face within inches of his, my body arched over his desk in a furious curve that stretched me so far that, fortunately, I couldn't reach any further. I'm very fond of Jeremy in many ways, but at that moment I could quite cheerfully have pasted him one.

'My dear Tim! There's no need to behave like this! Really! I make a mild criticism, the merest gentle reproof, suggest that you might take greater precautions, comport yourself more calmly, and you go right off the deep end! I sometimes wonder, you know, whether all these imbroglios you get into aren't having an effect. You're behaving like someone entirely *unhinged*.'

I opened my mouth, fairly wide, and then closed it again. Then I backed and sat down in the chair which I had just vacated, across the desk from him. We glared at each other unflinchingly. After a while he swallowed, opened his mouth, closed it and buzzed his secretary.

'We'd better have coffee,' he said. 'I'm not sure that you'd better not have a brandy with yours.'

I didn't answer. Words were quite useless.

'There's no need to sulk.'

'I am not sulking!'

'All right! All right. There's no need to shout, either. Coffee, thank you, yes.' He waited until his secretary left the room. 'You've absolutely terrified her. I've never seen her roll her eyes like that before.'

I managed to resist telling him that the eye-rolling had been in sympathy with me. Jeremy's secretaries know all too well what coping with him is like. He got up, went to his side-cabinet, got out two glasses, poured a liberal dose of Rémy Martin into each, handed me one and took a swig of his own just as his secretary came in and put down a tray of coffee. She gave us a significant second roll of her eyes and went out again. I drank a stimulating sip and felt a soothing fire purge through me.

'Brandy at eleven in the morning,' said Jeremy, suddenly cheerful. 'With coffee. Just like Spain? My Uncle Richard often had a split of champagne for his elevenses, you know. Said it was very good for you. I'm not sure I don't prefer a nip of brandy myself. Better for you.'

'Churchill thought so.'

'Ah, Churchill. And what of his uncle? The improvident Moreton Frewen?'

'Nothing new, really. Well, that's not quite true. Andy Casey knew quite a bit about him. From the cattle business. The Powder River ranch.'

'The what?' Jeremy was suddenly alert, coffee in one hand, glass in the other.

'The Powder River ranch. Where the Frewens ranched, in Wyoming.'

'Good God!' He nearly spilled his coffee. 'Of course! Hugh Lowther. The Yellow Earl!'

'What?'

'I'd completely forgotten. I heard that story at Eton.'

'What story?'

He stared at me. 'Haven't you read *The Yellow Earl* by Douglas Sutherland?'

'No, I can't say I have. What is it?'

'It's the story of Hugh Lowther, the Earl of Lonsdale. The boxer. You've heard of the Lonsdale Belt?'

'Of course.'

'Well, that was Hugh Lowther. He was a pal of Frewen's. Risked his inheritance to put money into the Powder River Cattle Company. It's a glorious story. Lowther took his wife Grace with him when he went hunting with Frewen on the ranch. One day when they were out in the wilds shooting, someone told them that a dreadful bandit and horse thief, called Little Henry, had been seen heading for the ranch house, where they'd left Grace Lowther alone with a female companion. This Little Henry was a notorious murderer. Frewen and Lowther were horrified; they drew their guns and galloped the whole way back to Frewen Castle, as it was called. They found Little Henry sitting in the living-room, having tea with Grace Lowther.' Jeremy started to laugh. 'It turned out that he'd been at Eton with Hugh.'

'He was an Old Etonian?'

'Absolutely. He was shot dead later, by Bat Masterson, in Dodge City.' He chuckled. 'You should read that book. Lowther was good with his fists; he knocked out the odd cowboy here and there.' He straightened his face. 'Look, I'm sorry if I was a bit of a bore just now, Tim.'

'Of course you weren't. I'm sorry if I was a bit touchy. I had Sue on the subject earlier and it ruffled the feathers a bit.'

He smiled and put down his empty glass. 'Good. That's all over, then. Now, let's hear all about Christerby's. I suppose they've convinced you that Chicago is essential?'

'Not quite. Here, let's go through these figures.' I slapped a sheaf of papers on his desk. 'There's a few aspects we have to discuss before I finalize my report.'

That was it. With Jeremy the changes are abrupt, and rancour never exists. He expects vigorous action and he behaves vigorously himself. The worst thing you can do when handling Jeremy is to be weak; he discounts weak people entirely. What he likes is high fettle, high spirits, no compromise. As long as you retain your nerve you can always deal with Jeremy. We plunged into the figures I'd assembled and he was alarmingly positive; after a while I could tell he'd grasped the essentials completely. There were still some bits of the picture that needed more work and we agreed to meet again to finish the whole thing.

'Excellent,' he said. 'My congratulations to Andy, and this fellow Carlton. Seems to have been very helpful. I'm off to lunch; sorry, I can't join you. One last thing.' He gave me a careful look. 'There's nothing more to do on this gold shares business, is there?'

'Nothing, Jeremy.'

'I mean, I'm sorry for Andy. Nasty business. But we're not involved?'

'Not at all. I mean, I never met Perkins. Never saw the shares. Andy is the one who's landed with all that.'

He heaved a sigh of relief. 'Thank heavens. With you safely back here, there can't be any more repercussions. It's a matter for Chicago. Well, I'm off. Keep me posted if there's any more news.'

'Right.'

He strode out, head up, leaving me to collect my papers and trot back to my office. His secretary gave me a wink as I passed. The business of the Bank was going on all around me, normal and grave, as any financial institution likes to appear, remote from the fisticuffs of Chicago, the art barter of New York and the bustle of Bond Street. I decided to work through lunch, and was deeply immersed in various erudite computations when, early in the afternoon, Andy Casey called me from Chicago.

'Andy! Hello. How are you?'

'Those stocks were worthless.' His voice was clipped.

'What?' I reared up behind the phone like a startled giraffe.

'Those gold stocks of Perkins's. For the mines in Utah and Colorado and Dakota. A letter came in from the specialist he'd sent the list to. Frank, his son, phoned to tell me. I made him read the list out and you can bet I've had it checked. Every damn item on it.'

'Worthless?' A stab of hopeful delight went through me.

'Absolutely. The mines they all relate to have been worked out for years. Companies have been wound up or defunct in some way. They have no value as mine stocks.'

'None? Are you sure?'

'None. They're just paper, Tim. Printed paper. The specialist says they have low value as collector's items, too. As a documentary record, some college might like them. For maybe a thousand bucks. No more.' He sighed, a long, deep sigh that brought the weariness of his condition all the way down a few thousand miles of telephone line. 'Maybe the University in Laramie or somewhere might like them. I thought we had something there. Our researchers found that a guy called Wood of Mobil Oil donated a pile of Frewen's papers to the University in Laramie. It seems a lot of English and Scots upper crust first ranched Wyoming as well as Frewen. Moncrieffes, Wallops—Lord Portsmouth —there were quite a crowd. But that's just history. That's all we here at OMC came up with: History.' His voice sounded disgusted. 'I just can't believe it. That people would murder poor old Perkins for worthless paper. I just can't believe it; it doesn't make sense.'

I spoke back cautiously, because I wanted to break out into a shriek of joy, but Andy was still upset and I felt for him, felt sorry for his distress because it's a situation I've found myself in before and it hurt me to see Andy in the same state. 'At least we had the luck that Perkins had put a specialist on to the shares before he was murdered and they were stolen. We might have gone on guessing for ever.'

'True. We have to be glad about that.' He sounded about as glad as the last man to cross the line in the Derby. 'I just can't accept it. It's so meaningless. So random.'

'What does Maguire say, now?'

'He says it confirms what they thought. That there was no connection between your attack, our break-in and Perkins's death. The murder is just another statistic to them. I can understand that. Maguire says if you knew what some of these crooks murder for, you wouldn't be sceptical. They murder for anything, for the hope of a few bucks. Well, he's a policeman. I don't believe it this time.'

'Andy, come on; don't let it get to you. It was a terrible thing, an awful thing, but it was one of those violent events you read about every day. It doesn't make it any better or more acceptable, but that's the way these things go.'

'I just can't accept it.' His voice was dogged. 'I'm not going to let it rest.'

'Now you're following a bad example. A very bad example.'

'Yours.'

'Exactly. It'll do you no good. Go home; go and play golf; try to leave the office for a day and get over it a bit. There's nothing you can do. It's over. It's another burglary murder statistic. Leave it to the police. Please?'

There was silence for a moment. 'I hear you, Tim. I hear you. But I'm not convinced. I'll give you a call in a day or two. OK?'

'OK. But please try to relax. The police will deal with it. One way or the other.'

He put the phone down. I didn't exactly dance round the office, because it isn't big enough, but I did leap to my feet and caper round my desk in unholy joy. Pure, unadulterated joy. There was no connection with me; the gold shares were worthless; it wasn't worth any planned, coordinated series of attacks; it was all random, unconnected. I pranced out and got two theatre tickets. I left a note on Jeremy's desk. I worked like lightning all afternoon and then I rushed out and bought a big bunch of flowers. Back at Onslow Gardens I presented the big bunch to Sue and hugged her delighted body to me to make up for the bad start to the morning. I swept her to the theatre and I took her to dinner. I laid it on with a trowel. There was music. There was atmosphere. We went to a night club. We drank champagne. We taxied back after two o'clock in a happy daze of romantic anticipation. I paid off the taxi and practically carried Sue up the stairs to the door of the flat, feeling her warm and soft and completely receptive in my arms.

The front door was open.

They had jemmied open the mortice lock with savage disregard for woodwork and paint. Splintered edges hung from the architrave.

They had gone through the flat like a whirlwind, opening, overturning, knocking down, wrenching apart.

They had left the paintings on the walls, the Clarkson Stanfield over the fireplace, the Seago and the Spencer Gore, the John etching of Dorelia, all the lady artists that Sue collects.

They had torn all the drawers open, the desk, the side cabinet, the newspaper rack. The kitchen looked as though a bomb had hit it and the bedroom looked as though it had taken the force of the blast.

They had pulled books out of the big bookcase on the wall, spilling them all over, hurling them, trampling them. There was one particular pile, separate from the rest, that Sue, cold and stiff and white, walked over to and knelt beside. It seemed as though the intruders had concentrated on that particular pile. They were shaken, ripped open, spreadeagled, hurled aside and re-scoured, as though the violator had been madly seeking some unimaginable inconceivable secret within them, contained on a slip of paper, a bookmark, a notation of some kind. Sue looked up from the pile. Her lips were thin and tight, like the voice that came from them.

'All these books are Anita Leslie's on the Frewens and the Jeromes. Don't tell me now—' her voice rose a pitch— 'don't tell me ever again, that this is all a coincidence. Pure coincidence. Only to do with America, you said? Nothing to do with you at all?'

CHAPTER 10

'Sporting, military and thespian specialities,' said Mr Goodston, smiling amiably at me over his half-moon spectacles. 'You know me, Mr Simpson.' He waved a plump arm in the direction of the dusty shelves around him, almost knocking over a teetering pile of books, one of several stacked on the desk in front of him. 'What is to be our pleasure this time?' His chair creaked as he sat back, revealing a stained and bulging checked waistcoat under his sagging corduroy jacket.

His Praed Street bookshop, just round the corner from Paddington Station, looks small when you go in, clogged with ranks and piles of gloomily subfusc bindings, only alleviated by the occasional bright jacket. Not much of Mr Goodston's stock is of recent origin. I rather suspect that he regards anything produced since 1945 as needing time to assess, like a port that has not been sufficiently mellowed. Only now and again does he have to accede to modern biography, memoirs of aged, retired generals and similar rather immature vintages. The shop is deceptive, because I happen to know that the floors above are also loaded with

ancient volumes, valuable many of them, carefully preserved
under lock and key, behind glass for the really rare ones,
not accessible to the public. I don't know why he has always
been so friendly to me, so helpful and encouraging. Perhaps
it is because the younger generation are not prominent
among his clients, particularly the collectors rather than
dealers, and he likes the idea, the concept of my building
up a collection over, say, the next forty years, in the manner
of nineteenth-century bibliophiles. He is a cautious, fat man
of great professionalism and wisdom, so in a sense he flatters
me by his encouragement. Perhaps that is part of his selling
style; pandering to one's conceit.

'It will be a thespian matter again, I suppose? Ellen Terry
perhaps, or did I provide you with sufficient material on
her and her, um, companion, Mr Godwin, the last time?'
He smiled a knowing smile. 'And Gordon Craig? I've
never really felt a permanent enthusiasm for the theatre in
you, Mr Simpson, though, I must say. It must be nearly a
couple of years since you seemed to be so keen on Ellen
Terry and her, um, associations. Is it something theatrical
this time?'

I grinned at him. He'd diverted me from the first question
I was going to ask and alerted me to something parallel, a
subject which might draw something of interest from him.

'Not really, Mr Goodston, unless, of course, you include
Lillie Langtry among your thespian treasures?'

His eyebrows shot up. His half-lights slipped a little
further down his nose. 'Lillie Langtry! Good heavens! Of
course I do. My goodness.' He waved his plump arm grandiloquently about him. 'The Jersey Lily. She is to be found,
I may say, ubiquitously among these shelves. She got about
a bit, Mr Simpson my dear young man, she got about a bit,
as they say, quite apart from her celebrated er, association
with his Royal, er, Majesty, Edward the Seventh.' He
chuckled rumbustiously. 'Sporting, military *and* thespian
specialities, ha-ha. She figures in all of 'em, my boy, all of

'em. My advice to you is to specialize. Otherwise you'll be buying up a major portion of my stock.'

'Come, come, Mr Goodston, that's a bit ungallant. As it happens, my interest is sporting, rather than military or thespian.'

'Understandable, sir, from a distinguished Rugby blue like yourself, but—'

'No, Mr Goodston. Not rugger. Hunting is my interest on this occasion. Fox-hunting. The Quorn, the Spottesmore, all that. Lillie Langtry was a, what shall I say, frequent guest at hunting parties. I have come to you as the oracle on the subject.'

He inclined his head gracefully. For all his other interests, I happen to know that Mr Goodston has a passion for fox-hunting memoirs, old racing books, legends of the Turf. Most of Mr Goodston's profits, if there are any, go into the betting shop across the road. He is a veteran punter. When Mr Goodston's shop is closed you know that there is a major meeting on somewhere, the jumps or the flat, it makes no difference. Mr Goodston is a racing man.

'Actually, what I came to ask you was a specific thing. A specific book. It's called *Melton Mowbray and Other Memories*. By a man called Moreton Frewen. Herbert Jenkins, 1924. You haven't got a copy, by any chance?'

There was a silence. Very slowly, he took off his half-lights and put them down on the desk in front of him. He sat forward and peered at me for a moment, giving rise to an uneasy feeling in me that I had asked for something forbidden, something accessible normally only to a secret coterie.

'Moreton Frewen,' he murmured. 'My goodness. Moreton Frewen.'

'It seems, Mr Goodston, that he was one of Lillie Langtry's earlier beaux. Among others. He and his future brother-in-law, John Leslie, took her riding in the Park.'

'Jack Leslie,' he corrected gently, almost absentmindedly. 'They called him Jack. Shy fellow, Irish baronet.

She fell off Frewen's park hack, Redskin, into Leslie's arms.' A smile came to his face. 'Part of her technique, they used to say. Falling into swoons, I mean. When a suitable gentleman's arms were available, of course. But good heavens! no one has asked me for a Frewen book for years. Not for years.'

'Do you have one?'

He gave me a reproachful glance. Picking up his comic spectacles, he put them on, hoisted himself to his feet and moved cautiously out from behind his desk. His bulk puttered along the shelves behind him and disappeared behind a sagging wall of loaded bookcases. The voice that came out from behind this bibliophilic screen was ruminative, philosophical, nostalgic.

'Melton Mowbray,' it said. 'Melton Mowbray. Jenkins. A green book, or rather, greeny-blue in the classic Herbert Jenkins design. Are you a reader of P. G. Wodehouse, Mr Simpson?'

'Of course. All true Englishmen are.'

'Then the book pattern will be familiar to you. Unmistakable Herbert Jenkins, long gone now, of course. Why, here we are. Melton Mowbray.'

He spoke the words lovingly, as though he were cutting keenly through the crispy crust of one of those renowned pork pies with a boiled egg in the centre, that carries the name of that celebrated hunting town. An eponymous pork pie, I thought humorously, of a type to which I am very much drawn. Mr Goodston, however, had emerged from his book-lined dug-out and was holding the volume under my nose, showing, sure enough, the well-known design with its black border line that any P. G. Wodehouse collector would instantly recognize. With a smile of triumph he opened it carefully, retaining it out of reach of my grasp, to show me a photograph of a party in hunting clothes standing posed outside the front door of a country house. 'A Hunting Party at Quenby Hall, Melton Mowbray,' he quoted, from the title under it. 'The tall, straight young man in white riding breeches on the right is Moreton Frewen. Next to him, seated, Lord Manners. On his left, seated, Mrs Langtry.' He smiled gently. 'Sporting, military, and thespian specialities. He introduced her to his future father-in-law in New York, you know. In the company of Oscar Wilde. Jerome was a connoisseur of fine women. Lent her his famous railway carriage to tour in. Frewen met her at Cheyenne and gave a party for her. A gala night.'

'People must have been very broad-minded in those days.'

He smiled secretly. 'Discreet. Discreet is the word you're looking for. The copy is fine. Yours for fifteen pounds.'

'Done.'

'Thank you kindly. Got all you need?'

'Oh yes. This will complete it, what with the Leslie books.'

He gave me a reproving stare. 'When you say you've read all the Leslie and Jerome and Churchill books, I take it that you mean you've got all the Anita Leslie ones?'

'Yes. Yes, that's it.'

'You didn't buy them from me.'

'No. Er, no. Sue, my girlfriend; she got them.'

'Humph. What about this then?' Triumphantly, he swept another small book into view, a hardback with a dust wrapper depicting a man in a bowler hat staring out directly under a title. '*The Splendid Pauper*,' he chirruped. 'Allen Andrews. It was Harrap over here but this is the Lippincott edition, New York, 1968. Have you read it? Have you got it?'

'No. No, I haven't.'

'This is good. Better, from your point of view. More detailed than Anita Leslie's; more factual. She was his great-niece, after all, so she was emotionally involved, and she was an Irish Leslie, so you tend to get quite a lot of the Irish aspect of things from her. Andrews is better on the business aspects; I'm sure you'll know that Ralph Martin, in his book on Lady Randolph Churchill, says as much.

Anita Leslie didn't bother with the detail of the businesses
so much. Being a woman she probably found them less
interesting, or maybe they were hard to grasp. She's very
readable, of course, a good writer, but not a modern bio-
grapher. Between the two of them, you'll get most of the
story, most of it that matters, anyway. Oddly enough, both
she and Andrews died last year, so you won't be able to
consult them.'

I nodded respectfully. 'I understand. I know she does go
on a bit about Ireland. It's a bit like Elizabeth Longford on
Wellington. Both she and Anita Leslie had a particular axe
to grind in that direction. We all tend to think of it as part
of the background, not relevant to the real story.'

He gave me a long, hard stare, holding the book firmly,
as though reluctant to hand it over to me. His eyes became
severe. 'My very dear young man, let me give you a piece
of advice before you jump to hasty conclusions on either of
those two lady authors. Whenever you are delving into the
past—or the present—history or situation of the British
Isles, never, but never, neglect what I call the Irish Dimension. Never. It is a fatal mistake.' He pushed his glasses
back up his nose and modified the stare, mellowing it down
a bit. 'Would you like me to tell you a story about Frewen,
to illustrate the point?'

I nodded as gracefully as my impatient urge to snatch the
book off him would allow. 'Please do.'

He beamed happily. 'Frewen's mother was Anglo-Irish,
a Homan from County Kildare. It may account for the fact
that her four sons were as wild as March hares. Frewen,
who was a Sussex Englishman, sat in Parliament as MP for
East Cork, but gave the seat back to Tim Healy. His nephew
Shane Leslie—' he pronounced it not as in the cowboy film,
Shane, but in the Irish way, Sean or Shawn—'Anita's father,
became a Catholic and espoused the Republican cause,
despite an Anglo-Irish baronet father and an American
Protestant mother, Leonie Jerome.'

'I see. A bit complicated—'

'I haven't finished yet.'

'Sorry.'

'Frewen's brother Stephen, the Lancer Colonel, had a daughter called Ruby. Moreton tried to get her to marry a rich Jewish man so that the wealth would bale out the family fortune, decimated by Moreton, and de-mortgage the family home, Brickwall in Sussex. Ruby refused and, when he hounded her, she married someone else.'

I realized I had been given a cue. 'Who?'

'Carson.'

'Carson? Sir Edward Carson? Wilde's prosecutor?'

'The very same. Carson of Ulster. So Carson had a double reason to distrust Frewen. There in the same family, you see, you have a bankrupt English gentleman with an Irish estate at Innishannon, near Cork; a Catholic convert Republican hereditary Irish baronet; and a rabid Ulster secessionist Protestant leader. A classic Irish triangle. Never neglect the Irish Dimension, dear sir, never. Do you follow my drift?'

'I do,' I said humbly. 'I do. Please may I see that book?'

'You may.' He handed it over. 'I would suggest that it is indispensable. It is in very good condition. It will cost you five pounds. *The Splendid Pauper*. The story of Moreton Frewen, by Allen Andrews.'

'Done.'

'Wise fellow.'

I held the book in front of me, barring his way for a moment. 'Tell me—why is it that you are so knowledgeable about Frewen? What prompted this encyclopædic interest?'

His eyes flicked slyly at me. 'You mock me, Mr Simpson.'

'No, no! I assure you. You quote chapter and verse, detailed family knowledge. How come?'

He smiled and took his glasses off again. A distant look came into his face. 'You're not a betting man? A gambler of any kind?'

'No. No, I'm not.'

'I thought not. Well, I'm sure you know that I am. I came across the name of Moreton Frewen many years ago, in a memoir of the famous jockey, Fred Archer. My historical interest in the Turf is long-seated, I regret to say.' He waved a hand about him. 'You see around you the accumulation of a lifetime's fruitless scholarship. A fruitless scholarship, but a happy one. Archer rode a horse called Hampton in the Doncaster Stakes of 1876. Friday the 13th of September. It was almost exactly one hundred and ten years ago. Frewen bet every spare penny he had on Hampton to win, having consulted Archer first. It's hard to understand how the English aristocracy gambled and how pointless their lives had become. Frewen knew it well. He had decided that if he won he'd take up an offer to be master of the Kilkenny hounds in Ireland. If not, he'd go to the West. The horse lost by a head. Frewen never reproached Archer or even batted an eyelid; he clapped the jockey on the back for riding a good race and left. My God, I thought then—this was before Leslie or Andrews wrote their books—a man who can lose that well has to have something sublime about him, even if it's lunacy. I read everything I could about him. There's something about his story, something fated and Greek-tragic about his luck, that rivets attention. He's a symbolic figure. He's the landed gentry's last throw of the dice, an heroic loser on a world scale. You can't help being attracted to him. He's the apotheosis of all we horse-gambling men who've lost forever, and he's more than that. Allen Andrews compares him to a Harold trying to stop the Norman Conquest, like a representative figure of an old doomed order, that in his case was the English Landed Gentry, especially its younger sons, trying to survive and prosper when their base of wealth had gone and their power was spent. Frewen tried to use the world and its resources to redress the losses of Sussex and Ireland and Leicester. He failed, but only just. By a whisker and not for want of courage. Terrific courage. Frewen is an example to all we poor timid half-hearted backers of today's gee-gees. This country will never turn out Moreton Frewens any more. Never again.'

There was a silence. I wasn't quite sure what to say. He turned away as I let him past. I'd never heard him speak like that before.

'I'm getting old and garrulous,' he muttered. 'Saying things like those to a strapping, brave young shaver like you. I'm sorry. You'll want an invoice for your books?'

'Yes, please.'

I waited in silence while he wrote it out and handed it to me in return for my cheque. His glance upward was shy and embarrassed.

'Thank you, Mr Simpson,' he said. 'I promise not to lecture you next time. If you come again.'

'I'll come again. And you can lecture me for as long as you like. It was fascinating.'

'Well—thank you. If it helps you in your pursuit of whatever it is that you seek, I am glad.' His eyes watched me curiously, begging an answer, a clarification.

'I'm sure it will. And to be honest, I'm not sure what it is that I'm looking for. Whatever it is, Moreton Frewen is a clue to it.'

He lowered his eyelids. 'Thank you. I wish you well in your researches. And may better luck attend you, whatever you do, than attended Moreton Frewen all the days of his life.'

CHAPTER 11

I got to the Tate Gallery just as they were closing. She was waiting for me in the entrance hall. She nodded to two black-uniformed porters who were closing in on me and they dropped respectfully into the background. She beckoned me towards the interior of the building, where lights were beginning to go out and autumn shades were suddenly jumping across high domed walls with pillars and cool marble around them.

'I came as soon as I got your message,' I said.

'You were out when I phoned.' Her voice wasn't accusatory but her eyes needed an explanation. 'You weren't at the Bank.'

'I was buying books. For our library.'

'Our library?'

'Yes. Books on Moreton Frewen. By Moreton Frewen. More comprehensive books.'

She compressed her lips, receiving the doubly unwelcome inference that Frewen was still an important unresolved subject and that the books she'd read so far were insufficient, with that carefully-revealed tolerance of men's clumsiness that is the hallmark of educated women.

'Follow me.' She made it a command.

I traipsed after her through the British Collection, starting with those splendid Elizabethan portraits of severe men and women in black, with white lace collars and ruffs, punctuated by the odd florid dandy or queen in red, yellow and green brocade. She turned right and headed through into the seventeenth century, then the eighteenth. Spiky chaps in breeches stared at me as they leant on their flintlocks. A couple of spotted dogs by Stubbs sneered at me.

'Where are we going?'

She didn't answer. She walked steadily ahead, carrying her satchel-handbag slung over her shoulder, the band cutting into the epaulette of her linen jacket a bit under the weight of whatever she'd got in the bag. Her ankles were very trim; I admired the rear view.

'Is it far?

Her heels rang on the parquet. Maritime battles slid past. John Singleton Copley's *Death of Major Pierson*, that great

Jersey skirmish, confronted me, its red-coated dying hero surrounded by stricken men.

'Copley was an American,' I said irrelevantly, as we flanked it and went round the back of it into the next gallery. A porter tacked out of the gloom, saw Sue, nodded respectfully and gave a curious glance in my direction. We marched on. Rows of Turners, sea-green to start with, followed by egg-yellow with red splashes, went gliding past. We were in the Duveen rooms. She stopped, pointed to a seat facing an end wall, a rather gloomy end wall, and then gestured.

'Sit there,' she said.

I sat obediently on the bench seat, quite comfortable it was, and looked at her expectantly.

'Don't look at me! Look at the paintings! What do you see?'

A huge gaffer in riding gear, wearing a top hat, peered down at me.

'Lord Ribblesdale,' I said. 'Vast, isn't it? Legs a mile long. There's a copy in the foyer of the Cavendish Hotel, you know. He was one of Rosa Lewis's favourites. After she'd been the family cook.'

She gave an impatient snort. 'What else?'

'Three other Sargents. That one with the children and the lanterns is called "Carnation, Lily, Lily, Rose". I remember that Sargent got so fed up with it that he called it Darnation, Silly, Silly Pose. Then there's that dim child. They're not nearly as good as the ones at the Whitney. They were in much better nick—ah! I've got it. You're going to re-hang the Sargents. That's why you made me go to the exhibition in New York. I must say that the collection at the Whitney was the best congregation of Sargents I've ever seen. Is that what this is about?'

'No.'

'What, then?'

'Can't you think? Doesn't it give you the faintest clue?'

I looked back at Lord Ribblesdale. He stared impassively towards me, an impeccable English milord in his riding kit and his black top hat. My neck began to get a crick in it. John S. Sargent painted on a large scale, with a lot of energy, for this kind of work. Lord Ribblesdale is enormous—the painting of him, I mean—stretching down a fair old expanse of wall.

'No. No, it doesn't.'

She made another gesture. It was like being in a school-room. I hate that sort of thing: tests, lessons, lectures. 'Try another tack. You're an educated man, or supposed to be. You love biography. What do you think of, when you think of Sargent portraits?'

'Society. High Society. He painted lots of 'em.'

'Who, for instance?'

'Now look, Sue—wait! I've got it! The Sitwells. There was an eighteenth-century painting of the Sitwell children by Copley at Renishaw. So they got Sargent to do one of the then Sitwell family, around 1900, I think. Sir George and Lady Ida with their children, Edith, Osbert and Sacheverell.'

'Well done. You are educated. Almost. In biography especially.'

It was just like school. Nine out of ten for little Timmy.

'What else?'

'What else? Is this what you got me here for? I don't know what else. Well, what I do remember is that the painting is totally unreal. Sir George is in riding kit, which he never wore. Lady Ida is arranging flowers, which she never did, in elaborate clothes, which no lady would have worn for horticultural activities. Sir George pointed out that Edith's nose was crooked, so Sargent, who was a kindly man, painted Edith's nose straight and Sir George's crooked. I don't know what else. Give us a break, Sue. What is all this about? Was it something I was supposed to see at the Whitney?'

She stood before me, a slender but full-bosomed siren with dark brown hair and blue eyes that fixed on mine with an intensity that I didn't like the look of.

'Sargent always painted in his Tite Street studio. His clients had to go there to be painted.'

'So?'

'So in order to be painted, the Sitwells came down from Derbyshire to London to stay. They rented a house for this purpose. Osbert describes it in *Left Hand, Right Hand*. The décor was mauve and it was full of pictures of Winston Churchill.'

'Eh?'

'Winston Churchill. The address was 25 Chesham Place. It got destroyed by bombs in the 1940s, but at the time it was the house of Mr and Mrs Moreton Frewen.'

'What?'

'Clara Frewen and Jennie—Lady Randolph Churchill—made mauve a fashionable colour.'

'Hang on. I'm not following this.'

'The Frewens rented the house out because they were hard up once again. They rented it to the Sitwells. For the time of the painting of the Sargent portrait.'

'Yes, but what—'

She came up to me and stood over me so that I had to peer up the charming elevation of her to look at her face.

'Keep with the Sargent for safety,' she said. 'Not sergeant. Sargent.'

'What?'

'Written on those gold shares. You never saw them. Nor did Andy Casey. You got the details over the phone. You *assumed* that the spelling was that way. Actually there are forty-seven varieties, from a spelling point of view, of the very ancient surname of Sargent. It was an old English family. Frewen was notoriously ungrammatical. He might well have misspelt it.'

'Oh no. No. This is absurd.'

She reached into the satchel-handbag and pulled out a large, solid copy of *Country Life* magazine. The Autumn Gardens Number, it was. 'It hit me when I was reading this. Look!' She held it open at one of the advertising pages and stuck it under my nose. I scowled at a long picture of a pretty woman in an expensive white dress. *Mrs Cecil Wade* it said, painted in 1886 in London by John Singer Sargent. Sold at Sotheby's, New York, on Thursday 29th May for $1,485,000 (£951,923).

'Nearly a million pounds,' she said. 'And the Sargent exhibition is on, right now, at the Whitney.'

I licked my lips. My mouth had gone dry. 'This is fantastic. Far-fetched. Ridiculous.'

She stamped her foot in fury. 'Sargent!' she practically screamed at me. '*Keep with the Sargent for safety!* Don't you see? Those gold shares and other valuables must have been kept somewhere with a painting that the Frewens owned. A painting by Sargent. It wasn't a police sergeant. Or a security company. Someone is after any clue they can get, on the gold shares, or from you. You particularly.'

'This is crazy.'

'You said,' her voice dropped a bit, but it was still vibrantly urgent, 'you said that those old shares are worthless now. Absolutely worthless. Why would anyone murder for them? Why?'

'We don't know. Well, it was—damn it, you've got me confused. It was a random break-in.'

'Oh yeah? Like our flat last night? And the grab on your bags at O'Hare? Tell me, Tim, what are you well-known for?'

'Me? Me? Nothing.'

'Don't be bashful. This is no time. Who found the Gwen John sculpture? The Whistler? The Norman Shaw? What are you to someone with an inkling of the existence of a painting worth a fortune?' She grabbed my hand. 'You are the competition! White's Art Fund. You are probably well on the track of the thing. Any information you've got is relevant.'

'But I haven't got any.'

'They don't know that. They think you're hot on the trail.'

I gaped over her shoulder at Lord Ribblesdale. His face hadn't moved. One and a half million dollars. I held the edge of my seat with my spare hand.

'This won't do. This is fantasy. It's because you work at the Tate.'

'Pah!'

'The Frewens couldn't afford a Sargent. They were always broke.'

Her face changed in triumph. 'Read your books; read them carefully. There are different definitions of broke. In 1904 Clara Frewen commissioned a cast of a sculpture by Saint Gaudens at a cost of £1800 for their house, Brede Place, in Sussex. Sculpture ran in the family. Their daughter, Clare Sheridan, became a famous one. Saint Gaudens was an American. He was a friend of—guess who? Sargent. American sculpture and American painting. Why not? You could commission a Sargent for £2000 then.'

'My God! Stop this. If there were such a painting it would be well documented. Is there any mention of one? Of the Frewens?'

Her face clouded. 'No, there isn't. At least, I haven't found one so far. Not all Sargent's portraits can be accounted for, though. Oh, I know what you're going to ask, and yes, I have. At least I've started. I've been working on it all day. I've been through Stanley Olson's recent book, but that's not a *catalogue raisonnée*. There's no mention of any painting of the Frewens by Sargent in that. But you know, Tim, you know better than anyone. Work leaks out of an artist's studio all the time. Not everyone wants a record kept. Not everyone. For all sorts of reasons.'

'It's a wonderful theory, Sue. I just can't grasp it.' My

voice seemed to echo in the empty gallery. Lord Ribblesdale regarded me solemnly, with perhaps a hint of mockery. 'I realize that a Sargent is possibly very valuable nowadays. From fairly recent times only, mark you; *Mrs Cecil Wade* was a world record for a Sargent. I agree that he does fulfil so many of the requirements of the New York market. He was American, but born in Florence. He was successful in Paris and London. He was celebrated in America. You've still got to be bloody fanatical to murder for one of his works. I mean, a painting can be traced.'

'Not if no one has ever seen it before. And you'd be fanatical, if it were an exceptional painting, even for a Sargent.'

'Exceptional? What do you mean?'

She stared down at me. Her face had gone pale with excitement. 'It's only a theory I've got. Something that occurred to me while looking at Carter Ratcliff's book on Sargent paintings. The one that you brought from New York.'

'What?' I was still held by the hand, tightly now. She looked fearful but very excited, a sort of feverish look that I didn't like at all.

'Sargent painted some famous threesomes, of women. The best known is the Wyndham sisters: Lady Elcho, of the Souls, Mrs Adeane and Mrs Tennant. But there were others. The Acheson sisters, the Vickers, Mrs Carl Meyer and her children, the four Boits, I don't know, probably others.'

I drew in my breath. 'You're thinking of the Jeromes?'

'Yes, Tim. Think of it! Think of a painting of those three sisters: Clara, the eldest, married to Moreton Frewen. Jennie, the middle one, married to Lord Randolph Churchill. Leonie, the youngest, married to Sir John Leslie of County Monaghan. Three famous beauties, daughters of the fabulous Leonard Jerome of New York. They took London society by storm at one time or another. Their connections are endless. What do you think the New York market would pay for a Sargent of them? All three together?'

I licked my lips again. 'A lot. A hell of a lot.'

'Exactly. And if such a painting does exist, and I feel sure it does, Tim, and if the Frewens had it or looked after it, you have been going around asking questions, as Tim Simpson of White's Art Fund, that must have set off the whole deadly business. And you acting all innocent.' She looked down at her hand, still tightly holding mine. 'The joke is that if there's one man who's most likely to find it, that man is you. So I'm not dropping out of this one. No matter what happens.'

CHAPTER 12

Jeremy White did a sort of two-step up and down his office. His face was congested. I've never seen him so agitated.

'Fantastic! Absolutely fantastic!'

'I know. It does seem far-fetched.'

'We have to find that painting!'

'What?'

He paused in his cumbersome effort at a hop, skip and jump. 'We can't risk missing it! The Art Fund must have it. It'll be the art scoop of the decade. Of the twentieth century.'

'You believe in it?'

'Of course I do. It makes absolute sense. Sargent must have painted Jennie at some time. Why not all three sisters? I've seen the Wyndhams one. The Souls! Damn it, Tim, I'm an Oxford man!'

'We've found no record of a Jerome painting to date. Not even a Jennie portrait.'

'Bah! It'll come to light. Tim, dear boy, you must get it. Forget everything else. It's your métier. This could be your finest hour. To coin a phrase. From their own family.'

'What? You, of all people! After all you've—'

'Yes, yes, I know! I know, but this is different.'

'How?'

He grabbed my arm. I'd never seen him like that before. He was like a terrier confronted by a barn full of rats. 'My dear Tim! Give me a guess—just a guess—at the value of such a painting? Bearing in mind that *Mrs Cecil Wade* fetched a million sterling. Guess?'

I sighed. I'd thought about that. 'Two million sterling? Three million dollars? In New York, of course.'

'At least! At least! I can think of five American museums who'd pay that. It's not only a superb portrait by an Anglo-American master. It's a social document. The Jeromes came from upstate New York. It's a—'

'Steady on, Jeremy. You're going to burst a blood vessel in a minute. Superb painting? You haven't even seen it yet. If it exists.'

'It exists! I know it exists! I feel it in my bones. It must exist. I believe in it.'

'That's what frightens me. You and Sue both jumped at the idea.'

He stopped his agitated movement. 'What do you mean?'

'It's so believable. Something a real forger could pass off so well. Sargent is a very paintable painter. There are plenty of photos of the sisters to use as models. A forgery like that would be well worth it.'

'My dear Tim! You are so devious, sometimes.'

'It wouldn't be the first occasion some clever criminal has laid a trail for Simpson to follow. Start me off with Frewen and lead me on to something exciting like this. You see, it's all such clever psychology. People who've bought forgeries, obvious forgeries like those Palmers of Keating's, have done so because they wanted those forgeries to exist. They wanted to believe in them, despite all evidence to the contrary, because the forgery fulfilled some romantic or material need. This is a bit like that.'

'Good heavens. You are a cool customer these days. The Art Fund is well guarded.' He smiled crookedly. 'We can muster experts for authentication, surely?'

'Indeed we can. Which makes us all the more dangerous to a forger. You've carefully avoided talking about danger, so far. This has become a game for very high stakes, Jeremy. You're sure you want to play, are you? I'm game, of course, but let's have no moaning at the bar if things go wrong.'

'Hm.' He stroked his jaw. 'Forgeries and danger. I don't want to expose you or Sue to danger. Which means that the sooner we resolve this the better. We have to get an idea where to start. Chicago is the obvious place.'

'Why?'

'The gold-mine documents. You said they turned up there in the 'twenties. Originally they were kept with the Sargent. It might be there too. Frewen could have sold the lot when he was out of funds.'

'It doesn't fit. A painting like that would have been recorded. He sold his mother-in-law's diamond necklace to finance his gold-crusher; that's in every book about him; don't think he wouldn't have told everyone if he'd sold the family painting too. Everyone has heard about the Holbein that was in the family home, Brickwall in Sussex. Moreton used to bounce a ball against it when he was a boy, but it's in the Metropolitan, or the Frick, now. That's famous. A Sargent would be, too.'

'You don't know.' His agitation was coming back. 'Don't be so negative. We must check every possibility—wait! I've got it! Get your coat!'

'What?'

'Donald. We never even started to tap Donald. We said we'd talk to him again. Come on, we'll take my car. He'll be delighted to see us. Donald is the fount of all knowledge on the Frewens, and he's a member of the family. There's no time to lose. The quicker this thing is ended, the quicker the danger will go.'

'What about the Bank? Today's work?'

'To hell with the Bank! Get your coat.'

Nothing would have it but that we had to rush down into the garage basement beneath the Bank immediately and roar off into the City of London in Jeremy's saloon Jaguar, him cursing at the traffic all the way to the suburbs. Once we got out on to the Portsmouth Road he calmed down a bit, enough to keep the speed at ninety miles an hour anyway, and to stop swearing. We drove through lunch-time and, the way Jeremy handled the car, the Devil's Punchbowl and Hindhead came up like landing lights on an aircraft runway. In no time at all we had turned off the road, bounced in a cloud of dust past the supercilious stallion and skidded to a halt at the front door, spraying gravel everywhere.

Donald White gaped at us in amusement as he opened the front door. 'Jeremy? Tim? What's this? Playing truant?'

'Want to talk to you.' Jeremy was brisk.

'Me? A retired old codger? I am honoured. What's up at the Bank? Business a bit slack?'

'No, no. Need your advice. Your memory. Can we come in?'

'Of course you can.' Donald held the door open. 'Have you had lunch? Can I get you something?'

'A coffee would be great,' I managed to get in before Jeremy refused any refreshment. 'Jeremy's short-circuited our lunch today.'

'In that case I'll do the honours.' He turned and beckoned us to follow him, limping his way ahead.

I didn't remember the house. I hadn't been inside before. The garden party had been literally that; with such good weather that Sunday, now seemingly distant, we had all stayed outside. The interior was a pleasant surprise, oak-beamed, tile-floored, smelling of polish. Good rugs, Kazaks, and Turkomans, lay on the tiles. We followed him through a hall, a sitting-room with an inglenook fireplace, a dining-room with an oak refectory table and a dresser I vaguely recognized, into a kitchen. It was small, compact, neatly-stowed. We had to stay behind a bar-counter while Donald went into a central area surrounded by the working instruments of the kitchen.

'Just like a ship's galley,' he explained. 'Crock like me can't do with others inside the working area. Everything to hand for one cook. Broth won't get spoiled that way. Here, have some cheese while I brew up your coffee.'

He wore a dark blue sweater and canvas trousers. His brown face regarded us shrewdly, and his expression, senior and experienced, made Jeremy remember his manners and keep his impetuous questions in check, to be held back until Donald indicated he was ready. When he had served us coffee and we were sitting at the kitchen counter, sipping from mugs and consuming fresh bread and cheese, Donald sat himself down on a stool opposite us and gave us both a keen stare.

'Now then,' he demanded, 'what's all this about?'

Jeremy cleared his throat. He'd restrained himself with great difficulty. 'It's your knowledge of Frewen we want to tap,' he began.

'Oh no! I thought you wanted my help as a banker. How disappointing. I thought I was going to be brought out of retirement.' Donald's voice was mocking but his eyes didn't twinkle. I sensed that his disappointment had more than a touch of reality to it.

'Well—sorry—you did say we could come back to you about Frewen.'

'Of course I did. Pay no attention to my howl of frustration. What about him this time?'

'Donald, did your father ever mention him in connection with a painting? By Sargent?'

Donald's head came up and his eyes widened. He put down his own coffee mug. 'Sargent? You mean John Singer Sargent?'

'Yes.'

'Good grief.' Donald seemed quite taken aback. 'A painting? What sort of painting?'

'We assume it was a portrait. Of him and/or his wife. Or—' Jeremy warmed to his enthusiasm before I had time to check him, to let any suggestion come from Donald himself and not to put ideas into his head—'of the three sisters, the Jerome sisters? Sargent painted several famous threesomes.'

'Good God!' Donald's eyes opened even wider and his mouth dropped. 'You mean Jennie Jerome? Lady Randolph Churchill? With Clara Frewen? And that other sister, the younger one, she married an Irishman, I've forgotten her name.'

'Leonie.'

'That's it. Leonie. Good grief. No, I can't say I have. How on earth has this idea come about?'

I explained to him very briefly how the whole thing had arisen. He listened in mounting incredulity. 'But I say! This is very tenuous, isn't it? I mean, good heavens, it must be possible, surely, to substantiate whether Sargent painted the three ladies or not?'

'Not so far. Well, to be honest, the evidence so far is contrary.'

'There you are! I mean, the idea of the writing being spelt the wrong way—though hang on a minute! Moreton Frewen was notoriously ungrammatical. He was a friend of Kipling's, but that didn't stop him from mucking up the punctuation of Winston's first book when he sent it to Frewen from India. Frewen got it published, but Winston was quite upset, because he said that after Uncle Moreton had checked through it, everyone thought it had been mangled by a mad proof-reader. I suppose it is possible that he meant a Sargent not a sergeant. But my God, it's hardly evidence, is it?'

Jeremy made an impatient gesture. 'Maybe not. But it's a possibility. Worth following up. Following up actively.'

Donald gave him an amused glance. 'You are becoming a fanatic, Jeremy. I can see that you and Tim put your Art Fund in front of everything.'

'No!' Jeremy stood up. He hates thinking in a seated position. Stretching himself to his full height, he stepped back from the counter. 'It's not that. Not that at all. I've got something here—' he tapped the side of his head— 'something nagging me. Something about Sargent. Something at the back of my mind. I can't put my finger on it, it won't come out, but it's something important. God, I wish I had the time to look into it properly.'

Donald gave me a meaning stare and a faint wink. 'You're quite obsessive, my dear chap. What sort of thing?'

'I don't know. Something someone told me years ago.'

'But come on!' Donald voiced an opinion I'd already given several times. 'If such an important painting was executed, it was commissioned by somebody, painted by Sargent, and paid for by that somebody. It didn't just materialize out of thin air. Sargent was a prolific and energetic painter. I accept that there must be a lot of his work still uncatalogued, but not something like this, this threesome of Jeromes. My God, every art foundation in America would be after a thing like that.'

'Exactly! Exactly!'

Donald shook his head. 'I've never heard of such a thing.'

'Your father never spoke of it?'

He grinned. 'My father only spoke of money lost on mad schemes like gold-crushers and tramways and opening up Kenya or Australia. Frewen had a fortune in his hands at Broken Hill and then let them cheat him of it. There were far greater dramas to talk about than oil paintings, let me tell you. Everyone was being painted by Sargent before the First War. It was no subject of conversation.'

'Damn it.' Jeremy was crestfallen. 'I felt sure you'd have some sort of lead for us.'

'Sorry, Jeremy. No can do.'

We finished our snack talking of Bank matters. Jeremy seemed to pull himself together and, realizing that Donald had been a bit disappointed at our avoidance of Bank consultation with him, made a real effort to brief him on current Bank affairs and to ask his opinion. It pleased me to see that side of Jeremy in action; he can be very considerate that way. After about half an hour he heaved himself up and announced that we must go, thanking Donald profusely.

'Oh, don't thank me. I'm sorry I've been of such little help.'

'Of course you've been of help. It's been jolly useful, hasn't it, Tim?'

'It certainly has.'

Jeremy looked about him. 'You've got a new dresser.'

Donald grinned. 'I wondered if you'd notice. Bought it at the rooms. Not yours, your competitors'. Always needed a good oak dresser in here.'

'It's very handsome.'

It was a large pot-board dresser of the early eighteenth century, with a frilly rack of shelves above. I realized that it was the one that had given me a faint pang of recognition but that it was a classic of its type, worth about three thousand pounds.

'What do you think, Tim?'

'Very fine. Fits in here perfectly.'

'Ah. Glad you like it.' Donald smiled at me. 'I turfed out a mahogany sideboard that didn't suit the house at all and it more than paid for this one.'

'Well, that's fashion for you. Mahogany is in, right now, but oak is out. The fashion for it, anyway.'

'It'll change, I suppose?'

'Oh yes. These things always do.'

He limped with us to the car, slapped the roof in a farewell gesture and moved across the gravel towards his horse. Jeremy drove out of the gates and turned towards London, biting his lip.

'What a waste of time,' he growled. 'There's something I simply can't place, Tim.'

'It's not Donald's fault. You have to consider that the painting might not exist.'

'Oh, Tim, really! You are the most negative man, sometimes. I—'

The phone rang, surprising him. Jeremy installed a car phone some time ago. He thought it would befit his senior and important executive role. I happen to know that he leaves it out of the car frequently, especially at weekends, because in his heart of hearts he hates the thing. There really have to be occasions when a man isn't available, and driving the car is arguably one of them. An expression of annoyance came out of him.

'Really! I did give instructions that I wasn't to be contacted on that infernal thing unless it was really urgent.'

'This might be.'

'Nonsense.' He wrenched the receiver off its fitting and put it to his ear. 'Hello? Now look here—who? Oh. From Chicago? Great heavens. And here we are in the car. You're patching the call through? How?'

'The miracles of modern technology,' I said.

He snorted and passed the instrument over. 'It's for you.'

'Me? Good grief. No escape for the wicked. Hello?'

The line was crackly but the voice was clear, quite undeniably clear and distinct so that, afterwards, there was no doubt as to what had been said. 'Tim? Hi, this is Andy. Andy Casey. I told you I wouldn't let this thing drop. I persuaded Maguire to carry out another house-to-house round Victor Perkins's street near the Sunset Valley golf course. It's a quiet, modest residential area. Four people picked out a photograph of Kamrowski as being one of three guys they'd seen hanging round the area before the murder. They held an ID parade yesterday. They were positive. All of them. Kamrowski was one of the people staking out Perkins's place before they broke in. Are you listening?'

'Yes, I am.' My mind raced and my hand shook a bit, but that might have been the car. 'The thing is that Kamrowski was the bag snatcher at the airport.'

'Exactly. There is a direct connection between the two events. You were a precisely-located target. It was not a random snatch, any more than our break-in was. You were a target. You most probably still are.' His voice was triumphant. 'I thought you ought to know that. As soon as possible.'

CHAPTER 13

'In principle,' I said, closing the report, 'the branch in Chicago is a high-risk venture. What we have done is to spell out how costly it is likely to be if it fails totally. In other words, if it attracted no new business at all. The other estimates are purely subjective. How much business do you think you will attract; how much you'll take from competitors; how long it will take; and so on. These are pure speculation, if you like, but speculation with an element of calculation in it. It quantifies the elements of timing and cost.'

I was beginning to sound like an accountant. Charles Massenaux gave me one of his secret smiles, half encouraging, half sardonic. Howarth rustled his papers at the other end of the table. Carlton sat on his right. The other directors sat or lounged in attitudes of keen alertness or laconic indifference as suited their individual styles. We were in the conference room over Christerby's in London, the room that is used for board meetings. Beneath and around us, the bustle of business could be heard; porters were moving chunks of continental furniture into the largest of the auction rooms for a sale the following week.

'You haven't said—' one of the alert directors with a

rather plaintive voice spoke to me—'how much business *you* think we'd get if this, this very expensive venture, I may say, were to be undertaken?'

'No, I haven't. Because I don't know. I am not an executive director of this company. It is for them and their managers to provide such estimates, and they have. Those estimates are included in the various projections in my report.'

'Hmph.' He didn't say it, but the inference was clear; Simpson was avoiding the issue. It wasn't a fair inference, of course, and I did have my own idea of what was realistic by way of achievement, but I wasn't going to commit myself at this meeting, in front of this lot. It was for Howarth and Carlton to do that, not me.

'On the other hand—' by speaking I brought the plaintive one's head up again, to look at me—'on the other hand, when you consider that we have regional branches in Britain —Edinburgh, Chester, Bristol and Worthing—a relatively small country of sixty-odd million people, it does not seem a conflicting principle to apply the same reasoning to the United States, a richer country of nearly, what, two hundred and forty million, with a much wider geographical spread.'

'Ah, quite. But you ignore the element of competition.'

'Not in my report I don't.'

'We're not without competition in Britain.' Howarth's voice cut in from the top of the table. 'We're keeping our place in the big four only because we are as efficient, as expert, and as well known as the other three. We're not frightened of taking on competition. The fact is that a business like ours either has to become a major force in the USA or expect, eventually, to become a branch of a big American auctioneer. The historical progression is inevitable.' He paused for a moment to let the contentious statement, with its wider cultural and psychological implications, sink in. Then he continued. 'What I'm sure we're all grateful to Tim for is doing an excellent job of work in setting out the facts and figures involved. We can all be quite clear in our minds just what, from now on, it is we're taking on.'

The phrase 'job of work' was so like the man. It brought to mind a smithy full of blacksmiths hammering out bolts of iron for a black boiler factory. I made a fractional bow in his direction as a response to his tribute. Charles Massenaux gave me another slightly mocking quirk of his lips and a meaningful glance, as though there were some deep, political significance or implication to which only he and I were party. I knew what the decision would mean to Charles; the radical alteration of the focus of the business, a powerful pull westward, the elevation of Carlton to a much, much more powerful position, providing that Howarth overcame the reservations he'd voiced to me in New York during my visit.

'Can we hear Mr Carlton on the subject?' The plaintive one's voice piped up bravely. 'I'm sure we all endorse Harry Howarth's feelings on the usefulness of Tim Simpson's figures but—' damning with faint praise—'it will, after all, fall to Mr Carlton and his team to, er, to execute this possible project and it is he, as the man on the spot, to whom we must all look for some sort of guidance, no, not guidance, er, commitment, perhaps?'

Aha, thinks Simpson at this point, he's getting you to stick your neck out, Alex, sliding the block beneath it so that, at some time in the future, if all goes awry you can take the chopper where it normally hits the turkey just before Christmas. Or Thanksgiving, in your case.

Carlton wasn't an American for nothing. He looked straight at the plaintive one through his gold-rimmed spectacles, which made his eyes look somehow barer and more intense than heavier frames might have done.

'I'm confident we can succeed,' he said in a flat, unemotional tone. 'We have the right people, we have the right backing, and our reputation in the States is growing every day. Tim's estimates are, necessarily, conservative. I believe we can achieve his first budget for break-even in two years and perhaps exceed it. Chicago and the mid-West is a relatively undeveloped area in our line of business. My people are keen to tackle it. We must go ahead.'

Howarth gave him a look that combined extreme satisfaction with what I detected to be an element of slight surprise. It was as though Carlton's commitment was much more positive than he'd been expecting. Howarth looked boldly down the long table.

'Good,' he said crisply, taking his cue at that moment and, sensibly, not waiting a minute more for anyone to shove an oar in. 'I move that we vote, then. The proposal is—'

And that was it. The board rallied to the flag. Considering it was a special meeting, that it was Friday afternoon going on six o'clock, and that we'd missed our Café Royal lunch, they behaved very well. I had a suspicion that some of them were disinclined to argue on the grounds that it might delay the start of their weekend, so that they all voted in favour. Howarth was as pleased as a dog with two whatsits, having got himself a unanimous board decision. He came up to me as they were clearing off and I was scraping up my papers, and clapped me on the back.

'Well done, Tim! Thanks for everything.'

'My congratulations to you. It's all gone very well for you and Alex.'

'It has indeed. I hope we won't have any ructions from Jeremy?'

'Oh, Jeremy'll be all right. For the moment.' I gave him a significant smile. 'It'll be in a year or so's time that you might have trouble with Jeremy.'

'No, we won't. We'll be very successful, you'll see.'

'I'm sure you will. Particularly with Alex so committed to it.'

'Indeed. He was very positive, wasn't he?'

'Very impressive. They couldn't say no after that—ah,

here he is. Hi, Alex. My congratulations. You're all set for the Windy City.'

'Thank you.' He gave me a broad smile. 'It will be a challenging time for us. I do hope your role won't end here? We'll be seeing you again in New York? And Chicago?'

'Oh, I expect so. You don't get rid of me that easily. I have to coordinate finance with Andy Casey and all that. There's plenty to do.'

'Good.' He gave me a long stare before turning to Howarth. 'What time do we have to leave, Harry?'

'Right now.' The other looked at his watch. 'Right now. There's a train from Paddington very soon.' He turned to me. 'Alex is staying on a day or so to go over things before he heads back to the States.'

'Good idea. I hope you have a nice weekend. See you both again soon, I'm sure.'

'Thanks, Tim. All the best.'

'Me too.'

I turned, to find Charles Massenaux standing beside me. 'I suppose,' he queried, with a tinge of the playful sarcasm that often colours his remarks to me, 'that you won't have time for a drink with a mere British company director? I mean, I realize that your thoughts are purely transatlantic now, but—'

'Enough, Charles! Enough. Of course I'll have a drink with you. Providing you are paying, of course.'

CHAPTER 14

Although it was Saturday morning, Mr Goodston's shop was deserted. He sat immobile behind his desk, his face concealed by a leather-bound volume. At the tinkle of the bell, his eyes came up over the top of the book and his half-moons widened at the sight of me.

'Mr Simpson!' The tone was of quiet surprise. 'Back already? This fine Saturday morning? I had imagined you to be somewhere out in the air, the field perhaps, water, or the moor? Not frowsting here in London, in my poor, dusty shop of all places.'

''Morning, Mr Goodston. I wished to consult you. Therefore I am here.'

'Consult me?' He put down the book, prised the wire frame of his glasses off his nose and peered at me before brushing vaguely at the rumpled waistcoat that contained the bulging, inchoate mass of his torso. 'Consult me? I am a poor bookseller, my dear sir, but my advice is available if you seek it. Provided—' he held up an admonitory finger —'you are not here to ask for a tip on the gee-gees. I have made it a rule, indeed a principle, never to give advice on matters of the Turf. One makes enemies that way.'

I smiled at him. He was so perfectly suited to his environment, to the dusty ranks of literature on the ancient wood shelves, to the grime-filtered light of his plate-glass window. It was a world removed from reality, a world of concept and memoir, of record and frozen image, long captured and petrified into numb, desensitized history.

'No tips for the races. I quite agree with you; such advice must be a hazard.'

He moistened his lips. 'Have you read the books you bought from me?'

'I have, thank you.'

'Did they provide the clue you were seeking?'

'No. I'm afraid they didn't.'

'Ah.' A cautionary look appeared on his face, as though he suspected that I might try to return them, but he suppressed the expression. 'I'm sorry. Is that the matter on which you have come to consult me?'

'In a way.'

'But not directly?'

I compressed my lips. 'The book by Allen Andrews was

—is—excellent. I agree with you and with Ralph Martin, whose book on Lady Randolph Churchill I have now read, in its two volumes. He says exactly what you say in his chapter notes. Andrews's book is more comprehensive, more factual, less involved than Anita Leslie's. On the other hand, Anita Leslie's is very readable and there are reminiscences of hers that add to the book by Andrews. In a way, the two are complementary. Anita Leslie doesn't really try to explain Moreton Frewen's vast, intricate and disastrous financial dealings. Andrews does so at length; it explains how Frewen's whole life, and tragically that of his wife and children, was poisoned by debts, legal action, entails, mortgages, bailiffs—it's like something out of Dickens.'

'Very true.' Mr Goodston sighed. 'Once the initial loss passes beyond a certain point, everything that follows is lost capital, sunk investment. In trying to recoup that vast initial loss, the judgement becomes impaired and the situation simply gets worse. It's a principle of gambling, you know.' His face sagged in knowledge.

'By initial loss, you're referring in this case to Wyoming?'

'Precisely. That crash haunted Frewen for the rest of his life. It wrecked his judgement. From then on he snatched at opportunities which were, many of them, premature.'

I stuck my hands in my pockets. 'In a way you can blame his brother Richard for Wyoming. If Richard hadn't insisted on pulling out, Moreton wouldn't have had to pay off his share. To do that he had to form a public company and raise capital over here, thus locking himself in. He lost his independence.'

Mr Goodston rolled his eyes. 'If Richard hadn't pulled out, Moreton would just have lost all their money instead of their money and that of all the other investors.'

'You're hard, Mr Goodston. But probably right. If he had inherited the estate of Moreton Old Hall in Cheshire from his godfather, as he should have, he'd probably have lost that too. Frewen's life is full of ifs.'

'Indeed. What did you think of his own book, *Melton Mowbray?*'

'I enjoyed it, even if the style is quixotically old-fashioned, and the memoirs remarkable for what they don't say rather than for what they do. He really must be unique in having had a personal one-man guided tour of the site of the Little Big Horn battle by Sitting Bull himself; to have had that sort of experience is incredible. I loved some of the horsey stories too. The other side of the coin is that it makes one so grateful for modern biography. In Frewen's day, public utterance and reminiscence had to be too circumspect, too cautious. Then there was that preoccupation with style. It's like Osbert Sitwell's memoirs, really; they only come to life, for me, when his father appears on the scene and Osbert is so upset and enraged by the thought of the old, eccentric devil that he forgets to use those long, convoluted clauses.'

'But the clue you were seeking: *Melton Mowbray* didn't provide it?'

'I'm afraid not. That's why I've come to see you.'

'Would you like to sit down?' He waved at a rather decrepit chair, birch-framed, but with frayed caning to the seat, that leant rather than stood against a bookcase near his paper-clogged desk. I sat down on it and opened my mouth, but he held up his hand.

'A moment. Do you, by any chance, drink sherry?'

'Of course.'

'In that case, may I offer you a glass? If you will forgive my observation, your face contains within it the traces of a serious preoccupation. Perhaps if we sip a glass of sherry while we talk, it may help to—to resolve the matter?'

'That's very kind. I'd love a sherry.'

He smiled broadly. 'Your acceptance gives me the justification for an indulgence which I regret occasions guilt within me.' He heaved himself to his feet. 'The law of England upon the hours of drinking in public houses has corrupted the independence of the nation's mind on its own habits. Before the First War, no one would have imagined that the population could be told when it could drink.'

'I quite agree. A Frenchman finds it absurd.'

'True.' He shuffled behind a sagging bookcase to a cabinet, out of my sight, and returned with a bottle of Celebration Cream and two large tulip glasses. A surprisingly clean white cloth emerged from the top drawer of his overloaded desk and he polished the two glasses with it carefully, holding each up to the light before placing them on a small clear area among the heaps of books on the desk's top surface. Then, with great precaution, he poured the sherry into the glasses, decanting perhaps a sixth of the bottle into each one. I made no comment on the quantity he had provided but held up my glass in a silent toast before I drank.

'Excellent,' I said. 'Just the ticket.'

He smiled again, slumping himself back into his desk chair like a collapsing bag of rumpled tweed cloth and individual checked waistcoat that insulated him from the air of the bookshop, cooler this morning due to a fresh breeze rustling down Praed Street on its way to Paddington Station.

'Tell me,' I said, working my way round to an idea that had occurred to me in the dark hours of the night, when with wide-open eyes I had listened to Sue's erratic breathing beside me, telling me Sue was having a bad night too, 'how much of the real nature of late Victorian and Edwardian high society has ever really been revealed to us?'

He put down his sherry glass which, I noticed, was already half empty. 'A large question,' he said. 'Rather too large a question, I think. Could you not perhaps be a little more, er, a little more specific? Which aspect do you have in mind? I mean—' he waved an arm grandiloquently at the millions of words which surrounded him—'sporting, military and thespian specialities. These you see are merely the tip of an iceberg. They recount, with varying degrees of veracity, spite, objectivity, truthfulness and downright lies, one part of one aspect of the doings of various people. The real truth, if there is such a thing, will never be known to us. Almost certainly never.'

'Indeed. I was thinking of something connected with the relationships within that society. The ruling part of society. It was quite a small number of people, really, who held all the power. I think Churchill said 20,000, or something like that.'

'Relationships?'

'Er, I meant sexual relationships. Between men and women. Very often married men and married women.'

'Ah.' Comprehension filtered into his features. '"Never comment on a likeness" perhaps, do you mean?'

'Exactly. If some of the literature is to be believed, London and country house society involved a great deal of, er, mixed bathing.'

'The Marlborough House Set, for instance?'

'Yes. And the hunting crowd. There was much tacit understanding, discreet bedroom arrangements. Provided no scandal ever ensued, everyone was quite reconciled to all their sort of—'

'Hypocrisy?'

'Well, we think of it as hypocrisy now, perhaps, but it was their accommodation with human nature.'

'There was—and is—much exaggeration, I believe. If many accounts are to be credited, the practice of calling on ladies at tea-time involved the most fevered adulteries, whereas—'

'Whereas, in fact, as Anita Leslie points out, the presence of servants and the cocooning nature of the clothes the ladies wore would have made the reality of the granting of favours very difficult.'

'You put it well, my dear sir. You put it well. I have no doubt that, as always, there were—what did they call it?—ardent, yes, ardent ones, who would behave promiscuously, as in any age. But there was, then, a great deal more truly romantic love, hopelessly unrequited love, than this modern age, with its insistence on instantly-gratified appetite, would tolerate.' Mr Goodston polished off his sherry with a smack of the lips and held up the bottle with a querying expression in my direction.

'Just a suspicion, thank you. I still have some.'

He topped up my glass and replenished his own. 'People then, men of wealth particularly, seemed quite content to worship married ladies, ply them with flowers and presents, in return for what was, quite often, friendly companionship. The men hoped, perhaps they hoped, but in a way, had their secret fantasy been granted, it would have destroyed the illusion, shattered the pure love. There's a story of Somerset Maugham's along those lines.' He glanced at his shelves. 'I include him for his theatrical connections.'

'Words can be difficult. The euphemisms they used. I mean "The King dined with Mrs X. last night." What did they mean? Sometimes it was clear, sometimes not. "The King dined with Lady Dudley," they said, the night—'

'The night Persimmon won the Derby! Ha!' Mr Goodston called it out excitedly, as though he'd been there himself. 'I think you can be sure of what the word "dined" meant that night! His horse had won the Derby and he savoured his triumph to the full. And yet, and yet; Lady Randolph twitted him for having been "jilted" by Lady Dudley. That was, perhaps, later. Or out of jealousy.'

'So you see, it's difficult to know.'

'Indeed.' He stared expectantly at me.

'Mr Goodston, I am trying to find a painting by Sargent. John Singer Sargent. It is possible that it is of the Frewens. It is also possible, perhaps more probable, that it is of the three Jerome sisters. At some point in their lives. I haven't found it yet, so I don't know.'

Mr Goodston made a bubbling noise. For a moment I thought that sherry was going to spout from him, perhaps from his ears. He choked at me for several seconds, going redder in the face and swelling like a frog in ecstasy.

'Are you OK? Shall I give you a tap on the back?'

He shook his head. An eructation shook him and the convexity deflated. He coughed, loudly. 'A Sargent! Of the Jerome sisters? My dear fellow! Such a painting would be extremely valuable.'

'It would.'

'I mean, think of his famous rendition of the Wyndham sisters. Astounding. God knows what that would fetch now.'

'I'm afraid it's not much use thinking. The Wyndham sisters are in the Metropolitan, in New York. Paintings as important as that don't come on the market. Not very often, anyway.'

'Who commissioned this canvas you seek? Leonard Jerome?'

I sighed. 'I'm afraid its existence is a speculation. We can find no evidence of it.'

'None?'

'None. Not so far. That's why I've come to see you.'

'Me? Mr Simpson, you run an Art Fund. I am a bookseller. Surely there is an antithesis in this?'

'A paradox, rather. But not such a paradox. Your speciality is certain aspects of society which, as it happens, were very important to the period I'm dealing with. I lay awake all last night. Sue—my girlfriend from the Tate—and I can find no record of such a painting in any work on Sargent. Neither Moreton Frewen, who was not an æsthete, nor Lord Randolph Churchill, nor Sir John Leslie, the husbands of the ladies concerned, appear to have commissioned such a work. Frewen's daughter Clare was painted by Emile Fuchs, one of Sargent's rivals. But no reference to Sargent can I find. Hence my line of thinking. Could someone else, another admirer, have commissioned it? And kept it secret? Could such a thing have been possible?'

Mr Goodston regarded me with what I recognized as a little awe. A thoughtful expression deepened on his face.

'Anita Leslie says her grandmother was always instructed never to comment on a likeness.'

Mr Goodston smiled slightly, his expression still deep and his eyes fixed on mine. 'Relationships were very interwoven' he murmured, almost to himself. 'Some conversations must have been minefields for the gauche and the ingenuous.' He gestured at the bookshelves. 'The tip of the iceberg. The tip of the iceberg.'

'That's what I was thinking. About the Sargent. And who commissioned it. And paid for it.'

'Could it have been concealed?'

'Goya concealed the nude Maja from the Duchess's husband. He only saw the clothed version. Anything is possible. Sargent was a fellow American. He could be discreet.'

Mr Goodston gave me a sharp glance. 'So who is your candidate?'

'For Clara, King Milan of Serbia. For Jennie, well, Edward the Seventh himself, or Kinsky, or . . . I don't know. For Leonie, the Duke of Connaught. Both Edward and Connaught were themselves painted by Sargent.'

'My goodness.' He took off his glasses. 'You have done your research well. Most thoroughly. I congratulate you. Those were, indeed, the principal admirers of those three ladies. Or, at least, the ones that history knows of.'

'The problem,' I said with emotion, for it had been plaguing me all night and all through all the books I had read, 'the problem is that I can find no connection between Sargent and any of the three Jerome sisters. None at all. If only there were a lead of some sort I could feel encouraged. As it is, I'm stuck.'

He frowned at me. 'I beg your pardon?'

'I'm stuck. I can't make a connection.'

His frown deepened. 'But you said you had read all the Leslie books? Your, er, friend, Sue got them for you?'

'She did. There's nothing in them.'

With a shake of the head, he put his glasses back. 'We

appear to be talking at cross purposes. You've covered the Leslie–Jerome connection?'

'Yes. All Anita's books.'

'No, no! Not Anita. Seymour.'

'Seymour? Who's Seymour?'

'My dear chap!' He heaved himself to his feet. 'I am most fearfully sorry! I made an assumption. Quite wrong of me, of course. Let me enlighten you.'

He shuffled sharply over to his shelves and skittered his fingers along them. 'Ah! Here we are! *The Jerome Connection*, by Seymour Leslie. He was Anita's uncle. One of Leonie's four sons. His memoirs are here. A rich source. John Murray, 1964. Blue cloth, fine. Surely, as I remember—ah! Here we are! Page 38. Opposite. Look, my dear fellow, look!'

He held the book under my nose. A strong charcoal sketch of a handsome woman, her face starting to thicken under the chin, her eyes down, met my gaze. 'Lady Randolph Churchill in 1900, as I first remember her, by John Sargent, RA,' the caption said. I could see the signature on the print: John S. Sargent.

'Mr Goodston! Jesus! Mr Goodston! He drew her! Is there any mention of a painting?' My voice roared through the shop, but Mr Goodston, smiling, shook his head. 'The acknowledgement is to Mrs Hugo Pitman for permitting reproduction of her uncle John Sargent's charcoal drawing of Lady Randolph Churchill. No mention of any painting. I fancy they would have used it if there had been one. The book—' his voice was mild but full of pleasure—'is yours for £20.'

'Done! My God! Done! I'll have it. We've made it! A genuine connection! Why the *hell* isn't it mentioned anywhere else? Not even in Martin's book?'

He shook his head. 'I've no idea. Perhaps it wasn't considered important. After all, Sargent went out of fashion for many years. Portrait-painting is such a fickle business I'm sure I don't need to tell you that.'

'I have to go!' I fumbled for my wallet. 'I have to get to Jeremy! He'll hit the sky when I tell him! Sargent certainly drew Jennie. Why not the others? Why not a joint portrait?'

'You'll find—' Mr Goodston's eyes were sparkling—'that Seymour Leslie isn't too keen on Moreton Frewen. An unwelcome relative who only came to borrow, I seem to recollect he calls him.'

'You don't know what you've done! I'm off! Mr Goodston, you are a jewel, a scholar beyond compare!' I hurled down a £20 note. 'Thanks for the sherry! Thanks for everything!'

'Mr Simpson.' His tone made me stop just as I reached the door.

'What?' I was all afire, eager to be off.

He waved a hand at the shelves. 'The tip of the iceberg. Some of this history is very recent. Very recent. You said yourself it's difficult to know. You talked of secrets. Anything is possible, you said, and you quoted "Never comment on a likeness." Much of history that has not come to light has not come to light for very good reasons, my dear young sir. Reasons of distress and upset, reasons that dictate that some of the past is best left alone. Surely I don't have to tell you, of all people? Digging up the past can be a very dangerous business. A very dangerous business indeed. I do counsel you to take care; I should hate to lose one of my most promising younger clients.'

CHAPTER 15

'I do wish,' said Sue crossly, as I hurled the Jaguar coupé into the first gratifying open stretch of the Kingston bypass, 'that Jeremy would not disconnect his radio telephone. Or his car telephone. It really is too bad that we have to spend the best part of our Saturday chasing about after him like this.'

'Jeremy is no fool. He wants the weekend off. Ergo, he has disconnected the phone. He will reconnect it again once he is at sea. For safety reasons. This is good news for us. It means he's still tied up at the jetty.'

'He's not at a jetty. His boat is on a buoy.'

Women are very contentious. Especially curators of art museums with feminist and teacher-like tendencies. They can't resist correcting you. This time, however, she was wrong.

'His boat normally rides on a buoy at the Hamble. I grant you that. It is not at the Hamble right now. It is at Chichester Harbour. That is why I am doing one hundred and ten miles an hour down the Portsmouth Road, not the M3 motorway. Oops!'

'That man shook his fist at you. How do you know that? About Chichester, I mean?'

'The children's nanny told me. On the 'phone. Jeremy and Mary have sneaked off for a sailing weekend. Well, they couldn't leave till lunch-time. It's one of the last fine weekends of autumn so they scarpered. Don't blame them; it'll soon be too cold for casual jaunts.'

'Why isn't the boat on the Hamble?'

'Because,' I said patiently, swerving round a car that insisted on staying in the fast lane at only eighty miles an hour, 'the whole point of sailing on the Solent is that you can put in for the night at all sorts of neat little places like Cowes and the Isle of Wight, or you can nip up the coast to Chichester and Dell Quay or Bosham and in all of them there'll be a pub and a dinner and a bit of convivial company. It's a mite tame for your ocean-going fanatic but for a nice, pleasant, safe weekend's sailing it takes a lot of beating. I expect Jeremy intends to sail back from Chichester to the Hamble so that he's in a position for the winter or something. He gets so little time for sailing at present.'

'He doesn't do too badly.' Her voice was still sharp. 'Mary gets a bit cheesed off with all that sailing sometimes.'

'But she goes with him. I realize that not many women are keen on the briny but I thought Mary was quite enthusiastic.'

She shot me a glance that said what would you know about what Mary or any other woman really thinks and what she shows by way of enthusiasms, it's all part of a vast, complex, carefully-planned manœuvering for position that only women understand.

'I still think it could have waited,' she said petulantly.

I ignored that. I'd already explained that a find as important as the charcoal sketch by Sargent of Lady Randolph Churchill meant that there might be a very good reason for spending time, money and resources in trying to locate the Sargent referred to on Frewen's share envelope, a Sargent whose existence she, indeed, had suggested. There are times when it doesn't do to over-emphasize these matters. A small affair of two million sterling doesn't stimulate your museum curator much, either, it seems; they live in a world of scholarship, you see. Nothing like ours.

'1900 seems to have been a key date,' I said hopefully, trying to stimulate her interest a bit.

'Why?'

'The Sargent sketch of Jennie says that was as he first knew her. It was in 1900 that the Sitwells rented 25 Chesham Place from the Moreton Frewens. To have their Sargent painted.'

'So?'

'So at least there is a connection with Sargent and both Jennie and Clara in 1900.' I was beginning to get a little narked.

'Oh, really, Tim. It's all so tenuous.'

'My God! Who was it, standing there in the Tate, with Lord Puddledock or Ribblesdale or whatever staring down at us, who said this was it, this must be it, a painting of the three Jerome sisters? Eh? Who was that?'

'I wish I hadn't, now.'

'Why?'

'I'll tell you why.' She turned to look across at me, full-face. 'Because it's dangerous, that's why. Damned dangerous, Tim. It isn't worth it. It isn't worth any amount of money. It frightens me; attacks and break-ins and murder.'

'Not in England.'

'No? What about our flat?'

'They obviously waited until we were out. Avoided violence.'

'They won't next time!'

'Sue.' I reached across to pat her with one hand but she avoided me and we were doing over a hundred so I had to abandon the attempt. 'Bear with me, please. Just for a day or two more. The quicker I get to Jeremy, the quicker it'll all be over.'

'Ha!'

'It will.'

'Some chance.'

A change of emphasis was needed. Art might help. 'I don't think that you like Sargent very much,' I said. 'I get the feeling that he doesn't turn you on.'

'He doesn't.' She's got firm views, has Sue; only the Impressionists really turn her on. 'He wasn't really an Impressionist, you know.'

'Eh?'

'Some people tried to make out he was one. Because he knew Monet and so on. But Monet always said Sargent wasn't one of them. And Degas was quite contemptuous.'

'Catty lot, artists.'

'I think painting came too easily to him. Sargent, I mean. People were jealous of that. He did experiment with Impressionism, though. Until he painted "Carnation, Lily, Lily, Rose". That's contrary to all the principles of Impressionism. Took him ages to paint it. He had to keep setting the children and lanterns up in the twilight and then rushing out to get a bit of the colour. Made that Broadway lot laugh a bit.'

'I didn't know it was painted in New York?'

'Oh, *Tim*. Really! Russell House, Broadway. He leased it with the Millets. There were a lot of ·Americans in the Cotswolds then. Sargent went there frequently. Afterwards he took a place at Fladbury. A rectory. That's in Worcestershire as well.'

'Broadway, Worcestershire? The Cotswolds?'

'Yes, yes, of course. What's the matter? Mind that car!'

'Nothing. I thought you said that Sargent only painted in his Tite Street studio? That's why the Sitwells and all those had to go there.'

'Of course. That was for *portraits*.' Her voice was impatient. 'Sargent did lots of *plein-air* paintings, out of doors. He was very good at that. In fact he got to hate portraits. They made his living, a lot of money in fact, but he found it a treadmill. Like your favourite, Orpen. Made Orpen drink himself to death.'

'Did Sargent marry?'

She shot me a glance. 'No, he didn't. But don't get the wrong idea. There's never been a breath of scandal about Sargent. I know your propensity for biographical investigation of that sort.'

'Mmmm. When was he in the Cotswolds?'

'Oh, the eighteen-eighties. 'Nineties. That sort of time. Why?'

'Just thinking.'

'Thinking what?'

It was time to stop this, so I quoted:

> 'Successfully she stopped him drinking,
> How can she prevent him thinking?'

'Tim!'

'Sorry. Uncalled for. Do you know that the Frewens had

to give up 25 Chesham Place, but they moved in Great
Cumberland Place? Number 39A, that was. Shortly after
1900.'

'What are you getting at?'

'Just that Jennie lived at 37A. And Leonie at No. 10. So
it is entirely possible, given the absence of their menfolk on
a regular basis, that the three could have sat for Sargent
with ease, round about then.'

'It'd have been a rather mature portrait. Clara would
have been fifty.'

'That's no impediment. Sargent often painted mature
women, mothers and daughters, that sort of thing. Three
famous Americans, at the height of English society, would
have been a great subject for him. He painted Jennie's
brother-in-law, the Duke of Marlborough, and his wife,
Consuelo Vanderbilt, another American, then. He belted
out portraits in England and America at an amazing rate.
Ah, that reminds me, you do realize that he painted Edward
the Seventh—who wanted to knight him but couldn't, because he was an American—and Edward's brother, the
Duke of Connaught, as well?'

'Yes. And I know what you're going to say about their
relationship with Jennie and Leonie respectively. I've read
Anita Leslie too, Tim, remember?'

'Sorry. Ah, we've arrived.'

Jeremy's yacht was parked, or moored, or whatever they
call it, in a harbour near Chichester that kept its level
against the tide by use of a lock built into a sort of dam, like
a breakwater. Within this flooded, peaceful basin, a series
of wooden jetties had been constructed so that the yachts
could be tied up and yachtsmen could walk on and off them
without difficulty. It reminded me a bit of the Connecticut
coast, which is full of creeks kitted out the same way. That
Saturday afternoon it was relatively empty because most of
the berth owners had already set out, anticipating that this
would indeed be one of the last glorious weekends of the

year, warm and sunny but with a fresh breeze that was ideal for sailing.

I pulled the car to a halt on the earth and gravel near the yacht basin and hopped out. Sue appeared on the other side of the car, pulling on a yellow windcheater against the breeze. The sound of ropes or halyards slapping against metal masts hit my ears. A smell of salt mud, fishy stew and wet boots spiked my nostrils. Big white clouds soared overhead, not obscuring the sun or the blue sky enough to lessen the bright glare and that very clear delineation of detail that you get when, later in the year, the sun is lower on the horizon and seems to pick out every leaf and blade or, in this case, every slapping wavelet and bobbing sea-bird that danced on the water.

'There they are!' Sue pointed and waved. 'There! At the end of the jetty. On their own! Hi! Mary! Jeremy!'

It was true. At the end of the third jetty along to our left stood Jeremy's sloop, preparing to leave. Mary stood on the jetty, holding a rope, preparing to cast off. The throb of the engine, starting up, came over the water.

'Hi!' I roared, running towards them with Sue close behind. 'Hey! Mary! Jeremy! Wait!'

Mary heard us. I saw the flash of her white teeth as she laughed and waved. Her head turned back to Jeremy, half-hidden in the cockpit, and I saw his cap pop up over a coaming. He did something with the controls, and came out over the side. I reached the start of the jetty, but Mary was skipping towards me, lightly hopping over the odd rope across the duckboards.

'Wait!' she called. 'Stay there, Tim! The jetty's very slippery. There's been some spillage.'

I grabbed Sue's arm just as her foot went on to the quay.

'Hold on!' Jeremy bellowed, striding towards us, clad in smart waterproof gear and those light rubber boots with castellated white soles that all that crowd wear. 'Wait there!

The jetty's lethally slippery! What on earth are you doing
here?'

'The Sargent,' I shrieked back. 'You're not going to
believe this, Jeremy. The Sargent. It—'

I didn't hear the next word. My ears went numb. It was
like concussion. I could see Jeremy, Mary, Sue's face, their
features working, Sue screaming, Mary's eyes white, Jeremy
lurching forward, out of control, on to his face in his water-
proofs, all in slow motion. I couldn't hear any sound. I saw
the yacht rear up in the water, great pieces flying off it,
small jagged bits sailing high into the air, water lashing
with compression and blast, surfaces churned white by
falling debris, rigging and spars and glass and shards going
skywards and coming towards us, so that I leapt to hurl Sue
and Mary to the ground, trying to cover them as bits
clumped down all around us. Sound suddenly returned: a
horrible, thudding, banging, screaming sound, air whistling
with projectiles, people shouting in fear, birds and gulls
shrieking and wheeling. Then silence again.

Sue was having hysterics so I clasped her first. Jeremy,
who had a huge mark on his face, was on all fours, shouting
at Mary, but she was all right. I got a glance at the remainder
of the sloop. There was nothing left above the hull and the
hull was missing all one side, so that, with the mooring rope
Mary had left in place still holding it, the shattered half was
sinking slowly into the water, held by the rope which,
obstinately, had not been severed. I realized then that the
sloop should not still have been tethered to the jetty.
It should have been out on the water, with its crew concentrated in it, in the cockpit, where there would be no
escaping the blast, where they would receive the full
impact of it. That was how the thing had been timed.
Just like the IRA did when they blew up poor old Mountbatten and his family off the west coast of Ireland a few
years back.

That was when it came to me. Holding Sue, who was

shivering and crying but calming down, and looking at Jeremy's desperate, contorted face as he held his precious Mary to him, safe and sound, the idea of Mountbatten and the IRA triggered back the memory of Mr Goodston's reproving words to me the first time I had visited his shop and made some comment about Anita Leslie and Elizabeth Longford. 'Whenever you are delving into the past—or the present—history or situation of the British Isles, never, but never, neglect what I call the Irish Dimension. Never. It's a fatal mistake.'

That was precisely what I had done. Despite names like O'Hare and Maguire and Casey, I had done just that. As people raced towards us and shouts arose, it hit me that I had completely and utterly neglected the Irish Dimension. Like an absolute fool.

It was time to put that right.

CHAPTER 16

The Aer Lingus flight from Heathrow to Cork takes off in the mid-afternoon so that, an hour or so later, when you are poised high to the south of that famous Irish city, you can squint out of the plane window to see, even further south, the valley of the river Bandon as it rolls towards Kinsale. On a clear day, when it is not raining, you might discern, far away below you, the village of Innishannon lodged on each bank of the river in a lush setting of superb fishing country.

Mostly, however, it is raining. It certainly was the day Sue and I flew in to Cork, so much so that they said we were lucky to get there at all. The airport had been closed all morning due to low cloud, which meant quite simply that the rain had become dense enough and heavy enough to blot everything out. It lifted briefly during the afternoon, enough for us to land anyway, and then it dropped again, the minute after we landed it seemed to me, so that when Johnson and Perrot handed the hired saloon over to us we had to scurry quickly inside it to avoid getting soaked. We untangled ourselves behind beating wipers that hardly kept the windscreen clear of the sluicing downpour, Sue shaking her wet hair and me pulling my wet trousers off my knees so that rheumatism wouldn't set in.

'I think I'll head straight for Cork,' I said. 'There's no point in going down to Innishannon this evening; everyone will be indoors during weather like this.'

She nodded in agreement and I headed the car towards town. I'm not sure when it was after the explosion at Chichester that I told Sue I was going to have to go to Ireland. Probably well after she had calmed down and the official inquiries had started, inquiries that got more serious and ominous as each piece of evidence came to light. Jeremy's yacht was not destroyed by a fuel leak or an accident. It was blown up by a bomb, a proper bomb, made from sticks of dynamite and wired to his ignition, his engine ignition, with a timer to ensure that he would be out on the water and exposed to the full force of the blast, as I had guessed. Jeremy was very badly shaken. In all the various problems I've had in the past it has been me, almost uniquely me, with Sue occasionally involved, that has been the target of the violence, and that was what, after Andy's call, I had assumed this time. Jeremy has never had anything directed at him before; the fact that Mary was with him had really rammed the danger home. Jeremy was in London, pondering on the hazards of life with the Art Fund and, after an hysterical and bewildered discussion with me, on the dreadful speculation that someone specifically wanted to do him in. I hoped it wouldn't put Jeremy off the whole enterprise, but I couldn't help being slightly amused; he'd blithely sent me off to pursue the Sargent without hesitation, never suspecting that the boomerang would head in his direction. There was a certain *Schadenfreud* in it all, from my point of view.

Sue had accepted the excursion to Ireland calmly. I was not nearly as calm about her insistence on coming with me, but reason would not prevail.

'Either I come with you,' she said, 'or you don't go.'

'You don't really need to come,' I responded. 'I can make my inquiries and be back within two days. You could stay with your mother. Or you'd be safe with Nobby and Gillian—'

'No!' Her voice was resolute. 'I will do no such thing. I will come with you. You have had a lucky escape. You have quite fortuitously saved Jeremy and Mary's lives. I believe that this whole thing has acquired a momentum of its own, a force that we must follow. It's like the other things in the past, only this time I feel it more strongly than ever before. I'm not letting you go alone. I don't know what you're looking for and I don't think you're very certain, either, but I'm coming. I said I wouldn't drop out, no matter what happened, and I'm not. You've set this whole train of events in motion and I'm keeping close to you.'

There's no stopping her when she's in that sort of mood and, on quieter reflection, I thought that she would probably be safer with me in Ireland than hanging alone around the flat in London. I booked the tickets and we sallied forth the next day. I'd never been to Cork before and, apart from remembering something vague from my school history books about Desmond and, later, Florence MacCarthy, and the Spanish occupation, and Winston's ancestor John taking the city for King Billy, and how the town always seemed to back the wrong side, the place was a mystery to me. All I knew was that it had the nearest airport to Innishannon, and that we could stay in a good hotel. I also remembered that Moreton Frewen, after staying overlong with Lillie Langtry when bidding a fond farewell to her on leaving for Wyoming, missed his ship in England but caught it at Cork

after a Sunday railway chase that had all Ireland betting
on the outcome. In those days the Atlantic steamers stopped
at Queenstown, or Cobh, as it is now properly called again,
in Cork harbour, before proceeding to America from England. Moreton had to catch the Irish mail train in London,
cross to Dublin, hire a special train, race to Cobh, leap on
to a sea-going tender and motor out to the departing steamer
to be hauled on board by his brother Richard and the
hunting party because his overnight farewell had caused
him to miss his proper embarkation. All in a day's adventure
to the cool-headed Moreton, who must have known Cork
well from his youthful days at Innishannon.

The city was grey and watery as we came into the old,
historic centre with the many bridges over the Lee and
found our way to the hotel. A silver-grey BMW nearly
collided with me as I altered course down St Patrick's
Street, admiring the quays as I crossed the bridge. In the
continuous rain it wasn't easy to be certain I had the right
way and I called an apology after the vanishing German
car as I turned again into MacCurtain Street, but the driver
wouldn't have heard me. We unloaded our cases and were
welcomed into the warmth, where an Irish whiskey and a
splendid meal of fresh fish soon dispelled thoughts of the
damp outside.

Sue was excited. She was almost feverish. She talked
animatedly, she ate ravenously, she insisted on going out
for a walk round the town in what had now become a drizzle,
she clutched at me in enthusiasm, she was like a terrier
nearing the end of a burrow for a rabbit. I realized that she
had the nervous anticipation of someone approaching the
end of a quest, someone convinced that a great quarry was
in sight. Since I wasn't sure myself quite what my own
instincts had brought me to, I tried to be a calming influence
without dampening her, but it was difficult, with her on
such a high key, not to be drawn into an enthusiastic reaction
myself. Especially when the effect upon her, after we had

retired for the night, was of an order that I won't embarrass anyone by describing. I've often pondered, in those gloomy moments that one gets, whether my attraction for Sue is due more to the excitement of the Art Fund's occasionally hair-raising acquisitions than to my scintillating personality, but it doesn't do to dwell on such introspective doubts. The fact is that of Cork itself I retain an affectionate, damply-grey memory, but the night that we spent there will never fade from my mind.

Mornings of joy are supposed to give for evenings of tearfulness. This time it was the other way round. The next day was cloudy but it wasn't raining. I woke with grave doubts in my mind. Sue gave me a rapturous embrace, leapt from the bed and practically drove me from the room in excitement. We had a splendid breakfast in which the local Cork-cured bacon and soda bread figured richly. I wondered what the hell I thought I was doing. I had terrible presentiments, irrational superstitious fears. Mr Goodston's warnings sounded in my head. We were in Ireland, we were here to dig up the past, we were going to intrude. Uncontrollable forces might be let loose. Sue golloped down the biggest breakfast I've ever seen her eat. She didn't seem to notice my qualms.

'Golly, I was hungry,' she exclaimed, giving me a flash of her blue eyes. 'Isn't this terrific? I feel marvellous! It must be the air. Come on, we've got to get going, haven't we? Mustn't waste time. Will we go on up north to Monaghan afterwards? To Castle Leslie? Buck up, Tim, I've finished. Drink up your tea.'

We got out on to the road, back past the airport, on to Ballinhassig and, with the signposts pointing to Bandon, we soon arrived at Innishannon, with a fork to the left down towards Kinsale.

There wasn't anything there. Nothing at all.

Oh, of course, I knew that the house had been burnt down by the Republicans in 1921. I knew that. I knew how

the Frewens came to own the place before Moreton was
born, taking it over from the improvident Adderleys in
return for a loan of £60,000 which could never be repaid.
I knew how old Thomas Frewen, Moreton's father, had
grumbled about good Sussex money lost on an Irish village,
but had none the less been a conscientious landlord and
repaired all the houses, maintained all the culverts, walls
and drains, replanted the woods. I knew how Moreton had
come here to learn all about salmon fishing as a boy of
twelve. I knew how he had inherited the estate when his
brother Richard was drowned while yachting off the Pem-
broke coast. I knew how he had tried to breed trout and
raise quail in this densely vegetated, heavily-poached, richly
endowed countryside. I knew how Clara preferred her be-
loved Brede Place in Sussex, never understanding Ireland. I
knew how their children had loved Innishannon, as Moreton
had, and how their daughter Clare, who married Wilfred
Sheridan and was quickly widowed by the First World War,
had come back in 1922 and climbed the garden wall to look
at the blackened ruin of their old home, just as I, now, was
sitting here, sixty-four years later, wondering what the hell
I was doing in this remote, damp and beautiful place with
the green hills and rocky walls and fisherman's river all
around me.

What I did first, after stopping to reflect on events and
to try and stifle my misgivings, was to go to the Innishannon
House Hotel. I thought it was the Frewens' old place,
rebuilt, but it wasn't. It was an old house all right, 1720 the
brochures said, right spang on the river, with smooth green
lawns and arched loggia windows, but it wasn't the
Frewens'. The proprietor was called Brian Macarthy and
he grinned sympathetically at me and Sue as we stood before
him.

'Oh no,' he said. 'This isn't it. The Frewens took over the
Adderleys' place—' he spoke as if it were yesterday—'and
pulled it down to build a new house in the early nineteenth

century. Riverview, I think it was called. It was burnt down in what we here euphemistically call the troubles. It's on the north side of the river, down a side road by the Catholic Church.'

'Is there anything left of it?'

He shook his head. 'No, I don't think so. It's a while since I last looked, but it was crumbled then and ivy grew all over the place. There's a modern house built in front of it. Clare Sheridan used to say how like the jungle it is round here. The vegetation grows like mad and covers everything so quickly. The whole place was encumbered, you know. To Barclays Bank. They still own a few houses in the village. There's a tradition that Winston Churchill came here because he was Frewen's nephew, but I don't know if that's true.' He smiled inquiringly. 'Are you members of the family? One of Moreton Frewen's grandsons was here a while back. From Australia, I think. Part of the Anglo-Irish diaspora, you might say. The British diaspora, indeed.'

I shook my head, warming to him. 'No, we're not members of the family. We're just doing some research. On, er, the family and its associations. Is there anything left of the trout hatchery?'

He shook his head vigorously. 'Indeed not. I'm afraid they did for that straight away. There were some very bloody-minded people about just then, you know. The fish bailiff—he was a Scot, I believe—was done for at the same time.' He smiled, the shy, apologetic smile of the Irishman trying to break the news gently to the English that things had been very nasty in our direction but that he really meant us well personally, even if in his heart of hearts he felt we might have deserved it.

'Is there anyone left in the village who remembers the house?' Sue was still eager, anxious. 'Anyone who worked there or anything?'

'Ach, no, I don't think so.' He smiled at her tolerantly.

'It was a long time ago, you know. Nineteen-twenty-one.
People have moved on and they'd be in their eighties now,
or have been children at the time.' His expression changed.
'Now that's a thought. There was a fellow called Coughlan
worked at the hatchery. His son's a poacher, towards Macroom. I've heard that he would remember the Frewens but
I've never met him. He's a bit of a legend as a salmon
poacher—they're a breed round here—being brought up
on the Bandon, but he's a very suspicious sort of an old
man. A recluse, almost.' He scratched his chin dubiously.
'He might talk to you. Do you want me to see if I can find
his address?'

'Oh, Mr Macarthy!' Sue hopped from one leg to the other.
'Please! Please! If you could! We'd be so grateful.'

He grinned attractively and looked at her eyes, sparkling
with excitement. 'How could a man resist that, now? Wait
here and I'll see what I can find out.'

I sat down on a hall chair as he disappeared into his
office. Ivy and a tangle of shrubbery had grown over material
relics of the Frewens here. The only traces that remained
were people's memories, laughing references to improvi-
dence and wildness, distant fated activities that bore no
relation to this world. I thought of the trails I had followed
before, to Somers Town and Meudon, to Hastings and Hove
and Bedford Park on similar pursuits, with similar instincts.
I remembered Small Hythe where there wasn't anything to
find, either; E. W. Godwin was just as evanescent as the
tall, handsome, hunting Frewen of such financial mayhem.*
Here I was, doing the same sort of thing again, for the remote
passing chance of a celebrated painting that somehow didn't
seem to get any nearer. There was nothing of me here; this
was a delightful foreign country where Englishmen like
me no longer belonged, had no presence, were part of
an uncomfortably-near unpleasant past, even if welcomed

* *The Godwin Sideboard.*

unreservedly as tourists, remote relations, by genuinely smiling people.

I was wrong. About my lack of presence, anyway.

'What a shame.' Sue's voice cut into my thoughts. 'They must have loved it here. Look at this super country hotel. I can understand why all the Frewens were so keen to come. It must have been a bitter blow. But they weren't the only ones. Lord Bandon was kidnapped and Castle Bernard was burnt down.'

'Mmmm?'

'You're lost, aren't you?'

'What?'

'You're lost. I can tell.' Her tone was decisive, still full of electric enthusiasm. 'Come on, Tim, buck up! This old chap Coughlan may have the answers. If not, we'll go to Monaghan.'

'I don't know. I feel apprehensive.'

'Oh, Tim! You of all people. I—ah, here's Mr Macarthy.'

He looked dubiously at a piece of paper as he came towards us, across the hall. 'I've tried to draw a map,' he explained. 'You have to take the Cookstown road from Bandon and then head towards Macroom. But it's a difficult place, up a country track. And there's no phone, of course.' He gave Sue the paper apologetically. 'I hope you can make sense of that. I got the directions from an old village woman but I can't vouch that they'll be right. You know how it is in Ireland; everyone knows the way but no one ever gets there.'

We laughed with him and, promising to return, we got back into the car. I drove back on to the Bandon road, just noticing the silver flash of a saloon turning by the Catholic Church as we sped our way past a roadside shrine set back in the loose stone wall bordering the route. It made me think of my near-collision the night before in the pouring rain, the symbolic sense of being partly lost, partly navigating by instinct, that comes over me from time to time.

Fortunately Sue interrupted any further thoughts with peremptory directions of a practical nature, so I had to concen-
trate on the specific way ahead.

We had to ask for directions twice. There was a smaller
road, signposted only in Gaelic, which made life a bit
difficult. Then there was a direction which seemed to be
doubling us back on ourselves. Finally, at right angles to a
side road to Macroom, a rutted track between two rough
stone walls, buttressed by banks of nettles and vetches, led
up a long green slope that steepened as it curved upwards
towards a distant cottage. Reluctantly I turned the hired
saloon up the track. The cottage was a fairly typical Irish
one, of a single storey, thatched, with a chimney perched
on the top of each thick, gabled end-wall. In the centre of
the whitewashed front was a door, with a small window on
each side. A thin whisper of blue smoke dribbled out of the
right-hand chimney and vanished into the damp breeze.
Behind the cottage loomed rounded hills and, as we painfully
lurched over the stony bumps between the walls, I could
see short, stunted trees half-circling the flat space behind
the building. The track levelled off a bit near the house and
I could see that it carried the single stony way onwards,
past the cottage and over the hill to some unknown destination out on the wet windy hills above the lusher vegetation
of the sheltered valleys.

I pulled the car up outside the stone cottage and drew
the vehicle off the track on to a bumpy green verge. Getting
out into the quick breeze, I noticed how much closer we
were to the clouds that drove across above us, and how
much barer the world seemed to be up here, scrubbed by
the wind. Water trickled out of the stone wall bordering the
road, crossed the track and disappeared into the wall the
other side, parting the nettles with a flat, wet, muddy groove.
Above the low stones there was a fine distant view over
green fields and wooded cloughs that must have contained
more streams, rivers, and fast-running water bubbling over

rocks. A fine prospect for a fish poacher, I thought, as I walked to the front door with Sue at my side.

No one answered my knock. I tried again and waited. Sue looked up meaningfully at the bit of smoke coming from the chimney but it was probably a peat fire of the sort they keep going all day. After a while I gave it up and tramped round the side of the cottage to recce the back, in case there was anyone there. I turned the corner of the building and pulled up quickly, short in my tracks.

An old man stood before me, braced with his legs apart among the vegetables clinging to the ground in that wind-swept back garden. Across his arm, with the ease of long habitude, lay an old-fashioned shotgun, a twelve-bore, smooth and polished with the wear of decades. On his head was a cloth cap, greasy with age. He was wrapped in an ancient, oiled coat of antique cut, with huge flapped pockets for game and pouches for ammunition. The face was lined, deeply weathered, shrewd and sharp, like a creature of the forest, heath or hedgerow. Very keen blue eyes, narrowed by ages of frowning into the weather, peered out from under spiky white eyebrows. His gaze flicked as Sue came round the side of the cottage behind me and she stopped, hesitant, to look at me. I realized that his positioning was careful and that the shotgun, though broken open, was charged with the necessary two cartridges. No one could have come round the side of that cottage and taken him by surprise. No one could have avoided his field of fire; he had a clear view of anyone trying to flank round the back of the house. He must have watched the car come all the way up the track, watched us get out and knock at his door, waited to see how keen we were to find him.

'Mr Coughlan?' I stood up straight, kept my face open, my voice as pleasant as possible. My arms were by my sides.

'I am,' he said.

His voice was quiet and middle-toned, without the hardness of Dublin or the north. Somehow I felt a confidence

that this man would listen to me, had a natural sympathy
that wouldn't tell me to get lost, like so many people might.

'I'm sorry to bother you. I'm from England. I got your
name from the hotel in Innishannon.'

'From England.' It was a statement, not a question. 'I
understand that.'

'And this, er, this is a friend of mine, Sue Westerman.
My name is Tim Simpson. We came to find you.'

'Simpson.' He seemed to muse slightly over the name.
'You're not a Scotsman, then?'

'No. I'm English. From London.'

Silence. He was waiting for me. I cleared my throat. 'I
was told you might be able to help me. It's a matter
concerning the time the Frewens owned the house at Innishannon.'

'The Frewens?'

'Yes. Moreton Frewen, actually.'

'That's a long time ago.'

'Yes. It is.'

'I was only eleven years old when they burnt that house
down.'

'Er, I suppose so. But I believe your father worked there
for a while?'

'My father worked there for thirty years.'

I didn't seem to be getting anywhere. He was staring at
me in an odd way that was disconcerting. I was wondering
whether it might be a good idea to get Sue to talk to him,
Irishmen being particularly charming with the ladies, when
he spoke again.

'You must forgive me for staring like this, but have I not
seen you somewhere before?'

That flummoxed me. 'No. Er, no. I don't think so.'

'I never forget a face.' His own brown, crinkled features
moved with a thoughtful, friendly look. 'I said to myself as
you came round the house, I said that feller with the broken
nose, I know him now, I've seen him before.'

'Really? I don't think so. I've never been here before.'

'I said to myself he's not a boxer, not the way he moves. If you'll pardon me, I know the way people move, it's like animals d'you see, you can tell from how an animal moves what it does, what it has to do to live, and it's the same with people.'

'Oh.' This is absurd, I thought, I'm standing in the middle of a vegetable garden at the back of an Irish bothy, probably on a wild goose chase, time's going by, and I'm not a step nearer, it—

'Rugby, now. That'll be a rugby player, I said to myself. Was I right? I'll never make a mistake about a thing like that. Will I?'

'You're right. I used to be a rugby player, but I haven't been for years.'

'Ah, but it leaves a mark, d'you see? A forward now, you'd be a forward. Wouldn't you?'

'I was. How did you know?'

A wide smile of pure joy came over his face. 'Ah, sir, 'tis unmistakable. Quite entirely unmistakable. My nephew, d'you see, he was a rugby forward. He played in England, too. To the pride of his entire family. After he left Cork. He'd be about your age, now.'

'Oh really? I'm afraid I can't recall, er, any Coughlan in my time. Who did he play for?'

'His name wouldn't be Coughlan. He was my sister's boy. She married a Horrigan, from Cork.'

'Horrigan? I can't—Good God! You're not talking of Mad Paddy Horrigan, the lock forward? Played for London Irish? Massive great bloke?'

The old man drew himself up in reproachful dignity. He shot me a look of grave affront. 'My nephew Patrick did indeed play for the London Irish side. With great distinction. After taking his medical degree.'

'About ten years ago? Maybe twelve?'

'Now I know it! I know it!' The old fellow slapped his

thigh, making the shotgun bounce and me jerk. 'I know where I've seen you! It's in the photograph. I've got it inside. It was an anniversary match—'

'Oh no! Don't tell me. O'Shaughnessy's XV versus the London Irish. An invitation side, at Richmond? They scooped me in at the last moment because they were short of a tight-head prop. Eleven years ago, it was. There was a photo afterwards. My God, Paddy was a powerful bug—er, fellow, he really was. A shocker to try and stop. Nearly broke my collar-bone.'

'Simpson! That's your name! You're in my house. My house right here. I remember Patrick spoke of you. If only that eejit Lacey hadn't asked that Englishman to join him, he said, we'd have done a lot better. He was forever blocking my way.'

'That was a match! And my God, afterwards! They destroyed nearly the whole of Soho. At one stage they got the chorus line from one of the musicals—*Hair*, I think it was, mind you, it might have been *Oh, Calcutta!*—and the girls —no, Sue's looking at me, I'd better not. What a small world!'

'But look at this! What will you think of me? Keeping you standing out here in this godforsaken vegetable garden in this keen wind without a thought of asking you inside? And you here all the way from England. It's disgraceful. I'm getting old, but it's no excuse. Come in, come in. No, dear lady, not the back door. I'm ashamed of that, it's such a mess. The front, if you please.'

He shepherded us back round to the front of the cottage and threw the door open with a flourish. We entered a dark but brightly-polished room with a deep fireplace, in which a peat fire smouldered dully. He put the shotgun down carefully on the butt inside the nook and snapped it shut, cartridges and all. I hoped the safety-catch still worked.

'Here we are!' he crowed, taking down a mounted photograph from a rank of them that lapped each other all along the mantel ledge framing the top of the fireplace. 'The names are all written on the back. I've looked through all these evening after evening. There's no telly here, you see. Thank the Lord.'

It was still quite fresh and bright. A black-and-white picture of a crowd of muddy rugby players, splashed and tattered, grinning cheerfully at the camera. Sue's hair brushed the side of my neck as I looked at it and I heard her laugh softly. 'My, but you were younger then. What a dreadful thug you look! How on earth did you come to play in such a match?'

I grinned at her and the old man. 'I was having a quiet beer in a pub on the Sunbury Road and four of O'Shaughnessy's side came in on their way to the match. I'd played with one of them at Cambridge. Tony Lacey, he was called, and he gave a great shout and said, 'Tim, you're just the man we need, we're short of a prop for the match.' The next thing I knew I was on the rugger field full of beer, with twenty-nine Irishmen knocking six bells out of each other and me the English punchbag in the middle. Shocking, it was, but they were a great crowd.' I stabbed my finger close to the group photograph. 'There's Paddy, er, your nephew Patrick. Cor, he was a big fellow. What's he doing now?'

The old man smiled happily. 'He's in Australia. He has a partnership in a medical practice there. Owns his own racehorse. He was always a fine boy and he still writes to me from time to time.'

'Send him my best, then. I didn't know him well, but I remember him vividly.'

'I will, for sure. Please have a seat. Let me give you a cup of tea? The young lady can use one, I'm sure?'

'Oh, Mr Coughlan—' Sue was at her most seductive— 'it'll be a lot of trouble, won't it? Please don't bother.'

'Of course it won't. Look—is the kettle not practically boiling on the hob already? A cup of Irish tea will warm you on a day like this. And an old man doesn't often get the chance of such fair company in his house.'

She blushed prettily and thanked him. It's a good job he's not forty years younger, I thought, otherwise there'd be problems, but he was putting teacups together and looking at me curiously as I sat at his cottage table in that simple but clean living-room. He picked up a fan of rook's feathers to liven the fire with, and spoke thoughtfully.

'Moreton Frewen, now. He and his brother Richard— they were fine men with guns and horses. Great tall fellers, my father said, when they were young they'd ride over anything. Wild, mad as hares, they were. Do anything for a bet on a race. All Ireland gambled on whether Moreton would catch the steam packet to America when he raced to catch it at Cork on a special train from Dublin.' He winked at me. 'The tale was that it was Mrs Langtry who'd detained him and caused him to miss the boat in England.'

'It's true.'

'Ha, I thought it was. They were wild all right.' He cocked an eye at me. 'My nephew Patrick was something of a prankster, you may say, but he had nothing on the Frewens. They were half-Irish, you know.'

I nodded. 'Their mother was a Homan, from County Kildare.'

'That's so. A tiny little woman, my father said.'

I tried to say it as gently as I could. 'Which made it all the harder for Moreton to understand.'

'What?'

'That they burnt his house down. It hit him hard. The Frewens were good landlords. Old Thomas Frewen spent a fortune on Innishannon. The village, I mean. Moreton loved the place. It hit him hard. He was an MP here once.'

'It hit him hard? Him?' Old Coughlan's eyes pierced mine. 'I remember the night it happened, young man! My father came in, crying. In tears, he was. I was eleven years old. I'd never seen my father cry. I was brought up to be a brave little boy, not to cry and all that. And there was my father, crying. "Sure, he said, we're destroyed entirely now. The house has gone. And everything in it. The Frewens'll never come back to us. It's finished for us. The trout hatchery will go, and the quails, the partridges and the pheasants. What will become of us?" They were terrible times. My father kept his shotgun—that very shotgun there—always to hand. He advised me to do the same and I always have. I'm ashamed to say that's life in Ireland and it isn't any better now. What with the economic troubles and the young folk all leaving once again and Haughey bound to get in at the next election because Fitzgerald, poor man, is too quiet for all of us.'

His eyes dropped and I shuffled my feet. 'I'm sorry. I didn't mean to open old wounds.'

'Ach, in Ireland you can't avoid it.' He gave me a faint smile. 'Let's be having our tea.'

The kettle, on an iron stand or trivet half into his peat fire, started to steam and spit. He stooped to lift it off with a thick pad and poured boiling water into an ancient brown teapot, filling it to the top so that leaves bobbed on the surface and a herbal, fragrant smell vapoured up to our nostrils before he dropped a stained lid over the brew.

'A fine strong cup o' tea,' he said. 'There's nothing like it.'

I stared at the photograph over the mantelpiece. Which philosopher can ever explain the consequences of our actions? As a result of that hilarious beer in a pub on the Sunbury Road eleven years ago, my photograph was lodged here, in this remote, isolated corner of Ireland, preserved, as the poet says, smaller and clearer as the years go by, to stare out in the blurred, youthful, cheerful ignorance of that day. Where else might my younger visage look unknowingly on the daily life of some family or pensioner, guardians of a favourite son or nephew's sporting past? Probably nowhere;

his was an Irish experience, the sort of thing that only happens to you in Ireland, on Irish days, with Irish people.

'Has it given you a turn?' Old Coughlan gave me a knowing smile and a lift of his eyebrows. 'Will it not be something to tell your grandchildren one day? Ye walked into a cottage in Ireland and find your picture on the wall? Hey, that's a thing, now. A thing to tell your grandchildren?' He winked at Sue, who winked back at him like a true colleen.

'It certainly will be. It's quite extraordinary. I don't know how to describe it. The most peculiar feeling.'

'Ha! The tea'll have pulled nicely, now. I'll pour it out. 'Twas fate, that's what it was. That brought you here, I mean. There's always an explanation for such things. There has to be. Will that be enough milk for you? It was destiny for sure. Say when, now, dear lady.'

'Super.'

'And you, sir?'

'Fine. Thanks.'

'There's too much we can't explain, so why bother trying? It'll all be clear one day, I've always said, but in the meantime look after yourself, look after yourself carefully. That's the thing.'

The tea was hot and powerful, restoring my slightly jaded metabolism to a more alert condition. The old man regarded me placidly, showing no desire to hurry the conversation or to inquire what it was that I had wanted with him. Sue, sensitive to mood as ever, had dropped into a quiet calm, sipping her tea and rubbing one foot gently down the back of her leg in a sort of soothing motion. The cottage room was warm and peaceful, its thick walls insulated the interior from the weather. I cleared my throat.

'Have you been away from Innishannon for a long time? Living here, I mean?'

'Oh yes. During the Troubles me father got a job in Kinsale. Then in Cork. He didn't like it; he was a countryman, d'you see. So we moved out to this region and he rented a little farm and then I did the same. So here I am. It's a simple story. I've never missed anything I wanted here.'

'Do you remember the big house at Innishannon? The Frewens' place?'

'Of course I do. I was eleven when it went. A boy's memory is always bright. It's a man's you can't rely on.' His eyes crinkled for a moment at his own wisdom and he sipped his tea. 'What was it you were looking for? If it's not an impertinent question?'

'A painting.' I'd decided to be direct. 'A painting of the three sisters. Mrs Frewen and her two sisters.'

His eyes widened and he almost glared at me for a moment before I realized that I had really given him a big surprise. He put his tea down on the scrubbed wooden table-top and looked from me to Sue and then back to me again.

'Now how the devil—pardon me, dear lady—but how the very devil did you know about that?'

Sue put her tea down and I sensed her tensing with excitement. I put a hand on her arm. 'I guessed it, mostly. But Frewen himself—Moreton, I mean—he made a note about it. Someone we know found the note.'

'Well I'll be damned! Indeed I will. I thought I was the only one left who knew about that.'

'You saw it? Was it hanging on the wall?'

He shook his head vigorously. 'Indeed it was not! It certainly never hung on any wall! It was a secret, was it not? A dire family secret. It was kept completely out of sight. That's how I saw it.'

'I beg your pardon?'

'It was covered over. It was in the top attic, right up in the roof. There was a scandal connected with it. I would never have been seeing it if I hadn't been a harum-scarum lad. We were always up to pranks. We used to play hide-and-seek all over. Up in the attics, sometimes, but the family and the servants, they used to give us a real hiding if they caught us.'

'But you saw it?' Sue was too excited to wait.

'Oh, dear lady, let me tell you, now. One day it was raining like hell, as it always does here in March, and my father was down at the trout hatchery doing something and I was bored, so I sneaked in the house for a piece of bread and butter from the cook. Drunk as a lord she was, brandy was her tipple, and while she wasn't looking I sneaked up the back stairs—all the big houses had a servants' staircase —and up I went, up and up, higher and higher, till I thought I'd reached heaven. But it wasn't, you see. It was the very top attic. I'd never been there before, the door was stiff with damp and dust and I could only just push it open a crack. But I was a thin wiry lad and I squeezed through and there were papers and boxes all strewn about. And a big frame with a cloth over it. So I pulled the cloth to one side and there they were, three angels they seemed. I really thought I was in heaven then, with them ladies in old-fashioned dresses looking at me. I found afterwards that was how they dressed before the war, with long clothes and folds and ribbons and things, but I didn't know then. And I asked my father that evening if rich folk always had angels up in the attic and he gave me a hiding like I'd never had. I howled so loud my mother cried and he was sorry. He really was. He took me in his arms and said he was sorry. Then he said I mustn't tell anyone, not a single soul, what I had seen, it would be bad luck, there was a curse and we'd all be ruined if I breathed a word. So I promised, of course.'

'Good grief. But you're sure it was the three of them? The sisters?'

'Oh sure. I recognized Mrs Frewen at once. She was younger, mind. They were in different poses, like, it's hard to describe, and I only saw them the once. But I eavesdropped on my parents afterwards, because my father had to comfort my mother, d'you see, for the hiding he'd given me.

I crept down out of bed. I was fascinated and I listened to them from behind the door.'

'What did they say?'

'Ah well. I was a lad, you know, and it were hard to understand these grown-up things. As far as I could understand it, there was a scandal about the painting. I don't know what, something to do with who paid for it, and one of the ladies' husbands was angry so it was put away in Innishannon for safety and to be out of sight. To be forgotten.'

'And so it was. Right up to the fire?'

'Oh, for sure. It went up with the house, God save us, although the roof and part of the wall fell out from that attic side, my father said, throwing papers and burning bits all over the garden. The painting went all right, because afterwards he found the charred pieces of frame and the black bits of canvas were still sticking to it. When they were clearing up the rubbish they found that. That was the end of it. My father was like a broken man anyway. It was a terrible time. They murdered the fish bailiff and my father took us away quickly too, first to Kinsale and then to Cork. Ah, it's hard in Ireland and it always has been. They were terrible times and the North's no better now. The Leslies, they're in County Monaghan, right up on the border, and my father always thought the painting might have something to do with them, with Lady Leonie anyway, but he never had time to find out. It's a strange thing, you coming all the way here to ask me this, you and your photograph here all the time. It's a day for picture stories now, isn't it? Fate it is, for sure.'

I found that I was staring at him with a fixed intensity that hurt my eyeballs and turned to look at Sue. She had an expression on her face that possibly only Ireland could induce. The mixture of emotions would have been laughable if I hadn't been near to exploding myself.

'Three million dollars,' I said it at last. 'Bits of charred rame and ash. Strewn all over the garden.'

'The painting. That beautiful painting.' Her eyes fixed on mine. 'Just like the Wyndhams, I'll bet. It may not be my favourite, but he was a fine painter. And that particular painting—I can't believe it. A wonderful work of art.'

'Oh dear.' Old Coughlan looked anxiously at us both. 'Sure I've upset you, now. Me and my—no, to be fair, I've never told anyone about that picture, not for donkey's and donkey's years. To think that you'd come all this way only to be disappointed. Isn't that a shame?'

'Mr Coughlan, you've been so kind.' Sue put a hand on his arm. 'It's not fair of us to spoil your story. It was a wonderful story. We're really grateful to you for telling us.'

'But—'

'No buts. It's helped to settle a long argument. To lay a ghost. And I'm sure you're right about Fate bringing us here. What an extraordinary experience it's been.' She smiled into his anxious eyes. 'Tim's photo and everything. We'll never forget that. The painting's only history, now, Mr Coughlan. Only history.'

'Oh, Ireland's got enough of that.'

'How right you are. I'm sorry, but could I have some more of this delicious tea? It really has done me good.'

'But of course!' His anxious eyes brightened and he got to his feet. 'I'll give the pot a boost right away. What about you, sir?'

'Tim, Mr Coughlan. My name is Tim. I'd love another cup, thank you. I rather feel I need it.'

He smiled at that and bustled about with the pot. It boiled again presently and he refilled our cups in triumph. I felt a sense of exhausting anti-climax, of unreality, but Sue was terrific in that situation. She drew old Coughlan out and chatted to him brightly, so that he soon was telling her all about the game and the garden and how the fish were to be caught. I thought of the car outside and the flights back to London, and the way the sky was going grey in the way that it does when rain threatens in County Cork. I thought about Jeremy and the Art Fund, dead Perkins, pieces of picture frame and charred canvas, the Whitney exhibition, Lord Ribblesdale, and beautiful women painted wearing their expensive dresses in rooms with high ceilings. I heard the compressive thud of Jeremy's yacht going for a Burton, Jeremy shouting, pieces of wreckage cascading down. I saw the face of the lumberjacketed man at O'Hare, my fists hitting him, violence, destruction. Mortal ruin.

'We've lost him,' old Coughlan said, and I realized he was talking of me.

'I'm sorry. Very sorry. I was miles away.'

'Ah well, have I not given you something to think about? Sometimes it's better not to bother with history. Some stories are best left untold.'

Sue was looking at me reprovingly for my manners. I smiled and thanked the old man again. 'We must be going. I'm eternally grateful to you. For closing a chapter for us. At least our minds will be at rest after this. Now that we know.'

'You're welcome. Of course you are very welcome. And come back, won't you? You can have a fine holiday here in the summer. I'll show you all the finest places. I'll have some fine salmon for you. Will you not come?'

'We will. We promise we'll come back.' Sue smiled brightly. 'Won't we, Tim?'

'Of course. And give my best to Pad—er, your nephew, Patrick, when you next write.'

The old man grinned. 'I'll do that, right enough. And remind him of his nickname. It's a few years since I heard it.'

'Sorry about that.'

'No offence. He was a wild boy all right.'

We went out through the low front door into the greying light outside and shook hands with him. We were moving towards the car when Sue stopped. Another car was coming up the long, stone-walled track towards the cottage. It was a bright silver BMW. It bumped its way carefully towards us with great caution, the tinted windows reflecting back the whitish-grey daylight and dark clouds, so that you couldn't see the driver's face. I couldn't have got our hired car past it, so I stood outside the cottage and took Sue's arm as I watched the BMW approach. Old Coughlan disappeared inside.

As the car got closer I could see that there were two men in it. Near to the cottage it stopped. I heard the driver put the hand-brake on. The engine was still running.

The passenger door opened and a man with gold-rimmed spectacles got out. I recognized the spare figure and dark hair of Alexander Carlton. He didn't smile or greet me; he stood a pace or two away from the BMW, closer to us, and stared at me. The driver's door opened and another man got out. I'd never seen him before. He was stocky and square, with very light hair. He had a machine-pistol in his hand and pointed it at me as he walked round the front of the car to stand closer to Carlton. Sue gave a small cry and then closed her mouth. I held her arm tightly.

'I'm afraid it's all been for nothing, Alex,' I said. 'The painting got burnt with the house. The Frewen luck again.'

His face was intent and serious. 'How do you know?'

'I guessed it. That's why I came here. But old Mr Coughlan, in there, has confirmed it. His father saw the bits after the fire. The Sargent was kept hidden in the attic.'

'Was it the three Jerome sisters?'

'Yes, it was. I'd forgotten that you studied in Florence as well as the other places. Sargent was born there. Has he always been an obsession with you?'

'Not an obsession. A lifetime study.'

'Must have given you a shock when I talked about it, all innocently, at the first board meeting. Shouldn't you be in Chicago, by the way?'

He didn't reply. He seemed to be thinking.

'You've been after it for years, I suppose?'

He still didn't answer.

'Well, it's too late now.' I began to feel garrulous, light-headed. 'It's gone. Since 1921.' I was repeating myself, trying to prompt a reaction. The light-haired man still held the pistol pointed at us. Sue made an involuntary movement and I restrained her. 'It's gone, Alex.'

'Oh no it hasn't,' he said oddly, still staring at me with that bare-eyed look his glasses gave him.

'I'm afraid it has. Old Coughlan can confirm that.'

'Only he can. And you. An English couple, snooping, and an old salmon poacher. Not likely to cause much excitement in Ireland.'

'Why? You've nothing to gain now.'

His face still showed no emotion. 'If I authenticate a Sargent, it will stand at auction. Whenever it was painted.' He turned his head towards the light-haired man.

'Stay clear of the door,' I said to Sue. 'Move to your left.'

'Kill them.' Carlton's voice was unemotional.

The fair-haired man raised the pistol slightly as I hurled myself round Sue, to the left, leaving the doorway clear. The blast made Sue scream. My heart nearly burst all its blood-vessels but the fair-haired man took the charge of shot right in the face. As he went bloodily backwards, the machine-pistol flew across to Carlton's side and he leapt for it, shouting. I had a fearsome glimpse of him bending, turning towards us with the weapon in his hands, screaming. Then the second blast burst his features horribly. I saw shattered gold spectacles, splashed with blood, circle through the air to fall into a clump of nettles beside a stone wall.

Old Coughlan stepped out of the doorway, breaking his shotgun open smoothly as he brought two more cartridges out of his pocket. 'I knew that was bad news as soon as I

saw the car,' he said. 'A BMW is always bad news in
Ireland.' He snapped the shotgun shut again. 'They'll be
from the North, I suppose?'

CHAPTER 17

'I don't quite understand.' Sue spoke quietly as I eased the
Jaguar out of the London suburbs to the south-east. 'Why
it is that you want to go to this Northiam place.'

'To lay a ghost. The ghost of Moreton Frewen.'

'I should have thought that you'd had quite enough of
that gentleman. Now that the whole thing's settled you
ought, surely, to be glad to let sleeping dogs lie.'

We had been back for several days. Ireland was sinking
into unreal memory, distant, unconnected, another place.
Another place so far from London, so different and remote,
that the memories had a dreamlike quality, as I imagine a
veteran's memories of war experience must become: remote
yet real, distant yet intensely personal. I won't tire you with
all the explanations that the Garda of County Cork had had
to have. It felt as though it would take forever. I had to
explain how old Coughlan had defended us superbly, how
there was no doubt about Carlton's intentions, how the
whole incident had come about. Days passed, days during
which the Garda contacted the whole world to check our
story. We were politely treated but confined to our hotel
until, finally, we were allowed to leave and assured that old
Coughlan would not be charged. Back in London, I was
at a loose end. Everyone connected with the Bank and
Christerby's was so shocked and horrified that they seemed
to be avoiding me. Jeremy was immensely relieved and
quite congratulatory, for him. The loss of the Sargent was
tempered by the safety of his situation, now that the danger
was over. Jeremy had visibly mixed emotions.

Corroborative evidence started to come in from all quar‐
ters. According to Andy Casey, the Chicago police knew of
the light-haired man; he was a professional killer. Loose
ends were being steadily tied up. Sue and I had been lying
low in Onslow Gardens, Sue recovering from a terrifying
experience but for which, as before, she accepted some
responsibility due to her own decisions. The weather was
still weakly sunny, but much cooler. It seemed to me that
any visit to Frewen's birth and burial place I was going to
make had better be made right away, to get the whole thing
over and done with. The climate didn't incline me to dawdle;
I headed into Sussex at a purposeful speed.

'What else have they come up with about Carlton?' Sue
demanded, after a while. 'I mean, I can understand the
greed for money, especially in an expert who saw everyone
else making fortunes that made his salary look puny, but it
still doesn't explain it completely. Not to me, anyway.'

'Sargent was an obsession with Carlton. I never realized
that until the very end. I knew that Carlton had studied in
Florence, which is where Sargent was born. His parents
toured Europe, permanently separated from America in an
interminable search for health. But who hasn't studied in
Florence these days? That was no criterion. Then Carlton
had studied in Paris. Sargent learnt his craft there, in
Carolus-Duran's atelier. So what? Who hasn't studied in
Paris, either? Or London? I mean, every darned art boffin
from here to Alaska has trailed round all three. Throw in
Venice and Carlton might have become a Whistler freak.
As it was, it seems he spent a lot of time in Boston, looking
at Sargent's murals for the Public Library. He spent all his
spare time tracking down every painting and portrait he
could record. I've no doubt he knew all about the charcoal
sketch of Lady Randolph Churchill at an early stage; how
he found out about the three Jerome sisters being painted
together is something we'll never know. He wanted that
painting for emotional reasons as much as for the money.'

'Yuk. He hired those criminals. That killer. Those thugs who attacked you at O'Hare. I suppose that vile pale man with the gun killed poor Perkins?'

'Oh yes. The bullets confirmed it. Forensic evidence. Kamrowski and the other two were just low-level bag-snatchers. They had no idea that Carlton was prepared to murder. Perkins must have seen or said or realized something they couldn't tolerate. The police in the States have tracked down Carlton's movements over a period and it all fits. They couldn't answer for his time over here, of course. He was a frequent visitor and it's hard to establish his exact itinerary in England each time.'

She shifted her sitting position in the car, so that I noticed her furrowed brow.

'What I can't work out is: why try to kill Jeremy? That seemed so vicious and so pointless. You, I can understand; you were in the way all the time.' She smiled at me. 'I mean, you were number one to remove.'

'Thank you. Very, much. But Jeremy became the motivating force. I work for Jeremy. Jeremy was mad keen to find that painting. With Jeremy removed the major impetus would have gone. And remember: Jeremy was and is in many ways much easier to remove than me.'

'Why?'

'Because I'm a much faster-moving target and I can look after myself. Especially with a guardian angel to watch over me.'

'Flannel! You won't soften me up that way. You're incorrigible. You don't really believe I can protect you at all. And my God, you—we—were lucky.'

'I know. What would I have done without you? You thought of the Sargent connection first. I mean, this whole adventure belongs to you, doesn't it?'

'You bastard! You absolute swine! Don't transfer the responsibility to me! If it hadn't been for you, barging your way around Chicago and New York, nothing would have happened.'

'Of course it would. And remember: Jeremy made me g‹
to Chicago and you made me go to the Whitney in New
York. To see the Sargent exhibition. Carlton must have
nearly had heart failure when I told him I was going there
on my afternoon off. Especially to buy the catalogue. No, I
think that you and Jeremy must take credit for the whole
sequence of events.'

'Tim Simpson, I shall get out of this car *now* if you don't
abandon that line of argument!'

That's typical of a woman, of course. They strut about in
the background, chi-iking you like mad to do this and do
that, handing you the ammunition, pointing out the enemy,
sending you over the top at O-six-hundred hours with
bayonet in hand, and then when you stagger back bleeding
and bloody they say, What, me? Responsible? What on
earth can you mean? Have you gone raving mad? I was
against the whole thing from the start. I abandoned the
conversation; there's no dealing with a woman once's she's
decided that you are to blame.

'The Cotswolds fooled me for a while. Harry Howarth
kept taking Carlton down to Broadway for the weekend,
charging off from Paddington. Right round the corner from
Mr Goodston's. Sargent was so often in the Cotswolds and
had such connections there that I couldn't help but be
suspicious. I thought that the painting might be tucked
away in Fladbury Rectory or somewhere like that.'

'How is Howarth? How's he taken it?'

'He's shattered. Absolutely shattered. Carlton was his
choice. He kept asking me yesterday, on the phone, if I
thought it was the expansion plans that sent Carlton off the
rails. Too much for him to handle; that sort of thing.
There might have been an element of that, you see. Charles
Massenaux warned me after the last meeting that some of
the New York managers didn't think Carlton could take a
lot of pressure. I don't think it was that. I think he was just
mad keen to get the painting for himself and then, when he

ew it didn't exist any more, to re-create it.'

'I simply can't believe that he would have got away with
a forgery.'

'Not in the long term, no. But as director of Christerby's,
New York, he'd have got his hands on a lot of cash. Look
how you all wanted to believe in that painting. Did believe
in it. Passionately. Read any history of forgery. It was a
natural.'

'Well, we were right, weren't we? It did exist. Had existed.
It must have been a terrible blow to Carlton when you
confirmed that it had been destroyed at Innishannon.'

'I'm sure it was. He was too far committed, by then, to
let us get away. Even if he hadn't wanted to produce a
forgery.'

She shivered. 'Don't, Tim. Don't bring up that awful day
again. How you anticipated old Coughlan's reaction I'll
never know. Come on, let's lay your ghost and call an end
to the affair.'

You come into the village of Northiam from the north,
after you have crossed the River Rother which divides Kent
from Sussex. After a quaint old hump-backed bridge which
crosses all that is left of what was once, hundreds of years
ago, a wide sea estuary, you follow the road along the flat
until it rises up the gentle opposite ridge past the former
tiny railway station, to which Edward, Moreton's brother,
returned in triumph from the Boer War. The initial approach to the village is flanked by post-war bungalows and
council estates which belie its rural nature. Like many
Sussex settlements, the houses straggle along a ridge for two
or more miles, so that you don't reach the church and village
green in this case until you are almost at the end, the south
side, where Brickwall House sits in the fork in the road.
Beyond the house, the park full of oaks stretches into the
distance until it meets a double line of chestnuts planted by
Moreton's father, Thomas Frewen, to mark the old road to
Beckley. In the great brick wall on the Hastings road you

can see his initials, T.F. 1838, but Brickwall has had its
name since the seventeenth century, when the Frewens first
moved into it.

I pulled the car up in front of the high ornamental iron
gates and railings at the entrance to the drive that leads
to the front of the house. A large three-gabled façade of
black-and-white timbering, very uniform in its striping, very
handsome in its fenestration, stood before us.

'That's a very fine house,' Sue said, peering over me.
'What is it now?'

'It's a school. The Frewens made it over to a Trust
after the First World War. Black-and-white timbering is
appropriate to Moreton; the Moreton Old Hall he never
inherited in Cheshire is much more complex and bendy
than this, though.'

'Is it all timbered inside?'

'Oh no, not *all*. There are Renaissance plastered ceilings.
The Frewens did a lot to the original house when they
moved in. They planted a topiary garden and put up brick
walls. Hence the name.'

'Who owned it before them?'

'Oddly enough, a family called White. No relation of
Jeremy's. A Frewen forebear became Archbishop of York
but the money to buy Brickwall came from a brother in
trade, in the City of London. Another Stephen. He bought
it from the Whites.'

'This is where Moreton was born?'

'It is. And he's buried in the church back up the road, in
a vault under the family chapel. The brothers had private
tutors; they didn't go to Eton. With riding wild here and at
Innishannon and in Leicestershire, with the avoidance of
school food and grinding discipline, it's no wonder they
were all a bit over-independent, and tall, and tough. Mr
Goodston was right; we shall never turn out anything like
the Frewens any more.'

'You and Mr Goodston seem to have formed quite a

elationship.' She put her hand on mine and smiled. 'I've never thought of you as a bibliophile.'

'It's a sign of age.'

'Well, there aren't any other signs.' She gave me a meaningful look. 'I can't see you settling down to be an antiquarian book-dealer. Not yet, anyway.'

'Give it time.'

I looked at the house, with its imposing gateposts capped by lions, its outlying stables, its walled gardens. This was Moreton's start in life, even though he knew it would never be his. What kind of psychological adjustment did a younger son need in those days? 'Some day, my son, all this will never be yours.' You grew up in it and got used to it and just when you had grown up and taken on all its style and bearing and social position they threw you out, into the Army, or the Church, or a dim profession, or something socially suitable. You knew it, of course, you were nothing if not hard-headedly realistic; you knew that the young dog fox must leave the litter and seek its own territory, like those on Ranksborough Gorse that Anita Leslie compared you with, but it must have needed toughness even though, in those days, the whole world was available as a territory. So you rode the prairie, steamed the Atlantic, smoked in the Pullman car, mixed with the string-pullers, frantic with energy to create your own Brickwall, your own place of respect.

'You're talking to yourself. He's really got under your skin, hasn't he?'

'Moreton? I suppose he has, a bit. His nephew, Shane Leslie, was correct. He's a study in sublime failure all right.' I let in the drive and the car moved off. 'Let's go and look at Brede Place, if we can.'

As it turned out, we couldn't. Brede Place is a private house, not the Frewens' any more, but it is still there, an ancient moated place, built of Caen stone brought over by the descendant of some Norman conqueror. It was Clara

Jerome Frewen, Moreton's wife, who fell for the dilapidated, uninhabited place in the 1890s and turned it back into a house, even if a wildly impractical house, with no heating, earth closets, freezing cold and draughty and uncomfortable, but wildly romantic and ghost-ridden. She persuaded Edward, who had inherited it with Brickwall, to sell off this one house and some land to her, so that she could make a home she could call her own after all the moonlight flits, the duns, the near-bankruptcy and the bailiffs which were always part of her life. To this, her place, came writers like Stephen Crane, Kipling, Wells and Henry James, politicians with Winston, and, from time to time at first and then more frequently, Moreton, who at last came back to Sussex to die. It had all come to nothing. His money and that of his brothers, his children and his friends and his enemies, had all been spent and lost, vast fortunes of it, gone forever. He used to sit under the huge oak trees and shout that he was dying; it made him angry to think of it, it wasn't fair, nothing that he wanted had come to him after all that effort and absence and risk, all that shrewd intelligence and amazing gift of prediction that he had wasted.

'And yet,' I said out loud, making Sue jump, for she had half joined in my reverie and was staring at the gates to Brede, lost in thought, 'and yet, most people live their lives in boredom and make no money anyway. Poor old Moreton, he did at least live like the splendid pauper that he was. Come on, we'll look at the church and then I will have laid the ghost. Once I've seen the place, somehow my mind settles.'

I turned and drove back to Northiam, parking in front of the old stone church that is entered via a bell-porch. It's quite a big church when you're inside, with a fine oak Renaissance altar rail and so on, but the Frewen family chapel is off to your left, built over a vault where generations of Frewens lie among their forebears.

Sue gave me a roll of her eyes, white in the gloomy

ᴧnterior. I gestured to the chapel door and we trod carefully across to enter the rather bare, simple annexe through a door in a glass screen. Up on the right-hand side there was a high Victorian marble memorial with mottled brown clustered columns flanking a long inscription. It went up to a Gothic point at the top, with frilly white marble decorations. It was an impressive affair, the biggest in the chapel, as befitted what was probably the most powerful landowner of all the Frewens, the summit of their condition.

'Moreton's father,' I said to Sue, my voice sounding loud in the empty stone chamber. 'You see? That's the old boy who had all the estates.'

We peered upwards at the inscription. *Sacred to the memory of Thomas Frewen, Esq*—that was him all right—*of Cold Overton Hall, Leicestershire; Innishannon, County Cork; and Brickwall House in this parish. Eldest son of John and Eleanor Frewen Turner. Born at Cold Overton Hall, August 26, 1811*—was that why Cold Overton was listed first? Why did it strike a dim chord?—*educated at St John's College, Cambridge*—a Johnian. Must have been a good man—*A magistrate for Rutland and Leicestershire*—hunting country all right, no wonder Moreton was such a horseman—*MP for South Leicestershire in 1832, High Sheriff for Sussex in 1839*—ah, we'd got back to Sussex again.

'*He married first in 1832*—' Sue's voice suddenly cut in on my thoughts—'*Anne, daughter of W. W. Carus Wilson, Esq. of Castreton Hall, Westmorland.*'

'She died in childbirth while he was taking the waters at Tunbridge Wells.'

'*Secondly*—' she ignored me—'*in 1847, Helen Louisa, daughter of Frederick Homan, Esq. of Hedenwood, County Kildare.*' *He died at Woodlands, Ore, near Hastings, Oct. 14, 1870.*

The solemn text continued, quoting Biblical extracts. Something was making me frown. I turned away from the big memorial, which reminded me of Albert's in Hyde Park, and saw other, simpler tablets, to other Frewens, ladies, wives, one of Charles Hay Frewen's wife, Frances.

'She was Moreton's aunt. He—Charles—was the Uncle Moreton calls pompous and futile in his book. He lived at Cold Overton Hall until—'

I stopped and walked back to look up at old Thomas Frewen's big impressive plaque, and there it was, as it was elsewhere, looking at me. *Sacred to the memory of Thomas Frewen of*—

Cold Overton Hall.

'What's the matter? You've gone as white as a sheet. Tim?'

Cold Overton Hall. I sat down on a nearby chair. Surely that couldn't be right? It must just be a coincidence.

'Tim? You look absolutely ghastly! For God's sake! What is it?'

Cold Overton Hall. There had been no coincidences in this whole business. I could see the auction catalogue in my mind, one that I had sorted in the office recently. It had a dark green cover with a photograph of an oak chair on it. The Cold Overton Hall Collection. Icy chills came up from the stone-flagged chapel floor. Above me the great frilly-Gothic memorial pointed its arch at the dark ceiling. Dead Frewens lay in the mausoleum below my feet. Frewens whom Moreton had rather light-heartedly written of. Frewens who had taken over the ancient family of Laton. Frewens who had loaned the Adderleys money and taken Innishannon in exchange. Frewens who included Moreton himself, since 1924 permanently down among the vaults. The Cold Overton Hall Collection. America and Ireland and, of course, England. The three places in which most of Moreton Frewen's life had been lived out. His daughter said that he was at heart an American, and should have become one. The Irish would laugh at that and say that he was one of them. But Frewen was an Englishman, whatever that may mean, like me. I hadn't looked nearly hard enough for solutions in England.

'You're shivering! You're not well! Come outside, Tim, quickly! You've gone so white! What is it?'

Cold Overton Hall.

'Get me out. Get me out of here.'

She got her arm under my elbow and I swear she practically propelled me physically through the church, past the bell-porch and out into the greying day.

'You drive,' I said abruptly. 'You drive, Sue. I'm not up to driving. Back to London. Please.'

'What's happened?' She started the car and I switched the merciful heater on full blast. The engine was still warm, thank heaven, and the rush of air struck my face as she moved off, so that my shivering came spasmodically now, instead of full-time as it had been doing. 'Tim! Tell me! What's wrong? You haven't laid a ghost; you look as though you've seen one!'

'Something I hadn't thought of. One of those irrelevant stupidities. An autumn catalogue that I saw. I'll have to get hold of Jeremy; I'm afraid there's much worse to come.'

CHAPTER 18

The horse whickered in recognition as I scrunched out of the car. It leant its bony brown head over a wooden top rail and stared at me before heaving its nose up and down in what is called a toss. You too, I thought, you give a toss as well, do you, brute?

Jeremy's saloon was already there and he opened the door to save Donald the trouble. 'Tim! Nip in smartly—it's turning chilly at last. Donald's put some coffee on; we're in the kitchen.'

I followed him into the hall and tramped through the dining-room towards the galley-kitchen, where Donald was

immured behind his counters to keep out the broth-spoiler
He looked up at me as I walked in. 'Aha! There he is! Come
in, young sir, come in. The legend is back. With another
scalp to its belt, I hear.'

'Well—hello, Donald. How are you?'

'Not too bad, not too bad. Shocking business. Dreadful.
That chap Carlton—who'd have guessed? A director. Member of the Christerby's board. Shocking.'

'Yes, it's been bad.'

'You're all right yourself?'

'Oh yes.'

'And that young lady of yours—Sue whatsername—is
she OK?'

'Sue's all right. Fortunately she's tough.'

'Good. Good girl, that. Look here—let's be civilized.
Take our coffee to the sitting-room. Better than perching
round the counter like a bunch of matelots. Use the vicar's
parlour.'

'OK, fine.'

Jeremy picked up a tray loaded with coffee things and
sauntered out to a sitting-room beyond an arch, a wide arch
that separated it from what I now saw was a dining area
rather than a separate room, timbered and half-panelled
like the rest of the old house. Donald and Jeremy sat on
easy chairs by a low circular table, where Jeremy had parked
the tray.

'You take milk?'

'Yes. Thank you.'

Donald sat down in his slightly awkward way, the artificial leg sticking out. He half-turned stiffly to peer at me,
twisting his face. 'Well, don't hang back, young feller. Come
on. Come and join us.'

'I was just admiring your dresser.' I stared at it where it
stood against the wall near the arch, its shelves loaded with
willow-pattern plates and its arcaded pot-board decorated
with a large tureen in a similar blue-and-white design.

'Oh, that? Fits well, doesn't it?'

'Excellently.' I walked across and joined them, to his evident relief—he settled back more comfortably in his chair —and Jeremy's slight impatience, evident by the way he peered at me with wrinkled brow. 'It's a pity you bought it from our competitors.'

'What?'

'From Sotheby's. It came from Sotheby's, didn't it?'

'What? Yes. Oh yes, I told you, didn't I? The last time you were here.'

'You did indeed. I wondered where I'd seen it before.'

'Really?'

'Yes. I didn't view the sale but I got the catalogue.'

'Have some coffee?' He passed a cup.

'Thanks.' I took it. 'The Cold Overton Hall Collection.'

'Sorry?'

'The Cold Overton Hall Collection. Sold at Sotheby's, Bond Street, on 10th October—this was part of it, wasn't it? I remembered it from the photo in the catalogue. An oak sale.'

'Yes, it was.'

Jeremy put down his coffee to look at me curiously. 'Cold Overton Hall? Wasn't that—'

'The Frewens'? Yes, Jeremy, it was.' I sipped some of mine. 'A long time ago. Cold Overton Hall, Leicestershire. Where Moreton did a lot of his hunting in his early years.'

'Oh yes?' Donald's voice was neutral.

'Yes.' I looked at him as best I could. 'I remembered that Jeremy said your family came from the East Midlands before the war. You rode to hounds there yourself. Until— until you joined up.'

'Yes.' He gave me a stare which implied that I was transgressing, moving on to forbidden ground, the delicate subject of his lost leg.

'You must have known Cold Overton.'

'Not really. We were the other side of Melton. Heard of it, of course. Renowned.'

'It hasn't been the Frewens' for years. Edward had to sell it in 1895 to pay off the debts and mortgages which had accumulated even by then. The agricultural depression and all that.'

'So I believe.'

'Odd that you didn't mention it.'

'I beg your pardon?'

'Considering all the information we were discussing. About Moreton.'

Donald stared at me without blinking. I sensed a shadow crossing Jeremy's face.

'I mean, there we were, rattling on about Moreton and the Frewens while all the time you'd just bought a dresser from Cold Overton Hall. Jeremy admired it specifically, and you never mentioned it. I realize that the place—Cold Overton —had belonged to someone else for years, in fact I remembered it used to be an antique place, I think it was Bill Stokes's. I phoned up Graham Child of Sotheby's—we do talk to our competitors, you know, quite a lot—and he said yes, most of the stuff in that sale had been collected together recently, of course, but the dresser went back a long way. It had always stood in a kitchen servery or something. Went with the house. This was the first time it had been sold separately.'

Donald put down his cup. 'I'm afraid I'm not following the drift of this. What are you getting at?'

'Just that it was odd. You not mentioning it. And I'm afraid I'm bad that way. When I thought about it—I was in Northiam Church, you see, looking at the memorials, and Cold Overton kept coming up, it was an important Frewen possession once—as I say, when I thought about it, I realized that if I hadn't seen that catalogue from Sotheby's, it would never have occurred to me.'

Jeremy's face creased. 'For heaven's sake, Tim. Come to the point, will you? Whatever the point is.'

'Just that if Donald didn't tell us about that, what else didn't he tell us about?'

Jeremy looked from me to Donald with a bewildered expression. Donald had set his features into a hard look, like a yachtsman who was heading into an irritating squall.

'Good heavens, you are a strange fellow. I bought a piece of oak furniture I liked at auction, that's all. The Frewens haven't been at Cold Overton for years. Not for years. They sold it in 1895, as you say. It never occurred to me that there was any significant connection.'

'I'm afraid I think there was. I think that Moreton Frewen and anything to do with him is a very important subject to you.'

Silence. Donald was beady-eyed now, his coffee forgotten. 'I've told you all I know about him. And my father's disastrous investments in his schemes. There's nothing else. I rather resent this.'

'Ah yes, your father. Was it he who told you about the Sargent painting of the Jeromes?'

'What?'

'He saw it, presumably, when Sargent painted his portrait together with his first wife. Around 1900 or so? I got Sue to check, you see. We were thrown the first time, because Sargent painted a White, Mrs George White, she was the American ambassador's wife in London, in 1883, and they were a well-known couple in society. It didn't occur to us at first to look for other Whites. Sue found the reference somehow two days ago. Took her a hell of a time. Your father and stepmother were painted by Sargent. A long time ago. You never told us. But I guess—just guess—that your father must have seen the secret painting of the Jerome sisters and told you. That's why you knew, didn't you, the day I came here and blabbed about the gold shares being kept with a sergeant. You knew it was a Sargent, didn't you?'

'Rubbish! Of course I didn't. What are you implying? Eh?'

'That's why you tried to kill Jeremy. I've thought about that for two weeks. Why would anyone want to kill him? I thought it was because he was pushing me; the motivating force to find that painting. Then I remembered. The day we came here together to ask you about the Sargent, Jeremy was trying to recall something. Something he'd dimly remembered from family talk about a Sargent. It was your father's. That yacht bomb was a military job. The sort you might have learnt in the Army. You didn't want him to remember anything at all.'

'You're mad. Raving mad.'

'You remembered it, though. Very well indeed. If you could get your hands on the three Jeromes, you'd be back in funds.'

'You're mad! It was Carlton who did all that. You proved it yourself.'

'Oh, Carlton was one prime mover, of course. Your partner. I'm afraid Graham Child blew the gaffe on that for you. He was amused when I inquired about the Cold Overton dresser. "What's up with you lot?" he asked me. "Both Jeremy's cousin Donald *and* your New York chap, that new one, Carlton, all after the dresser. Now you, Tim, asking about it. What's the story?" He saw you, you see. Together, you and Carlton, at the sale, buying the dresser. Carlton knew about the Sargent from his research. He was a Sargent freak. You knew about it from your father, and you had all the Frewen knowledge. You pooled your resources. I imagine that he first contacted you when he was doing his research into Sargent's work. He found out about the portrait of your parents in the same way as Sue did. When did he ask you about the painting of the Jerome sisters? He must have raised the subject with you. Didn't he? You knew, of course, that one of the ladies was Moreton Frewen's wife because your father had told you all about that. You were

y useful to Carlton and he must have been very useful to
ou. Mobile and able to supply the materials for the bomb
you planted on Jeremy's yacht. That had to be you; one
more yachtsman down at Chichester would have been quite
unremarkable. Everyone knew you. And you knew Jeremy's
yacht of old. Military training has its peacetime uses, especially if you've been in the Armoured Division.'

Donald drew back in his chair. 'This is intolerable!
Jeremy, I—'

'If it hadn't been for Moreton Frewen, you'd still be a
director of White's Bank, wouldn't you?'

His face changed. I can't describe his expression. It was
vile. Horrible. It gave everything away. Unfortunately, I
had forgotten to keep a close eye on Jeremy. He spoke, just
managing to get words through his dreadful shock.

'Mary. Mary was with me. You meant to murder her.
You—'

I was too late as I jumped to stop him. He's big, is Jeremy,
and years of City business lunches have been tempered by
strenuous yachting, so that he's not weak, not by any means,
and he had Donald by the throat. The flesh bulged over
Jeremy's vice-like fingers. It was a horrible couple of
minutes, Jeremy roaring in murderous rage, his hands
clamped round Donald's throat, Donald shaking and twitch-
ing, going white and red and black, me fighting and shouting
as I tried to get Jeremy loose, to break his hold.

'Jeremy! Stop! It's not worth it! Let go!'

It was damn near death for Donald. I managed to get
between Jeremy's hands, so that, fighting and shouting and
hating me, he was finally manhandled off, away, into his
chair with me pinning him down. It took all the strength
I've got, I can tell you.

'Jeremy, listen! Listen! McIntyre. No, look at me! The
puce old johnny. You remember? At the garden party? The
one fuelled on Singapore Slings, you said. Him. Major-
General McIntyre.'

He tried to struggle free, but his face was close to mine and I forced him to look at me. 'What about him? Let me go!'

'His son plays rugger. I contacted him. The General isn't a sawbones any more. He used to be, but he's not, now. His speciality is psychiatry. Psychiatry. He's not a sawbones, Jeremy, he's a shrink. A *shrink*. One of the Army's best, apparently. Donald is a patient of his.'

Jeremy's eyes looked into mine for so long that I had to blink. It was as though he was examining the back of my brain. Then his limbs slackened and I let go of him, so that I could stand up, all ruffled and bruised and shaken, in the middle of the room.

Donald lay in the chair where I had torn Jeremy off him. His artificial leg stuck out at an angle, making him look like a broken doll. His clothes were torn and his face, congested and purple, twitched as he stared at me in hatred. He managed to croak at me, though.

'Smart Alec! Bloody smart Alec! Think you're damn clever, I'll bet.'

'You hate both of us, don't you? As much as Moreton Frewen.'

'Yes I do! If it hadn't been for Frewen bamboozling my father we'd still have had our block of shares in the Bank. We had to sell a lot of them to pay off the debts. Otherwise, we'd still have control. Then you—*you*—wouldn't be strutting about the Bank! You'd be out on your ear, in the gutter, where you both belong! Scum!'

'When did the Sargent go for sale? Of your father, I mean?'

'In the 'forties. My stepbrother needed money. Sargents went for nothing, then.'

'So your father did tell you about the Jeromes painting?'

He leered at me. 'You're so clever! Work it out for yourself!'

'Mary.' Jeremy managed to speak directly to Donald at

st. 'I can understand, now, why me. But Mary. My wife. Your bomb would have—'

'Mary!' Donald's voice mimicked him. 'Mary! Your precious wife! That traitress! Uncle Richard's secretary. Feeding you with what you needed in your dirty game to take over the Bank. Stabbing Richard in the back. Working for you, to get me out. Your whore. Your treacherous whore!'

Jeremy leapt, but I had him half way that time. I got him round the waist with both my arms locked and dragged him back, fighting and heaving, to his chair. I had to hold him there for a full two minutes before he stopped, with tears of rage and sorrow on his face. Donald grinned, a horrible grin of triumph and knowledge that made me feel hideously murderous too, but I managed with an effort to straighten up and stare back at him. There was only one weapon I could use against Donald and I had a mind to use it, fairly or unfairly, if he pushed me too far.

He did. 'What can you do?' It was a sarcastic question, put in a triumphant tone.

'Nothing.'

'Nothing? Nothing?'

'No, nothing. This is a family matter. It's not for me to decide. I am not a member of the family. I shall do nothing.'

He leered. 'What you mean is that you have no proof. No proof you can use. Don't wave the family at me.'

'It's not that.'

My head was in a turmoil. I had planned to hand the whole thing over to Jeremy at that point. He was the boss. It was his family, his feud. I was just a retainer. But Jeremy was sitting stiff in his chair, face congealed. Horror suffused him; his will and nerve were temporarily out of action. I would have to handle this myself. Donald had not only tried to blow Jeremy and Mary to Kingdom Come; he and his accomplice had arranged for that trio to meet me at O'Hare, to kill me if they couldn't get my papers any other way.

'What, then?' Donald's next question goaded me.

'You're not well, Donald.'

'What?' His face changed. A look of unease came over r

'You haven't been well for years. The black dog, you cal.
it, like Winston Churchill. It will do White's Bank no good
to have a sensational court case, cousin trying to blow up
cousin, spread all over the papers. We can't have that. I
prefer the quieter course.'

'What the hell do you mean?'

'We'll talk to General McIntyre. I expect him to explain
that the years of pain and frustration have cracked you.'

'You bastard!'

'It'll mean treatment. White's will look after that.'

'Treatment? What treatment?'

'For your own good. A Crown Court would do precisely
the same, so why go to all the trouble and expense and
publicity? You can be put quietly away.'

'Wha—I'm not—you—'

'It'll be quite a nice institution. You haven't really got
any choice. You're obsessive, Donald. Criminally obsessive.
About Moreton Frewen. About the Bank. About Jeremy,
and Mary, and me. About your horse and riding. But mostly
about Frewen and the financial havoc he wrought on your
father's money. The loss of the Bank shares. Buying that
dresser was an obsessive act. An act of obsession. It was
something of the Frewens from the area where you'd done
all your youthful riding. Something the war put paid to.
Killing the man who had the gold shares you hoped would
provide a clue was obsessive, too; Carlton was like you. I'm
sorry for you, actually, Donald.'

'What? You? You dare to say that to me?'

'You'll be put in an institution. There won't be any choice
once we get to McIntyre. With modern drugs you'll calm
down. Eventually. We have to leave, now. This has been a
dreadful shock for Jeremy. I'm taking him home. Now.'

I hated this. I had really liked Donald. I hated it. I'd
hated it since I'd sat on that chair in the cold Northiam

.rch, the truth dawning, and Sue had had to drive me
.ne. The shock had affected me. Just as it now had Jeremy.
  took him out of the house, telling him he wasn't fit to
drive, and I sat him in my car with his pale grey face,
speechless. I shut the front door of the house, leaving the
interior, with its dresser and Donald stiff inside it, turning
over the things I had said to him in my mind. I thought
about McIntyre and the army and Rommel and Donald
stuck smashed in his armoured car where it might have
been best if he'd died and I shook that thought out of my
head. But then the horse whickered in the paddock once
again, staring at me, and my thoughts repeated the same
line of the verse once more, the verse I'd thought of and Sue
had taken up. An unprophetic verse, but it made me shiver
as I got into my car to take the silent Jeremy away.

> I 'listed at home for a lancer,
> Oh, who would not sleep with the brave?
> I 'listed at home for a lancer
> To ride on a horse to my grave.

CHAPTER 19

Donald White died the next day in a shooting accident. He
took his twelve-bore down the meadow to hunt rabbits,
passing the big brown hunter on the way. His daily cleaner
saw him stroking the horse's head as he stood talking to it
in the middle of the field, letting its big soft lips search him
and the pockets of his poacher's jacket for a lump of sugar
until he handed one over. She said he was there for quite a
while, then she saw him limp away in the grey autumn light.
When the shot went off she thought he'd bagged a bunny
for the pot. The stable boy found him much later. It seemed
that he'd clambered over the fence and his artificial leg had

hampered him somehow, caught in a wire on the top rur
He'd fallen and the gun had gone off right into his ches
killing him instantly. It was so unlike Donald, they all said,
carrying a loaded and cocked shotgun like that, but he might
have seen a rabbit, tried to bag it from the top of the fence
and lost his grip or his footing. No one knew. People get
careless; it was an accident.

There was a laudatory obituary in *The Times*. The tip of
the iceberg, as Mr Goodston would say.

Jeremy didn't speak to me for ten days. He went to the
funeral and he came to work erratically, looking pale and
tense. I knew he knew that none of it was my fault, I hadn't
even started it, but it was a family thing and I had been there,
inside it, intrusive. It was hard to take, despite everything we
had been through together before. He didn't avoid me
obviously, but he didn't speak either, so I stayed away as
tactfully as I could until one evening, it was after six and
the secretaries had gone, I had to get him to sign some
papers. I went into his office, put them in front of him, and
while he signed them I stood staring out of the window into
the London dark, a London dark full of wet lights, red buses,
black taxis and scurrying people heading towards stations
to get home. The phone rang and he picked it up, grunting
a bit until he turned and spoke to me.

'It's Mary. She says she can't stand this any more and
will you and Sue come out to dinner with us tonight?'

'We'd love to.'

He turned back to the phone. 'He says they'd love to.
About eight? All right.'

He put the phone down and went across to the cabinet
against the wall, pulling a key out of his pocket. 'Drink?'

'Yes, thanks.'

The veneered doors swung open and he peered at the
glazed interior, scowling as if in thought.

'Whisky?'

'Yes, thanks. Just ice.'

He nodded absently, picked up a large tumbler, then other one, put ice in both, and then practically filled the glasses with a torrent of whisky. He carried them across to his desk and motioned me to sit down, putting the glasses on the desk-top. As I picked mine up, he reached across with his and touched it gently, causing an icy chink of a toast to sound in the room. I toasted him back silently and drank. He put his glass down after a considerable swallow.

'Making enemies is a vile business.'

'It is.'

'I never believed that Donald—I—I always thought of him as a soldier. And a sort of uncle. A soldier-uncle.'

'I know. If you can, it would be best to leave it like that. Think of him as a soldier, I mean. A long time ago. He was ill, later.'

Jeremy picked up his glass. 'God knows what sort of enemies Moreton Frewen must have made.'

'Mmmm. Obviously, there were some bad ones. Lord Wharnecliffe was one. But quite a lot of his losers never seem to have held a grudge, despite lost fortunes. Tradespeople must have loathed him. Lowther forgave him; Grey supported him; Donald became obsessive about him.'

Jeremy smiled wryly. 'If he hadn't brought that dresser from Cold Overton, you might never have considered Donald.'

'True.'

'You are an amazing fellow, Tim. Poking about churches.' He cleared his throat awkwardly. 'I've got to ask you something.'

'What?'

'I've had a call from Harry Howarth. The Christerby operation in New York needs a new chief. Someone who can run New York, manage the expansion in Chicago, and probably later in Los Angeles. He asked if he could have you.'

'Me?'

'Yes, you. He says he can't think of anyone bett'
equipped to do it. You understand the art market, you'r
young, you're tough and you have all the figures in your
head. He also says he thinks he can get on very well with
you, which is perhaps the most important thing of all. This
Carlton business shook him up considerably. He wants
someone he can trust.'

Jeremy's face was dark and preoccupied in front of me. I
stared at him in some bewilderment. 'What did you tell
him?'

'I said that of course I would put it to you. For you to
make the decision. It's not that I don't need you here; I do.
You know my plans for the Bank. I'm going to need every
good man I can get. But I must be fair to you; I don't want
you to go, but I must be fair to you. And there's the territorial
imperative.'

'The what?'

'The territorial imperative. The male territorial imperative.' He gave me a humorous look. 'You and I are both
fairly direct characters, Tim. Sparks are bound to fly. They
have flown between us, and they'll fly more as you grow in
this business, as you have grown, and take greater things to
deal with. Then, to be fair to you, you should have the
opportunity of doing your own thing, at least for a couple
of years, to prove to the main board that you're not just my
dummy, my shotgun guard.'

I opened my mouth, but he held up his hand. 'Don't say
anything now. Think about it. A couple of years over in the
States, making a go of Christerby's there, would do your
career a power of good. You could come back here perhaps
and join me in the final putsch to take over White's Bank.
It might fit in very well. I can't keep you here, under my
wing, for ever. Not for your own good, anyway. And not for
both our goods, come to that.'

My first thoughts went to Sue. There was no way Sue
would abandon her career at the Tate, not for me. Sue left

once, to go to Australia because of an opportunity there,
a whole year. For her career. If I went to the States the
chances were I'd go alone. It was the classic modern yuppie
problem, career versus love, the only difference being that
because Sue and I aren't actually married, the legal damage
would be minimal. Perhaps it was because of considerations
like this, intimations or intuitions she'd had, that she'd
always held off marrying me, to limit that sort of damage.

The emotional damage was another matter.

'I thought you and I got on pretty well, Jeremy.'

'We do.' He took it seriously. 'Better, to be honest, than
any of my other, er, colleagues. I realize I'm not always
easy. But I have to put this to you, Tim. You don't have to
take it. There will be other opportunities. It's just that I
should draw your attention to Howarth's enthusiasm for
you and the opportunity is a good one. I suppose we've
never discussed your career strategy until now.'

The young dog fox must leave Ranksborough Gorse. To
make the dangerous run to wherever he could find his own
territory. Like Moreton Frewen. The world never changes,
the laws of nature are supposed to be ineluctable, if that is
the right word.

Jeremy was staring at his desk, face dark and gloomy. To
hell with nature; it was time to put him out of his misery.

'I've got a low boredom threshold, Jeremy. You said so
yourself. I don't see myself as a full-time auctioneer. If it's
all right with you, I'll stick around here at the Bank for a
bit longer.'

His head jerked up.

'After all,' I went on, 'I'm still on Howarth's board and
there are all my other activities to think of, and Sue, and,
most important, who on earth will keep you from going
barmy? You'd be bored to tears without me here.'

'You're sure?' His face was lightening.

'Positive.'

'My dear Tim! I do realize that you do have other, er,

considerations. I—I can't say I'm sorry, but I didn't w
to influence you. Poor Howarth is caught very short, thoug
and you do seem to get on well. Perhaps you could help hir.
temporarily? As I said from the very beginning, we have to
get on with this business: expansion into Chicago is vital for
Christerby's if they are to get ahead of the competition.
There's no time to lose. I—'

His eye caught mine, saw the look in it, and he stopped.
A sheepish smile came to his face. There was a pause
and then we both burst out laughing, slightly hysterically
perhaps, but laughing the laughter of those who need it as
much for an emotional release as for the enjoyment of a
rich, mutual joke.

Eventually, he managed to stop. 'Here! Have another
drink. If we're going to make a night of it, let's make a night
of it.'

'Why not?'

He refilled the glasses and held his up in a toast to me.
'Here's to more happy days! That reminds me: something
you've never explained.'

'What's that?'

'The painting by Sargent. Of the Jeromes. You've never
said who commissioned it.'

'We'll probably never know.'

'But you must have an idea? Come on, Tim, you of all
people! Who do you think the gentleman was? Their father,
or an admirer? It must have been an admirer, surely?'

'Well, Leonard Jerome died in Brighton in March 1891.
I don't think it was him. For once, Brighton had no part in
all this, by the way.'

He waved an impatient hand. 'So who was it? Which
admirer?'

'Come on, Jeremy. It's not very gallant of you to speculate
on such matters. Even old Moreton Frewen could be discreet
when it came to affairs of the heart. Perhaps that's why he
looked after the painting. Or maybe it was Clara who put

way, not to upset him. Her admirer, King Milan of
bia, left England in 1897 to go back to his own country,
t he continued to write to them both and he didn't die
ntil 1901. He might have sent the commission to Sargent
from Serbia and then—he died suddenly—not been able to
receive the painting. I do believe it was painted around
1900. Somehow I rule out King Milan, though. That leaves
the Duke of Connaught, who had a long and touching
affection for Leonie Leslie, and his brother, Bertie himself,
Edward the Seventh, who was Jennie's admirer and frier.
Jennie would have been married to George Cornwallis-West
by 1900. He went off with Mrs Pat Campbell, and she had
other admirers, of course. Kinsky was still about—oh hell,
there's endless speculation one can go in for. Anyway, this
business has taught me a valuable lesson.'

'You? A lesson? What's that?'

I grinned at him and stood up, to be able to stare out at
the shiny, wet, dark London outside. 'Digging into the past
seems to be a very dangerous business, Jeremy. Besides, you
wouldn't want to upset the Royal Family, would you?'